PLA

A JIM LOCKE NOVEL

P. F. HUGHES

PLAYING WITH FIRE

by P.F. Hughes

Email: paul@pfhughes.com
Web: www.pfhughes.com

First published in 2021 by Punch Publishing
Cover photographs © Shutterstock

To you, reader, for choosing to spend your time with something that came from my head.
Thank you.

Fire

noun

1.

a process in which substances combine chemically with oxygen from the air and typically give out bright light, heat, and smoke; combustion or burning."his house was destroyed by fire"

2.

a burning sensation."the whisky lit a fire in the back of his throat"

HEAT

CHAPTER ONE

Y ou see them everywhere. Men and women, out on the piss, so sick to death of the nine to five that when they finally manage to get out, it can sometimes get out of control. A few too many and perhaps the odd pill or line thrown in and before you know it, bang. It hits them at a hundred miles an hour. Lads get rowdy, girls get mouthy, hard cases get silly. It never stops. You can see it all from my office, hear the night alive with revellers at all hours. It's no good for my health. Neither is the heat.

I sparked up and let the smoke curl out of the window. Crowds spilled from bars, out into the thirty degree night. Beats pounded across the pavements, the punters dizzy with summer dreams. And it wouldn't quiet until the sun began to rise. I checked the clock on the dash. 00:37. No sign of the cheating bastard - yet. If he didn't come out soon, I might have to go in there and drag him out myself. I learnt long ago that it's better to let them come of their own accord. You get a feeling for it, like a sixth sense. This one wouldn't last until closing time.

I dragged deep, let the nicotine course through my over-

heated blood. Felt like I could boil from .the inside.
Unscrewed the cap on the White & Mackay. Sipped, swallowed, felt the burn. It was so good I wanted more. I allowed myself another, throwing it down my throat before returning the cap and tossing the bottle in the back. A young woman caught my eye, mini skirt so high I wondered if it could still be called a skirt at all, purple eye shadow and mascara running down her pretty face. I wasn't met with her approval. Gotta say, I couldn't blame her. I knew this was a waste of my time from the beginning. And I'd been driving nowhere but driving myself crazy. I told myself it made sense to sit behind the wheel as it gave me a good vantage point from down here and I had a clear view across the street. It was the perfect location for surveillance. Laura had her eyes peeled from my office, zoom lens pointed right at the door to capture him leaving, and who with. It was a good view, but I was easily prone to distraction. The flesh on show was enough to bring on the sweats, never mind the heat. At least I still knew I had blood pumping through my veins.

I couldn't wait to put this one to bed once and for all. It was all just about the evidence now. The camera never lies. My client, Gloria, would be given the bad news just as soon as I could e-mail the photographs to her. I guess anyone could do this job, though. Stalking cheating partners was so easy, a monkey could do it. It took nothing special. But then I suppose she felt better handing it over to a private investigator, someone who could do it professionally and get the job done quickly. Although she could've done it herself if she had the inclination, I suppose emotions could get the better of you. It can't be easy seeing your husband wining and dining someone much younger and more attractive than yourself. So I agreed to do it for her, for a price, and prove her suspicions were correct. And I wasn't complaining, not at all. This kind of thing was my bread and butter. She was paying good money - silly money, even - just to have him caught red-handed. I could get away with dragging it out for weeks, if I really wanted to. And she would keep paying too. But this was week three and by now I was bored. There was only so much sitting in cars I could do. The heat of the night was calling, and I needed a cold beer. Would be just as well to step in to the bar and prop it up while I snapped away on my iPhone. Once I'd found him, it would be easy enough from then on. If I got a shot of them exchanging a kiss, all the better. Straightforward it may be, but I should be thankful for small mercies. The three grand Gloria had paid me already was burning a hole through my pocket. I only ever charged a higher rate for the ones who could afford it and were gullible enough to pay. Besides, it was small change to her. I'd have been a fool to turn the job down.

The phone rang then. I picked it up from the little well beside the gear stick and answered.

'Yeah?'

'I've got him right between the eyes. Gin and tonic for her, some kind of wanky cocktail for him. She's clearly got him reeled in, Jim. Won't be long before he's signing his prize riches away. Gotta give her her dues.'

'Is he that clueless?'

'Seems it. Wouldn't surprise me if she left without him, to be honest.'

'Classy chick.'

'All part of her game.'

'So what does she want to gain, exactly?'

'His money,' she said. 'A bit of lawyer cock. And he knows what he's getting into as well. Doesn't seem phased about paying for her drinks all night, probably more. It's flirting based on a business agreement, by the looks of it. Not like you and me.'

'No.'

'Anyway,' she said. 'There's someone been in the office tonight. Looking for you.'

'If it's any more insurance jobs or cheating husbands, tell them we've got enough on our plate. Can't be arsed with this now.'

'No, no. He wasn't the type. Black guy, seemed a decent bloke. Said he'd call in again soon.'

I wracked my brains for anyone I knew, anyone I might've pissed off somewhere down the line. I couldn't think of one. The girl with the miniskirt and running mascara was still eyeing me like I'd just pissed on her chips or something. Didn't know what her problem was, just that I seemed to be the centre of her universe.

'He say when? Hang on, wait.'

'I see him. If only he knew what we know.'

'Laura, you are just my secretary, love. Not my sidekick. It's not Batman and Robin. Far from it.'

'You'd make a shit Batman, anyway.'

She wasn't wrong. I was no superhero, but reckoned I could hold my own when it mattered. And Laura had seen me do just that, yet she'd been less than convinced I'd gotten away with my life without any damage. She knew the score, had seen me almost fall between the cracks. She'd helped to heal the scars, both physically and emotionally. I knew she loved me, and God knows why–but she did. Perhaps a bit too much.

'He's flagging a cab,' she said. 'Now's your chance, unless you want to drag it out even further?'

'No chance of that. I'll be back in ten minutes.'

'That's what you always say.'

I hung up and took the keys from the ignition. Locked the motor and stepped down Thomas Street with the camera app at the ready to catch him with his mistress, whoever she was. That didn't matter. I weaved through the crowds filling the pavements and got that bit nearer. There was enough noise and action going on for him not to take any notice of me snapping a few photographs. I edged back against the wall of a bar that wanted to be a pub and took several quick shots as they stood at the pavement's edge trying to flag a cab. Even took some film footage too, just a minute or so to really put him in the shit. No one batted an eyelid. Everyone was too busy knocking back shorts and smoking. I had what I needed. When a black cab pulled in and they got in the back, I dropped into the bar cum pub– The Bay Horse–and wrestled my way to the front.

It was so hot in here I was certain there were droplets of sweat dripping from the ceiling. When I finally ordered–a long, ice cold pint of Spanish beer–I slumped into the shadows and downed half of it in one. Spotted the girl with the running mascara peek her face around the door, then move her way inside. She was obviously looking for someone. I could only hope it wasn't me. I wasn't going to hang around any longer to find out. I'd had enough of it for one night and the place was too hammered for me to bother getting another. Besides, Laura and I had a bed to get home to. Better to upload what I'd gotten on the phone to the Mac before I called it a night. The Volvo would be fine where it was, for now.

I finished the beer and left the empty on the bar before battling my way back through, a thousand voices ringing in my ears.

M y office was merely a stone's throw down the street, tucked away behind a string of bars and sitting next door to a tattoo parlour. There was a cheap curry house around the back and the smell of Madras and Vindaloo was gradually replaced by the strong aroma of stale brandy the closer I got to the top floor. From the back window of my office itself, I could see out into the back alley and the rusting fire escape. The fire escape came in handy when I wanted to make a quick exit, which, when Laura was around, was more often than I'd like.

I went in through the little side door beside the tattoo place and took the stairs, the only things keeping me fit these days. When I reached the top, I almost coughed up a lung. I knew the smoking was finally taking its toll and I should do something about it, but I just couldn't bring myself to pack them in. By way of a reward, I sparked up on the landing before heading down the narrow corridor to find Laura slumped on the tatty leather couch I had brought in last week. She was sleeping, bless her. I slung two teaspoons of instant coffee in a mug and flicked the kettle on, which I kept on a little side table beside a filing cabinet, before crossing the landing and powering up the Mac. It was Laura's job to do all my office work, but I wanted to upload the photos for Gloria and send her the e-mail before I finally got my head down and put it to bed once and for all.

When the kettle boiled, I made it black and added a shot of brandy from the bottom drawer of the filing cabinet as Laura stirred. I looked at her, wondering how the hell I'd gotten involved with her at all, then remembered how she'd looked after me during the dark times. Remembered, also, how I ended up sharing her bed and decided it was no bad thing after all. She spoke up just as I was addressing my sugar craving.

'It'll be the death of you, Jim,' she said, nodding at the bottle on the side. She was talking like I didn't know it. 'I wish you'd just try. You could make the effort to cut down, at least.'

She was right, I knew. I could, and I had tried in the past, of course I had. But the pull of the burn was strong right now, and this Armagnac was a good one. Maybe I'd consider it when I reached the bottom.

'So tell me,' I said. 'This guy who was in asking about me. He give you a name?'

She scrabbled around on the couch as she shook the sleep away. Found a piece of paper she'd scribbled on down one of the cushions. 'Lloyd,' she said. 'Had dreadlocks. Absolutely stunk of weed. I almost asked him to hang around.'

Lloyd. Now there was a blast from the past. He was a volunteer at one of the soup kitchens I used to drop into during the dark times. Hadn't seen him since I made a visit there to catch up with an old friend who helped me out on the Angel case. But what the hell he wanted with me, I didn't know. I asked Laura.

'He didn't say. Said he'd call in again tomorrow. Didn't give a time.'

I sat down and drank the coffee. Sparked up and smoked as the night owls howled at each other outside. Gave Laura the iPhone and she got to work on uploading the photos to the Mac, ready for sending to Gloria.

'That reminds me,' she said. 'Another cheque arrived from her this afternoon. It's in my bag.'

Laura was pretty much my secretary these days, though she assumed otherwise. She dealt with the finance side of the business, filed reports, took in referrals from potential clients while I got on with the important stuff. She was also my partner, my lover. It seemed to work. She'd made it clear how she felt about me, but I wasn't entirely sure how I felt about her. But she kept me sane, just. And I knew she cared. I cared about her too, massively so. I just wasn't certain I loved her back.

'Can you cash it tomorrow?'

'No.'

'Why not?'

'Because,' she said, 'tomorrow is a Sunday. The banks are shut. And you're supposed to be taking me out for dinner.'

I'd forgotten. There was no way she'd forget. But maybe it would do us both good. This Gloria case had been getting right on my tits for weeks now. I suppose I needed to redis-cover what I saw in Laura in the first place. I checked her out quietly as she moved from the Mac to the filing cabinet, then back again. It had been a while since we'd thrown caution to the wind. Especially here in the office.

'Come here,' I said.

She turned, smiled. 'It can wait, Jim Locke. At least until we get home.'

But I wasn't sure I could. All that flesh on show outside was making it unbearable. I knew I should be thankful I was still in working order.

I flicked on the fan beside the couch and slung my shirt off. The heat was too much, even at this hour. Unprece-dented, they said on the news. It had been great for a while, but thirty degrees at half past midnight was a bit much. There seemed no end to it in sight.

'Done,' she said. 'All sent. I uploaded the ones form the Nikon too. Want a look?'

But I couldn't be arsed. I felt my eyes closing and

concentrated on drawing in breath. Wondered what Lloyd wanted with me. He was always someone I had time for.

'Jim?'

'Yeah?'

'Do you want to see or should I close it down?'

'Close it down,' I said. 'I need to sleep. You do too.'

'Oh no. It's home time.' I heard her dangling keys over my head. 'We're not crashing here again. You'll never get it up if you fall asleep on me.'

We locked up and she drove the Punto home—a new one after I'd gotten her sister's old one blown up. Fifteen minutes later we were both in bed, the sheets gathering at the bottom as the heat rose up a notch and Charlie slept soundly next door.

CHAPTER TWO

B ut I hardly slept a wink. Even with the windows wide open and the fan I'd picked up down the market two days ago switched to level three, the sweat seeped out of me like I had a bad case of malaria. I snatched a few hours after Laura wore me out but then the heat, with no sign of diminishing, had roused me again around four a.m. and it was there I lay, watching her sleep beside me as the evening's events went in and out of my tired brain.

I was glad to put the Gloria case to bed once and for all. She wouldn't be happy, but I was just the messenger. Her suspicions were confirmed, finally, and she'd have to get on with her life and start divorce proceedings. Something told me, though, that she wasn't the type, and I wouldn't be surprised if she confronted him the hard way. Revenge is a dish best served cold, they said. In Gloria's case, she'd probably serve it up freezing. I'd love to be a fly on the wall, just to see the bastard's face.

Then there was the girl with the mascara. A young woman, really. There was something strange about that. About *her*. I couldn't put my finger on it, but it was the way she was looking at me. And then she turned up in the Bay Horse, of course. I had to admit to myself that one of the reasons I'd left, perhaps the only reason, was because she showed her face in there too. I'd learned to trust my instincts over the years, and they told me she wanted something from me. What, I didn't know. But I didn't expect it to be our last encounter.

Around six a.m. I'd had enough of the voices in my head and jumped in the shower. The incessant bird chirping was the final straw. Felt a bit lightheaded, so took a few painkillers to take the edge off. Went out into the backyard to smoke and downed about a litre of ice cold water I'd kept in the fridge. Scorchio wasn't even close. The rising sun had already warmed up enough to send a fine mist ghosting into the air. The temperature was already twenty-six and was expected to go higher, much higher, by late afternoon. It didn't bode well for my mood. Sitting in the shade of the backyard, I was just about coping. Take me out into the world itself and I'd be climbing the walls by midday.

I dropped inside and threw some bacon in a frying pan. Got a pot of coffee on too. I never used to be a great coffee lover, but now I was an expert. Laura had seen to that when I moved in. We divided our time between this house, which was actually her sister's, and Laura's flat. Sara was off her meds again–I suppose we should've seen it coming after last time–and had been back at Laureate House for the past two months. The Angel case had sent her over the edge. Her friend's murder had almost gotten me killed too, and I'd almost called the whole private investigator thing off. Believe me, I'd have liked nothing more. Except Laura got giddy about it and by the end of Christmas day we were plotting where we were going to have an office. Most of my work covers insurance fraud, conjugal affairs, internal investigations–all that kind of shit. There are many methods I adopt, of course. Surveillance, tracing, and generally a lot of driving around and following people. I've seen it all. Saw it all before I was kicked off the force, too. Only now I was my own boss and I liked to keep it that way. It keeps us in food. It pays the bills. The lack of competition in this city keeps enough work coming in to keep me busy. Kept telling myself I'd knock it on the head one day and get a proper job. Who was I kidding?

It must've been the smell of bacon that had roused Charlie, because he came bounding down the stairs as I dropped two slices of bread in the toaster. I'd become quite attached to the kid. Sara, his mother, was in no fit state to look after him at the moment, and we hoped that would change in the future. So for now, he was Laura's responsibility. I chipped in for moral support and a fatherly influence, though I questioned my ability in that department since Karen, my ex, had upped and left with our daughter Nicole. At least we were now on speaking terms and I had some contact. Not a great deal, but it was better than none at all. I planned to keep it that way this time.

I sorted the boy out with some Rice Krispies and a beaker of juice and put together my bacon butty and a large coffee, black. Left enough in the pot for Laura. Got to admit, I was tempted–only tempted–to add a dash of brandy, just to give me some fire in my balls before getting to work, but I didn't. It could wait until dinner, since Laura had pointed out that I'd promised to take her out this afternoon. I'd almost forgotten. Though I'd need to be at the office at some point today if Lloyd was going to call in again. Strange day, Sunday, to be mithered about going anywhere, let alone calling in to see a PI. I suppose he had his reasons, but I don't know why he didn't just leave a number. And late last night was a strange time to drop in at the office. It had been six months since I'd last shared the same space with him, after I'd had to seek out the soup kitchen as part of the Angel case. Got to admit, he had me intrigued.

I sat and watched the news while Charlie ransacked the kitchen until Laura finally rolled from her pit almost two hours later. I must've gone through three coffees already by the time she'd gotten dressed. I'd always been a fan of Sundays, but not today. The heat was getting to me already and by the time I left in the Punto for the office I was sweating so badly I felt I needed a change of clothes. Wouldn't be at all surprised if I ended up with heatstroke before the week was done.

Town was just about stirring when I parked up around the back of the office. Most of the bars were already dumping their tables and chairs on the pavement, ready for the day's drinkers and diners, and it wasn't even eleven yet. I'd give it an hour before it got busy. The Northern Quarter was that kind of place. It had a good mix of residential flats and restaurants and bars that it usually got vibrant around lunchtime, especially in the summer. Christ, even the tiniest bit of sunshine was guaranteed to bring the punters out.

I made a short walk down Thomas Street and found a parking ticket stuck on the windscreen of the Volvo. Tossed it into the nearest bin on my way back. Would've made no difference anyway as I wouldn't be paying.

When I made it back to the office, out of breath and desperate for a smoke, I fired up the Mac again. Gloria had replied to Laura's e-mail, the one with the attached photographs of her husband doing the dirty on her. She said she wasn't surprised and thanked us for the service. Even said she would recommend me to all her friends, which was good to know. I could only smile at the thought of similar ladies queuing up to get their spouses in the frame. Was music to my ears.

Opened all the windows and flicked the fan to number three. If these temperatures were to carry on for much longer–and according to the experts, they were–I'd have to think about some better air con. All I wanted to do these days was spend my time in the shade. I was getting very little work done. Every time I came across a bar, which around here was a common occurrence, I wanted to join in. Nothing better than a cold beer in the hot sun. Maybe today would be that kind of day, after all. There was nothing on other than the boring surveillance on disgruntled employees for a bloody insurance firm. I couldn't give a fuck if they were disgruntled or not. I'd been there myself. But I didn't agree with what the insurance firm was doing. What right did they have to go spying on their staff? It was all money in the bank but a far cry from what I'd seen as a copper.

Maya, the tattoo artist from next door, came in to borrow some sugar. At least that was her excuse. I reckon she just liked the company when she didn't have any busi-ness. She'd struck up a good friendship with Laura, though, which I was pleased about. Since she was so close to her sister Sara, it was good for her to have another woman to confide in now Sara wasn't always around. I knew she didn't like to discuss Sara with me, which was just as well. I wasn't fond of it either. So Maya was a godsend and a breath of fresh air. She was one of those rocker types, a walking tattoo.

'You know,' she said, standing in front of the fan so it blew her dyed red hair all over the place, 'there was a guy hanging around here last week, looking for you. Rasta. I forget his name.'

'Lloyd,' I said to myself. 'Jesus, he must be keen. Did he say what he wanted me for?'

'Nah, just that he wanted to speak to you. Seemed a bit... strange.'

'In what way?'

'Just... I don't know. Paranoid?'

'That'll be the weed.'

'No, it was something else. He didn't seem stoned. Just really on edge.'

'He showed up last night,' I said. 'Laura was here.'

'So you know him?'

'Kind of,' I nodded. 'Well, yeah. But I've not seen him in a while. Look, are you on all day? Only I promised Laura dinner later on. If he turns up, can you give him my number?'

She nodded. 'What is it this time? Italian? Spanish?'

'She can have a Sunday roast and be happy.'

'Might be tempted to join you.'

'Well, you're welcome to. If you like. The more the merrier.'

She said she had an appointment to attend to at half twelve but could be free after that. In a way, it suited me. I just hoped Lloyd turned up before then. I wanted to know what he wanted before I ate and the booze got the better of me later on. I hated nothing more than not knowing what was going on, and I'd be prone to distraction as I got stuck into my roast potatoes. Laura, I knew, would want my full attention. If Lloyd was around last week, it had to be important. If he had any sense, he'd show up sooner rather than later.

But Laura turned up first, five minutes after Maya had gone back down. Charlie's dad had picked him up this morning shortly after I left. We both knew it was good for the kid. He was on his way to an all-star fun day out in Blackpool, and would spend the night there. No complaints from me. As much as I liked the kid, he could sometimes be a handful. We were both glad of the time off and it would give us free rein to hit the town for a few hours this afternoon, all being well.

Aunty Laura, of course, was more than a bit giddy by the time she arrived. She'd already treated herself to a chilled white wine in the bar across the road, just to get her in the mood for her dinner. I suppose that's what I liked about her–the fact that she liked a drink as much as me. The difference was that she knew when to stop.

'I've booked us a table at Hawksmoor for four o'clock. I believe they do a cracking roast beef.'

'Better make it a table for three. Maya's joining us.'

'Oh, great!'

'She's downstairs. Been in asking for you.'

She nodded as she made the call. 'That guy been back in yet?'

I was beginning to wonder if he'd turn up at all. But just a few minutes after Laura had made her way down to Maya, in he walked. Straight away, I knew he wasn't himself. This wasn't the Lloyd I once knew. He looked scared for a start. More than that.

He looked frightened to death.

———

I sat him down on the tatty leather couch. Gave him a coffee and he sparked up a joint like he owned the place. Almost worded him about that but when I saw his hands shaking, I waved it. I could see in his eyes he needed to talk and talk good. I wasn't sure if I was too keen on hearing what he had to say.

'Laura said you'd called. Maya too. I've been wracking my brains wondering who the hell you are.'

'It's good to see you, Jim,' he said, blowing potent ganja smoke around my office. His Jamaican patois bellowed thickly around the room. 'I've been trying to find you all week and when I finally discovered where you were, I couldn't get hold of you.'

I nodded, sat myself opposite. 'Been a while, eh? How are things at the shelter?'

'Things are good, you know. Busier than ever, man.'

The weed smoke was making me lightheaded. 'So, what brings you here?'

He looked down, took another long drag like it was a life support. 'Got some bad news, I'm afraid. I knew you'd want to know about it. Some of the other guys have been asking about you, too. Word's gotten around, you know?'

'Word? What word?'

'What you do, you know. Private investigator and all that. People want to know if you can help in any way. Police don't seem too concerned about it, you know what I mean?'

'Hang on a minute, Lloyd,' I said. 'You're not making much sense, man. Come on. Spill it.'

Massive sigh and another long drag. Clouds of skunk smoke filled the air. 'It's Stevie.'

'Stevie?'

'You know Stevie,' he said. He was damn right. I'd slept rough with him behind Ho's bakery for a few months not too long ago and he'd been a key part in the Angel investigation. Guy helped me out when I needed it most.

'Course I do,' I said, fearing the worst. Stevie had a major issue with the drink. We had that much in common, but it took him down roads I'd not even seen myself. I could picture him now, his long hair and beard making him look like a clapped out Jesus. 'He okay?' But I knew what was coming.

Lloyd looked me straight in the eye. 'He's dead, man. Stevie's dead.'

I knew it would have to happen sometime. 'Shit, man.'

He nodded, sighed, took a sip of his coffee. 'That's not it, though. They found his body down by the Irk. Was almost unidentifiable.'

'Must've been there a while,' I said. I knew he liked to kip beneath the arches down by the river. Stevie was known as a bit of a free spirit. He liked it on the streets. Liked being off the grid. He'd never have lasted in his own tenancy anywhere. I knew a lot of homeless people like that. When the drink or drugs took you, it really took you. He'd probably passed out or fell over a wall or something. Could've had a heart attack or anything. 'Poor bastard. I suppose it had to happen sometime. How old was he?'

'No,' he said. 'Apparently he'd only been there less than twenty-four hours. He'd burnt to death, Jim. Burnt to death, man. Some say he was burnt alive.'

'Fucking hell...' I got up, paced the room until I could pace no more. Sparked up and added a dash of brandy to my own coffee. 'Jesus, Lloyd. You better tell me more.'

'Well, that's just it,' he said. 'No one knows any more than that. He was burnt to death, may have been burnt alive, and as far as anyone knows, that's it. There'll be a funeral on Wednesday. Southern Cemetery. I'm just glad I got a hold of you before then because I knew you'd want to be there.'

He was right. I wouldn't miss this for anyone. 'I'll be there, Lloyd. Absolutely.'

'It's at ten o'clock.'

I nodded, took a long drag. Felt like a blast on Lloyd's joint then thought better of it. 'When was he found?'

'Few weeks back. A lot of the lads are really upset about it, you know?'

I wasn't surprised. 'Police been around?'

'Occasionally, but nothing like I'd have expected, you know. Spoke to a few of the guys and that's that. People have told them what we know, which was nothing much, and they seem satisfied with that. But a lot of people aren't happy with it. They want explanations, Jim. Someone gets burnt to death, people want to know why, you know what I mean?'

I wanted to know too. I drank the coffee and smoked down to the filter, thinking. Thinking of the possibilities more than anything. Could it have been an accident? Stevie wouldn't have taken his own life. I knew that much. And he'd have to have been crazy to set himself alight. It all pointed to something much more sinister than that. I wondered what on earth he could've been doing before his death. Who did he know? What had he been up to? Had he pissed anyone off enough to get himself killed?

'We just thought...' he said. 'Well, we just thought that with your connections to the police, you might be able to find out what went on. You know, dig around a bit. You must still have some contacts, yeah?'

I did, but I didn't want to go there. Not one bit. Not after what happened to Phil Young. DI Rob Robertson had had it in for me for years, long before the Angel case. Not only had I been pushed off the force, I'd become a laughing-stock and a big pain in Robertson's arse. The corruption at GMP went deep. Too deep for my liking. After the Angel case, I thought things would've settled down. But they hadn't. I knew they were keeping an even closer eye on me than I really deserved. One of their own and my one time mate on the force had been found out by yours truly. Taking his own life had been a convenience for them, especially Robertson. Yet coppers didn't forgive or forget. Phil Young had murdered Angel in cold blood and they'd covered it up. But she'd been just another missing girl in a long line of missing girls. Since I'd exposed it all, my cards were marked. I spent a great deal of time watching them as they watched me. The last thing I wanted was to go prying into their investigation on Stevie. As hard as it was, it wouldn't bring him back. And besides, a part of me reckoned Stevie was better off dead, anyway.

We sat in silence for a moment. I could barely believe what I was hearing, but Lloyd had no other reason to be here.

'Where was he found, exactly? Do we know any of this, Lloyd?'

'It was young Kyle Faulkner who found him. He went down to do the same, you know—sleep under the arches. Down by the water. When he went to the spot where he knew Stevie would be, there he was. He said the smell knocked him sick. He didn't know it was Stevie, of course. The body was too badly damaged. It must've been smouldering all night.'

'Jesus...'

'I know.'

I watched as Lloyd's eyes darted around the room, then out the window into the blinding white heat of the afternoon. He'd been rocking nervously since he'd arrived, which was as far away from Lloyd as you could get. He was a well known gentle Rasta who, rumour had it, could handle himself. Remembered what Maya had said about him being paranoid. Could've been the weed. He'd been smoking it for long enough to have done some serious damage to his brain. But then...

'Is there anything else, Lloyd? Something you're not telling me? Only you seem a bit on edge. I know I've not seen you for a while but this isn't like you, man.'

He looked down at his feet, took in the rest of the joint before crushing the dimp between his fingers and tossing it out the window.

'I think there's someone been following me,' he said. 'And I don't know why. Seen him a few times now. It can't be just coincidence.'

I drained my coffee. 'Back up a bit. From the beginning.'

'Jim...'

'Could be important, Lloyd.'

'I should get going, to be honest with you. Got the kids to see to.'

'Lloyd,' I said, looking him square in the eyes, 'spill it. A problem shared is a problem solved. You know that.'

He sighed. 'Seen him around the shelter a few times.'

'Exactly how many times?'

He thought for a moment. 'Twice. Wednesday just gone and the Monday before that.'

I took out a notebook from my desk drawer and started writing. 'Description?'

'He was big,' he said. 'White guy. Looked like he worked out, you know. I don't just mean to stay fit, I mean...'

'What, a proper body builder?'

'Yeah,' he said. 'Looked like he could do some damage, you know. Like a bouncer or something. Pure muscle.'

I nodded. 'Go on.'

'Really big guy. I reckon, what? Six foot? A bit more, maybe. And bald. Like it was razored bald, proper shiny.'

'He speak to you?'

'No.'

'So what makes you think he's been following you?'

'I don't know, you see. Just... he's been hanging around. Parked across the road.'

'What does he drive?'

'A big white Range Rover. Souped up, you know.'

'Okay,' I said. 'But it doesn't mean he's been following you, Lloyd. Could be anything, could be totally innocent.'

'Just a coincidence?'

'Yeah,' I said. 'Just that.'

'So why is he parked outside, then?'

'What?'

He tossed his head towards the window. 'See for yourself.'

I looked out into the street and there he was. Or at least the Range Rover was. I felt queasy all of a sudden. 'What does he want?'

'I've no idea.'

'Thought about asking him?'

'No,' he said. 'It just doesn't feel right, you know. Don't ask me why.'

'Think it's anything to do with Stevie?'

'Well, he only showed up after Stevie had been found dead. So what do you think?'

'He tried speaking to you? Any of the other lads?'

'Not that I know of.'

I jotted down the number plate and brought myself back in. The heat was rising. I needed a cold one.

'I was driving home one day,' he said, 'and I spotted him in the mirror, you know. Right behind me on the Parkway. There was another guy driving, and he was the passenger. I would put it down to coincidence, but Manchester's a big city. Doesn't seem right to me.'

Me neither. And I knew where he was coming from, too. I'd been a victim of such intimidation tactics myself.

'So what about the other guy? What did he look like?'

'Similar. Muscly, stocky, as far as I can tell. Hard to say since I've only seen him behind the wheel.'

'They threatened you at all?'

'No,' he said. 'But they always seem to turn up whenever I'm out. They're definitely following me.'

'No wonder you seem paranoid.'

'Got stuff to be paranoid about.'

'I'd think about giving up the weed.'

He laughed at that. 'You can see for yourself, Jim. They're onto me for whatever reason and it's fucking with my head.'

'I'm not surprised.'

'What, that they're following me?'

'That it's fucking with your head,' I said. 'Right, back to Stevie. Can you tell me anything else about that? I mean, any of the lads know the last time he was seen alive? Had anyone spoken to him in the days before his death?'

'You'd have to call in at the shelter, man. You know how they all come and go. If there's no beds you sometimes won't see anyone for a week.'

'Things still busy down there, then?'

'Busier than ever.'

'When was the last time Stevie had a bed there?'

He scratched his head and stared into space. 'Now you're asking. You know what he's like—was. I think about three weeks ago but I'd have to check.'

'Give me a ring when you've done that,' I said. I handed him my card. 'I'll speak to some people at the funeral, I

suppose. But I can't promise anything, Lloyd. You know
that. The police aren't very forthcoming with the truth
when it suits them. Especially when it's me digging around.'

'But you'll look into it?'

I sighed. Can't say I wasn't interested, but this was too
hot to handle, by the sounds of it. Except Stevie was a mate,
and I owed him. 'Maybe,' I said. 'I'll do what I can. In the
meantime, what about him?' I arched my head to the
window. 'He been following you this morning?'

'Must have,' he said. 'Though I haven't seen him until
now, really. I parked up around the corner and when I got
here, he was already parked outside. Must've known I was
coming here.'

Which had me thinking. Did he know why Lloyd was
here? 'Have you mentioned this to anyone? You know, that
you were coming to see me about Stevie?'

'It's common knowledge at the shelter. Everyone's keen
to know what's going on. Not only that, people want to see
your face at the funeral, you know. So there was that too.'

I nodded. Offered him another coffee, but he declined.
As far as I was concerned, a cold beer was the order of the
day right now.

'I'd better get back,' he said. 'Supposed to be taking my
son to football in an hour.'

I jotted down his mobile number and added it to my
iPhone. Said I'd walk with him to his car. The fire escape
would be ideal and would save him leaving by the front
door. But before we went anywhere, I hung out the window
facing the street and took several shots of the Range Rover
on the phone. There was no sign of the guy Lloyd had
talked about.

We crossed the hallway and into the other room, where

the Mac was. I lifted the old window frame up and we stepped out onto the fire escape.

'Don't look down,' I said.

We were on the ground in less than a minute and took a shortcut back to his car. It was only a stone's throw away round the back of the craft centre on Copperas Street.

'Ring me,' I said, once he was buckled in. 'If anything else comes up. And I mean anything. Otherwise, I'll see you at the funeral.'

He nodded. 'Yeah, man.'

'Any time, day or night. And I want to know when Stevie last had a bed.'

'I'll check it tomorrow.'

We shared a look. 'I can't believe he's dead,' I said. 'Not like this. Not Stevie.'

'Just wait until it sinks in, man. Then you'll start to get angry.'

I could feel it rising already. After he drove off, I walked the short distance back to the office and took the fire escape back up. I switched everything off but kept the window to the street open. The place needed some serious air. There'd been two missed calls from Laura. I reminded myself I should always remember the phone. Old habits.

I dialed her back and stepped up to the window, but when I checked the street, the Range Rover was gone. I could only wonder if it was tailing Lloyd again and why. I didn't know if they had anything to do with Stevie's death, of course, but it was more than unusual they'd started watching the shelter since his body was found. I knew then that it wouldn't be the last time I'd see it.

CHAPTER THREE

We spent the rest of that Sunday afternoon having dinner and doing what came naturally–getting drunk. Which was just as well, because I couldn't get Stevie's face from my mind. By the time Laura and I got back to her flat, a tiny one bedroom job just a mile or so from her sister Sara's, it was gone midnight. I don't know what we were thinking, going back to the flat, but we probably thought, in our drunken state, that it would be quicker to get to from the centre of the city. Besides, we hadn't stayed there for a while, at least three weeks, so it sort of made sense for us to drop in and check how things were. It was, after all, Laura's own place. We'd been house-sitting for Sara for too long now, and I'd probably spent more time there than the flat. It still felt strange to me.

I can't speak for Laura, but I was asleep as soon as my head hit the pillow. And by the time I'd woken, the morning was over and it was edging into afternoon. Laura had left me a text message to let me know she'd gone shopping. But that was two hours ago and with the clock ticking by–it was now 12:17–I had to wonder where she was. Depends what she was shopping for.

I was surprised I'd slept this long, especially in this heat–it was now thirty degrees again, according to the radio–but then a flashback of the night before came back to haunt my battered head. It was Maya's idea to get on the Sambuca shots, which at the time I knew would be a mistake. It turned out to be true because my head was pounding and when I shifted my legs out of bed, I instantly felt queasy. It was lucky I didn't throw up right there and then.

Couldn't face any breakfast. It was way too late for that anyway, so I just made a double strong instant coffee, dived in and out of the shower and dragged on my jeans and a tee-shirt. Laura had been hassling me to put some shorts on and said I was mad to be wearing jeans all the time, but I just couldn't bring myself to wear them. I was a private investigator and it required appropriate attire. I just didn't feel at home in anything else, blazing sun or not.

As far as the rest of the day went, I had nothing much planned. I'd decided to put the insurance job on hold in order to put some feelers out about Stevie. He'd been on my mind most of the time since Lloyd called to see me.

He'd even been in my dreams last night. I recalled him whispering to me down in the alley behind Ho's bakery, the place we used to bed down. In my dream, it was cold. Winter time. I watched him as he drank from a bottle of Whyte and Mackay, part of his face obscured. He was whispering either to me or to himself and when I called out to him, he turned to me, the other half of his face black and blistered, the smell like burnt pork fat.

I put it from my mind, but I knew it would be back.

I picked the Volvo up and tossed another parking ticket

in the bin. Didn't bother calling in to the office. It could wait until later. The best thing about being my own boss was that I could pretty much do what I wanted when it came to office hours. I called the shots, didn't need to answer to anybody except Laura. She was enough to keep anyone in check. But I liked that about her. I knew that if I couldn't bring myself to face the day, she'd be in my ear about it. Nine times out of ten, if I wasn't in the office, she'd be there holding the fort, taking referrals and answering the phone. She kept the operation professional–most of the time. Which was more than could be said for me.

I took the Volvo a short distance up to Cheetham Hill Road and parked in the grounds of the hotel on the corner before making my way back down behind it. Stevie's body had been found beside the waters of the Irk below, the river which ran beside the train tracks. I descended the steps that led down from the road, entering the staircase via a hidden alcove in the structure of the old iron bridge. The waters were treacherous. As I made my way down the steps, I thought about how easy it would be to fall in. Especially if you were unstable and unsteady on your feet. Perhaps for the desperate and lost, only a step off the edge would surely lead to a nasty drowning. It was deadly, and one of the many reasons I never slept under the arches here. But I knew others liked it for that very reason. A man was less likely to get hassle down here and only a select few would doss down. Stevie, I knew, was just one of them. I had to wonder if there'd been anyone else around the night he went up in flames.

I could smell the stale, burnt odour before I reached the bottom. Felt it in the back of my throat. I knew I was near to where he'd been found. There was a sharp sweetness to the air, and the sound of the crashing water was making me dizzy.

When I reached the stone bank below and turned right into the darkness of the arches, the smell got much stronger. Even in the darkness, the scorched and blackened brick wall stood out, and I could hear the flies buzzing. The flames must have licked high, easily as high as the ceiling above. I looked up, saw the black charcoal brickwork dripping damp droplets to the floor. I could taste that burn now. I retched and spat bile away before I sparked up and turned to the spot before me, the place where Stevie had lay burning. Blew smoke out into the dank air and felt a nicotine rush.

It was a foul mess, and it clearly hadn't been just any fire. I wondered if the melted grey waxy substance was the remains of his fat that had melted into the brickwork. If the oily residue at the base of the wall was what was left of his bodily fluids. If the blistered and cracking black and red stuff at my feet was what was left of his flesh.

There would have been scenes of crime officers here as soon as he was found, of course. And a forensic examination would've been carried out in detail. The body removed, the remains cleaned up. Maybe the mess that was left behind was just my imagination, nothing more. I'd never been to the spot where a man had burned to death before. It was ugly and brutal and there wasn't just the overbearing smell of decay, but petrol, too. And death. I was certain it was made worse by the heat.

I took out my phone and snapped away. Got several pictures of the charred walls and floor, the oily mess around it. I took pictures that would've been from the victim's point of view as he lay burning. Another arched wall directly ahead of him, the crashing water of the lock beyond. The graffiti all over the place.

It wasn't lost on me that there was a lot of it around, but I hadn't expected to see a crude red swastika daubed onto the wall just a few feet from the scorch marks. And beneath that, a horizontal lightning bolt and the letters E.N.D. scrawled in blue.

End?

End of what? His life?

I took some more photographs, got some closeups of the graffiti before I felt the shivers down my spine. There was a sudden gust of wind through the arches, and the noise of the crashing water had me mesmerised for a minute as I took the sight in. I couldn't help but feel there was something else not quite right about the whole picture, but I couldn't put my finger on it.

Took one last drag and flicked the dimp into the darkness, pocketed the phone and turned back towards the steps. Had the weirdest of feelings, like I was being watched.

I wondered if anyone else had dossed down here since he'd been found. And I knew I'd have to speak to Kyle Faulkner sooner rather than later, maybe even today. I was still waiting on a call from Lloyd about the last time Stevie had taken a bed at the shelter. I knew I needed a timeline of events leading up to his demise here.

As I looked around, a sudden depression hung over me. He'd died here alone, the victim of a brutal and cowardly attack. I don't think anyone knew why. It made no sense.

I felt that chill again and another gust of wind had sent the dust particles up from the ground, the scent of burnt decay filling the air and the sound of buzzing bluebottles and crashing water cutting through the afternoon. I felt cold all of a sudden.

Couldn't get away quick enough.

I drove back down to the office so I could upload the pictures I'd taken to the Mac. I could still smell the burnt charcoal, sickly and sweet, as I joined queuing traffic at Shudehill. When I got to the office, I found Laura emptying out shopping bags full of clothes she'd bought herself. Asked her if anyone had been in touch. She said no.

I left her to try on her things and fired up the computer. Before it came to life, my phone rang. It was Lloyd.

'I got the information you wanted,' he said. 'And I spoke to Kyle Faulkner, too. Told him about you wanting to meet up with him, you know.'

'Go on.'

'Stevie last had a bed twenty-four days ago. So a little bit longer than first thought. It was a Friday night. Thirteenth of June. No one saw him since until Kyle found him dead.'

'Which was?'

'Friday the twentieth of June. Though could've been the twenty-first, early hours on the Saturday.'

I checked my calendar. It was now the seventh of July, which would've put it at just over two weeks ago. And it would've been just over three weeks since he'd last had a bed at the shelter. Question was, what was he up to in the week between his last stay at the shelter and the night he was burnt alive?

I remembered how quick the white Range Rover had disappeared from the street once Lloyd had left yesterday. Asked him if he'd seen it again.

'They followed me most of the way home,' he said. 'As far as Hulme, you know, then I got away from them on the Parkway. You know what the traffic can be like on there. Couldn't see them in my mirror by the time I rolled up home. But then I saw them again when I dropped my son off at Hough End for the football, you know. They were parked up near the changing rooms.'

'They say anything?'

'I didn't hang around.'

'And what about your lad? He say anything?'

'Nothing.'

'Seem okay to you?'

'He seemed fine, man. But I'm thinking of going to the police.'

I sparked up. 'Lloyd, I think that's a bad idea. For now, at least.' He didn't sound convinced. 'Lloyd?'

'I understand, man.'

'They haven't threatened you.'

'Not directly, no. But then I don't want them to, either.'

'I don't think it'll come to that.' Though I reckoned I could be wrong. 'Look, let's sleep on it. For the time being. Let's get the funeral out of the way then take it from there.'

'Okay.'

'Now about Kyle. He's been around the shelter then?'

'Was here this morning. No beds tonight so he's gone walkabout.'

'He say where?'

'Nah, but a few reckon he kips down by the canal, you know. Piccadilly basin.'

I knew it was a well-known cruising ground for gay men, but I didn't think Kyle was the type. Though sometimes, maybe, if he needed money or drugs...

'Okay,' I said. 'Thanks. Unless you need me, I'll see you on Wednesday for the funeral. And if you hear of anything else, ring me straight away.'

He said he would and hung up. I took a long, hard drag on my smoke and tried to decide about where to go next.

There was no guarantee the Faulkner kid would be down by the canal this minute, but if he was anything like most homeless men, he'd be sorting out his doss about now. Or at least getting strung out on something strong.

Laura handed me a coffee, black. The sound of the whirring fan was making me dizzy. I still felt hungover. Perhaps it had been a bad idea to visit the spot where Stevie died. It had brought a dark cloud hanging over the day, and I felt more than just queasy. I drank the coffee and smoked while Laura hovered around me with new dresses and shoes. I needed food, something fast and bad for you, so I sent Laura out for a couple of chicken kebabs while I jotted down some notes and uploaded the photos. I created a file specifically for the Stevie case and crashed back on the couch, sweating with the afternoon heat despite the fan on number three. Not for the first time, I thought about how none of it made any sense. Wondered if the heavies in the white Range Rover had anything to do with it, and if so, why?

What did it all come down to?

I couldn't rule out suicide, of course, though I doubted very much that even if Stevie had intended to kill himself, he would choose to set himself on fire.

Laura came back and we ate quickly. She said she had more shopping to do, as if two dresses and a pair of sandals weren't enough, and had arranged to meet up with Maya again. The hours were ticking by and by the time I finished the kebab, it was nearly half two. I knew I had nothing better to do than find Kyle Faulkner. I didn't know the kid, but I knew his face well enough to recognise him, even if it was obscured by a bottle of white lightning, though I'm told alcohol wasn't his drug of choice.

'I'll phone you when we're done,' she said. 'Don't forget, Charlie's back tonight. I'll need to pick him up.'

I nodded, told her about Kyle and how I'd spent my afternoon so far. 'Take your time. I need to find him. I should speak to him soon.'

'Can it not wait until the funeral?'

'If push comes to shove,' I said. 'But that's two days away, and a lot can happen in two days.'

'And the police?'

'Not interested, according to Lloyd. I might check them out, see what they've got to say.'

'Probably not much.'

'No.'

She looked at me. 'What's your gut feeling, love?'

What was my gut feeling? I wasn't sure but answered her, anyway. 'I think he was murdered, all right. The why of it all is a different matter entirely.'

'Isn't that always the case?'

'Sometimes it's more straightforward. This doesn't feel straightforward at all.'

'You'll work it out,' she said. 'Isn't that what you do?'

But this didn't feel right to me. And when something didn't feel right, I had to find out why.

I left her to her shopping and headed out on foot towards the Piccadilly Basin and the Rochdale Canal. Smoked keenly on the way and craved a cold one as the afternoon sun beat down and the cool new bars made a killing. Kept telling myself it could wait.

My route took the back way, down Dale Street and Tariff Street. Almost took a wrong turning down Back China Lane, which brought back bad thoughts about my recent run in with the Chinese on the Angel case. As far as I knew, I was in the clear, but my friend Bob Turner hadn't been so lucky. Interpol and the Spanish authorities were still looking for his body. Needless to say, it kept me looking over my shoulder.

I took a shortcut over the water, taking a bendy bridge to the Rochdale Canal, and trudged through the housing complex beside it. Further along, under the narrow tunnel that went under Great Ancoats Street, the scum had washed over the side, making it slippy underfoot. I knew it was a notorious place for scoring drugs or sex or both. Usually in as many varieties as you could count. Crack, smack. Whatever you needed to get you through the night. Most took comfort in the fuzzy, warm glow of brown. But then when the shakes came, and there was no smack to go around, it wouldn't take long before the sweats got bad. You could sometimes hear the cries of anguish late at night, and not even White Lightning could quiet it. I knew plenty of homeless men and women that could only survive the streets with something to get them high, make them forget.

And there was the sex too, either selling it or buying it. A suck or a fuck didn't come cheap these days, and there were plenty of punters who would willingly hand over decent cash to the likes of Billy Kelly. Yet there was often danger involved. Rumour had it that young Billy had gone missing last winter and hadn't been seen since. It was assumed he was lying at the bottom of the canal somewhere.

It was dark in the tunnel and I was glad to reach daylight again on the other side. When I found my way onto the canal tow path I saw three disheveled looking men sitting on a graffitied bench beside the lock up ahead. Even in this heat, one of them was wearing a mud coloured bubble coat that had seen better days. Another had his bare feet to the air, except when I got closer I could see they weren't feet at all. They were stumps. Poor bastard had no toes, probably taken by the cold in the depths of a harsh January. Or perhaps something more sinister entirely. He had a set of crutches beside him and a plastic bottle of white cider in his arms.

The younger man was just a kid. He was pacing up and down and talking animatedly to the others. They clocked me as I approached and shared a look. I couldn't be certain the younger kid was Faulkner, but his face looked familiar. I introduced myself and asked him.

He nodded. 'Lloyd spoke to me. Said you'd want to see me.'

'That's right. The sooner the better. Just so I can try to jog your memory of events.'

'This about Stevie?' It was the guy in the bubble coat. Faulkner nodded, said it was. 'Bloody awful. He didn't deserve that.'

He wasn't wrong. No one deserved to go out like Stevie did. Seemed they all knew him and when I asked if they were at the funeral Wednesday, they all nodded solemnly.

'So, Kyle,' I said. 'Just run things back a bit. What happened the night you found him? Lloyd said you came across the body.'

He spat into the water beside us and took a seat. The guy with the stumps, so thin you could mistake him for a scarecrow, handed him a smoke. I sparked up too.

'He was still smouldering,' he said. 'You know. Burning. At first I didn't understand how a simple fire like that could really burn. It was fucking hot, man. The temperature coming off that thing... like nothing I've felt or seen before, ever. I couldn't even get that close, know what I mean? And then I saw his head. It was definitely a head. A face, you know?'

I nodded for him to go on, blew smoke into the summer sky and gritted my teeth.

'I couldn't believe what I was seeing,' he said. 'Couldn't be sure it was a body at all. It was as if it was burning from the inside. And the shit coming out of him, man. It was like lava. Fucking unreal, mate.'

He couldn't have been any older than twenty. I asked him.

'Nineteen, I think.'

'You think?'

'Doesn't really matter, especially out here.'

I knew that, of course, from my own stint pounding the pavements and sleeping behind Ho's Chinese bakery.

'So, when you found him—what did you do then?'

'Got the fuck out of there,' he said. 'Gotta admit, I was pretty scared. There he was, burning to death. Dead already. And there was no one else around, as far as I could tell, so—'

'You thought you might be next?'

He said nothing, and the others turned away. The guy with the stumps bared a mouth empty of teeth except for a handful of molars. Rotting cavities wasn't even close. I finished my smoke and crumpled it beneath my boot.

'I flagged a police car down,' he said. 'They're always going up and down Cheetham Hill Road. Showed them where it was, then the fire engines came and they closed it all off.'

'You give a statement?'

'Yeah. They had me waiting for four hours.'

Sounded about right. I glanced at the other two, Bubble Coat with his head down and Stumps letting a line of drool drip to the floor. I guessed they were both strung out on some shit or other and didn't want to talk, but I asked them what they knew anyway.

Bubble Coat shrugged. Said his name was Dennis. He had a lip as fat as the bubbles on his jacket. 'I didn't know him,' he said. 'Only by sight to let on to.'

'Same here,' Faulkner said. I caught a nod from Stumps too.

'Bad shit, man,' said Dennis. 'He seemed like a nice guy.'

'He was a drinker,' Stumps said. He ran a needle marked arm across his mouth. 'Everyone knew that. Could've gone to sleep. Might've been dead before he went up in flames.'

'Almost seems pointless being cremated,' Faulkner said. 'Poor cunt's been melted from the inside out already. I don't know what made him burn like that, but he must've suffered. Unless he was dead already, like Shaun said.'

The possibility he'd been dead already had crossed my mind, but without the autopsy results I couldn't possibly know. There was probably nothing left of him for the white coats to examine anyway, so I doubted they'd come to any other conclusions. Seemed any evidence on this one was hard to come by. To identify the reasons why he was killed—if indeed he was killed—would require piecing together the days and weeks leading up to his death. Were there any significant events prior to his demise? If the police weren't asking, it was my job to do so. I asked the three guys before me to jog their memories a bit more.

'Now you're asking,' Faulkner said. 'Hard to say what he was up to, really. Kept himself to himself, you know. He'd call into the shelter for soup and a bed, if he could get one. Like most of us. Some of the lads would spot him out and about. You'd never know where he was from one day to the next.'

'Where had he been hanging about the most lately?'

'He slept under the arches a lot,' Stumps said. 'He was a well-known face down there. Sometimes he'd turn up in Rusholme, Platt Fields, places like that. Was known to doss down under the Mancunian Way.'

'To sleep?'

'Yeah,' Faulkner said. 'Or to chat, you know. Was never really without a drink, was he?'

When I knew him, he was never without one either. 'Can you remember the last time each of you saw him?'

'Had to be about three weeks ago,' Bubble Coat said. 'Might've been longer. I saw him walking down Market Street, dragging his shit behind him.'

'You talk?'

He shook his head. 'Just a wave across the street. I was heading out of town and he was heading in.'

I looked to Faulkner. 'You?'

'It was a Thursday. About three or four weeks ago.'

'Three or four?'

'Shit, man, I don't know. Four? I lose track of the days. Four weeks is a long time. He was walking through the Northern Quarter. Just near that fucking burger place all the hipsters can't get enough of. I let on to him. Got a grunt back.'

'Not in the best of moods, then?'

'He was always like that,' Stumps said. Yet it wasn't the Stevie I knew.

Faulkner was nodding. 'Didn't expect much in the way of conversation,' he said. 'He just didn't seem the type. Had his head down a lot of the time, you know. Like I said, I knew his face, he knew mine. Recognised most of us, I think. Just to let on to, you know. Nothing more than that.'

I nodded. Felt the sweat drip down my neck. 'Any of

you notice anything strange about him? You know, any people around him you didn't recognise, anything like that?'

'Not really,' Faulkner said. 'Sometimes he was in a good mood, sometimes he wasn't.'

'He never said anything about anyone else,' said Bubble Coat. 'No one we didn't know, like.'

'He gave no indication of any problem he might've had?'

They all shook their heads. I suppose I shouldn't have been surprised. They were all strung out on something. And what did they care, anyway? They weren't exactly Stevie's friends, despite him being one of them. He was just an acquaintance. And now he was dead.

I got the feeling I wasn't going to get much else from these three, as the silence between us lingered. They were sorry he was dead, sure, but they weren't exactly clambering for answers, like Lloyd had implied. I wondered, though, if his death had affected them in other ways. Were they now looking over their shoulders too?

Faulkner shrugged when I put it to him. 'Nah,' he said. 'I think most of us are better off dead anyway.'

It wasn't too long ago when I'd thought the same myself. I've stared into the abyss too, just like these guys, just like all of them, and found myself wishing for death, even going as far as tipping myself over the edge, quite literally. But Stevie, so I'm told, was never suicidal. It just wasn't in his makeup and I doubted he had the balls to do it, anyway. So someone wanted him dead for a reason.

'One other thing,' I said. 'Lloyd's told me about a white Range Rover that keeps showing up, especially since the body was found. Any of you shed any light on that?'

'I've seen it around,' Bubble Coat nodded. 'Outside the shelter. Doesn't mean anything.'

I decided not to mention the fact that it had been tailing

Lloyd for days. Instead, I sparked up another smoke and thanked them for their time. 'See you at the funeral.'

They said nothing as I walked away into the baking sun.

The heat was making me feel dizzy as I walked back to the office, and my hangover was weighing me down. My legs felt heavy, and all I wanted to do was sit in the shade with a cold one. I ran the conversation through my mind as I walked, thinking about the places he'd doss down in. I knew there were plenty of others who knew Stevie, were perhaps acquaintances or shared a bottle during the cold nights, just like I did. I'd maybe call in on all the places he'd get his head down. Someone had to know something. Maybe he'd been scared about something and had talked before he went up in flames. And if it was a random attack– as crazy and sick as it was–maybe there was no reason for his death at all. Was there some sick bastard out there simply getting his kicks by setting people on fire? None of it made sense, and I wondered what the police knew, if anything. I knew I'd have to speak to them, though knew it wouldn't go down well, especially if DI Rob Robertson turned out to be the SIO. But Stevie was one of the good guys, good enough for me to call him a friend. I had every right to go poking around.

It struck me right then, as I dodged the traffic on the way back through town, that I didn't even know if Stevie had any next of kin. A Mother? A Sister? A Brother? I guessed if he had any family members or friends from a previous life, they'd show up at the funeral. If they even knew he was dead.

I dropped back into the office and added a few notes to

his file. There were no new e-mails. Laura sent me a text to let me know Charlie's father had dropped him home and he was now settling in for a sleepover with his little mate next door. Laura said that she'd gone out with Maya. She didn't say where to, but the night was ours. It was all I wanted to hear. I flicked the radio on as the early evening commute got in full swing. That was one thing I didn't miss about being a copper. My time was my own and I could work in the quiet hours if I wanted to.

I dropped two fingers of brandy into my coffee mug and knocked it back. I needed a livener to get the thoughts ticking over. Made myself a black coffee, just to tell myself I didn't need another drink, but then I added another shot to it for good luck. I knew I'd need it if I was to call in at GMP. My old work colleagues were never happy to see me these days, particularly DI Rob Robertson. Yet he knew I had one over on him. In fact, all the force did, especially after the ramifications of the Angel case. The damage to their integrity had been immeasurable, and they had very little credibility after the corruption was exposed. Still, I knew I'd have to tread carefully where they were concerned. I wouldn't put it past them to have me tracked. They'd done it before, they'd no doubt do it again.

I knew if I were to get any answers, I'd need a cast iron legitimate way in, which was where Stevie's next of kin came in. Trouble was, I didn't know if he had any. I don't ever remember him talking about any family he had. He'd always preferred to avoid that subject, and I suppose he had his reasons. I'd maybe call Lloyd again, see if he knew. The shelter kept records, so I guessed he might know something.

After half an hour of staring into space, I must've drifted off for a while and only came around when the news head-lines chimed into the room. It was six o'clock. I paced the office, checked my phone for messages, gazed out into the city. The evening was busy, and the summer had brought the punters out again. I watched as the bars slowly filled up, even on a Monday, and made that call to Lloyd. There was no answer. I was beginning to feel hungry and called Laura, but she wasn't answering either. It was as if the whole world wanted to be disconnected. I sometimes felt like that too.

I thought about my ex wife, Karen, and our daughter, Nicole. Thought about how disconnected we were. Opened up my text messages to my daughter and hovered my thumb over the screen, trying to think of something to say. I hadn't seen her in a while and the gap was getting wider. When I couldn't think of anything, I closed up the office and took the Volvo back to the flat, picking up six bottles of ale at the off license on the way. A new case often brought the unexpected with it and I knew tonight could be my last chance to relax before I got in too deep to get out quick enough.

CHAPTER FOUR

I spent the evening drinking alone. Laura had called me around nine o'clock, only to inform me she was staying out for a curry with Maya and I shouldn't wait up. I wouldn't have been able to anyway because I passed out in front of the news at ten and only woke upon her return. She was in a good mood and insisted I come to bed immediately, but I declined what was on offer and instead got my head down. Didn't manage much sleep though, thanks to the heat, but finally got off again around eight the following morning and slept like a baby for six hours. I didn't see much point in going anywhere by the time I'd showered and come round, so I just hung around the flat for the rest of the day while Laura went visiting her sister.

I'd dreamt of fire and smoke and whisky, a jumbled mess of brick walls and bluebottles and marijuana. It was a heady mix. I lay on the couch, completely deflated with the heat of yet another scorcher. There was no way I could venture outdoors, not on a day like this. Outside, the sounds and smells of summer filled the air, but I wanted no part of it. This kind of weather was for lizards only. The papers and TV were all full of it. You couldn't hang your head out the window without taking the news in. Seemed global warming had come to bite us on the arse. We were repeatedly told that everyone was happy and the sunshine brought out the best in all of us. I was just amazed anyone could function at all. There was no end in sight and at this rate, they'd call a countrywide drought soon enough.

I was happy to lie back with nothing on but a pair of nineteen eighties briefs and Laura's laptop for company. It was hardly work, but I kept telling myself it was. With the fan on number three and a bucket of ice in the corner–I'd give anything a go–I waded in to researching Stevie's tragic demise. I had to start somewhere.

I read a few articles about how bodies burn. The flames dance across the skin for several hours before penetrating the lower, dermal layers. Then the fat oozes from the cracked and blistered flesh, a good source of fuel, certainly enough to keep it burning through the night. Any clothing would act as a wick and whoosh. Just like barbecued pork.

If someone had dropped a flammable liquid over Stevie before throwing a spark, I very much doubt he'd have died without suffering. It would've been a blessing if he was killed in some other way first. There was no way of knowing now. I thought about my trip to the spot where he was found. Thought about the oily residue coating the concrete, the waxy substance on the walls. The fat bluebottles. The cascading water that would've drowned out the noise of the crackling flames. Wondered if anyone else had seen something prior to Faulkner. I'd be interested to know if the white Range Rover had been spotted in the area at or around the same time or in the hours before he burned. I knew there was a hotel within walking distance. Getting my hands on some CCTV footage–that's if GMP hadn't got it first–could prove invaluable.

I realised I needed to delve deeper, but I didn't even know Stevie's surname, let alone his last whereabouts before he left this world. I needed to call Lloyd. I grabbed myself a shit beer from the fridge–Laura's purchase, not mine–and flipped the cap before taking a long drink and scrabbling for my phone, which I finally found under the couch. There were several missed calls, all from an unknown number. The phone had been on silent. Most likely a Nigerian computer engineer out to know my bank details. I deleted them and brought up Lloyd's number. Dialed and waited.

He answered just as I was about to hang up.

'Lloyd? It's Jim Locke.'

'Yeah, man,' he said. 'What can I do for you? Not seen it today, in case you're wondering. Did you catch up with Kyle?'

I realised he was talking about the Range Rover. 'Yes, I did,' I said, 'but that's not why I'm calling. It's something else. Stevie in particular.'

'Go on.'

'You have records there, don't you? You know, you keep notes and stuff. Family details, next of kin, all that.'

'Yeah,' he said. 'Got a whole file on him. Anyone who comes here–or used to come here–has to consent to providing information, you know. We refer to other services when required, so we need a history of our client's lives. Health conditions, drug and alcohol use, that kind of thing. Previous tenancies, debts, criminal records, stuff like that. Pretty much a case history.'

'Even better than I thought. Listen, I'd like to have a look, if possible.'

'Well, I'm not supposed to, man.'

'Lloyd, it's important. Could be something in there.'

'Well, it's confidentiality and all that, you know.'

'I get that,' I said. 'But I want to find out why Stevie had to die. If there's anything in that file that can provide answers, I want to see it.'

There was a pause on the other end. 'I'll see what I can do. Maybe I can make an exception in this case.'

'If you can bring it tomorrow, that would be great.'

'We'll see...'

'Okay. But listen, I need something now. Just to get me started. What was his surname? And did he have any next of kin?'

'I'd have to check the next of kin, but I'm sure he had someone. And I'm surprised at you, Jim. Surname is Kennedy. I thought everyone knew that. Like the President. Though he might have changed it since being on the streets. A lot do.'

'Kennedy?' I said. 'Irish connection?'

'Only the whiskey, as far as I know.'

'Any middle names?'

'Not that I know of.'

'Okay. That'll do for now. Don't forget the file.'

I ended the call and went back to what I laughingly called research. Typed Stevie's name into Google, which brought up a lot of Facebook and Linked In profiles but not much else. Stevie had been on the streets for a long, long time. Much longer than any social media website. Perhaps even longer than the Internet itself. I doubted he had any kind of presence on there at all. He was always one to live off the grid. Being online in any capacity would likely be his worst nightmare. Giggled at the thought that, if he could see me now, he'd think I'd finally lost my mind. He wouldn't be far wrong.

Instead, I closed the laptop down and paced around the flat. Finished the beer I'd opened and cracked open another. Turns out it wasn't such a shit beer after all. I underestimate Laura too much.

Got to thinking about the conversations we sometimes had when I was on the streets myself. We'd often share a place to bed down, but he never revealed much about himself. Never had any enemies, as far as I knew. He was just overcome with the drink. It consumed him. I knew that feeling all too well. When I first met him, I kept a lot of things to myself. Being a copper–ex copper by that point–I was used to being guarded. Took a few months before I told him about my marriage breakup, and losing the house and everything else that came with it. Stevie had said that most people off the grid were there because of a breakdown or a drug problem or a combination of those things and some-times a mental health disorder for good measure. I knew as much as anyone that a few months bedding down on concrete would send anyone nuts, if they weren't nuts already. Throw in a dysfunctional upbringing and the recipe was a potent one for a life in the gutter. And Stevie had his demons. I knew that much. He just didn't like to share whatever was on his mind, at least not with me. I couldn't speak for anyone else.

Plenty chose the off grid lifestyle, for whatever reason. I think Stevie was one of those, too. Having spent most of his young life in care homes, he'd simply decided to take matters into his own hands and live anywhere he wanted. I suppose that was true freedom. I could see how it would appeal. But if the pattern of his life was written any other way, if he'd had a normal childhood and upbringing, perhaps he'd have lived a different life, taken a different path. It was all 'ifs', and no one could go back and change anything, least of all the man himself. I doubted he'd change anything, anyway. He was what he was, and now he was dead.

I dug out my funeral attire from the wardrobe, a black three-piece suit and tie. Put it all on and added a pair of sunglasses. I looked like a gangster from some sixties black and white film. Wanted to remain inconspicuous, but this get up would make me stand out like a sore thumb. I doubted anyone who knew Stevie would turn up in black, either. Toyed with the idea of not wearing black at all. I knew Stevie wouldn't give a fuck, but I kept hearing my mum's voice in my ear. Make yourself presentable and pay your respects in the traditional way. I ditched the waistcoat.

I opened the laptop again, twice, then closed it again. I wasn't quite sure what I was looking for, but knew there was something. It would come. My phone rang several times with that unknown number and when I answered it on the third occasion, ready to spit venom down the line, the person on the other end–there was definitely a breath–hung up quickly. On the fourth occasion, it rang out before I could get to it. I'd had my head deep in the fridge, looking for something to eat but bringing out not so shit beer number five instead.

Got to thinking about the calls. Either someone was playing silly buggers, out to piss me off, or someone wanted to get in touch sharpish. I didn't know anyone who needed me in a hurry, and there were only a handful of people who knew my personal number. It had to be cold calling gone mad. There was no other explanation, and yet–there was something just a little bit odd about it. They were getting more frequent and more annoying by the day. Whoever it was knew how to push my buttons. Considered Karen, my ex wife, a potential culprit. Then I brought myself back to reality. She avoided me like the plague these days, so it couldn't be her.

And there was no one else. No one with an unknown number. I guessed that whoever was doing it didn't want to be contacted. I'd tried calling it several times, only to find no connection. It was a mystery. I'd gotten so sick of it that I turned the phone off and fired a quick email to Laura to let her know it was out of action. But then I realised it was a stupid idea to turn it off and turned it back on again. Bloody thing was getting on my tits, but I knew I'd need the phone on in case of emergencies. Thought back to when I was off grid myself and no one could get in touch. Part of me preferred it that way. There were definite benefits to being invisible.

Had a short nap on the couch and talked myself into leaving the flat when I woke up. It was early evening by now and Laura came back soon after, but only for a flying visit. She showered and changed and moaned at me for lying around virtually naked all day. Didn't have the energy to put up much of an argument as she inspected my funeral attire and hung it out, ready for tomorrow.

'Charlie's full of the break with his dad,' she said, running an iron over the shirt. I sparked up and let her talk. 'So I'm heading back there for tonight, even though he's next door for this sleepover. Thought it best I be nearby, you know. Don't mind, do you?'

'Of course not,' I said. I was thinking of heading out anyway and told her as much. 'I'm gonna head down to the Park Inn as soon as the sun goes down. See if anyone around there can tell me anything about the night he burned.'

'So you're really taking this one on?'

'Yeah,' I nodded. 'Why wouldn't I?'

'Well, no one's paying you.'

'Yet,' I said. 'Anyway, it doesn't matter. He was a mate. Money isn't the issue.'

She nodded and smiled. 'Might start calling you Dracula.'

'Dracula? Why?'

'You only come out at night.'

'I like it that way,' I said. 'And it's too fucking hot.'

'You're weird.'

Maybe I was, but I wasn't complaining. And it was too hot for me to work. Could never focus in the heat and with no end to the heatwave in sight, I'd have to get cracking in the cool hours before the case got further away from me.

'And Jim,' she said, grabbing me and kissing my nose as the iron steamed on its rack. 'You're drinking too much. Have a break, eh?'

Wasn't it always the way? 'It's not that bad,' I said. 'And it's only a few beers.'

'But then we know what that leads to, Jim Locke. Don't we? You've got a funeral to go to tomorrow, don't forget. You don't want to turn up drunk.'

I couldn't think of a more suitable occasion to get pissed. 'I won't. I've got work to do. *We've* got work to do.'

'Oh, so I'm your partner in crime when it suits you?'

'I just need you to man the office, just while I get my head into this. Got a long list of adulterous husbands to investigate and clients like Gloria wanting immediate results. I need you to put them off for a bit. It'll be a few weeks at most.'

'In other words, you want me to leave you gallivanting around the city while I do your paperwork...'

'You know me too well.'

'Not well enough,' she said, putting a hand beneath my balls. 'It's been too long.'

'I know,' I said, 'but not now, eh? Got stuff to do.'

She shook her head and went back to the ironing board. 'Fair enough.'

'Sorry, babe,' I said. 'But you need to get back to Sara's. You said so yourself.'

'You don't love me anymore.'

'You know that's not true.'

Which is how it went on until I'd finally gotten dressed and she kissed me goodbye for the night at the door.

'We're like ships passing in the night these days, Jim. I don't like it.'

'I'll make it up to you,' I said. And I meant it. 'I promise. I'll ring you from the funeral, let you know what I'm up to.'

I watched from the window as she crossed the street and the descending sun turned the road to gold. Then I sparked up, threw a shirt on, and left to meet the city.

———

The road felt longer than it should and the heat was still so bad I had to undo a few buttons on the shirt before striding on. I was feeling out of breath as the punters streamed out of The Band On The Wall to smoke on the pavement and I reckoned my best days were behind me. I didn't realise I was this unfit, and when I sparked up and took a break at the bottom of Swan Street, I saw stars dancing around my head after a coughing fit. It wasn't a good sign.

The bars and cafes were busy but when I reached the Cheetham Hill Road corner, right at the end of the Arena, I slipped into the main entrance at the Park Inn and settled myself down on the couch in the main hall to get my breath back. It was laid out for the evening meal, but I didn't see any guests. It was cool and quiet and the traffic had become a hum. It was still fairly light out, but I knew I wouldn't feel quite myself until the moon was high and bright. I was thirsty, so I ordered a pint at the bar and passed a business card to the barman behind it.

'Jim Locke,' I said. 'Private investigator. I'm looking for the manager, or anyone in security.'

He poured me a cold one and glanced at the card. 'Don't get many private detectives in here. What are you looking for?'

'Answers,' I said. I gave him a look. He gave me one back. I took the head off the pint and let it sink in. 'As I said, I'm looking for the manager, or anyone in security. But preferably someone in charge.'

'The night manager's not on duty until nine. And Graham's off sick.'

'Graham?'

'Head of security.'

I glanced at the clock on the wall behind the bar. 'I suppose I'll wait for the night manager, then. Who is?'

'Louise,' he said. He squirted himself a coke and took a drink. 'She'll probably be in soon.'

It was gone eight thirty, so I guessed she'd turn up just as I finished the beer. Told him I'd wait.

'Anything I can help you with?'

'As a matter of fact, yeah.'

'Go on.' He leaned in. 'As you can see, I'm not exactly rushed off my feet.'

Sat myself down on a stool and took another drink. 'A man died recently. About three weeks ago. Found burned to death around the back of here, under the arches.'

'Burned to death?'

I nodded. 'Just by the water.'

'Near the tracks?'

'A stone's throw away,' I said. 'He was homeless. Had been for a long time.'

'Not exactly missed, then.'

'He was a friend of mine,' I said, eyeballing him. 'So yeah, he's missed. By a lot of people.'

He looked away. 'Right. Sorry.'

'The bottom line is, he burnt to death. Someone set him alight and it's my job to find out why.'

'Isn't that what the police are for?'

'You'd think so,' I said, 'but in the case, it seems not. I've been hired by some friends to look into it myself. Think of it as a separate investigation.'

'So you want to run it by the manager?'

'You're a sharp man,' I said. I glanced at his name tag. 'Luke.'

'Well, I don't know anything about it,' he said. 'Not heard anyone else mention it, either.'

I nodded. 'I suppose it can be easily overlooked. I know there's a lot of activity around here at night. Easy to miss it.'

'There's always something going on,' he acknowledged. 'Look, it depends what time all this happened. We might've had guests staying here who could've seen something, but they'll be long gone by now.'

'No doubt. But you've got CCTV here, yeah?'

'Yeah.'

'I could do with taking a look.'

'There won't be much chance of that.'

'Why not?'

'We can't just show it to anyone. And like I said, Graham's off sick. He's the one deals with all that.'

'But I'm not anyone. And what about Louise?'

He nodded. 'You better ask her yourself.'

I turned and saw a plump woman, probably mid-thirties with an ice cream addiction, stepping out of a Mini. I drained the beer and removed myself from the stool as Luke called her over. Handed her a business card as the young barman explained, as best he could, who I was.

'Private investigator,' I corrected him. Offered her my hand and she reluctantly shook it.

'Well, this is... unusual,' she said. 'I don't usually get this kind of excitement when I turn up for work. Here's me thinking about the bloody paperwork I've got to do and instead I get a private eye waiting for me. Luke, I'll have a coke if you don't mind. So what can I do for you, Mr. Locke?'

'In brief, I want to look at your CCTV. But I'll need to explain first. Got an office we can use?'

She took the coke, which was loaded with ice, and suggested I follow her.

She led the way around the back of the bar and down a darkened corridor before taking us through a door marked PRIVATE and another one marked STAFF ONLY, which she had to unlock. She dumped her briefcase and shoulder bag full of shopping and gestured for me to sit down. Fired up the computer and kicked off her shoes. I guessed she was in for the night.

'Mind if I smoke?'

'Sorry,' she said, not looking at me, but at her screen. 'So, what can I do for you?'

I told her what I'd told young Luke, and more. 'His

name was Stephen Kennedy. A drinker. Been homeless for a long time so you might've even seen him around.'

'Who's to say. You got a photo?'

I didn't and quickly realised I'd better get one. Gave her a description instead. 'He was in his early forties,' I said. 'A lot of people knew him on the streets. Hard to say if he was burned alive, and I'm hoping that's not the case, but... well, we just don't know.'

'And so you're working with the police, you say?'

'Well, not quite. I'm conducting my own investigation. Used to be a copper myself, so I know all about this type of enquiry. The CCTV would be of some use, if there's anything on it worth looking at.'

'Well, that's a tricky one,' she said. 'I can't just let anyone look at the CCTV. You could be anyone.'

'You've seen my card.'

'Yes, but the police are usually the ones conducting murder enquiries, aren't they? They were here a few weeks ago. Not sure why, but Jackie would've dealt with it. She's the day manager.'

'They look at the CCTV?'

'I don't know,' she said. 'I'd have to check. I could call Jackie but hate to ring anyone when they're not on duty.'

I nodded 'Look, I'm not intending to waste anyone's time. I'm just trying to build up a picture of events.'

'But you said he was found under the arches behind here. By the water, yeah?'

'Correct.'

'So I'm not sure our CCTV will give you anything, anyway. It's not pointed at anything behind the hotel.'

'I'm just wanting to connect the dots on the night he died. That's all. I'm looking for a white Range Rover in particular.'

'There are a lot of white Range Rovers, Mr. Locke.'

I dug around in my pocket and pulled out my notebook. 'Registration CV15TYK. I take it you keep records of your guests' car registrations?'

She sighed and picked up the phone. 'Not really. Give me ten minutes.'

I took in the walls as she dialed and listened when the other end of the line picked up.

'Jackie, it's Lou. Yeah, hiya. Look, sorry to bother you, but I've a private detective here and... Yeah, I know. It's just like a film.' A long pause while Louise listened. 'Someone was killed behind the back of the hotel. You know the arches? Yeah. Yeah, I know. Terrible. He was burnt, yeah. Anyway, I remember you saying the police were in. Was a Tuesday, wasn't it? Wednesday? Oh. Right.... Yeah.'

'Can I speak to her?'

'Okay, yeah. Hang on, I'll just put him on.'

I took the phone and put my notebook down. 'Hello.' Got through the small talk of what I wanted and cracked on. 'Yeah, as Louise says. She said you had the police in and I was wondering if they'd gotten anywhere when you spoke to them.'

'Well, it was a Wednesday afternoon,' she said. 'About two-ish. They already looked at the CCTV and said that was that, they didn't need it from that point.'

'They seem interested?'

'They didn't really tell me much, to be honest with you. Just that it was a part of their enquiry and that was that.'

'Were they looking for anything in particular?'

'They didn't say.'

'Right. Look, Louise says she can't just show me the CCTV. Is that how you understand it?'

'Yes, but... well, you could ask Graham. He knows more about that side of things than we do, to be honest with you.'

I told her I wanted to look at the night he burned in particular.

'It should be on record, but we might have to download it. Graham will probably need permission from high up.'

'Your head office?'

'Yeah.'

'Well, can he get it?'

'You'd have to ask him, like I said.'

I handed her back to Louise and jotted a few notes, thinking that nothing was easy when you wanted to find stuff out.

Louise ended the call and turned to me. 'I didn't think it'd be much help.'

That was an understatement. 'Can you call him?'

'Well, like I said, he's off sick and I don't want to bother him.'

'It won't take a minute. I just need a quick yes or no from him.'

She sighed again and left the swing chair to reach into a filing cabinet. She plonked a file on her desk in plain view, and I got my notebook ready. When she dialed Graham's number, I made a note of it as she tapped it in when her back was turned. She sat down. Ringing. No answer.

'Try again,' I said. When she did, I jotted down his address. I knew it well enough. 'Still no joy?'

'I'm afraid not. You might have to call in tomorrow or something, but then I don't know when he'll be back.'

'Is it just a twenty-four-hour thing or something, you reckon?'

'I'm sorry?'

'Graham,' I said. 'Do you expect him back soon?'

She shrugged. 'I hope so.'

I thanked her for her time and she saw me out. Told her I was staying for a quick drink and she left me to it. By now, Luke was only slightly busier than before, and there was a whole table of diners that had very little effect on the massive, empty room. Thought about having a quick whisky but knew I'd find a better atmosphere in a funeral home. I gave Luke the thumbs up and stepped into a darkening night.

I thought about walking the short distance to the office so I could phone Graham from there, but instead descended the steps behind the hotel once again, venturing down into the darkness like I was being pulled there by some invisible force. The sun was almost down entirely and a half moon had risen, casting a pale white light across the cascading water and the train tracks beyond.

Yet it wasn't the only light.

As I reached the bottom, I could see the flickering orange flames blink across the walls, and I was a bit apprehensive about stepping any closer. I stopped and sparked up. Took that shit in deep. Over the din of the crashing water, I could hear voices, neither muted nor loud, but enough for me to know there were more than a few men around. I stepped into the shadows and crept along the wall's edge, past the place where Stevie had burned not long ago. I could almost feel him standing behind me. The stench of burnt flesh still hung in the night air. As I reached the end of the wall and peered around the corner, I saw the three of them standing around an oil drum fire, all drinking their lives away under the quiet of the bridge. They were swearing and laughing and there was another one, a woman, seemingly asleep against the wall. I knew it was a popular dossing place, and I guessed this spot was theirs. I couldn't recognise anyone in this light, and it was hard to guess anyone's age. But I could only guess that they knew Stevie too.

I cursed and dropped back into the shadows when my phone burst into life and when I pulled it from my pocket, it went clattering across the concrete. I grabbed it and slipped away, back towards the steps. I was at the top and on the main road before any of them had a chance to work out where the noise had come from. I stood above them, on the bridge, as the traffic moved steadily by, and studied my phone.

'Fuck's sake.'

It was another 'unknown' caller, probably the same annoying twat as before. I tried calling it back but just got a dead line. I looked around me instinctively, but there was no sign of the homeless I'd almost stepped in to question. They were hanging around so close to where Stevie had burned, so casually too, that I'd considered stepping from the shadows to see what they knew. The bloody phone trilling away had caught me off guard and I'd panicked. The last thing I'd wanted was to spook anyone. Not when we all wanted the same answers.

I walked on, considering my job for the evening pretty much done. There was nothing much I could go on until I had Stevie's doss house file in front of me, but I decided to make a call to Graham when I stopped off at the Ducie Bridge for a thirst break. Got myself a pint of snakebite and took a seat on an empty bench on the pavement outside. Took out my notepad and dialed him up.

I let it ring for a minute and was about to give up when he answered.

'Hello?'

It was noisy, and I could hear a lot of chatter and music. 'Is that Graham?'

'Who's this?'

'Jim Locke,' I said. 'Private investigator. Listen, you don't know me but I've just been to speak with your boss and she tells me I needed to run it by you first.'

'My boss is a man so you haven't spoken to anyone, is my guess.'

'I meant Jackie. And Louise. At the hotel?'

'Oh, right, I get you. No, they're nothing to do with me. Not employed by the hotel, you see. Anyway, what's this about?'

'I'm investigating a serious crime and I think you might be able to help me out.'

'Oh yeah, in what way?'

I told him in brief about Stevie and his lonely death and why I was investigating. 'So I need to look at the CCTV from the hotel going back a few weeks. Just one night in particular will do.'

'Not sure I can do that, Mr. Locke. You'd have to run it by my boss's boss, if you know what I mean. And because you're not police, you don't get to dictate.'

'Sounds busy where you are,' I said, and it did. 'Where are you exactly?'

'At a birthday do, why?'

'Right, it's just that they told me you were off sick, that's all. Funny place to be for a sick man.'

There was a pause, then 'Shit.'

'I'm sure your boss would be interested to know you're

out on the piss when you should be tucked up in bed with a bottle of Lucozade and some chicken soup.'

'Fucking hell...'

'But it doesn't have to come to that.'

'How did you get my bloody number, anyway?'

'I'm a private investigator, it's my job to find these things out. Not hard. But listen, Graham, I can make it worth your while.'

'You'll be wasting your time,' he said. 'The police have already viewed the footage and found nothing.'

'Yeah,' I said. 'But I'm looking for something completely different.'

'Oh aye?'

'When are you planning on going back to work? Or are you off to the races or something tomorrow? Jolly Boys' outing lined up or something?'

There was a long pause and a big sigh down my ear. I took a long drink of snakebite.

'Tomorrow,' he said. 'I suppose.'

'And you'll help me out?'

'You won't find anything.'

'We'll see,' I said. 'And cheers, Graham. Much appreciated. I'll be in touch. Hang on, is that 'Come on Eileen' I can hear? Better get back to it.'

I let him go and sparked up, but before my phone's light could even blink off, it rang again. It was 'unknown' again on the end of the line. Grabbed it and answered fast.

'Right, you cunt.'

'Hang on, hang on.'

'You've been ringing me for fucking days now. Who are you and what do you want, twat?'

'Steady on, lad. Jesus, your temper's ballooned.'

'Who is this?' But I knew. I'd recognise that voice anywhere. I just wanted to hear him say it.

'Right, lad. You know who. Meet me in the King's Arms tomorrow at five o'clock.'

'Salford?'

But he'd hung up.

CHAPTER FIVE

I never liked funerals. When we buried my dad, I was drunk before we even got to the crematorium, having spent most of the night before staring down a bottle of Islay single malt, and one of the very best too. I'd told myself, even at three a.m., that dad would've understood, and I continued to pour dram after dram of the good stuff down my throat, almost two-thirds into the bottle by six on a cold and wet February morning in ninety-nine just as mum's alarm blared into life and I was just about coming to terms with the day we faced and the utter dread I felt with it.

Several years later, just a few months into my new police career, we buried a young DS who'd been stabbed to death while off duty after a row with a group of coked up kids when out on a Saturday night with his wife. I wasn't the only copper who'd gotten off my face that day. The injustice of a life destroyed and the lives of his wife and son torn apart never left a lot of us.

And then there was Maureen, my ex wife's mother. Taken by cancer just weeks before Christmas and at a time when I was particularly fucked up myself due to the Angel case. I'd made sure I was sober for that one, as hard as it was. But I didn't want Karen to think I wasn't fit to see my daughter anymore. Strange that it took my former mother-in-law's death to bring me closer to my kid.

And now, just last night, the one person I'd thought was a certainty to be dead and whose funeral I'd probably never attend due to the fact that his body had never been found, calls me out of the blue and wants to meet me for a pint.

As I stood there in the flat, examining my funeral attire in the bedroom mirror, the past came back in waves. Losing dad, losing coppers, losing Maureen. I'd always been reminded of my own mortality when we buried someone close. And now here I was, about to say my formal goodbyes to a friend who'd had nothing and had perished in the most terrible way imaginable. I guess, in many ways, we get what we deserve in life. But Stevie didn't deserve that.

I took the Volvo and drove over to Southern Cemetery. As I drove down the Princess Parkway, I thought of Lloyd and the white Range Rover that had seemed to be following him. More importantly, it was the two men occupying it that bothered me. Then my thoughts returned to Stevie's file from the soup kitchen. I hoped Lloyd had remembered it because I needed a damn sight more to go on than this.

And then Bob Turner and his phone call from nowhere. It was this that I thought about the most, driving on autopilot towards the south of the city. I was very keen to hear what he had to say. I thought he was dead. We all did. After he went to press about the corruption within GMP, he fled to Spain, where he stayed until I finally got a phone call from him last Christmas Eve. The gunshots down the line and the subsequent dead tone immediately afterwards all pointed to one thing. The journalist had been shot dead and Interpol, despite months of searching, had never found his body. For weeks and weeks afterwards, I did my own searching. I spoke to his friends, his acquaintances at the paper. Everyone assumed the worst. I resigned myself to the fact that he was dead and I was partly to blame for it. I should never have gotten him involved in the Angel case, though if it hadn't have been for him I wouldn't have known what I know now. And I probably wouldn't have found out who her killer was. So for him to just turn up out of the blue was a shock, to say the least. I was almost ready to kill the bastard myself after what he'd put me through. If he hadn't died that night I'd taken his last, desperate call, then what the hell had happened and what had he been doing since?

I pulled into the Southern Cemetery Crematorium via the entrance on Barlow Moor Road and parked up in a space beside the rose bushes skirting the perimeter of the gardens out front. The service would begin in less than twenty minutes and already there were a handful of disheveled looking men and women hanging around the front door to the building. I thought about what young Kyle Faulkner had said about it being pointless to cremate him since he had already burned from the inside out and there had to be nothing else left of him to bother with. But it was the service that mattered, a way to finally call time respectfully on a life that had been taken too soon.

I locked her up and made my way over to the group, spotting Lloyd before he spotted me. I was right about no one else wearing black, too. I pulled him aside.

'Morning, man,' he said. 'You look the part.'

'Thanks for noticing. You bring the file I asked for?'

He nodded. 'It's in the car. But I'll need it back.'

'Obviously,' I said. 'I'll get what I need and return it straight away.'

'I could get sacked for this.'

'Lloyd, you're a volunteer. It's not as if you're getting paid for helping out in a soup kitchen.'

'It's not the point,' he said. 'Just get it back to me as soon as possible.'

I told him I would and looked around. There were familiar faces from my time on the streets. God, Faulkner, Dogends and a few others I recognised but didn't know. Bubble Coat and Stumps hung around nearby with a few women who had a lot of teeth missing. I wondered just how many of the people here were using the hard stuff and what kind of lives they led away from such peaceful surroundings. And then the pit of my stomach turned over when I saw DI Rob Robertson step out of his BMW on the opposite side to where I'd parked myself. Our eyes met for the briefest of moments, and I thought I saw him smirk, which would be about right for him. He was much thinner than the last time I saw him, back when we were on the force together. Perhaps the pressure of the job had taken its toll.

I suppose I shouldn't have been surprised that there was police representation here and, in my experience, it was usually the SIO who showed up in such circumstances. So now I knew who it was and I wondered if he had a team of minions on the case. I kept my eyes peeled for anyone I recognised from the force, but couldn't see anyone. When people began shuffling into the crematorium for what I suspected would be a short service, I followed at the tail end and took a pew at the back. Lloyd sat beside me and kept his head bowed.

I looked around, deliberately choosing my position so I could take in exactly who was attending.

I nudged Lloyd and whispered. 'Any family here?'

He nodded. 'Down the front. His sister.'

I took a look and saw who he meant. It was the woman from the other night, the one with the purple eye shadow and the mascara running down her face. The girl who'd followed me into The Bay Horse. 'His sister?'

'That's what she said. Name's Shannon.'

It was exactly what I needed in order to probe the police, but I hadn't been expecting any next of kin to be her. Maybe I should've known, though. The fact that she'd been hanging around me the night before I even knew of Stevie's death had me raise my eyebrows. She obviously knew who I was and what I did, so our brief contact had to be more than mere coincidence. She was the only other person in black besides myself and when she looked around, our eyes met. Perhaps she could feel my eyes on her because she nodded in acknowledgement before turning around to face the altar and the priest who stepped out onto the carpet.

'The only family he had left, apparently,' Lloyd whispered as we stood, and the reverent organ music played solemnly around the room. 'She hadn't seen him in years.'

Which begged the question of what she'd been doing herself. I was keen to find out.

———

The service was brief, no more than half an hour. There were only two speakers. His sister read a poem by William Blake and one of Lloyd's colleagues from the shelter offered a short eulogy. There were no tears, even from his sister, and only respectful observation from everyone else. The priest made all the right noises and before long, a standard pine coffin rolled back behind the curtain, accompanied by a large framed photograph of Stevie that no one recognised because his hair was short and he was clean shaven and clearly much younger than when anyone in the room knew him. I could only assume that Shannon had provided it. It looked as if it had been blown up from a smaller print, perhaps one she had privately kept in her purse.

A few gathered outside following the service, and I hovered near the door for Shannon. Lloyd stayed beside me to make the introductions. She was the last to leave, perhaps saying one more private goodbye once the room had emptied.

'We're sorry for your loss,' Lloyd said when she appeared. 'Stevie was a good man.'

I nodded. 'One of the best.'

'Shannon, this is Jim Locke. A few of us wanted him to make his own enquiries around your brother's death.'

'I know who you are,' she said, directly to me. 'Steven had mentioned you the last time I saw him.'

Which was news to me. 'When was that, if you don't mind me asking?'

'It's okay,' she said. 'A week before he was found. He'd come to see me at my flat.'

'I saw you,' I said. 'A few nights ago.'

She nodded. 'I was drunk. Sorry about that. I'd thought about coming to see you after I realised what you did. Looks like some of his friends got there before me.' She smiled at Lloyd. 'Thanks.'

There was a silence between us, and I wondered how best to fill it. 'Look, it might be good if we can have a chat about Stevie. About his death. In private, I mean.'

She placed a hand on my arm. 'I'd like that, Mr. Locke. He spoke fondly of you.'

I insisted she call me Jim.

'Miss Kennedy.' It was a voice I recognised. I gritted my teeth and turned to see Robertson stepping our way. 'It was a lovely service. I'm sure your brother would've been proud.'

I wondered what he was after. It made good PR to attend a murder victim's funeral, to put in a show of support. But I suspected there was another motive for his attendance.

'Jim,' he said. 'I'm surprised to see you here. Pub not open yet?'

I knew it was an attempt to stir the pot, and I wasn't falling for it. 'Stephen Kennedy was a friend of mine. I wouldn't have missed my chance to say goodbye. Especially given the circumstances.'

'It's never easy to let a family member go,' he said to Shannon, before glancing at me. 'And I can assure you that we will get to the bottom of what happened.'

'Made any progress?'

He turned to me. 'I'm sure I don't need to remind you that these investigations can take some time. We don't need any unnecessary distractions.'

'What do you mean by that, detective?' Shannon said.

But I knew exactly what he meant. He didn't want me poking around his case.

'There can sometimes be things outside of our control,' he said. 'Little things that can get in the way of an investigation. But we're determined to get to the bottom of it and bring the perpetrator to justice.'

'So you're admitting he was murdered?' I said. 'Or at least there was someone else involved?'

He put his hands to his hips and I watched his fingers

tighten around his belt. It was a sign he meant business. 'I wouldn't quite go that far yet, but you could say there are certainly signs that there was definitely somebody else involved in his death.'

'Well, it couldn't have been suicide,' I said. 'He wasn't capable. Someone else must've started him off, for whatever reason. Burning to death isn't exactly right up there in the top ten of methods to top yourself.'

He smiled, looked me in the eye. 'With all due respect, you don't have the best track record in this type of investigation. And I trust Miss Kennedy would not find your choice of wording appropriate either. Excuse me, Miss Kennedy. I'm sorry for your loss. I'll be in touch.'

I watched him walk back to his BMW, wanting nothing more than to sling a punch at his thin, smirking mouth. Yet he was right about my comments. Sensitivity wasn't exactly my best trait.

'Look, he's right,' I said. 'I could've chosen my words more carefully. I'm sorry.'

'Not at all.' She reached into a shoulder bag and put a long cigarette to her lips, sparking up and blowing a cloud into the summer morning. 'You're right. It couldn't have been suicide. He wasn't capable, and he had no desire to take his own life. I don't believe that he would. Not my brother. He's been through far too much in his life to just kill himself. And he's an arsehole. He's got a nerve to show up here. I've only seen him once since they found him dead.'

It didn't surprise me, but I kept it to myself.

'Sorry to interrupt,' said Lloyd, 'but some of us are going back to the shelter. A few drinks, you know. I wouldn't call it a wake, but you'd be welcome to come, Shannon. You too, Jim.'

'Thanks,' she said. 'But I just want to be on my own today. I do appreciate it, Lloyd.'

'About that chat,' I began. Offered her my card, which she pocketed in her jacket.

'I'll call you tomorrow. You can come to my flat.'

'That would be good. I'd like to know more about your brother and was hoping you'd be able to help me trace his whereabouts in the days before...you know.'

She nodded. 'How long have you got? Tomorrow, Jim.' Then she turned and walked away.

By now, the rest of the attendees had dispersed and I made my way back to the Volvo, collaring Lloyd, who was chatting to a tiny woman I didn't recognise, on the way. He asked me to give him a minute and, right on cue, the passenger door opened a moment later and the big man sat down and handed me a green file.

'It's all there. Everything we'd been given by other agencies and everything he'd told us, at least. Previous tenancies, the care homes he'd been in. Pretty much all we know.'

'I appreciate it, man.' I flicked through. There wasn't a great deal of information, probably no more than twenty pages, but it was infinitely better than what I had.

'I'll need it back,' he said. 'Like today.'

'Today?'

He nodded. 'Get it photocopied or something. Whatever. But if anyone finds out it's gone, I'm fucked. And not only that. This isn't exactly moral, is it? I'm sure Stevie wouldn't want us poking around his private stuff. It's confidential, Jim. I'm uneasy about it.'

I started her up and left the crematorium grounds before he had a chance to protest, easing my foot down towards my destination half a mile away.

'It's not immoral if any of this information helps to catch

his killer, Lloyd. You wanted me to look into it and I am. This is the best start.'

'Where are we going?'

'Post office.'

I left him stewing and probably craving a thick joint while I took copies. I bought an A4 brown envelope and filled it, dumping it in the glove box when I got back in. Handed him the originals and told him to relax.

'Easy for you to say. I saw it again.'

'The Range Rover?'

He nodded. 'This morning. It was parked in a little bay around the back of the cemetery.'

'They see you?'

'I don't know. Maybe.'

I nodded. Thought for a moment. 'Have you tried speaking to them?'

He almost laughed. 'Nah, man. What you take me for?'

'Wouldn't do any harm.'

'Yeah, well, I'm still thinking of telling the police. It's harassment, Jim. I can't prove that but...'

'Have you got a camera? Or better still, a smartphone?'

'Got the latest Samsung.'

'Right. So, do yourself a favour. I want you to photograph it every time you see it and make a note of the date and time. Film it if you have to. Build up your evidence before going to the police. That way they're less likely to laugh you out of the station.'

'So you think I'm being foolish?'

'I never said that. And you're far from foolish, Lloyd. But it has to stack up if you want to be taken seriously. Trust me on that. And anyway, they haven't approached you, have they? It could just be a coincidence that you keep seeing them.'

'Coincidence,' he laughed. 'Come on, man. You're better than that.'

I did a u-turn and took him back to the Crematorium, where he'd parked his car. The day was hot, worse than yesterday, and I wanted nothing more than to lie down in the shade. I had a lot going on in my head and wanted to get stuck in to Stevie's case history before I met Bob. His return out of the blue had knocked me for six, and I was very keen to hear his excuses. Plus, I was eager to speak directly with Shannon tomorrow. Her final comment before leaving had got me more than intrigued, and there was the implication she had a lot to discuss. The arrival of Robertson on the scene had only galvanised me more. Perhaps it was the kick up the arse I needed. And I understood Lloyd's concerns. Strictly speaking, whoever was in the Range Rover hadn't broken any laws as far as I knew. But then I wasn't the one being followed. Lloyd's anxiety was plain. I wondered if he was keeping something else quiet.

'I'm just wondering why they'd be following you,' I said. 'I mean, why you?'

'They only started showing up after Stevie's body was found. I don't know what they want, but I'm guessing it's something to do with that, eh? You're the detective, Jim.'

'Not anymore.'

'You know what I mean.'

You could say he was right, but I didn't feel like it. I hadn't been involved in a murder inquiry for a long time. The Angel case was different. It was the fact she'd gone missing and then turned up dead that got me involved. With Stevie, I could call him a mate to begin with, in fact, a mate who'd helped me out on the Angel case too. And I couldn't say no to looking into it when I was approached by the man sitting beside me. Maybe Robertson was right. I didn't have the best track record, and he should know. Yet I also knew he was trying to put the seeds of doubt in my head, make me feel out of my depth. I hadn't seen his smug face since I got the boot from GMP. Nothing would please me more than to wipe that grin off it.

Now that I had more to go on, I told Lloyd as much. 'Which is why this file helps big time. And the Range Rover - I'm trying to look into some CCTV from near where Stevie was found. If the car's on it anywhere the night he died, I might link it to why they're following you.'

He nodded. 'They just keep turning up out of nowhere and I don't know why.'

We were silent for a moment as we both watched a group of mourners waiting near Lloyd's Vectra. The sky was deep blue, and the heat was rising. I slung the tie I was wearing into the back and undid several buttons.

'I said I'd give them a lift back. A few want to say goodbye properly, you know. Come and join us.'

'No,' I said, thinking about Bob Turner and The King's Arms. 'There's some stuff I need to do. Look, thanks for this. You didn't have to. It's appreciated.'

'You think it'll help? You know, find his... his murderer?'

'It's a start.' I looked back at the crematorium. It was hard to say if the service had done Stevie any justice. It was over for him now. 'A way in.'

After Lloyd left to return to the shelter, I drove back to the flat to get a cold shower and a change of clothes. It was still late morning, and the sun wasn't yet high, but the humidity was enough to stop anyone from taking life too seriously. I reminded myself that at least I still had one.

I was tempted to hide away in a dark room and out of the sun but reckoned I was developing a deficiency in vitamin D. Instead, I downed several pints of water and hit the road again, this time on foot and with Stevie's photo-copied file in my pocket. Sparked up on the street and made my way down to the Park Inn again to speak to Graham the security guard about the CCTV I wanted to look at.

There was flesh on show everywhere you looked, which made for a pleasant walk, but I had serious business to attend to as well and I knew I wouldn't get anything done if I couldn't keep my eyes from wandering.

I was also more than tempted to grab a table outside the Ducie Bridge and settle in for a quick pint as I passed, but kept walking. It was hard in this weather, and especially having said goodbye to a mate, but I knew that if I had one, another two would follow. There was time for that later when I met up with Bob.

Instead, I dialed up Graham as I walked. He answered immediately.

'Hello?'

'So you turned up then?'

'You what?'

'Jim Locke. Private investigator? We spoke last night when you were on the piss at a - what was it? - birthday party?'

A sigh so long and noisy, I thought it was a gust of wind. 'What do you want?'

'Good morning to you too, Graham. CCTV. Remember? You said I could have a look.'

'Did I?'

'Yeah, something about you being off sick.'

There was a long pause, followed by something mumbled under his breath that sounded a lot like 'fuck' until finally, the reply I needed. 'I suppose you'd better come up.'

I found him around the back of the hotel, sitting outside a Portakabin that overlooked the arches where Stevie had burned. Beyond, the waters of the river Irk glimmered in the sun and you could see the heatwave pulsing over the rail tracks. He was smoking casually and drinking from a dirty mug.

'Shouldn't take too long, Graham,' I said as I approached. 'I just want to see one night in particular.'

He shook his head, spat on the floor, and tossed his smoke. 'Yeah but... look, I'd appreciate it if you didn't mention any of this to my boss.'

'Your secret's safe with me, Graham. If you can show me what I've come to see.'

'You've got a nerve, Mr. Locke.'

'Only way to get things done. Shall we?'

He nodded and stood, his wiry frame almost skeletal and his stubble, which was old man grey and stinking of nicotine, sharp like the bristles of a brush. 'Just in here. I need to download it from our system, which could take a while. What exactly are you wanting to see? And by the way, I don't need to remind you–I could get a proper bollocking for this.'

'The night of the 13th of June. Between the hours of eight pm and four am would probably cover it.'

'Shit, that's twelve hours. You'd be here all bloody day. No can do, I'm afraid.'

'We can skim through most of it.'

'And what exactly is it you're looking for? Nothing ever happens around here.'

I told him.

'So if this relates to a murder inquiry or whatever, why aren't the police here instead?'

'They've already been, or so I'm told by the hotel,' I said. 'This is a separate investigation.' I pulled two twenties from my wallet.

'Some would call that bribery, Mr. Locke.'

I smiled. 'I couldn't give two fucks. Now are you gonna roll the tape or not?'

He snatched the money from my fingers so fast I thought he might be moonlighting as a magician at weekends. 'You'd better sit down.'

I took up a plastic chair and sat beside him as he messed around with the computer a few minutes. Soon after, a little bar in the corner of the screen told us it was downloading information, and a digital clocked ticked down. Moments later, the screen had split into four, with a timestamp in each corner and a different view in each section. It was night. The clock showed it was 10:33.

'Can I smoke in here?'

He dug around in a drawer and plonked a glass ashtray down. 'Not supposed to, but...'

I sparked up and peeled my eyes. The images were in black and white. Grainy footage illuminated by streetlights and the glow of a summer moon. Top left, a view of the main Cheetham Hill Road. Top right, a view from the back, overlooking the rail tracks and the nearby apartments. Bottom left, a view of the yard and fire exits. Bottom right, an interior view of the main entrance. It was enough to go on for now. The yard was still, as was the rear of the hotel overlooking the tracks. But it was the traffic I was interested in. It wasn't the best of angles, but at least it offered something and the vehicles could all be seen clearly.

'Move it on,' I said. 'A couple of hours.'

He messed around with a control pad beside the computer, and the images whizzed by. Stevie had been found, still smouldering, on the Saturday morning, and from what Lloyd had said, the police reckon he'd gone up in flames sometime in the early hours. My guess was anywhere between eleven p.m. and two a.m. I got Graham to stop fast forwarding around the midnight hour.

'A brew would be nice.'

'Now you're just taking the piss.'

I glanced at the tea stained mugs in the little sink at the back. 'Second thoughts, don't bother.'

It was clear the guy was on edge. He left me to view the monitor while he paced up and down and poked his head out the door. During that time, he smoked four fags to the filter as I watched nothing much happen on screen. I wondered if he was on meds for anxiety. And if he wasn't, perhaps he should be. The guy was a walking heart attack with a bad case of the Heebie Jeebies. I guessed he was a bit nervous about me being here at all. I did wonder how he'd got this gig. I was about to suggest ways he could relax when it flashed across the screen so fast I almost choked on my own smoke.

'There it is.'

He turned back in from the sunshine and almost tripped over the step. 'There's what?'

'Just what I'm looking for. Rewind it a minute. Can you pause it when I say?'

He did as I asked and I took that nicotine in deep as I dug out my notebook from my front pocket. Grabbed a pen off the desk.

'Play it.'

It was top left I was interested in. The traffic rolled by, and there was quite a lot of it too, given the hour. I suppose I shouldn't have been surprised. We were just a stone's throw from the city. There was a lull after several buses and a truck passed from right to left, then seconds later, from left to right, a white Range Rover.

'Pause.'

I was looking right at. I'd jotted the number plate down from when Lloyd had called at the office. CV15TYK. I couldn't be sure, but a closer look would help. From this angle, it was hard to make anything out at all on the plate, except for the first two letters.

'Can you zoom in?'

He messed around with a mouse and the image filled the whole screen. Then he zoomed in two hundred percent. There it was, or at least the beginning of the registration. CV15TYK. I had my man. Although it didn't prove anything, at least I could say for sure the Range Rover was nearby the night Stevie died, which put whoever was behind the wheel in the frame. The time stamp in the top right corner read 00:43:31. Almost a quarter to one in the morning. Still early enough for a lot of people to be around, but late enough to go halfway to being unseen, especially around the back of here, down under the dark arches. The question remained, though; was Stevie burning right then and if they were responsible, had they just left? Or were they on their way to do the job?

Of course, I had no definitive answers. I couldn't prove anything in terms of who'd set him alight. But the Range

Rover being both here on the night he died and tailing Lloyd like a dog on heat ever since didn't seem right at all. They had to be connected, whoever they were.

'Can I get a printout of this?'

'I don't know about that,' he said. 'I've done enough already and I shouldn't have let you - '

I pulled another tenner from my wallet. 'The most expensive printout I've ever had the misfortune to get. You've made yourself a pretty penny here, Graham.'

He snatched it like a frog catching a fly. 'Pleasure.'

While it printed, he let the footage run on. I was thinking about calling Laura to let her know my plans when the bottom right screen caught my eye. There was a group of men exiting the main entrance, one of whom looked a big lad compared to the other two. Big and bald and full of muscle, like a bouncer. He fitted Lloyd's description of the guy who'd been following him perfectly.

'Stop it, Graham. And rewind it.'

He handed me the printout, which I folded and pocketed before sparking up. Once he took it back a few minutes, I peeled my eyes once more. Told him to pause on my signal and get ready to print again.

The first two were relatively well built, and both had short hair. They walked straight out the main entrance, keenly followed by our bald guy. His head was so shiny it reflected the neon light. I got Graham to pause it so that all three were in the frame. There was something that had caught my eye, but I couldn't put my finger on what it was. I got him to run it back one more time.

'Can you make it go slo mo?'

'What am I, a fucking whizz kid? Give me a minute.'

He messed around with the mouse until it played back at half speed. I watched the three walk towards the exit again, the two smaller guys in front and the baldy trailing behind.

'Pause it.'

I leaned in to get a closer look. I had to think for a minute about where I'd seen it before, but I didn't have to think too long. It was written on the wall beside where Stevie had burned to death. Tattooed on the big guy's neck, as if stamped there, was E.N.D. There was a horizontal lighting bolt right below it.

CHAPTER SIX

Graham printed out what I needed, but not before seeking assurances that I wouldn't grass him up to his boss. I told him I didn't know what he was talking about and left with a wink. I headed back to the office. I needed a long lie down to think things through before I even considered what the evening might bring with Bob. I was still gob smacked he was still alive and for him to just rock up out of the blue like he had seemed like an elaborate practical joke had been played on me. But it was no joke.

Laura was going through some book-keeping, her lipstick stained mugs cluttering her desk. Asked her to scan the printouts Graham had given me on to the Mac and link them to Stevie's file. She asked how the funeral went as I made myself a coffee, black.

'The usual, you know.' I sparked up. 'A modest affair, which was to be expected. He has a sister. Shannon. I need a long chat with her.'

She wrapped her arms around my waist and kissed me. 'I missed you. Charlie's missing you too.'

'Same here.' I kissed her back long enough to want to

take her clothes off right there and then, but it wasn't the time. Didn't feel right after a funeral. 'I'll see you tonight.'

'You better had.' She kissed my nose and put her hand between my legs. 'Because I need this.'

'It's a promise.' A promise I intended on keeping. 'But in the meantime, you won't believe who's finally turned up.'

She left my arms and went to the Mac. 'Your ex?'

'Bob Turner.'

I told her everything I knew - which was pretty much nothing other than the fact he'd been trying to contact me and I was meeting him within hours - and she was as shocked as I was. Although she knew of Bob, she didn't know him like I did. But she did know he'd played a big part in the Angel case and had apparently paid for it with his life. We'd been keeping close tabs on Interpol's investigation, as well as that of the Spanish Police. As far as anyone knew, he was stone cold dead. I heard the gunshots myself on that Christmas Eve, which begged the question: if it wasn't him, who the hell was it?

'You said he was dead. Everyone did.'

'That's right. Everyone, not just me. No one had seen or heard from him in months and months, not even his own family. Believe me, kid, I want to know the truth more than most.'

'And where are you meeting?'

'King's Arms, Salford way.'

'More drink. Figures.'

'It was his suggestion. And anyway, that's not all I wanted to tell you. I've been poking around. About Stevie. I think I may have a significant lead, which is why I want those printouts scanned into the computer.'

She wanted to know more, so I told her. About the Range Rover, about the graffiti where he'd been found -

E.N.D. and the lightning bolt - and the same thing tattooed on the back of the bald guy's neck.

'So you think it's connected?'

'Well don't you? Pretty strange coincidence.'

'But why kill him? A homeless guy? No harm to anyone?'

'That's what I want to find out.'

'And what the hell does E.N.D. mean?'

'I've no idea.'

'Sounds weird.'

I wouldn't quite put it like that, but I knew what she meant. It obviously stood for something. I sat down on the couch beneath the window and let the noise from outside flood over me. Combined with the heat, it was making me sleepy. The coffee was strong though, and I hoped it would spark something. I needed a wake up call.

I took the photocopied file Lloyd had given me from my pocket and pulled the coffee table over. I began leafing through the paperwork. Though there wasn't much to go on, there was enough here to keep me busy for the time being. The front page was simply a table of contents before we got to the meat and bones, beginning with the basic stuff–full name, date of birth, other official particulars–and ending with the more historic stuff like the care homes he'd been in since childhood, hostels he'd bedded down in and some documents related to all that. In between was a fair amount of information about drug and alcohol use, mental and physical health including various hospital records, and a lot of case notes by various members of staff, including social workers and nurses and GPs. I thought all of this stuff might be interesting. The opening pages gave a background to his life, and I jotted some notes down as I read. It was clear he'd had more than his fair share of troubles, even at a very young age. I was surprised he'd made it this far at all.

His mother, a Dublin woman called Angela Kennedy, had died as a result of complications during childbirth when she had Stevie at St. Mary's on 31st July 1973. Steve and his elder sister, Shannon, were subsequently taken into the care of social services because it was deemed their estranged father was too unfit to look after them. A number of care homes followed, beginning with St. Joseph's House, an organisation run by the Catholic Church in the Rochdale Diocese. But that was back in the mid-seventies and I doubted it was still around today. According to the notes, both children were taken in straight away. Their father, one Donal MacGuire, had disappeared, it was assumed, back to rural Ireland before Angela could even think about buying a second hand pram.

There wasn't much information on their stay there—almost four years—other than a page of medical notes that didn't amount to much and a letter from the chairman, a Mr. Peter Reynolds, to his counterpart at Ivy Brook Residential Home, a privately run charity in Salford.

I skimmed through the letter. There was nothing of note until I got to the final paragraph, which was a cursory warning that Stevie's behaviour could sometimes be troublesome and concerning. But then he could be no older than five at the time, and what kid doesn't misbehave at five? Besides, this was the seventies, and I understood practices in care homes back then would be very questionable these days. I wondered how the kid would be punished for his 'troublesome' behaviour, and just how troublesome it was. I guessed this Mr. Reynolds was alluding to something other boys his age weren't presenting. The information was sparse, but the warning was there. I could only assume the two men had other conversations in person or over the phone about Stevie, but as far as his early care home life was concerned, the only stuff I had on paper was this. There was nothing from Ivy Brook and no other documents until he was fourteen, almost ten years on. Either there were documents about his early life elsewhere, hidden away in some dusty vault or basement, or they didn't exist anymore, or perhaps at all. I wondered if Shannon could fill in the blanks.

I skimmed through most of it, stopping once or twice to read hospital notes and care plans–he'd been sectioned under the Mental Health Act in 1989–and it seemed he'd spent several months on a locked ward. The diagnosis was Schizo-affective disorder. There were entries from a psychiatrist who reckoned Stevie was suffering from paranoid delusions, though it wasn't clear what exactly his delusions were. He'd been on antipsychotics and SSRI's and had even undergone ECT to address his problem. There was a suicide attempt prior to his admission (by ligature, it said) and he had a history of self harm by cutting his flesh. The whole thing was depressing to read. I had no idea he'd been through any of it. No wonder he'd turned out a drinker. I knew he was self medicating with whisky, but I had no idea about the extent of his problems. The man had been through some deep, deep shit. Troubled wasn't the word.

I closed the file and sparked up. I'd read enough. In some ways, I wondered if it wasn't a blessing that he was dead. I knew it wasn't going to be a pretty read, but I wasn't expecting this. I knew he'd had some mental health issues, but I always thought it was a depression thing. Seemed it went much deeper than that.

My thoughts turned to Bob Turner and our impending meeting. I was looking forward to seeing my old friend, and

I guessed it would take my mind off the case, at least for a while. There was a lot going around my head. The coffee gave me a buzz, and I could feel the nicotine seeping through my bloodstream. The afternoon humidity was getting dizzying, and I knew I needed a few cold ones to help keep the heat at bay. But I also knew it could be a dangerous cocktail. The sun had brought out plenty of nutters already and the world didn't need another joining them.

When Laura had finished scanning what I needed onto the Mac, I got her to bring up Google.

'Type in E.N.D. Let's see what we get.'

She did. We got nothing but pages of acronyms meaning different things, obscure German bands, engineering industry websites and other such nonsense.

'Try 'horizontal lightning bolt'. That could be better.'

'If we knew what it stood for, we might have a better chance of finding something.'

'You'll never make a P.I.'

She typed in what I asked. We got pretty much the same rubbish again. Aside from a lot of stuff about lightning and the odd thing about a car company and science organisations, there was nothing. We scrolled through six pages of the same such stuff before I had to leave the desk. I suppose E.N.D. and lightning could mean next to fuck all, but it was the context I'd seen it in that bothered me. The graffiti on the wall where Stevie had burned and the tattoo on the big guy's neck. I couldn't ignore the connection.

'Let me see,' she said. 'You go out and give me a few hours. I'll do some poking around. There's got to be something to link it all together. You know how impatient you are with these things.'

I suppose she was right. And I could probably use the

help. She might have a screw loose and made your average dizzy blonde look like a genius, but sometimes she could surprise me. I still fancied her, too.

I slapped down Stevie's file on her desk. 'Have a read through that. See what you can find out about the care homes. Ivy Brook and St. Joseph's. And you'll find there are gaps. If you can fill in the blanks, love, I might just give you a promotion.'

'Is that all you're going to give me?'

'It's the heat, isn't it?'

'What?'

'Nothing like the summer to get you going.'

She smiled and licked her lips. 'I love you, Jim Locke. And I want you in my bed tonight.'

'I'll see what I can do.'

'Romantic...'

I gathered up a few things—smokes, wallet, phone, keys—and headed to the fire escape window. 'I'll keep you updated. I've not seen him in a long time, remember.'

'And he's supposed to be dead.'

'There is that.'

'Don't be home too late,' she said. She ushered me back with a finger. We kissed. 'And keep your phone on. You never know what I might find.'

Just before I left through the fire escape, she called out that Maya might be around later so she wouldn't be on her own. Gotta say, it pleased me.

———————

As far as pubs go, you could say the King's Arms in Salford was a bit of a hidden gem. I took a stroll there through the afternoon sunshine, avoiding the crowds at every opportunity by taking as many backstreets as I could. It still felt like ninety degrees in the shade, but it was cooler than walking in the glare of the blazing sun. And I couldn't stand weaving my way through the main streets, dodging the people traffic with every step. I had to cross Deansgate to get to Bridge Street, but from then on, it was pretty quiet. Once I made it to the rail bridge at Salford Central, pausing for a precious moment under the cool of the ironworks, I could see the pub standing down the side of Chapel Street. It was big and old and built with solid brick. Had probably seen lots of blood, sweat and tears too. I wondered if Bob would be waiting inside or maybe I'd made it here before him. It wouldn't be the first time.

It was cool and quiet when I entered, a bit too early for the after work rush but well into the afternoon for it to be occupied by the mix of regulars who had nothing better to do.

I stepped up to the bar and got myself a pint of Holts from the young barmaid. She had a student, eco warrior look about her, her hair dyed pink with streaks of blue and several piercings in her ears and nose.

I looked around for any sign of my old friend and poked my head into the snug, but aside from a couple of construction workers and a pair of old chaps playing dominoes, there was no one. I took a glance out the back, through the door to the beer garden. Could hear muted voices, so stepped down the corridor and out into the cobbled yard. There was a group of young lads, probably students from the nearby Salford University, each babysitting a pint. Took a seat on the adjacent table, the one out of direct sunlight, and sparked up.

I thought about the events of the day. The funeral, the CCTV stuff from the hotel. Stevie's file from the shelter.

Although there seemed to be enough to put two and two together, I was only making five so far. There was the Range Rover and its occupants, and the fact they'd been tailing Lloyd ever since Stevie had been found, and the graffiti and tattoo, of course. But I still felt like I was wading through quicksand. The heat wasn't helping. I really needed this drink, and I looked to the heavens before taking the pint halfway down. I had a quiet moment for Stevie. God knows what the lad had been through the night he died. God only knew what his sister was going through now. I reminded myself to call her tomorrow. Had a feeling she had some information I needed to hear.

Before I could drain the last of the beer, I caught a familiar smell in the air, just for a moment. And then it was gone. I thought briefly about where I knew it from, but didn't have to think too long. Montecristo cigars were always his smoke of choice. I took a long drag on my own smoke before turning to see him standing right behind me in the doorway, holding two pints aloft.

I'd imagined before now that he hadn't changed much, that he still had those same lines on his face, the same Fedora on his head. And before that, I'd pictured his lifeless body, stiff with the passage of time, decomposing and lying in a Spanish ditch in an orange grove somewhere near Seville. But he wasn't dead. He was very much alive and looking very different to the last time I saw him, when he'd left my car to walk in the pouring snow on a gridlocked Oxford Road.

'Hello lad,' he said, stepping closer. He put the pints down and we embraced, the way blokes do–awkward and brief, with a pat on the back. 'It's been a while.'

It had been a relatively short period of time since I last

saw him, and I truly believed, like we all did, that we'd never see him again.

'I thought you were dead. Everyone did.'

He nodded. 'I nearly was.'

He took the head off his pint while I took him in. A considerable paunch had been added, and his face had filled out. I reckoned he'd put on at least three stone. And now he'd grown a beard, thick and grey to match his shoulder length hair. His felt Fedora had been replaced by a Spanish leather one and his overall complexion was a healthy tan, the skin benefitting from what I assumed had been an olive oil heavy Mediterranean diet. He looked like an elderly, fat Jim Morrison or a Father Christmas after too many pies. But it was Bob.

'Jesus,' I said. 'You've changed.'

'I may look like Jesus, lad,' he said, 'and believe me, I feel like I've been resurrected from the dead. But that's as far as the comparison goes.'

I looked him in the eye. 'I want to know everything.'

He glanced at the students on the table beside us. 'Later.'

Eyeballed him. 'Bob, for six months we've done nothing but wonder where the hell you are. After that phone call on Christmas Eve, and the gunshots, for fuck's sake...'

He grimaced. 'Keep your voice down, lad.'

'We thought you were dead. For all anyone knew, you could've been lying in a bloody ditch or thrown overboard at sea. Jesus, Bob, the police have been all over it, searching Spain high and low for your corpse and all you can say is 'later'. Fuck's sake, have you any idea what we've been through? And all the time, no word at all from you. Nothing. I mean, what were you thinking? Where have you been hiding?'

'I said we'll speak later,' he whispered. 'It's complicated.'

'I think I deserve better than that.'

'What's a couple of hours?'

I took up a fresh pint and drank. 'I don't believe you.'

'Look.' He put his pint down, looked around before leaning in. 'I know there's a lot to discuss. But now isn't the time or the place. You don't know who might be knocking about.'

'Sounds ominous.'

'Oh it is, lad, I can assure you.' He sparked up a new cigar. Blue smoke curled into the summer afternoon. 'And it's not over.'

It only seemed like yesterday when he'd blown the lid on the corruption across several UK police forces, not least my former employers and our very own GMP. The Angel case had driven him to the edge when his own grandson was given a lift home by several Triads in a black Mercedes. The veiled threat wasn't lost on the former Chief Crime Correspondent, and so he blew the lid once and for all and fled to Spain, leaving me high and dry to deal with the mess.

And he'd been there ever since.

'You've put on weight,' I said. 'And it's not like you to go without a shave.'

'Good living,' he said, patting his belly. 'You know how it is. There wasn't much else to do but eat and drink.'

I didn't believe him. I could still hear those gunshots late at night before I drifted off to sleep. He may have seen some good living before those shots, but I guessed he hadn't ever since that night. He was hiding nothing. He'd always been one to watch his weight and liked to be well presented. Now he looked like he'd let himself go. I wondered if it wasn't on purpose.

The students to our right had decided to take their party

elsewhere, which left us alone. Bob removed the leather Fedora and took several enthusiastic puffs on the Montecristo before undoing another button on his shirt and wiping the sweat from his brow.

He tossed me a twenty. 'Patience is a virtue, lad. Anyone ever tell you that? Get us another round in. Actually, make it two. I've missed this stuff and what I'm about to tell you may take a while.'

'Are you okay?'

'Just get the beers in and pin back your ears.'

I did as he asked, keen to get back and finally get to the bottom of why he'd disappeared. My phone buzzed as soon as I ordered the pints.

'Jim?'

'Christ, you're keen. I've only been gone about an hour.'

'Yeah,' said Laura, 'but I said I'd call if I found anything. I did some digging around. Bob there yet?'

'Yeah, I'll fill you in later. So, spill.'

'Well,' she said. 'I might be wrong–and I hope I am–but I found some stuff after going through about forty pages of shite online. Don't know if it's relevant, but then I looked at the photograph you uploaded of the graffiti again. You know, where he was found?'

'Go on.'

'And there was a swastika there. You remember?'

I did. A very crude version, spray painted on the wall. I didn't like where this was going. 'I remember.'

'Well, apparently, a horizontal lightning bolt is a symbol of fascism. As is the swastika.'

'Yeah, after the Nazis hijacked it.'

'Anyway. Just thought I'd point that out and how it might be relevant.'

'It's an interesting link.'

'But there's more. I went on YouTube and typed in 'horizontal lightning bolt' and 'E.N.D.' Have a guess what came up.'

The eco warrior barmaid put four pints down and I paid her. 'The trailer for some new superhero film? I don't know. Enlighten me.'

'Amongst all the other stuff, a rather shaky bit of footage from a far right rally in Liverpool. Jim, there's bloody lightning bolts everywhere. Flags, tee-shirts, you name it. And then there it was, painted on a bed sheet in red.'

'What?' But I had an idea.

'E.N.D.,' she said. 'Or to give it its full meaning–English National Defence. I think we might be dealing with a load of far right nut jobs here, Jim.'

I felt a sudden chill travel down my spine. In the back of my mind, I wondered about that graffiti, but the swastika passed me by. Back in the eighties, when I was just a kid, it was the kind of thing I saw daubed on most walls. Or maybe it was just the kind of town I lived in. Combat 18, the National Front. All that shit. Seems like it had never gone away.

'I'll show you the footage when you're back,' she said. 'There's more where that came from. When are you back, by the way?'

'I don't know,' I said. 'I'm waiting to hear why Bob isn't dead after all first. I'll let you know. Listen, have you found anything else on Stevie? You know, through the file?'

'Not yet, but I'm on it.'

'No rush.'

'Well Maya's calling in as well later on, so...'

'It's fine...'

'And something else: didn't really want to spring this on

you, but Karen called. Something about Nicole being in trouble at school.'

'Shit...'

'She might call your mobile.'

'Did you tell her I was at an important meeting?'

'I was hardly gonna say you were in the pub, was I? Not after your... well, you know.'

Our break up. All down to the drink and a lot more, if my ex was to be believed. But at least we were now on good terms and I had access to my daughter again.

'Okay, love,' I said. 'Gotta go, but good work.'

'Jim, why would a bunch of fascists want a homeless man dead?'

It was a good question and one I couldn't answer. 'That's what I'm gonna find out.'

'I don't like it, love.'

And neither did I. But the girl had done well and it was a lead with a route worth travelling down. I just wasn't entirely sure I wanted to take it. 'Nor me,' I said. 'Listen, we'll speak later. Keep me updated if you find anything else.'

'Will do. Love you.'

She hung up before I could tell her the same.

When I went back out to Bob, he was examining his passport. I sat down and he handed it to me.

I studied the photograph and the information on it. It was definitely him. Either that or he had a Spanish twin. 'Alvaro Eusebio Garcia?'

'What do you think?'

'I think you've finally lost your fucking mind. Is this a fake passport, Bob?'

'You're quick, lad, I'll give you that.'

I turned it over. It was embossed with the Spanish

equivalent of our British stamp. There was even a microchip inside, too.

'Bob, how... I mean, what possessed you to–'

He took it back. 'I needed it. I was desperate. Let's just say I called in some favours and took it from there.'

'Woah, hang on. Favours from who?'

'It's strictly on a need to know basis. I can't tell you, lad. All you need to know is that I called in some favours while I was out there and the favours came. At a price, mind. Cost me a fair do to get this shit sorted out.'

'Need I ask why?'

'I'm getting to it.'

'Come on then, Alvaro. Spill it.'

He took a long drink and a drag on the Montecristo like it was an oxygen mask. Blew a cloud above us. 'Okay. Now, just listen. No interruptions, lad.'

'Go on.'

He nodded. 'When I went out there, after it all kicked off...'

'The corruption stuff?'

'The corruption stuff,' he said. 'Twenty-odd years we'd been working on it, but anyway, I digress; when we went out there, I thought that was it, all sorted. Margaret could spend her days down the market and I could finally write that spy novel I've been meaning to get stuck into. But then they started following me.'

'Who?'

'The bloody Chinese, lad. The Triads, you know. Half the reason I left the country in the first place. It's no secret they were in cahoots with the police and some of it - not all, mind - came out in the wash when we went to press. But there were one or two who followed me out to Spain. They made it bloody obvious, to be honest with you.'

'Made what obvious?'

'That they were following us. We'd spot one in the same restaurant or they'd be on the fucking beach or something just when we were. It got to the point when I didn't want to leave the villa. Neither of us did.'

'In case?'

'What do you bloody think?'

'Why didn't you just go to the police?'

'And tell them what, lad?'

'The truth.'

'It's a bit more complicated than that. And anyway, I said no interruptions.'

'Go on.'

'So. We were being followed and didn't want to leave the villa. Well, I didn't. Margaret was a bit more down to earth about it than me. She thought I was nuts, to be honest with you. Put it all down to me being retired and getting silly, paranoid thoughts about the things I'd written about in the past, digging up memories that were best kept there.'

'And were you?'

'What?'

'Paranoid.'

'Well, I wouldn't call it that, lad. Finely tuned is the way I'd describe it, and rightly so as well, because if it wasn't for my suspicions in the first place, I wouldn't have got in touch with Sergio.'

'Who's Sergio?'

'A need to know basis, lad. But someone I knew a long time ago.'

'Someone who owed you a favour?'

'Yeah,' he said. 'You could put it like that. Anyway, I needed some help, and he came up with it.'

I took a drink and sparked up. 'I'm all ears.'

'He got hold of a gun for me.'

'Jesus...'

'Let me finish.'

'A gun...'

'And got some boys to keep an eye out for me. You know.'

'For protection?'

'Something like that.'

'Well, either it is or it isn't.'

'I thought I said no interruptions?'

'Bob, are you fucking mad?'

He gritted his teeth and blew another cloud above us. 'Just shut up and listen. Protection, yeah, I suppose, if you want to put it like that. And I bloody needed it, too. Oh aye, I did. Turns out they weren't around to protect me on bloody Christmas Eve, though.'

The night he finally called after I'd put the Angel case to bed.

'The gunshots...' I said.

He was nodding. 'They came for me, lad.'

'The Chinese?'

'The Chinese. Well, one of them. I still don't know where the other one is.'

'What happened, Bob?'

He finished his pint, then promptly picked up another. Took a drink, then sighed. 'Well, as you know, it was Christmas Eve. Margaret was down the local bar with her friend Isabella. I stayed at home. I'd just poured myself a glass of Marques de Riscal when I heard something hit the back window, out in the kitchen. I went out into the garden and there he was, marching towards me with a long looking blade.'

'Jesus...'

'So I ran back inside, locked the bloody doors as fast as I could and called you.'

I remembered it well. Shit, I couldn't forget it. It was snowing that night and I remembered I'd stepped outside to take the call and get some air while Laura danced around Sara's living room to Wizzard. Bob, in a blind panic, wanted me to contact his friend at the paper, George Thornley. Said he had a message for him but he didn't get that far. That's when I heard the gunshots. I hoped it wasn't just the line that went dead.

'I went upstairs,' he said. 'To our bedroom. I got the gun out of the bedside drawer. It was a good job it was already loaded because I wouldn't have had a clue and by that point, it was too late. He was already making his way up the stairs. Smashed the kitchen window in, you see, and just waltzed in like he owned the place.'

'Christ, Bob...'

'So by the time he was at my bedroom door, I had no chance. I had no choice, either. It was either me or him and I wasn't gonna let Margaret find me like that.'

'Like what?'

'Dead, lad. What do you think? The fucker had a bloody sword, didn't he? And he was gonna use it as well, so I got in first and shot him.'

'Bob...'

'Right between the bastard's eyes, several times.'

'Fucking hell...'

'Oh, he came off worse, all right. I told you they'd be on to me, lad, didn't I? You thought I'd lost it. Every bugger did, even Margaret. But I wasn't wrong. Needless to say, our Christmas was ruined.'

I almost laughed. Almost. We were silent for a moment as he let me take it in. We drank, we smoked. I shook my head in disbelief. It's not that I didn't think he was capable, it was that it had happened at all. And I was surprised he was even telling me. Me, an ex copper.

'He was gonna kill me, lad. No doubt about it. I didn't want to be the one to find out what it was like to get my head cut off. Because, believe you me, he would've done it. So I pulled the trigger and watched him die on my bedroom floor.'

'Jesus, Bob.' It felt like the only thing I could say right then.

'I tell you what, lad. There's a part of me enjoyed it too. I'm not afraid to say it. But what came afterwards was not pretty at all. Or easy. That's where Sergio came in, calling in some of his own favours. And I'll tell you something else. I may have been a lot of things in my lifetime, but I never thought I'd end up a murderer.'

I got us another round in while I attempted to get my head around what he'd just told me. Bob, a murderer? I knew he had connections that wouldn't hesitate to do the killing for him, but to pull the trigger himself? No. I wouldn't have believed that, and the thought had never once crossed my mind in the six months since that Christmas Eve phone call. Yet here he was, telling me everything, and I had no reason to disbelieve him. I knew Bob, and I knew he wouldn't lie to me. If what he was saying was indeed true, I had to wonder why he didn't just stay in Spain. When I returned, I asked him.

'You said so yourself,' he said. 'Everyone was looking for my corpse. After we got rid of the body–'

'We?'

'Sergio and me... I had no choice but to lie low. I had to go into hiding, lad. Here I was with blood on my hands, a killer–'

'You're not a killer, Bob.'

'A killer, son. I killed a man in cold blood.'

'Yeah, defending yourself! He was gonna kill you!'

'Doesn't matter. He's dead, and I pulled the trigger. So I'm responsible for another man's death. I've got to live with that for the rest of my life.'

I shook my head and drank.

'Bottom line was that I'd killed a man, son. Murder. I was scared. Fucking hell, lad, I was bloody terrified. If the truth came out, I'd be buggered–or getting buggered in some Spanish jail.'

'I don't know how you can joke about this, Bob.'

'Because,' he said, tapping a finger to his temple, 'I'd go crackers otherwise.'

I was beginning to think he was crackers, anyway. I wanted to voice it but didn't. Instead, I asked him to go on because what I'd heard already wasn't quite enough.

'Strangely, the first thing I did when I realised what I'd done was to go back down to the kitchen to drink the wine I'd just poured. By that point, of course, he was just slumped there on the bedroom floor, his blood seeping into Margaret's favourite bloody Persian rug. I drank it quick. I wondered why my face felt wet and it was because the blood had sprayed into it when I shot him. I clocked it in the mirror when I went into the hallway to phone Sergio.

'I picked up the phone and got him on his mobile. He was at home with his mother. When I told him what had just happened, he went quiet for a minute and then said he'd be round straight away with some friends of his. They turned up ten minutes later in a Mitsubishi pickup truck.

We were just wrapping him up in the rug and mopping the rest of the blood off the floor when I looked up to see Margaret standing in the doorway. I've never felt so much shame in my life, lad. I love Margaret just as much–perhaps more so–than the day I married her, and I'll never forget the look on her face or what she said to me as we rolled him up in her bloody rug, which she loved.'

'What did she say?'

'She said I was a stupid bastard. She was right.'

I would have to agree. He was far from stupid, but he'd done a very stupid thing, certainly by his standards. And yet, could I really blame him? Given the circumstances, and the fact that he would've quite possibly been killed himself, it was no surprise he'd acted the way he did. Perhaps I'd have done the same. He said he'd been followed for weeks, so had made plans for this very scenario. When it came down to it, Christmas Eve had turned out to be as eventful as he'd expected. Defending himself, sure. But I wasn't too convinced any of this could be relied upon in court. And given the fact that they'd dumped the body, indicated he was guilty as charged. It was written all over his face. He'd pulled the trigger, yes, but to try and cover it up afterwards was a big mistake. Instead of maybe getting away with manslaughter, there was absolutely zero chance of that now.

'I'm still listening.'

'There's not much left to say, lad. We left Margaret at home with her head in her hands and drove twenty miles east to the coast. A couple of Sergio's boys took a small fishing boat out to sea and tossed him overboard into the Med. We thought that was it, job done. We went back, and I convinced Margaret we had to leave the villa for the mountains, and we went on with our lives in the middle of nowhere under Sergio's watch. But then the remains washed up on a beach last month and when we got wind of it, that was it. I knew I was assumed dead, so it was the logical choice from that point. We managed to get a new identity and here I am.'

'Back home.'

'Back home,' he said. 'But without a roof over my head. That's where you come in.'

'Oh no. Forget it.'

'Just for a few weeks. I've got some things to sort out and then I'll be gone.'

'I'd be harbouring a murderer, Bob.'

'Oh, so I am a murderer now?'

'You know what I mean.'

'One minute I'm not, the next minute I am.'

'I could get sent down for a long time if anyone finds out where you are.'

He took a long pull on the Montecristo and downed his pint before starting off another. 'And I could too. But I'm hoping it won't come to that. Listen, do you really think I want to be here? When I went to press with all that corruption shite I thought, right, that's it, I'm retired now and no more pissing about. I can put my feet up and relax, finally get around to doing the things I want to do. And then these bloody bastards show up and now look at me! I acted in self defence, lad. Anyone would've done the same.'

'I see that, Bob, but to dump the body...?'

'What else was I gonna do?'

'Go to the police.'

'Oh, and tell them what, exactly? I panicked, lad. I'd just killed a man, for fuck's sake. I would've had to bring Sergio into it and all sorts. It would've very quickly gotten worse.'

'It's gotten much worse than that now, anyway. If he's washed up, they'll inevitably link it back to you.'

'That's why I'm here.'

'But they'll trace you anyway.'

'Not unless I'm dead.'

'But you're not.'

'But they think I am.'

'No,' I said. 'They don't. Surely not now, not after he's showed up as half eaten shark food. I take it the bullet holes are still intact?'

He shrugged. 'I don't know. Maybe. Does it really matter?'

It was my turn to sigh. 'Look, I'm not exactly hot on forensics, but as far as old school detective work goes, it wouldn't surprise me if they weren't onto you already.'

'Or putting two and two together and making five. I hope.'

'You better cling onto that hope, Bob. I've a feeling it's all you've got.'

CHAPTER SEVEN

W e talked through the evening until Bob got paranoid about who might be listening to our conversation. I had to get him to repeat some of what he'd said, especially the stuff about how he came to be Alvaro Eusebio Garcia. The real Mr. Garcia, it turned out, had died in a farm accident in nineteen eighty-two. At least that was Sergio's story. It wasn't clear how the deceased's official documents came into Sergio's possession, and Bob explained that he didn't want to question it, given Sergio's background. The Spaniard didn't elaborate on how the new identity came about. He just turned up at the safe house where Bob was hiding one day and gave him his new passport. No questions asked.

'I was just glad to have been given an opportunity,' he'd said. 'I knew not to question it. It was an unwritten agreement. He offered to help me out, and I accepted his help. That was that. And anyway, by this point, I couldn't care less who Alvaro Garcia was, or whether he was alive or dead. And if he was dead, fine. Through me, he would live again.'

I suppose the sensible thing to do would be to tell him I couldn't help him, that he was better off going back to Spain and handing himself in to the authorities. But I couldn't do that. He was a mate, albeit a stupid one, but he could also come in very useful too. I knew, though, that if I put him up in the flat, he couldn't stay for too long. It would be madness to allow him any longer than a few weeks. The last thing I needed was the law on my case. So I told him I'd put him up but to not expect miracles.

'It won't be for long,' he said. 'I promise. I've just got a few things to sort out. Family stuff. And then I'll be gone. I promised Margaret I'd be back within a month. I can't leave her there on her own.'

'Is she still in the safe house?'

'No, a different one. On the coast, hidden away. And I'll be joining her as soon as I can.'

Now, as the beer garden filled up in the evening sun, and our talk had turned to my current case, the alcohol was reaching the edges. We were both pretty drunk. I welcomed it. I think he did too. But the jitters had set in. He said he couldn't be too careful and I agreed with him. I knew what it felt like to always be looking over your shoulder. I hoped it wouldn't catch up with me again.

We walked back to the flat, picking up a takeaway curry on the way. I called Laura as we walked to explain why a wanted murderer would be staying on our couch. She wasn't best pleased, but I sensed she found it a bit exciting too. It wasn't the first time I thought she was a girl who liked to live on the edge.

'But what if anyone finds out?' she said. 'And haven't you got enough to think about?'

'No one will find out. And anyway, it won't be for too long.'

'Do you trust him?'

'With my life.'

'He won't shoot you, will he?'

'I'm sure he won't, no.'

'How can you be sure?'

'Laura, we've been through this. He's not some cold-blooded killer. He's just Bob, former crime correspondent and, let's not forget, a pensioner.'

'But he's killed a man, Jim! Have you completely lost your mind?'

'Have you lost yours? He's a mate, and he's kipping on the couch. Now that's the end of it.'

Bob fell asleep halfway through his chicken madras, while I carried on where I left off. It was a mistake and I knew it, yet I couldn't resist the pull of an eighteen-year-old Glenfiddich. I left him sleeping on the couch while I stood at the window and looked out into the night. The light was fading, but there was still plenty of life out there. Traffic too. I thought about Stevie. It had been a long day. Thought about his body, burning there under those arches in the dead of night. Saw his coffin roll beyond that curtain in the crematorium, whatever was left of him burning all over again. It was no way for any man to die.

I poured another dram. It was a sad reminder of my own father's funeral. Threw it back, poured another. Switched on the TV, then switched it off again, preferring to look out the window instead. I could hear the revelry of the night kicking in, almost wanted to be a part of it, but knew I didn't belong there anymore. Those days were long gone. I was edging closer to my forties, and the closer I got, the less I cared about hitting town. I only had time for Laura and myself these days. The work kept coming in, thankfully, and I was grateful for it. But I was way past investigating murder. Maybe Robertson was right. Maybe I was out of my depth. With every passing hour, I felt it more. The self doubt creeping in. The fear of failure, of fucking up. Yet everything about Stevie's death set alarm bells ringing.

On the other side, why should I even care? He was dead and he would stay dead. I could do nothing to bring him home, couldn't turn the clock back. I wondered if all of this was pointless. A waste of time and energy. But then I thought of Shannon and the homeless friends he'd left behind. I thought of the injustice of it all and how unlikely Robertson was to even give a fuck. To him, Stevie was just another body in a long line of bodies. All that paperwork, dotting the I's and crossing the T's. He was just another number, didn't matter.

But he mattered to me.

I downed the whisky. Felt the burn. Laura had sent me the link to the YouTube footage she'd found of the E.N.D. far right rally in Liverpool. I took out my phone and opened up the e-mail as I stepped into the bedroom. I slung off my clothes and crashed on the bed as Bob slept in the room behind me. Clicked on the link and saw half a dozen knuckleheads draped in union flags and bedsheets that had been daubed in crude fascist slogans. I hardly knew Liverpool like the back of my hand but it was clear they were somewhere in the city centre, marching down some road that wasn't too far away from the Liver building, which I could see in the distance, its unmistakable bird sitting high above.

They were chanting some indecipherable shit, fists punching the air, flags waving above their heads. A gathering of cunts, if ever I saw one. And then the film ended, right in the middle of some song slagging Muslims and the Irish. I sparked up and played it again, looking for some standout faces. I didn't really know what I was looking for. I suppose the bald guy from the CCTV at the Park Inn, the one with the tattoo on his neck. Or any of his associates. I contemplated walking over to the office to dig through the printouts Graham had kindly sorted, but then I was half drifting off to sleep and I knew the Northern Quarter would be at its liveliest about now.

I must've slept for a while but was thankfully woken by my phone chiming a text message just before it slipped from my hand. It was a good job because the smoke was slipping too. I dragged in deep and rubbed the ash into my palm before checking the text. Rubbed my eyes.

THEY'RE HERE

It was from Lloyd's number. I called him straight back, half asleep and half drunk, but there was no answer, just the phone ringing out. I sat up then, stumbling through the half light and scrambling for my jeans. Fired off a quick reply.

WHO?

I dressed quickly, calling Laura as I pulled a shirt on. The night was hotter than ever. She answered almost immediately.

'The law caught up with him, then?'

'What?' Then I realised she was referring to Bob. I glanced into the living room as I paced around, looking for my keys and wallet. 'No, but listen. I need you to come over to the flat. I need you behind the wheel.'

'Oh Jim, you don't half pick some stupid times...'

'It's Lloyd.'

'Who?'

'Never mind. Just get over here. I've had too much to be driving. We just need to get over there, he's not answering his phone.'

'And?'

'Laura, I've not got time for this, just fucking get here.'

She said something about twenty minutes before the line went dead, but I was already sparking up again. I checked on Bob. He was now on his front, snoring hard. Thought about waking him but considered he'd be a liability in his condition. I doubted he'd be up for the excursion, anyway. I tried Lloyd again, but it continued to ring out. I could only hope all was normal and he wasn't near his phone. That had to be it, though I somehow doubted it too.

I paced around, smoking, until Laura unlocked the door ten minutes later. Bob remained almost comatose on the couch throughout our brief conversation, which was mainly Laura moaning about having to be dragged out of bed.

'So what's this about?' she said as we left the flat. I'd left Bob a little note beside him on the coffee table. 'What's so important you have to drag me out at this time?'

'It's hardly late.'

'It's late enough,' she said, showing me her watch. It read 10:47.

I explained Lloyd's message and why it made me nervous, particularly since he hadn't been answering my calls.

'Do you think he's okay?'

'That's what I want to find out.'

'And you said they'd been following him for a while?'

I nodded. 'Since Stevie's body turned up.'

'Doesn't seem right. Why didn't he just tell the police? Come to think of it, why don't we just ring them now?'

'And say what? They'd laugh us off the phone. It's a non emergency.'

She shook her head. By now we'd reached the Punto and she got behind the wheel. I let my window down.

'Doesn't make sense to me.'

'Just drive.'

'Where to?'

I told her.

We skipped the city centre and came up to Deansgate via Trinity Way. Lloyd had said they were having a bit of a gathering at the shelter following the funeral. I hadn't expected it to be party central, and I wasn't wrong. By the time we pulled into the little cobbled area beside the building–a small place down a side street off Blackfriars–there was little action going on inside, just a handful of rough sleepers gathered around a coffee urn and a couple of workers sharing a joke over a cup of tea and an iPhone. I left Laura in the car and popped inside. A bespectacled lefty type looked up from his phone.

'Can I help?'

'Friend of Lloyd's,' I said. 'He around?'

'No, I think he left a few hours ago.'

'By himself?'

He nodded. 'Far as I'm aware. I've not been here long. Anything I can help you with?'

'It's okay,' I said. 'If you hear from him, tell him to call Jim Locke.'

'No problem.'

'And one other thing. I know he's been holding a gathering today. A wake after Stevie's funeral. I don't suppose you've seen a white Range Rover around, have you?'

'Can't say I have, to be honest. But I've only been on duty since ten, so...'

'Okay. Tell him I called.'

I got a few nods of recognition from some of the homeless guys on my way out. It was fast becoming an epidemic in the city and something I knew about all too well.

'Well?' she said, as I got back in the car.

'Gone a few hours ago.' I lifted the phone to my ear and dialed. 'Let's go.'

We drove across the city but without a destination it was pretty useless. I knew Lloyd lived somewhere in Moss Side, so I directed Laura to the Princess Parkway for any sign of him or the Range Rover. I knew it was a long shot. With the night being hot and summer at its height, the local youth were out in force, hanging around in groups and circling the streets in souped-up, tinted cars. The air was pungent with the thick aroma of burning weed. We drove the length of the road, then back again before turning into the Alexandra estate for any sign. Just as I was getting anxious, the phone pinged again. It was another text, this time with a video attached.

'Pull over.'

She pulled up beside a damp-looking council flat. Although it was dark, and a residential area, there were still a handful of locals dotted around, several of whom were looking in our direction from someone's front gate just fifty feet or so away. I could hear hip hop music rumbling from a house nearby.

I opened the message.

SEE THIS, L. DON'T COME FIND ME.

I clicked on the video. It took a moment to download.

'What is it?'

I pressed the PLAY button and set the phone in the well between us as we watched. It took a moment to recognise what I was seeing, but then I saw that it showed the view through the rear windscreen of Lloyd's car, a Vectra. I could hear him breathing. He sounded out of breath. He zoomed in–assuming he was filming this from his driver's seat–through the back window at a narrow and quiet street that was dark and poorly lit. I didn't know if that was a good or bad thing. I could see stairwell fire escapes going down one high brick wall. The buildings on either side looked like old Victorian warehouses. Then the Range Rover came into view, rounding a bend less than two hundred metres away. We watched it creeping slowly, could hear Lloyd's heavy breaths with my own.

'Fuck.'

There was a rush of light, then darkness as the image was catapulted around before coming to a stop, presumably as the phone was thrown onto the passenger seat. The screen had turned black, but we could still hear him.

'They're following me again,' he said. There was the sound of the car moving off, changing gear. We shared a look between us. 'Jim, if anyone gets this, I'm driving through town. I'm coming up to Portland Street right now, and the Range Rover is right behind me, man.'

The image changed again, and suddenly the street came into view. He pointed the camera at the rear-view mirror. Sure enough, there it was, creeping up behind him. By now, the view through the windscreen had become bright with city lights, illuminated by neon advertising screens and traffic of all kinds. There were a lot of people on both sides of the road.

'Why the fuck they're following me, I don't know,' he said, his voice tinny through the phone's speakers. 'You see that? They're right behind me, man. That's twice today! I don't know what to do.'

'Evidence, Lloyd,' I said. 'Drive to the police.'

I was urging him on, but I knew this event was already over. The video only had a few minutes to run and it was coming to an end already. I was acutely aware that wherever he was now, time could be running out for him too. We watched as the clock ticked down.

'I'm gonna put my foot down now,' he said. 'I'm gonna try to lose them, see how fucking good their driving is. Jim, if you get this–'cause I'm gonna send it to you, man–I'm going to Lower Broughton, okay? Got a mate there who can back me up with this shit.'

'Lloyd, no...'

'He sounds scared,' Laura said.

'He is.'

The video ended. It abruptly stopped when he held the phone back to the rear-view mirror and focused on what was in it. It was them, all right.

'Start her up.'

'Where're we going?'

'You heard the man.'

The Punto hardly purred, and when she put it into gear, it struggled to even meet it as we moved two hundred yards down the road.

'Where the fuck's Lower Broughton?'

'Salford.'

'And how do I get there?'

'By the seat of your fucking pants, Laura. Just drive.'

'I like it when you're angry.'

I didn't reply, just directed her to where we needed to be. Back down Deansgate to Blackfriars and on to Salford. It occurred to me that we could've wasted so much time. There was nothing we could do now.

I dialed him up again. It rang out. Called Bob. That rang out too. I was getting more anxious with every passing moment. There was no doubting that Lloyd was scared. And for them–whoever 'they' were–to be following him since Stevie's remains had been found didn't bode well for what was now occurring. I felt that pit of dread in my stomach as the world moved by outside. Something had gone wrong.

I urged Laura to put her foot down. The place was like a ghost town and almost eerily quiet. I didn't like it one bit. We crossed Trinity Way and headed into the estate. The world felt like a lonely place around here. As we drove further in, we could see a black plume of smoke rising into the summer night. It was near too, and we both choked as we approached.

When we reached Albert Park, there it was.

'Pull over.'

We left the car and ran through the park entrance, the acrid smoke billowing. Seemed the entire sky had turned black. Lloyd's Vectra was sitting there on the grass, beyond the football pitches and beside the kids' playground. It was burning. I could feel the heat as I neared, my mouth covered. Could hear the bodywork warping and cracking. As I edged closer, my eyes watering, I could see there was a hole in the windscreen, a spider-web crack across the glass. Could see the blood splatter across the inside too. It was sparkling in the dead moonlight. When I looked through, just catching a glimpse through the smoke, he was sitting there in the driver's seat, his face a mess of blood, a bullet hole in his forehead.

'Oh fuck.'

Laura was already on the phone. I could hear her, half a world away, screaming down the line. I turned to her but was blinded by headlights. She was nothing but a silhouette. Behind her, the Range Rover hummed and revved.

She was trying to pull me back but I wouldn't let her, except when I fell to my knees, and the glass shattered, the red hot flames licking over his body and out of the blown out windows, I let her pull me to her and drag me away.

It wasn't just the car that was burning.

'It's gonna fucking blow up, Jim!'

It was then we ran, and I could feel the heat now as the Range Rover sped off somewhere into the night.

I fell to my knees and watched Lloyd burn. I was sure I could hear him screaming, though I knew he couldn't have been. He was already dead, though probably hadn't been for long. By now, a crowd had gathered. No one could touch it. I was aware of Laura beside me as I stared hard into the flames. The fire had really taken hold.

There was a blast of heat when it finally blew, the petrol tank adding an intensity. The fire was hungry. It consumed him. I wondered if anyone else knew there was a dead man inside.

PAIN

CHAPTER EIGHT

'I'm telling you, it was a white Range Rover, registration CV15TYK. What the fuck else do you want me to say?'

'I want you to say you'll stay well away from a police investigation, Locke. We've got your number. You're not a copper anymore.'

'Bollocks.'

'That's exactly what it is,' Robertson said. He'd reached the crime scene, now cordoned off with blue tape. The SOC crew were busy beyond, all white overalls and scientific gear. 'Now do us all a favour and fuck off. Pub'll be open soon.'

I watched him march off towards the burnt out Vectra, Lloyd's remains probably still sitting in the driver's seat. Always one to get a sly dig in. If I had a fiver for every time I wanted to punch the bastard, I'd be filthy rich.

'Ignoring the evidence again, I see,' I called as he marched off. 'Some fucking D.I. you are.'

I turned away and sparked up. Took that shit in deep. Events had taken a serious turn for the worst, and having spent the last five minutes arguing with Robertson, showing him the clip Lloyd had sent me (which he outrageously said proved nothing), I'd come to the sorry conclusion–and not for the first time–that the police were just as useless now as they were when I was a copper. Except it was dangerous to ignore evidence. Either Robertson really couldn't see the wood for the trees, his judgement severely marred by his deluded hatred of me, or he was as corrupt as they come. Probably both.

It wasn't even past the rush hour, and the sun was already blazing. Working in heat like this was making me feel sick, and coupled with the dank odour of burnt flesh and a dampened down petrol fire, every time I inhaled, my eyes watered and my throat stung and all I wanted to do was throw up.

When I got back to the Volvo–I'd decided it was time to get back behind the wheel–Laura was sitting in the passenger seat with a takeout coffee and several painkillers in her hand. I took them all. The coffee was hot and bitter, just like my mood, but it tasted good and it would serve a purpose.

'Bob insisted on coming along,' she said. 'So I told him I reckoned that was a bad idea.'

I wasn't listening. I couldn't get Lloyd's face out of my head. I could hear him now, telling me all this was going to happen all along, that he'd told me over and over again about the Range Rover.

I should've done something sooner.

And now here we were with two dead men, both of whom I knew well. There was no telling Stevie had taken a bullet in the head like Lloyd had done, and I supposed I'd never really know. But I'd seen Lloyd's gunshot wound myself, before the car went up and took him with it.

It made me wonder if I was on their radar as well, whoever 'they' were. For Lloyd to be stalked, gunned down, then finally burnt to death in his own car told me these people meant business, whatever their business was. All I knew was that Lloyd hadn't deserved any of it. If he'd gone to the police earlier, insisted they look into it, perhaps he'd still be alive. Instead, his wife and kids were waking up without a husband and father.

'He said he'd phone you later. And by the way, did you ring Karen?'

Karen. Shit. I'd forgotten about Nicole being in trouble at school. 'Forgot,' I said. 'It won't make me look good.'

'You'd better call her.'

I could see the SOC guys hovering around the burnt-out car. A tent was being erected while a chief fire officer was going over the details with a woman I didn't recognise, probably a DS. Robertson was standing, hands deep in pockets, gazing into the blackened metal.

I put my phone to my ear and dialed. She answered on the fourth ring.

'Shannon?'

'Yes?'

She sounded like a woman who'd been up all night.

'It's Locke.'

There was a pause and a deep breath.

'I've been waiting for you to call. Do you know Churchill Way? Pendleton, near the precinct?'

I told her I'd be there in half an hour.

I dropped Laura back at the office, by which time the city centre commute was in full swing. Even Maya had opened up early, sitting outside with a dirty mug of tea and a bearded bloke with even more tattoos than her. I asked Laura to hold the fort while I went to visit Shannon. She said she was scared for me. I didn't see the point in telling her I was scared too, which I was. Driving through the city, it was clear there were a lot of Range Rovers around, and I expected one on every corner. I didn't believe it was just the heat that was making me sweat.

I decided that Bob tagging along wouldn't be a bad thing after all, given my current disposition. Yet I was all too aware that travelling with a wanted murderer in my passenger seat wasn't going to do much to dampen down the Heebie Jeebies. But I needed someone to be my eyes when I wasn't looking, and he was a good ally. Perhaps my only real ally.

'There's no bloody coffee, lad,' he said, when I called him en route to the flat. 'Do you expect me to drink PG bloody Tips?'

'Listen, it might not be a bad thing after all.'

'Look, lad, with my hangover only the darkest, strongest coffee will do.'

'I meant to come with me.'

'Oh. Well, here I was, resigned to sitting around this miserable flat with nothing but daytime TV for company, so I'd much prefer to tag along. Gotta be better than the bloody Jeremy Kyles of this world.'

'Be ready to leave in five minutes.'

'Aye, right.'

But I was there in less than three. I hung up and took a right down Thompson Street. When I approached the flat four hundred yards beyond in Ancoats, Bob was hanging out of the window, a Montecristo between his lips. I couldn't quite believe how he looked now. The weight he'd put on had filled him out. It was all by design, of course, and I suspect he'd taken great pleasure in letting himself go. Throw a patch over his eye and he'd be a pirate on the high seas. The fog of a heavy night's drinking hung around him, but we'd soon put that right. I called up, told him to just slam the door shut. Minutes later we were pulling into a petrol station that had a drive through coffee place attached–I needed fuel anyway–so he got us both a strong one while I filled her up and threw back half a litre of freezing cold water.

'I couldn't have sat indoors all bloody day,' he said, as we moved off. 'Especially on a day like this. Jesus, it's hot. Bloody hotter than Spain for this time of year and that's saying something.'

'Been like this a few weeks now,' I said. 'I don't like it.' I drove us back to Lower Broughton and pulled over at Albert Park so that he could witness the crime scene himself. By now, the tent had been erected.

'Got any spare?'

He was referring to the sunglasses I'd dropped over my eyes. I nodded to the glove compartment where he found an old and battered pair of Ray Bans. Nodded to the white SOC tent which now no doubt still concealed the burnt out Vectra and Lloyd's charred remains lying stiff beside it. I filled him in on last night's events in full. By the time I finished, I had to down the rest of the water I'd bought.

Twenty minutes later, thanks to the traffic, we turned into Churchill Way, a quiet road that ran beside a bank of high-rise flats that overlooked Salford Shopping Centre, more commonly known in these parts as The Precinct. The place wasn't much more than a bus station skirted by betting shops, charity shops, pawnbrokers and a Poundland or two. Throw in a Greggs and a KFC and a small indoor market and that was what passed as a 'shopping city'. The giant supermarket beyond had done nothing but shove small businesses out of the way. As we left the Volvo and found Shannon's block down a side road, the exhaust fumes of a hundred knackered buses hung in the air. It was enough to make anyone consider giving up smoking. Almost.

We found our way through Birch Court and made it up to the second level in a few minutes. I could see Pendleton Police Station beyond the fried chicken place and the big roundabout beyond that. The air was heavier than the traffic. Even at this early hour, we both had a sweat on. I rang the bell and waited. It didn't take her long to answer.

'Jim,' she said. She opened up and let us through into a cool and dark lounge. The stale smell of vodka and knock off cigarettes hung in the room. It was a good job there was a window open. Shannon looked like she'd been up all night, and I guessed she had been, though for reasons I didn't expect given she'd just buried her brother. A naked, tattooed kid kicked the bedroom door shut when he saw me poking my nose in. Took that as my cue to sit down. I sparked up and tossed her one, too. Bob stuck his head out of the window and took in the view.

'Thanks,' she said. 'For coming, I mean. And for being Stevie's friend.'

I nodded. 'It was easy to be his friend. He was a good bloke. He helped me out when I needed it most. I won't forget that.'

She looked down at the carpet, lit up her fag. 'Can I get you a coffee?'

I was about to decline, but Bob said he'd love one. She disappeared into the kitchen, giving me a chance to have a look around the room. I called out and asked her if she'd mind me recording the conversation. She said it was fine, so I took out my iPhone and hit record on the Dictaphone app.

There wasn't much to see, and certainly no photographs of Stevie. A wall unit full of junk, a stack of vinyl records in the corner. A child's rocking horse placed against the wall near the window. The couch we sat on was ragged and needed springs replacing. Aside from a print of a crying boy on the wall, there was nothing much else upon them other than a wallpaper that looked like it belonged in the nineteen eighties. But it was her home. Though sparse, it was clean, and she was clearly comfortable here, and I guessed it was probably the only proper home she'd had, given what I knew of her history, which wasn't much. When she returned with the coffee, I asked her about it.

She almost laughed. 'Been in and out of care homes most of my life,' she said, brushing her black greasy hair over her ears. She inhaled deep, blew a cloud above us. 'Though there wasn't much care going on, I can tell you that.'

'Was Stevie with you all the time?'

'Oh yeah,' she said. 'They never split us up. Except for this one time when I had to go to this bloody convent for a month. That was in the eighties.'

'Do you remember when?'

She took a long drag and looked to the window. Finally letting the smoke out, she said, 'Not really. It was a long time ago. Probably the mid-eighties.'

'Where was this convent?'

'Chorlton,' she said. 'I don't think it's there anymore.'

We paused for a minute, both of us wanting to get to the meat and bones.

'Anyway,' she said. 'It was a long time ago. The police never asked me about any of that. The care stuff, you know. We were in and out of so many places when we were young. It settled down a bit as we got older, into our teens and that, but it never really did anything for us. They were horrible bastards, some of them.'

I wanted her to go on, to tell me all she could remember,

but I also wanted to know of Stevie's last whereabouts in the weeks before his death.

'You said yesterday that Stevie had been to see you. Before it happened.'

She nodded. 'He came here a few times. Asked for money. I fed him once or twice, and he had the spare room a few nights, but you know what he's like–what he was like. He wasn't even that comfortable in his own skin, let alone under a roof. Any roof, really. He was like some kind of nomad. A wandering spirit without a home. It was the system that did that to him, I think.'

'The care homes.'

'Yeah,' she said. We all had a drink of coffee before she went on. 'He didn't like the routine. The rules, the way things were supposed to work, you know. They had one rule for this and another rule for that. You name it. It was like being in the fucking army or something.'

'A regime,' Bob said.

'Exactly.' She nodded, took a long drag. 'Like a regime. Bed at eight, up at six. All that shit. It was hard to even feel human at all.'

'Were they all like that?'

'Pretty much.'

'And do you think that's why Stevie ended up on the streets?'

'Well, don't you? On the streets, he could do whatever he liked. It started with petty theft, I'm sure. And he used to be into his speed so he had to fund it somehow. Then it was booze, of course. Anything to escape, really, because he couldn't escape in care.'

'And once he had a taste of the freedom it brought...'

'There was no going back,' she said. 'You see, Stevie never knew our mum. But I can just about remember her.

And he looked like her, you know. Not having a mum–or a dad–broke us both from the very beginning. But it was worse for him, I think. He never knew her at all. He never saw her face. At least I could dream about her sometimes. All he knew was the system he was in. Didn't know anything else, never had done. So when he broke away from it, he meant it. He wasn't fucking about. He just cut himself off from society and lived off the grid. He cut himself off from me too.'

'For how long?' Bob said. 'When did he come back into your life?'

'Well, he never did come back. I only saw him about six times since he was twenty, the last time being a week before he was found. I got a knock on the door and the police told me they'd found him.'

'They must have been able to identify him,' I said.

'Yes.'

'Must've been hard for you,' Bob said.

She looked away before scrambling for a cigarette on the coffee table. Lit up and blew smoke up to the ceiling. The silence was interrupted by the bedroom door creaking open and the young man she'd been sharing her bed with creeping out. He told her he'd phone later before leaving quickly, a blast of heat moving into the room before cooling again. I thought about Lloyd, burning in that car.

'He was my brother,' she said. 'So yes, it was hard. Still is. I can't think about him without seeing him burning. The other memories, the ones I have of us as kids, well, it seems like they're locked away in a dark room forever and all I have now are the ones I don't want. The police knocking on my door. The images I have of him burning under those fucking arches.'

'The times he came to see you,' I said. 'The most

recent. What do you remember of that? What was he like? Different? Scared? On edge? Did he talk about anyone else?'

She left the couch and walked to the window. Gazed out across Salford as she smoked and gathered her thoughts. Bob and I exchanged a look. I was thinking bout Lloyd and whether to tell her about him too.

'Hard to know what he was like, really,' she said. 'The first night he came, that is. A Monday, I think it was. What was going through his mind, I mean. It had been so long since I'd seen him that, in a way, I'd come to forget what he was like at all. Who was the real Stevie, you know what I mean? I saw him a few times the week before he died. So on the Monday he came to me asking for money, a few hundred quid, though he denied it was for drugs or anything like that. I wouldn't have been bothered if it was, to be honest. I knew he needed stuff.'

'Did he seem desperate?' I asked.

'Maybe,' she said. 'A bit scared, it seemed, though he wouldn't tell me anything that was on his mind. We had a talk, about a lot of things. He slept over and I got us a take-away–kebab for him, chippy for me–and we had a drink but nothing too heavy.'

'What did you talk about?' Bob said. 'If you don't mind me asking...'

'When we were kids, that kind of stuff. Reminiscing, you know. All the shit we had to put up with. Had a good laugh about the time he fucked off to Blackpool on the train when he was fourteen and they had a search party out for him. He seemed to enjoy talking about that, but then got pissed off with me for bringing up Ivy Brook. His mood got quite dark then, and he snapped. I had to change the subject quick but when I started talking about mum, he just went to bed. When I woke up the next morning he was gone.'

'What was it about Ivy Brook that made his mood dip so much?'

'I don't know. But he was never happy there. Neither was I, if I'm honest. They're the bastards that sent me to that bloody convent. There were a lot of other kids that weren't happy there. We weren't the only ones. Some kids were seriously fucked up.'

'In what way?'

'Just... weird. Quiet, depressed. Mental problems, you know.'

I nodded. Can't say I was surprised by any of this, given recent reports about the care system back then. I knew there was a lot of abuse around. Of all kinds. Stevie had even talked about it with me back when we used to doss down behind Ho's Chinese bakery together. He never talked about himself being a victim of it, though. And maybe he wasn't. Maybe he just knew people that were. But I couldn't help but think, sitting there in his sister's flat, that Stevie had taken secrets to his grave.

'A couple of people took their own lives,' she said, and suddenly I was back in the room. She was nodding, staring into space, the ash on her cigarette dropping to the carpet. 'Not back then, but recently. What I heard, anyway.'

'Go on,' Bob said.

'A couple of blokes,' she said. 'One a few years ago, can't remember his name. But then another lad just a few months ago as well. Carl McDermott, he was called. I don't know anything about how he died, just that he was found in his flat one Sunday morning. He lived around here.'

'Did Stevie know him?'

'Oh yeah, Stevie knew him. He was at Ivy brook with us

for a few years. Stevie was mates with him. Not best mates but... you know, he knew him.'

'You said he came a few times before his death,' I said. 'On the Monday, and then, after that...?'

'Friday night,' she said. 'A week later, he was dead. Excuse me a minute.'

She disappeared into the kitchen and we could hear her opening cupboards and stifling sobs over the sound of the kettle coming to the boil. Bob said 'Christ' and sparked up a Montecristo. I followed with my own. I was feeling drowsy. The heat and conversation didn't go well together. I knew the whole mess was too close to the bone for her, so soon after the event. It was for me, too. Yet there was stuff here that needed to be dealt with. Putting a timeline of events together, however fragmented the picture had become, was needed now more than ever. Whoever had torched her brother must have had a motive for setting him alight. Must have wanted to make sure he was dead. But then for Lloyd to have lost his life too, well that was a bit too much to handle. And I couldn't see a connection. I decided I wouldn't mention Lloyd to her at all just yet.

She came back in with more coffee and, although neither of us wanted one, we both obliged. Bob knew as much as I did that we needed to get to the bottom of Stevie's last meeting with his sister.

'So,' she said, settling down once more onto the couch. 'The Friday. He wasn't himself at all, I don't think. A bit twitchy, you know. He turned up with some other guy, who didn't hang around.'

'Another man?' I said. Now we were getting somewhere. 'Go on.'

She was nodding. Sparked up again and took a long drag before continuing. 'He turned up with this guy. I've never seen him before. When I answered the door, this man was with him. But when Stevie came in, the guy said he'd wait downstairs. Outside, you know. Which I thought was a bit weird, really.'

She wasn't the only one.

'He went down to the ground and waited in the road. I watched him sit on the kerb, smoking.'

'Did it seem like he was just waiting for Stevie?' Bob said.

'Oh yeah. He could've come in. I had a meat and potato pie in the oven and everything but before I could say anything, he was off down the stairs.'

'Did you get his name?' Bob asked.

'Stevie said he was called Liam. At least I think that's what he said. I asked him where he knew him from, but he didn't say much apart from that he was just a mate. I assumed he meant from the streets.'

'Did he say much else about him?' I asked.

She shook her head. 'Nothing. He just marched in and started pacing around. He said he wanted to use the phone, so I gave him my shitty mobile and he spent five minutes in the kitchen but I didn't hear him talking.'

'Where were you when he was on the phone?'

'Just sitting here,' she said. 'I looked down into the street at Liam, or whatever he was called, until he came out. He went in the bathroom for a few minutes, then came out and asked me for money. Two hundred quid, like before. I only had seventy odd on me, so I gave him fifty of that and left myself the rest. He didn't stay long. He said he had to go but didn't say why or where to, just that he had to go.'

'Do you know who he was trying to call?' Bob said.

'Well, that's just it. That's why I turned up at your office that night, Jim. When you saw me drunk in the street.'

'What do you mean?'

'He'd been trying to phone you. He said as much himself when I asked him, but I didn't know who you were then. It was only when he'd... after he'd died... that I checked what the number was and it turned out to be your office.'

'Me?'

She nodded, took a long drag. I sparked up again and shared a look with Bob.

'I did wonder who Jim was when he mentioned you as he'd never talked about you before.'

'Did he say... well, did he say for how long he'd been trying to contact me?'

'No,' she said. 'I assumed it was just that day, that night. He just said you were someone he knew, that you might be able to help him out. I asked him what he needed help with, but he just shrugged it off. Said he was fine, there was nothing to worry about. I was being overprotective, as usual. All that stuff.'

'Was Stevie the type to confide in you?' Bob asked. 'Confide in anyone?'

She almost laughed. 'Confide? Fuck no. About what? No, he was the last person to want to talk to anyone about what might've been on his mind. He was very private like that. Didn't see the point in sharing his problems. Too proud, you know.'

I let what she'd said go around my head and tried to piece things together. He'd seemed a bit stressed out and on edge. Didn't want to talk about Ivy Brook, visited his sister sporadically over the years so their relationship could have been very different to the one they had in his previous life. The fact he'd been trying to get a hold of me gave me chills. I had no recollection of anyone desperately trying to get in touch, let alone Stevie. No frantic calls in the night, no banging on my door. I would need to ask Laura about it, since she was always the one manning the office. I was keen to know more about how he presented on that night.

'Cast your mind back, Shannon,' I said. 'And I know you don't want to have to think about it, but was there anything else about that night? Something he might've said about anyone? Anything at all? Were there any other people mentioned or did you discuss anything else?'

She was silent for a moment, just staring at the carpet. Couldn't tell whether she was thinking or emptying her mind. Perhaps she'd forgotten or deliberately blocked stuff out.

'He was scared,' she said. 'I'm certain of that. He had a cough, but that wasn't unusual. Had the shakes and that wasn't unusual either, given he was a drinker. But he was in a hurry. The pacing around, you know. Like I said, he just wasn't himself. He was anxious. I asked him if he was okay, of course I did, but he just kept silent. Said it didn't matter. He wasn't quite the Stevie I'd known, but then you have to remember that I hadn't seen him in a long time.'

'I'm curious about this Liam,' Bob said. 'Can you describe him?'

She looked into space for a moment, gathering her thoughts, searching for the right words.

'He looked like a weasel,' she said. 'Shifty, you know. He was thin, full of tattoos and had bad skin. I could smell booze on him, which made me assume, rightly or wrongly, that he was a mate from the streets, you know. Short hair, blonde brown. Mid forties, probably.'

'Have you seen him since?' I asked.

'No,' she said. Shook her head. 'But I have thought about him, a few times. I wondered if he'd turn up at the funeral, but he didn't. Imagined him knocking on the door, but he hasn't.'

'Just one last thing,' I said, sensing she'd had enough by now. 'I just want to know how it was when he left. I mean, did he say goodbye at the door, anything like that?'

'He made it quick,' she said. 'He didn't hang around. He'd gotten some money, so as I watched him leave, I just thought, there he goes, off to buy drugs with this Liam, you know. He didn't say goodbye. He normally would've done, but he was off, waving over his shoulder as he turned to head down the stairs. Normally he'd say when he'd try to call back again, but he didn't this time. It was almost as if he knew he wouldn't be coming back.'

CHAPTER NINE

'So what do you think?'
    'Could do with finding out who this Liam character is,' I said. 'I'd like to know just how well he knew him.'

When we reached the Volvo, I glanced up at Shannon's flat and saw her move away from the window. Going over it all again couldn't have been nice for her. As we left, she asked me to keep in touch. I assured her I would. I decided not to mention Lloyd. I wasn't entirely sure how she'd take the news, and I was in no mood or shape to drop the bombshell. Wasn't sure it would do any good, anyway. It would be big news soon enough, if it wasn't already. Shit had just gone up a notch. I didn't like it one bit.   •

As we drove back to the office, I called Karen on the way. I'd put it off for too long already. By now it was midmorning, the commute over, but Salford Crescent was still hammered with traffic. The sun was blazing, the sky a deep blue. Bob smoked a Montecristo in the passenger seat, mulling over the conversation we'd just had, while I let my ex-wife rant down the phone. It had to happen sometime.

    'Nice of you to enlighten us with your presence,' she

said. Her voice boomed through the speakers. 'Meanwhile, while your daughter has been expelled from school, it's fallen on me to find her a new one.'

'I've been caught up in something,' I said. 'I did mean to phone yesterday.'

'Caught up in what? A lock in down the pub?'

'Uncalled for, Karen.'

'No, Jim. It's uncalled for you to not be there when your daughter needs you. It's uncalled for to let me deal with it all when you haven't bothered to see her in months. In months, Jim. It's uncalled for -'

'All right, you've made your point.'

'Oh, I've not finished yet, Jim Locke. I've not even started.'

'Is there a point to this?'

'You cheeky bastard.'

'It's just that I can't see any point in you going on at me when we're trying to find a solution to -'

'I called you two fucking days ago!'

'It's work. I've had stuff on. I just forgot, love, okay?'

'Who are you calling 'love'? I'm not your 'love', Jim. And don't you forget it.'

'So what's happened?'

'Oh, like you care.'

'Karen, if you can't be civil, we won't talk at all. I'll speak to her myself.'

'You never change, Jim.'

That's when I hung up. She called back seconds later.

'Just who the fuck do you think you are?'

'I thought it might give you a chance to simmer down.'

'You really haven't changed, have you? You're still a total fucking prick.'

I glanced across at Bob, who was looking at me,

eyebrows raised. 'If I could get a word in, we might be able to discuss this like adults.'

'So you're calling me a kid now?'

'Well, you're fucking behaving like one...'

'Oh piss off.'

She went quiet then. We could almost hear her seething down the line, grinding her teeth. There was a momentary pause before she spoke again. 'Right,' she said. 'Nicole has been expelled for fighting with not just one other girl, but three. And she's not been in class on several occasions when I thought she was in school.'

'Three?' I said. 'What, at the same time?'

'I don't know. I think so.'

'Well haven't you spoken to her teacher, found out what's gone on?'

Big sigh. 'She's not been right for a while, Jim. I've spoken to the school and they've said that she's been misbehaving in class a lot and skipping lessons. Whole days, Jim!'

'Have you spoken to her?'

'I've tried, but...'

'But what?'

Another big sigh. 'She's just... she won't speak to me. She's been giving me the cold shoulder for weeks.'

'But Karen, she's only seven, for fuck's sake! She's a kid!'

'All the more reason why you need to see her more often than you have been.'

I could hold my hands up. She was right about that, and it had been in the back of my mind. But then Karen and Chris did like their weekends away with my daughter. Sometimes it felt I couldn't get a look in. I'd be a liar if I said it didn't sometimes suit me.

'Look, I'll come over,' I said. 'Tonight, if need be. That all right with you?'

'No good. I've got a PTA meeting I can't get out of.'

Parent and Teacher's Association. I always thought that sometimes, her precious career could get in the way of her real life. I wondered what Nicole thought of her mum being a teacher. How much time she spent with her. All that marking she did, all that preparation. Did she have any time left over for her own daughter? Back when we were still married, and I was still in the force, there were times when we had words over her commitment to her job, rather than to her family. I hadn't expected her to have changed.

'Tomorrow, then?'

'Out of the question, I'm afraid. We're doing interviews for head of year nine. Got to prep with David.'

'David?'

'The head teacher, Jim.'

It was my turn to sigh. I turned to Bob, shook my head, mouthed Can you fucking believe this? 'Look, Karen. You can't let the job take over your life. No wonder she won't talk to you if you're never there for her.'

'I am there for her! Bloody hell, you've got room to talk! You fucking just disappeared!'

'You threw me out!'

'Didn't see her in two years...'

'You wouldn't fucking let me, if you remember.'

'Because you were off your face on booze.'

'No thanks to you.'

'I beg your pardon?'

'Nothing.'

I let the stony silence hang between us. The air felt like lead. Although we'd had the same arguments over and over before the end of our marriage, having it all over again now almost brought back all the hurt. Nicole had been in the middle of it then, and she was in the middle of it now when she needed her parents the most.

'Look,' she said, finally. 'I'll check my diary, okay? I think I'm free on Sunday but I'll have to check with dad.'

'And what's your dad got to do with it?'

'Well, she's staying with him at the minute...'

'What? What do you mean, she's staying with him!?'

'I told you we weren't talking, Jim.'

'Yeah, but you didn't say she wasn't even in the same fucking house! Jesus, Karen, what's happened to you? I'll phone your dad and arrange it with him.'

'No.'

'Just leave it now,' I said. 'Get back to your bloody school, Karen.'

I hung up again, left it there before I said something I would regret. She didn't call back this time. It was a good job because I was fucking pissed off. She had some audacity, she really did. Some things in life never change.

Back at the office, I uploaded what I'd recorded to the Mac and we listened back over strong coffee. Laura had been busy going through the accounts and had confirmed that several clients had paid up. She transferred some money from the business account to my own account, which gave me a fair whack to play with. Now would be a good time to pay Bob back for what he'd done for me during the Angel case. I made a mental note of it before showing him the YouTube video of the far right rally Laura had found. He watched it twice as I read through Stevie's file, the one I'd photocopied in the post office as Lloyd sat sweating in my car.

And now I'd need a file on Lloyd. I got Laura to create a new folder while I crashed on the couch and sparked up. Thought about the big man burning in that car. He'd come to me for help and I'd failed him. I let the noise outside wash over me, let the heat envelop me. Now that shit had gotten deeper, I didn't know where to start. I felt like I was wading through quicksand and needed someone to throw me a rope.

I let the nicotine seep into my bloodstream. Wondered what the hell I could say to Lloyd's wife and kids should I have to explain why I did nothing to help him. What I'd say to Robertson when I got my hands around his scrawny fucking neck.

'The English National Defence, eh?' Bob said. 'Look like a real bunch of physics academics, don't they?'

'Is that a euphemism for "Twats"?' said Laura.

'Well, when you put it like that...'

'It still doesn't make any sense,' I said. 'I mean, why? Why Stevie, why Lloyd?'

'Why follow Lloyd around like a bad smell,' Laura said. 'Then kill him.'

'Laura...'

'I'm sorry.'

'But you're right,' Bob said. 'Why indeed. Do you really suspect that they're a part of this far right group, Jim?'

'It's as good a lead as any. The only one I've got. And some of these people in the rally film, they do resemble the occupants of the Range Rover. And there was that crude graffiti where Stevie was found. As far as motive goes, I haven't got a clue. Lloyd, being black, could maybe fit their profile. A hate crime, you know. But Stevie?' I shook my head. 'Not a clue.'

'But what about what Shannon had said,' he went on.

'About their past. The care homes, the abandonment, all that. And then this Liam character...'

'You think Stevie might've known him from his past?'

'That wasn't where I was going but... why not?'

'It's a possibility, I suppose.' I was only saying it for the sake of it, but then when I gave it some thought, it became a real line worth investigating. I leafed through the file in my hands. I'd only had it since yesterday morning and now here we were, twenty-four hours later, and the man who'd given it to me was now probably lying in a morgue. I owed it to him to look deeper. What secrets, like so much about this case, were hidden within it?

I sat up, drained my coffee, and finished my smoke. When a job needed doing, it needed doing head on. I knew I'd have to go back sometime.

'Laura, do me a favour,' I said. 'I want you to see if you can find anymore on this E.N.D group while we go on a little excursion.'

'Can I not come with you instead?'

'It's a case of too many cooks,' I said. 'And I need you here.'

'Where are we going?' Bob asked.

'The Police.'

'The Police? Have you finally gone mad? Have you forgotten why I'm even here?'

'It's all right, you can wait for me. I just want to get something off my chest.'

We took the main stairs out to the street, where I'd left the Volvo parked on double yellows. Maya and her bearded friend were sitting out in the sun. They both nodded and Maya said she'd pop up to keep Laura company later. Given that I didn't know when I'd be back, I thought it was a damn good idea.

The Greater Manchester Police Headquarters was just a few miles north of the city centre. Two enormous buildings housed thousands of officers and personnel, special units, a large proportion of civilian staff, and hundreds of police vehicles. It was a huge complex, built on an old train yard that had lain derelict since the sixties. I hadn't set foot in the place since I was booted out on a day not too different from this one. I'll never forget Robertson's smug face when I took the walk of shame down those HQ steps. Back then, like myself, he was a DS, but family in high places soon saw to it that he'd be given a quick promotion and a heady rise through the ranks. Now a Detective Inspector, the weasel would finally have his own office to play in. No doubt the promotion happened quicker than most would've liked, so soon after I'd gone. I'd heard on the grapevine he wasn't well liked and that more than a few grievances had been made against him, which didn't surprise me. He had the kind of face you wanted to punch, and for good reason. So as I climbed those steps once again, it was no surprise I'd had my fists clenched.

I half expected the flashbacks to come once I was inside, but they didn't. Instead, a desk sergeant I didn't recognise looked up from her paperwork before looking away again. I approached the desk, the memories flooding back. Looked around for those familiar faces, but it was as if I'd stepped into some parallel universe where everything was different. Two years was a long time in the force, when anything and everything could change. Since my departure, it looked like things had.

'Can I help you?'

'Locke,' I said, handing her my card. 'Jim Locke, former DS, now PI. I'm here to see Robertson. He around?'

'Detective Inspector Robertson, I presume?'

'The same,' I nodded. 'Although our definition of inspector may differ. I believe he's the SIO on the Stephen Kennedy investigation. I'd like a word with him. I have some evidence I think he'll be interested in.'

'I'm not sure that'll be possible, Mr. Locke,' she said. 'Do you have an appointment?'

I knew I'd have to come here and wing it somehow. There was no way Robertson would give me the time of day if I'd gone through the correct procedure and channels. Turning up like this would catch him off guard anyway, which was what I wanted.

'I'm afraid not,' I said. 'As is usually the case with these things, needs must. Something has recently come to light that I thought he'd be very interested in.'

She nodded, taken in, or at least it seemed that way. I held her gaze for a moment before she looked away and picked up the phone. It was my cue to turn around, casual as fuck, as she dialed internally. I listened with one eye firmly fixed on Bob, parked up across the road and dragging on a Montecristo like it was a life support.

'Someone here to see you, sir,' she said. I could feel her eyes upon the back of my neck. 'Yes. That's right. A Mr. Locke, sir.'

I could picture him now, cursing in his office, beads of sweat rolling through his comb-over.

'I'm not sure. Yes, I'll tell him. Of course, sir.'

I half expected her to tell me I should leave immediately, that the pub would be open soon, that I was to never set foot in here ever again.

'Third floor,' she said. 'Take the lift. You've got ten minutes. The lift's over there by the -'

'I know where it is, Sergeant Ball,' I said, looking at her badge. 'And thanks.'

It was odd setting foot back in this building. I recognised it well enough, and the glass and chrome and carpet hadn't changed as far as I could tell, but it felt wrong being here again, almost as if it was the setting for all my miseries, and of course, it had been once. I spent many unhappy hours inside these walls, my marriage hanging by a thread, a booze addiction clouding my every judgement. It felt claustrophobic being here, and as I rode the lift, the heat giving me a headache, I had to remind myself that things were different now. For the better, too. I didn't belong here, never did. I never thought I'd ever come back, especially in these circumstances, but as the lift doors parted, I smiled at the ridiculousness of it all, for that's how it felt. The past has a way of coming back to haunt you, and I knew that all too well. But it was cathartic too. In some ways, I wish I'd come here sooner to banish the demons for good.

I walked down a long and familiar corridor, where on either side of its walls sat officers from the Serious Crime Division. Some didn't look up from their work, never casting a glance as I passed. One or two did though, and I recognised a few faces, saw them look away before whispering to the officer beside them. Not that I gave a fuck what any of them were saying now. I eyeballed a few before I fixed my gaze firmly on Robertson's door. I didn't need to knock. It opened right on cue, a tearful and worried looking WPC scurrying out, leaving a gap for me to peek through.

Robertson caught my eye. 'I suppose you'd better come in.'

'Robert,' I said, stepping through. I shut the door behind

me. 'Glad I caught you. I was beginning to think you might actually be doing some work for a change.'

'You're wasting your time, Locke,' he said. 'But since you're here, we may as well go over this again. You know as well as I do that you have no jurisdiction in this investigation. And if you think you can stroll in here calling the shots, you can think again.'

'I'm not calling anything.'

'You're forgetting that we used to work together. I know you, Locke.'

Yeah, and you were a prick then too, I thought. 'I'm only acting on behalf of my client.'

'Who is?'

'Shannon Kennedy,' I said. 'And Lloyd, the man who burnt to death in that Vectra last night. Shot in the head too.'

'There's no evidence of that.'

'I saw it with my own eyes.'

'I'd be careful what you say.'

'Fuck's sake, what's wrong with you?'

'This is a police investigation and you have no part in it.'

'Robert, two men are dead. Burnt to death, for reasons that are not apparent. You'd be a fool to just ignore what's in front of you.'

'You've got nothing to offer, Locke, and you know it.'

'Lloyd sent me footage,' I said. 'From his phone. Has it been found yet?'

'What's it to you?'

'It's a part of my investigation. He sent it to me, to this very phone, as evidence. And you're choosing to ignore it.'

'It's not as simple as that.'

'Oh, come on!'

'You know it isn't, Jim. Just because this white Range Rover is on that footage, it means fuck all. And you know it.'

'They were following him for days. Weeks, even.'

'There's no evidence of that.'

'I saw them with my own eyes,' I said. 'I've got photographs of them outside my office window.'

'Means nothing.'

'When Lloyd was inside telling me about them following him.'

'I don't know what else you want me to say.'

'And then they turn up in this footage -footage with Lloyd's voice on it - and just hours later, he's dead. I saw them speed off, for fuck's sake! They had me in their headlights...'

'Like a frightened rabbit?'

'Oh fuck off.'

'No, you fuck off,' he said. 'Pubs opened an hour ago.'

I could've grabbed a chair and slammed it right in his weasly little mouth right there and then. Instead, I counted to ten, gritted my teeth and put my thoughts into words. Leaned into him, both hands on his desk.

'Listen, you cunt. Everyone in here knows how you've managed to get yourself this job. If it wasn't for daddy, you'd be nowhere fucking near it. You're out of your depth, Robert. You know it, I know it. The whole force knows it. You think anyone out there has got your back?' I laughed, and I meant it. 'You're sitting here in your little office, choosing to ignore the evidence in front of you because you're too blind and too proud to admit that I'm better than you, and always was. It's pathetic and right about your level. Now I may have no jurisdiction, but I'm here to represent my clients. One of them is dead. The other buried her brother yesterday. Both have burnt to death. And as far as I can tell, you're doing fuck all about it.'

'Have you finished?'

'No,' I said. 'I've only just started. Did you know these men in the Range Rover have connections to a far right group?'

He had his hands over his ears, shaking his head, pretending he wasn't listening and going 'la la la'. Which summed him up in every way. He had become exactly what I knew he would. A man who couldn't see the wood for the trees.

'Oh, come on. Jesus, Locke, give it up. Your police career is over, thanks to your little addictions, and you've only got yourself to blame. Just stop playing at being a copper and leave it to the professionals, eh?'

'You're fucking deluded, Robert,' I said. 'You're the one playing at coppers - and making a right tits up of it. The two men in the Range Rover fit the profile of members of this far right group, the E.N.D., which, incidentally, had sprayed graffiti on the wall where Stevie was found, not to mention the swastika...'

'What the fuck are you talking about?'

'... and the lightning bolts...'

'You're pissed, aren't you?'

'You just can't see it, can you?'

We were silent for a moment. I stared hard into his smug face while he tried to stare back into mine. A beam of bright sunlight cascaded through the window, and I could feel the sweat prickle the skin on the back of my neck. I had to try very hard to not throttle the bastard.

'One last time, Locke,' he said. 'And I won't repeat this again and again. This is a police investigation, of which you have no part. So, please. You carry on with whatever nonsense you're convincing yourself of and leave the real work to us. Do I make myself clear?'

'Crystal.'

'Now do us a favour and leave the premises, or I'll have you arrested for wasting police time.'

I didn't hang around. Figured there was no point trying to reason with a blind man and a fool. I knew it could be a nasty combination. There would be no mutual respect or professionalism in any meeting between us, let alone a sharing of ideas and evidence. It would be a long fall for him, and he couldn't even see it. I pitied him, but the pity only lasted as long as it took me to leave the building.

The WPC who'd left his office crying as I arrived was standing under a smoking shelter, blowing a cloud across her tears between sips of coffee. She held my gaze for a moment before turning away.

I found Bob half covering his face with his fedora as he neared the end of his Montecristo. Got in the car and drove us away from the place.

'Well?'

'Like talking to a child.' I filled him in on what the conversation entailed.

'But you're covering your back,' he said. 'At least you've offered him what you know. If he's not interested, it's his problem. Incidentally, did anyone mention me? Please tell me I'm not on a poster or something.'

'You're not on a poster,' I said. 'You might be a pain in the arse, Bob - they don't call you Bob Piles for nothing - but as far as they're concerned, that's all you are. I'd say they're pretty clueless about the murder you've committed, to be honest with you.'

He went quiet then as we drove and I realised, halfway back to the office, that I'd brought it all back for him.

'Okay, manslaughter,' I said. 'I'm sorry.'

He was shaking his head, looking out the window. 'What have I done?'

'What anyone else in the same position would do. It was self defence, Bob. The mistake you made was trying to cover your arse afterwards.'

'I panicked.'

'I know.'

But he had blood on his hands. I didn't want to admit it, but I found myself looking over my shoulder, too. And not just for the law. If any of the Chinese had gotten wind of Bob being on English soil, they'd be after his balls quicker than you could knock up a chicken chow mein. And they'd want mine too. I was guilty by association. And after the events of the Angel case, it would be no surprise if they had me in their sights. I was beginning to feel as paranoid as Bob.

He asked to be dropped at the flat. Said he needed to freshen up and make some phone calls. I half believed him and he didn't elaborate on the phone calls he was going to make or the favours he was calling in. I had a feeling he would run out of favours soon enough, which worried me. Still, I couldn't watch a mate suffer. I'd promised him a bed and that's what he had.

When I got back to the office, I dropped a little brandy before going any further. Then I sat and smoked hard while I thought about Lloyd and Stevie, their charred remains, their liquified fat. The bullet hole in Lloyd's brain. The people they'd left behind. I played the conversation we'd had with Shannon over and over. Something was troubling me. When I picked up the phone to call her, I knew what it was.

'Shannon?'

'Yeah?'

'Shannon, it's Jim Locke. Listen, I've been thinking about something.'

'I wasn't expecting you to phone so soon.'

'I know, I know. But I keep thinking about those men you talked about. Those suicides. And I want to ask you some things, just to get it clear in my head.'

'Okay.'

'Okay.' Laura had spun around in her chair to listen in. 'Those men. The ones who committed suicide. Can you tell me anything about them? Anything at all?'

She was quiet for a moment, and I heard her spark up. 'Carl McDermott,' she said, blowing smoke out. 'They found him in his flat on a Sunday morning. I don't know how he died - what state he was in, you know - just that it was definitely suicide. A lot of people knew him, me included. And Stevie.'

'You said he was at Ivy Brook with you...'

'That's right,' she said. 'For a good few years. He was okay. Quiet, you know. Never troubled anyone, wouldn't say boo to a goose. Stevie knew him better than I did.'

'And the other guy,' I said. 'Did you know him?'

'Not personally, but some people around here did. He was at Ivy Brook too, apparently, but not when we were, I don't think. I suppose he could've been.'

'Do you think you can find out? You know, ask around or something?'

'Course I can, yeah, but... well, do you think it might be

connected? To Stevie, I mean? Oh God, you don't think Stevie killed himself, do you?'

'No,' I said. 'I don't think that, at all. No, I just think it's a bit strange these two men were both in the same care home, that's all.'

'And Stevie was there as well?'

'It's just something I think is worth looking into.'

'Could be just a coincidence.'

She wasn't wrong, but I had that feeling again. That intuition, that itch. 'Maybe,' I said. 'Of course. But can you ask around? See what you can dig up?'

'I'll be in touch. I'm going down to the Wilton Arms tonight. Karaoke. My mate Claire goes mad for it, especially when she's pissed...'

'Well have a good night.'

'Just that everyone knows everyone's business in there,' she said. 'Someone's bound to know something.'

The pub sounded like a damn good place to start. 'Let me know if you hear anything as soon as you can.'

She said she would, and we ended the call. I hoped something would come of it, though really I was just clutching at straws, trying to find a motive, anything at all, that would link someone to Stevie's death. But then there was Lloyd now too, someone I definitely know didn't go to Ivy Brook. But after the white Range Rover had me in its headlights, and the footage that was on my phone and now on the Mac proved they had been on his case, I don't think there was any doubt as to who his killers were. Robertson didn't seem to think so though, which worried me. How could a DI be so incompetent? I'd have my work cut out making him see what was in front of him. Yet I knew he was choosing to ignore it because it was me bringing it to his desk.

He couldn't let a sacked copper get one over on him, let alone a sacked alcoholic one. And that's how he would see it. I was someone who couldn't be trusted. Someone who was out to prove them wrong. Someone who wasn't a reliable source.

If that's the way they wanted to play it....

'Promising?'

'Maybe,' I said. 'Let's hope her karaoke night pays off.'

'Well,' she said, rising from her seat. She went over to the coffee pot and poured us both a strong one. 'I've been busy looking into the E.N.D. while you were out. Anything come of that, by the way?'

I shook my head. 'Without going into details, the guy's a dick. End of story. So, you find anything?'

'You'd better get your notebook out.'

'Sounds interesting.'

'One way of putting it...'

'I'm all ears.'

She brought me my coffee and sat beside me on the couch. 'I've been doing a lot of digging. And there is plenty of shit out there on the web about these freaks, if you know where to look.'

'Go on,' I said. I took a drink, sparked up, settled myself in. 'How bad are we talking?'

'The worst kind,' she said. 'Honestly, some of the shit they believe... I started with that YouTube clip. Seemed as good a place as any. Anyway, there were some links attached to the video, you know, links to various websites and such. Even a Facebook and Twitter page. A lot of the websites were pretty much a potted history of the far right. Various groups, political opinion, supremacy stuff, nazism. You name it. But as far as digging anything up on the people in the footage, or on the printouts you got from that hotel CCTV, I hit a brick wall. Until...'

She had my full attention. I'd been feeling uneasy about this whole thing since the beginning. The lightning bolt, the swastika, everything. Could Stevie be a victim of their vile hatred? A one off murder victim thanks to a mindless act of violence? But for what reason? Being homeless? It didn't make sense. Whatever their opinions were, did it really surmount to one of them - or even a few - burning a harmless homeless man to death? I doubted it. Nutters though they undoubtedly were, they were probably more likely to see him as a victim. A white victim put on the streets thanks to an influx of refugees and immigrants in this green and pleasant land. He could even be a poster boy for their twisted agenda. And then there was Lloyd, of course, whose killing made even less sense.

'Until what?'

'The deeper down the rabbit hole I went, the more I found. And the more frightening it became.'

'So..'

'Hold your horses,' she said. 'I'm getting to it.'

'I've not got all day.'

But then maybe I did. The landline rang out then, but I said to ignore it.

'So I clicked on the Facebook page. It was a closed page - invitation only - but I could see there were a couple of hundred members attached to it, from all over the country. A bit of simple digging around brought me to a bloke called Simon Anderson. One of the members daft enough to be very lax with his privacy settings. Bespectacled thirty-year-old in a suit and tie on his profile picture, ever the young politician. But strip the suit away and underneath you've got sixteen stone of muscle. A Tory - or worse than a Tory if that can be possible - on steroids.'

The thought terrified me.

'Jesus, Jim, will you answer that fucking phone?'

Had to admit, it was getting on my tits too. I got up to answer, but it rang out just as I got to the desk.

'Carry on.'

'So, Simon Anderson. With me so far?'

'Get on with it.'

'Right. So I have a good nosey around his Facebook pages and it's pretty clear where his political opinions lie. Thinks anyone that isn't white is to blame for the world's ills. Hates Jews, Pakistanis, in fact anyone who 'doesn't belong here'. Thinks it's only the 'indigenous' people of Britain that should be allowed to live here.'

'As if Britain has ever been indigenous.'

'Exactly. So you can see why this guy's pissed off given the current refugee situation, Syria, Iraq, yadda yadda yadda...'

'Yep.'

'And don't get him started on immigration and Europe and the Muslims and all the rest...'

'You're going round in circles, love. I get the picture.'

'So, anyway,' she said. 'I'm looking around to see who his friends are, and lo-and-behold, there he is. At least, I'm pretty sure it is.'

'There's who?'

'The guy on the CCTV. The bald guy. Tattoo of a lightning bolt on his neck. And not just him, either. There's a bloke who also resembles one of his mates, you know, one of the other guys on that printout from Graham. A few faces I recognise from that YouTube footage too.'

'Can you show me?'

'Anytime, big boy.'

'Laura,' I said, 'now's not the time or the place.'

She winked, kissed me quick. 'I've left the computer running.'

We moved over to the desk. 'You got a name?'

She nodded as she opened up Facebook. 'Colin Black. Although he could be using a false name, I suppose.'

I pulled up a chair and watched as she clicked through page after page of meatheads, bent MP's, blatant racists and no holds barred neo-nazis. It was somewhat troubling to see it all right there in open view on the Internet, but then I also knew that whatever nastiness was lurking out there, some-thing good could come of it in equal measure. If any of this information was going to help us find Stevie's - and Lloyd's - killers, then I suppose it'd be worth the pain of having to sit here looking at such sorry excuses for humanity. It crossed my mind whether our friend Liam could be one of these faces scrolling before my eyes.

She opened up a page for Simon Anderson. Sure enough, there he was in a flash grey business suit and a pair of expensive specs. Straight away, I could see what she meant. He had that air about him. A smug grin, a perfect face. Good looking and well built; a small-time gangster with ideas above his station and political ambitions, judging by the stuff plastered across his page, that could maybe one day see him rub shoulders with the most corrupt bastards hanging around Westminster.

'So,' she said, scrolling down. 'Anderson. Not connected in any way to the deaths as far as we know, but if you scroll through his friends list, we can come across a man who could very well be who we're interested in.' She stopped. 'And here he is. Colin Black. Now, tell me if that isn't the guy on the CCTV. And look here.' She clicked on his profile page, another empty head lax with his security. 'Lots

of photos of his tattoos, including the lightning bolt one on
the back of his neck.'

I looked hard at the information in front of me. There
was no question he was the guy on the CCTV. If I really
was looking at the man who'd taken Stevie's and Lloyd's life,
then I wanted to hunt the bastard down and kill him myself.
This image was much clearer than the one I'd been given,
and now I had a name too. Colin Black.

'Can you print this off?'

'Already have.'

'Great,' I said. 'What else is lurking on here?'

'I've not been through it all yet,' she said, as the landline
started ringing again. 'But I've already printed off everything
I can get my hands on with this guy. It's in the filing cabinet.'

I rummaged around and picked out a green file. It
wasn't loaded with stuff, but she'd copied photographs -
many of which were of his tattoos - and had also printed out
various conversations he'd had in other groups and chat
rooms. It would take me a while to sift through this stuff, the
writings especially. A quick scan through showed him up
for what he was, though. Racist, homophobic, and totally
deluded. A dangerous combination. His tattoos were
further evidence of his hatred. Besides the lighting bolt,
there was plenty here to show his fascist leanings. A huge
eagle across his back, a swastika, an SS symbol. Even a
portrait of Hitler on his thigh.

'Will you answer that bloody phone!'

'Can't you?'

'I'm busy!'

I grabbed it before it rang out again. 'Jim Locke, private
investigator. Hello?'

The line was silent for a moment. The last thing I

needed now was another bitter housewife out to catch her husband.

'Hello?'

'Mr. Locke?'

'Yeah?'

A pause again. I could hear her breathing down the phone. 'Look, you don't know me,' she said. 'But I know you. At least, I've heard a lot about you.'

'Glad to hear it but I'm pretty busy at the moment.'

'Meet me,' she said. 'You know the Castle? In town?'

It was a pub I knew well. 'What's this about? And who are you?'

'Shall we say eight? It's important.'

I had that itch again. That gut instinct. 'Okay, but how do I know...?'

'I'll be waiting for you.'

She was waiting for me in the piano room, a parlour space that sat snug behind the bar, across which were several pumps of real ale and artisan beers. The top shelf sparkled with obscure rum and whiskey and vodka. I tried hard to look away but threw caution to the wind and knocked back a measure of Woodford Reserve before carrying my Guinness through. When I laid eyes on her, I did a double take, wondering if this really was the woman who'd insisted I meet her, or maybe it was just a coincidence she was here. Perhaps she knew me better than I thought, because she'd chosen the location well. Yet a part of me panicked and I almost turned around and walked straight out again. But it occurred to me that she might be useful, that she could maybe do with a listening ear too. Seemed Robertson had done little to give the girl any confidence. She timidly waved at me when I popped my head in to find a seat. A brief thought hit me. What if she's lured me here for him?

'Mr. Locke.'

'Jim,' I said. I sat down to save her from standing.

She was halfway through her pint. I liked the fact that she didn't seem to be a half a lager girl. Said a lot about her character.

'So I suppose you're wondering why I wanted to meet you, eh?'

'You must be a genius,' I said. 'It's usually a well-known trait in rookie coppers.'

She laughed nervously. Glanced around the room at the other occupants. Three long-haired students on an adjacent table and a loved up couple in the corner. None looked our way.

'Can't be too careful,' she said. I wasn't sure whether she was joking or being serious. 'But to be honest with you, I'm past caring.'

It was a strange situation. I didn't know what the girl was playing at, but something about her reminded me of myself. I couldn't put my finger on what it was. She was pretty. Shoulder length black hair and smooth skin. No make up. She was wearing a plain black top with jeans, civilian clothing that didn't stand out. Simple and modest. She also might've been a bit drunk.

'It's Fiona,' she said. 'WPC Fiona Watson. Though how long I'll be a copper now is anyone's guess.'

Was that what the tears were about? 'I saw you,' I said. 'Leaving Robertson's office.'

'I know, I... was a bit upset. You might've noticed.'

I nodded. 'Is it him? Robertson?'

'You could say that.'

'He should pick on someone his own size,' I said. 'No offence. Look, what's this about? Must be important if you've had to drag me out like this. Although I'm not complaining.' I took the head off the pint. 'Speaking of Genius.'

'He's out to get me,' she said. 'For fucking up on a murder investigation. Well, not just that, but that's his excuse. It wasn't my fault, but he thinks it was and he's got on my back about it. Threatened me with all sorts, taken me off the investigation, put me back on the bloody beat. And I'm better than that.'

'It's a steep learning curve,' I said. 'Being a young copper. But to be honest with you, Fiona, I'm not sure what this has got to do with me.'

'I'm getting to it.' She shook her head, took a deep breath, drained the pint and stood up. 'I'll get us another.'

Gotta admit, this was odd. I looked around into the corridor beyond for anyone else who might look like a copper. Anyone who stood out like a sore thumb. Someone who might be watching. But all I saw were the same people. It was all retro clothes and hipster beards. Maybe I was just being paranoid, but I had good reason. The police had been onto me before and given the way Bob had blown open the corruption within GMP, I wouldn't put it past them to have someone go undercover to watch out for anything I did that was even slightly illegal, just to get their own back. Or just to keep me looking over my shoulder.

I took out my iPhone and opened the dictaphone app. Set it to record and placed it on the table before she returned.

She came back and sat down with a heavy sigh. I took a mouthful of the black stuff and studied her. Seemed this was gonna be a hard conversation for her, judging by the anxiety written all over her face. She opened her mouth again just as New Order came on the jukebox.

'Look, I know this must seem weird,' she said. 'I'd think so too. And believe me, I feel such a dick for phoning you and dragging you out to see me. But I'd heard a lot about you and I thought we might be able to help each other.'

Eyeballed her. 'Heard what, exactly? Get to the point, love.'

'Everyone on the force knows you, it seems.'

'Oh yeah?'

'Everyone's got an opinion on why you were pushed out.'

I knew this too. 'And what's yours, Fiona? If you don't mind me asking?'

She swallowed, took a drink. 'Fancy a smoke?'

I made sure I brought my phone with me, resting it in my jeans so the microphone could pick up our conversation. The night was hot. No change there. We stood out on the street, which was relatively quiet. The odd bus swept past as the queue for the comedy club up the road stretched towards us.

'My opinion,' she said, 'is that you were a good man swept away into a bad place. A good detective. A lot of people thought so.'

'Can't say I remember you, Fiona,' I said. Sparked up, took that shit in deep.

'Well, you wouldn't. I was brand new when you were forced out. I'd barely qualified a fortnight before. I'd heard about you, though. Plenty of coppers filled me in.'

'Did they indeed?'

'Detectives too,' she said. 'We're not all bastards, Jim.'

'Just a few.'

'Yeah, and I think you know who they are,' she said. 'Which is partly why I'm here.'

'Go on.'

'Robertson.' She almost laughed. Shook her head and dragged hard. Launched the beer down her neck. 'What a twat. He came on to me. Well, more than that. Six months ago. Tried to stick his tongue down my throat and touched me up in the toilets.'

'What!?'

She was nodding and shaking her head at the same time. Took another hard drag on her smoke. 'At the annual awards ceremony. Said he could help me get to where I wanted to be, you know.'

'What!?'

'With my career, you know.'

'Fuck's sake...'

'I know.'

'I mean... well, have you told anyone?'

'No!'

'Well why the fuck not? Fiona, Jesus, he can't go around behaving like that! You need to tell professional standards. Report the bastard.'

'No, I'm gonna do better than that,' she said. 'Besides, I don't trust those bastards, either. You know yourself they look after each other.' She took several hard drags before tossing her smoke into the gutter. 'See you inside.'

I finished my smoke, checking for texts as I did so. Bob had been in touch, wondering where the hell I was. I gave him a quick call and told him to meet me here and be as inconspicuous as possible. I wanted him to hang around, just observing while I had this meeting with Fiona. I didn't quite know if I could trust her and needed a keen eye to watch my back. Now that I had a taste for a drink, I wanted to get back inside.

'So,' I said, sitting back down. I placed my phone on the table between us. 'How are you gonna do better? The man needs bringing down a peg or two. That's sexual assault. He can't be allowed to get away with it.'

'Oh, he won't get away with it,' she said. 'Far from it. But I'm gonna make it as slow and as painful as I can. I want him to sweat.'

'What happened, exactly? I know this must be hard for you to talk about but -'

'It's not hard,' she said. 'He followed me into the toilets and grabbed me.'

'Grabbed you?'

'From behind, as I'd just stepped in. Said he thought I'd like it.' She laughed, shook her head. 'You believe that? Then he had me against the wall and went to kiss me, touching me... groping me down there as he did so. I pushed him away, told him to fuck off, and ran out. It all happened so quick. He must've just followed me in. I don't know where he went after that.'

'Jesus...'

'But then later, at the bar, he came up to me and apologised, said he thought I wanted it, it wouldn't happen again. Not to mention it to anyone. It would be silly and pointless. All that.'

'I bet he did.'

'Yeah, so... I'm not stupid. I know I could bring him down but I'd need evidence, otherwise all of it is just my word against his.'

I nodded, sank a mouthful of Guinness.

'And he'd get away with it if that's all I had,' she said. 'Friends in high places.'

'Not to mention his father.'

'And his rank. He's going for DCI, or so I'm told, and he won't let a little copper like me get in his way.'

'DCI?'

She nodded. Took a drink.

'Do you believe him?' I said.

'Believe what?'

'You said he thought you wanted it.'

'No,' she said. She laughed, shook her head. 'Wanted it? Did I fuck.'

'You've not given him the wrong impression, anything like that?'

'Absolutely not. No fucking way, Jesus!'

'Because you have to make sure you didn't give him the wrong signals.'

'Jim,' she said, 'you must be living in cloud cuckoo land if you think I've been giving him these ideas. No. Just no. There is no way on God's earth I'd let that vile creature anywhere near me.'

'Seems pretty clear.'

There was that almost laugh again. I wasn't that surprised by his behaviour, just surprised he thought he could get away with it. The guy had some audacity.

'He thinks he can go around doing whatever he likes,' she said, as if reading my mind. 'You should see him. Swanning around like the big chief. Like he owns the place.'

'He was always like that.'

'I dread to think how things will be if he makes DCI.'

'Do you think he will?'

'Not if I've got anything to do with it,' she said. 'I suppose I'm just waiting for the right moment.'

'Right moment? Right moment for what?'

'To reveal my hand,' she said. A smile creased her mouth. I was beginning to think I was wrong about this girl. She wasn't timid at all. Got the impression she knew exactly what she was doing.

'Which is...?'

'I've been watching him. For the last six months, actually, ever since he tried to get his hands into my pants. And believe me, I've got stuff on this prick you wouldn't believe. He's dangerous, Jim. Thinks he's untouchable.'

'Tell me more.'

'Look, I'm not sure I can. It's too sensitive at the minute.'

'What have you got on him, Fiona?'

'Wouldn't you like to know.'

I took a drink. Studied her expression, wondered what she was hiding. 'You need to be careful,' I said. 'Sounds like you've got your work cut out. The axe could fall on you at any time. These people are big players. You're a little fish in a big pond. You're not indispensable, love. If you value your career, I'd be very careful about who you reveal your information to. You can't trust the police.'

Now she really did laugh. Hard. Maybe the joke was on me.

'Don't try that private detective shit on me, Jim,' she said. 'Jesus, you're so predictable. Look, I know you want information on him, so I'll give it to you, for a price. Some of it, anyway. You'll just have to trust me on that.'

'And if I don't want the information?'

She shrugged. 'Means nothing to me. But come on. Think about it. It'd be like being a copper all over again.'

'So you want money from me, is that it? That's why I'm here?'

She nodded. 'Money for information. Sensitive information. I thought you'd jump at the chance.'

She wasn't wrong. Shit, had she been keeping an eye on me, too? What exactly was she offering me here? To be her 'inside man'? I'd be a fool to ignore the opportunity, but still... could I trust her? And there was no telling she was doing this to give me false information, for whatever reasons she had. This whole tale could be a bluff.

'How do I know you're not lying?'

'What, about Robertson?'

'Yeah,' I said. 'Any of it. All of it.'

There was a pause as she drank. I saw Bob peek into the room, wink, then leave again.

Fiona reached the bottom of her glass and looked at me directly. 'I suppose it comes down to trust,' she said. 'That's all I can say.'

'The best you can do?'

'It's enough, for now. Look, I can tell you that he's been at it before.'

'Another copper?'

She shook her head. 'A colleague in forensics. She approached me about it, actually. Said she saw how he was with me at the awards ceremony and had been keeping an eye on me.'

'Did she see him grab you?'

'No. But she overheard his grovelling afterwards. Put two and two together. Then she came to me and told me about her experience as well, which wasn't too different from mine.'

'Evidence, though...'

'Exactly. Which is why I've been following him around for the past six months. When I've been off duty, of course.'

'Sounds like you've been busy. Did you find anything worth keeping?'

That smile again. For a brief moment, I thought she might be flirting with me. 'Look,' she said. 'I'll come clean about some things, Jim. But it works both ways. I'll help you if you help me. I can't say fairer than that. Yes, I need the money, and yes, I want to see this corrupt bastard rot.'

'That's something we both have in common.'

'Yeah,' she said. 'The whole force knows you hate each other. And believe me, he's not without his enemies.'

'Okay,' I said. 'How much are we talking? What exactly do you want from me, Fiona? And you should bear in mind, this kind of shit can ruin a career.'

'Well, that's just fine,' she said. 'Because I don't want a police career anymore. I'm quitting. But I'm quitting on my terms, when I'm good and ready.'

'You're serious?'

'Deadly. What, after all that stuff that was blown wide open? It's the coppers that are bent, Jim. Give me some dignity. I came into it for all the right reasons and as soon as I get my head around the job, bang. All of a sudden, I work for scum. You can't be a copper in this city without getting abuse. I even lost friends through it all. So, no. And especially now, after he's put me back on the beat. I've taken two steps forward and three steps back with this job. If you don't fit, you're fucked. So I suppose I might as well be fucked and walk away with my pride intact. On my terms.'

I liked her style. Told her I'd get us one for the road. I wasn't wholly convinced - yet. And I'd need to know more before coming to any kind of agreement.

I stood at the bar as the pub filled up. The place was getting lively and I welcomed it. Felt good to blend in to the background and watch the night kick in. Bob shimmied in next to me as I waited to be served.

'Well?'

'She's a copper,' I said, sensing the fear rising in him. 'Come to dangle me a carrot. Offering me information for cash.'

'Really? Are you gonna take it?'

'Well, I can afford it,' I said. 'It's just whether I can trust her with whatever information she gives me. But it would be good to have someone on the inside, Bob. Could be invaluable. With her access, I could get these bastards nailed.'

'It's a dangerous game, lad, and you know it.'

I got him an ale too and suggested he sit down out of the way. Mentioned what Laura had found online and was keen to hear his opinions just as soon as Fiona left. As he disappeared, I wrestled with my indecision. My conscience was clear. And I had a recording of her offering this service to me just in case it came back to bite me on the arse. But I wanted to hear more first.

'You've still not told me what I can help you with,' I said. 'Isn't the money enough?'

'As I said, I need the money. But I need you to back me up, too. I've got stuff in my possession, Jim, that would be very damaging to Robertson and his career. Not just his career, either. His marriage, his reputation. It'd be sure to send him down. I think it could be very useful for you.'

'What stuff?'

'Files. JPEGs, surveillance footage, recordings. Written and signed testimony. Evidence, Jim. Enough to send him down for a long time. And I know he's deliberately avoiding this burnings case because of you.'

'Not surprised,' I said. 'He knows what he's up against. But these files,..'

'I need someone to look after the copies, Jim. Someone I can trust. You see, he's onto me. I know he is. I think that's the reason he's taken me off this murder case. Not that I was doing much anyway, but that's not the point. He's out to get me because I spurned his advances. I think he wants to damage me, actually. Make me feel small, you know. And there's someone watching me too, I'm sure of it. I don't know who, but I know they're on my case. So I've done copies of everything and I need someone to keep them safe.'

'Me?'

'No, I was hoping you could put me in touch with someone who can. For fuck's sake, Jim, of course!'

'Jesus, hang on a minute. You want to give me incriminating evidence of a GMP Detective Inspector. Me? But why?'

'You've not seen the files yet,' she said. 'And believe me, when you do, you'll want to kill the bastard.'

'And what's the price, Fiona? If I keep these copies - putting myself at huge risk, by the way - then what's in it for me?'

'I can get you the stuff you want,' she said. 'The job doesn't matter to me anymore. It's worth the risk to see this through.'

'But if you're caught, Fiona, you could go to prison too. Have you thought of that? And why should I pay you anything? You want me to look after these files, taking a big risk, and you also want me to pay you for the privilege?'

'I'm willing to accept going to prison because I know that what I'm doing is nothing compared to what he's done,' she said. 'But I don't think it'll come to that simply because of what he's done. If anything, they should give me a bloody medal. And anyway, I can't stand by and watch him keep doing it, knowing the damage it's causing. Jim, I won't rest until I see that bastard destroyed. I want him behind bars.'

'How much do you want from me?'

'I'm just asking for your help. Help me nail him once and for all. Five hundred a month will keep me going, keep me afloat, so I can bide my time for when I do quit. Which could be sooner than you think. For information, anything you want. But you have to back me on this, Jim. Believe me, it'll be worth it when we see the evil bastard finally sent down.'

'Anything I want?'

'Anything I can get my hands on.'

'Access to the PNC?'

'If I can, I will.'

'Files on me?'

'If I can, I will.'

'Five hundred a month - cash only - until when?'

'Until I can get him arrested. Or as long as you want me to get you information.'

'What's the catch?'

'There's no catch.'

'And you say they're bent?'

'But this is for the right reasons, Jim,' she said. She reached into her handbag and pulled out a small black box with a cable attached. A hard drive. Placed it on the table. 'You can walk away now and that'll be the end of it, or you can take this with you and help me nail him.'

I sat and stared at it. I realised that this was the chance I'd been waiting for, to finally get one over on Robertson so that he'd be the one looking over his shoulder. Revenge is a dish best served cold, they said. And if what was contained on this hardware was as good as she implied it was, it could be gold dust. I was willing to take the chance. There was no hesitation. I'd always been a risk taker. In the back of my mind, I knew it could be highly damaging for myself, yet it would be worth it to see justice prevail. Poetic justice at that. And if Fiona could get me what I needed, when I needed it, all the better. The worm had turned.

'There's a cash machine around the corner,' I said, standing. I took the hard drive and pocketed it. Clocked Bob watching me from out in the corridor as Fiona raised a smile. 'Shall we?'

I withdrew five hundred quid from two separate ATMs and handed it over.

'Trust me,' she said. 'You're doing the right thing. You won't regret it. And I won't let you down.'

'You'd better not.'

She shoved the hefty wad of cash into her handbag before shaking my hand. It felt tiny in my own. A wave of doubt washed over me, but it soon passed. 'You've got stuff there that will change everything,' she said. 'A power shift, Jim. Protect it well for me.'

We exchanged numbers. I told her I'd be in touch. To begin with, there was plenty I wanted to know about this case and what they had. Not least, I wanted more on Colin Black.

I watched her walk away towards Piccadilly as I kept my hand on the black box in my pocket. Pressed STOP on the dictaphone app and called Bob.

'Well?'

'Get the beers in,' I said. 'We've a lot to talk about.'

CHAPTER ELEVEN

There was a pint waiting for me on the same table I'd occupied with Fiona. Bob was waiting for me too, stroking his beard and staring into space. Bad Moon Rising came on the jukebox as I took my seat. I hoped it wasn't an omen.

The hard drive - no bigger than a large matchbox - was safely tucked away in my pocket. I could see by the look on Bob's face that he was eager to talk. To hell with it. I'd tell him everything. I knew I could trust him. I might be breaking the law by withholding this information, but fuck it. I was never one for sticking to the rules. You never grass a fellow copper up, they said, when I began my career. But they couldn't stop me now. If this was going to put their noses out of joint, then good. So these were good reasons, and if Fiona was to be believed - that what was contained on the hard drive could potentially send him down - I wanted to be the one swinging that hammer. Plus, I was more than intrigued about what the hard drive contained. Not to mention what Fiona could bring to me. The thoughts were tumbling through my head like falling rain. Felt like I was on the edge of something extraordinary.

'You look happy, lad,' Bob said. 'I take it you've taken that carrot she was dangling?'

I tapped the hard drive. 'Changes everything.'

'Do you think it's wise?'

'Bob, you're a journalist,' I said. 'Don't tell me you wouldn't have jumped at the chance back in the day. This is gold.'

'You don't even know what's on it yet.'

'I will soon.'

'Could be nothing, lad. An empty box. You thought of that?'

'It won't be. I know what this bastard's like. I know what lurks in his history.'

'Do you?'

I filled him in quickly on what Fiona had told me before putting it to bed - for now. I wanted to get the hard drive back to the safe at the office before I was four pints in and ready to party. Just as soon as I got through this one.

'So anyway,' I said. 'Laura's been delving deep into the E.N.D. Dug up several possibilities on an ID for the men in the Range Rover. I think she may have found something well worth pursuing on Facebook. I believe we might've found our killer. Goes by the name of Colin Black.'

He sat and thought for a moment. 'No, can't say that name rings a bell.'

'No, nor me. But why would it? Anyway, it could be a false name. I know these people are stupid beyond measure, and their belief system is totally backwards in the twenty-first century, but you'd think if he had any sense, he wouldn't use his real name at all.'

He was nodding. 'But having said that, you just don't

know. This kind of delusion is powerful. Of course, they wouldn't agree they're deluded, not in the real sense. But one can't help but consider them troubled. In the strongest possible way, lad. So maybe they are daft enough to use their God given names. I wouldn't put it past them.'

'And going back to Shannon this morning,' I said. 'The suicides she mentioned.'

'I'm glad you brought that up.'

'Yeah? How come?'

'Because it struck me as significant,' he said. 'You won't remember this, but back in the late seventies, there were a lot of suicides over a three-month period. Two main areas - Lancashire and North Wales. Young men, you know. It was all over the papers at the time. They put it down to the economic situation, low standards of living and educa-tion, poverty, drug abuse, all that. A tragic signature of the times we were in, you know. But in a lot of the cases they failed to notice the connection with a lot of these young men.'

'Which was?'

'They all lived in care.'

'You're shitting me...'

'Well, maybe not every single one, but a good seventy percent, I'd say. So what she said this morning just brought that back to me. Not that I think these suicides are connected to that in any way. It just brought back a memory.'

'But that's where I was going with it,' I said. 'You know, how these suicides were connected in that way. That they both went to Ivy Brook.'

'Like Stevie did.'

I nodded. 'Like Stevie.'

'And do you think he could've killed himself, too?'

'I suppose it's possible,' I said. 'But unlikely, given the nature of his death.'

'Suicide by fire.'

'Not a common method.'

'But a violent one,' he said. 'And statistics show that violent suicides are most common in men, especially young men. Hanging, jumping off buildings, throwing yourself in front of a train, that sort of thing. Quick methods, you know.'

'But burning to death,' I said. 'I can't think of anything more agonising.'

My thoughts turned briefly to my own dark past. Standing on that ledge until Angel came to bring me down. Looking out across the city and preparing for the jump...

'Which makes it highly unlikely he took his own life.'

'I believe he was killed, no doubt about it,' I said. 'The real question is why. Not to mention Lloyd. Bob, they shot him in the head. Drink up.'

'I was just getting started.'

'We'll get a few beers on the way back to the office.'

'You know how to show a bloke a good time.'

'I need to get this uploaded to the Mac,' I said. 'And I want to see what's on it.'

The heat had continued unabated for weeks now, and it was still showing no signs of stopping. After picking up a case of beer from the local express shop around the corner, we walked the short distance to the office through the cooler back streets of the Northern Quarter. The sun shone on the red brick buildings, turning the stone to twilight gold. The evening was in full bloom, as were the women on show at every turn. The bars were filling up, their tables loaded with bottles of cider and large chilled glasses of white wine and crisp, ice cold beer. I decided right then that it was time to enjoy a cold one.

As we climbed the staircase, we heard voices. One was Laura's but the other's - a man's - I didn't recognise. I could only hope trouble hadn't caught up with us. We hesitated a moment before continuing. As I stepped through, Laura was sitting at her desk, accompanied by Maya and her bearded friend, the one who had more tattoos than her.

'So, it's that easy,' he said. They turned as Bob and I stepped in.

'What's easy?' I said.

'Jim, I'm glad you're here,' Laura said. 'You won't believe what we've found. Dave will show you.'

Dave spun around in the chair, all hipster beard and full sleeve tattoos on both arms. A row of piercings down his left ear and a spike through his nose, his checked shirt pretty much open all the way down, revealing more tattoos beneath. He held his hand out, and we shook.

'Dave's a mate of mine, Jim,' Maya said. 'Works in I.T.'

'Web developer,' he said. 'But I was a programmer before that for about ten years.'

'Yeah?' I said, wondering why the hell I should be interested.

'We've been on the dark web,' Laura said. She sounded excited. 'After what I found on Facebook. But when I tried to get on to this website, it wouldn't let me and kept throwing me out.'

'Which is where Dave came in,' Maya said.

'Right, hang on a minute. Just back up. What website? Start at the beginning.'

Bob passed me a can of beer. Cracked it open and downed half of it in one. There was just enough space for five of us in the room. Bob and I took the couch while Maya, Dave and Laura occupied the office chairs. I glanced at the Mac's screen. It showed a Facebook page from earlier. Beside it, though, was a battered looking laptop I knew didn't belong to us. On that screen was a rather crude looking site, like something you'd see in the early days of the Internet. The simple fonts were in red and green over a black background. No pictures, no video. Just a lot of jumbled content in neon colours.

'The dark web,' Bob said. 'A hive of criminal activity.'

'You guys know much about it?' Dave said.

I couldn't keep my eyes from the spike through his nose. Made my eyes water just looking at it. 'Not a great deal, to be honest with you.' I stood and made sure the hard drive was safely in my pocket. 'Other than child porn and gun trafficking, what else is there lurking out there?'

'A lot, man. You think Google can find you this kind of shit?' he said. 'No chance.' I tossed each of them a beer and sparked up. 'Hey, nice one. So, what's on there? Probably much easier to say what isn't. You've got international terrorist cells, drug trafficking and dealing, porn of all kinds, fraud on an epic scale, you name it. You can buy weapons on the dark web. You can score heroin. Sell it too. You can learn how to make a pressure cooker bomb and buy the parts. Fuck, there's loads of stuff on there, like you wouldn't believe. But you've gotta know how to find it. And crucially, how to access the sites. Which is where the software comes in.'

'You've lost me already,' I said, joking.

'That's what I thought,' Laura said. 'But then it made sense when he explained it. And this site here, Jim, is what I wanted to get to but couldn't without this software Dave is on about.'

'And what's the website?' I said.

'It's a forum,' she said. 'But I'll let Dave explain.'

'He's a geek with this sort of thing,' added Maya.

He took a long drink, asked me if I minded him smoking. Pretty much on cue, we all sparked up.

'Right, imagine a giant fishing net,' he said. 'It gets hauled in on the beach and it's got crabs, big fish, lobster, a tuna, whatever in it. But the vast majority of the catch in the net are prawns. Thousands of them. Yeah?'

We nodded.

'So I want you to think of the deep web as just that - all the prawns in the catch.'

'Dark web, you mean...'

'No,' he said. 'I mean deep web. With me so far? The prawns are the deep web. Everything else is just your normal Internet, the stuff on the surface. Like when you use a normal search engine, that's the portion of the catch you will get. But the prawns - what represents the deep web - is all the stuff, billions of pages of data, that lies hidden beyond what you normally see when you log on. The stuff not indexed by your average search engine. It's the hidden stuff on the World Wide Web. With me so far?'

'Go on.'

'Right,' he said. 'So. You've got common usage stuff like Internet banking, e-mail, locked sites where you might need a paywall to get into them, locked video streaming, legitimate sites that aren't live for whatever reason... yeah?'

Gotta say, it was going over my head.

'Like an iceberg,' Bob said. 'The surface web - in other words what the average person in the street uses - is on the surface, but the iceberg, the deep web or whatever, is much bigger below the water.'

'Bob, you don't even know what Twitter is,' I said.

'But he's right,' Dave said. He stood up now, took another long drink and a hefty drag on his smoke. 'It's a good analogy. So that's the deep web. But the dark web, well... going back to those prawns. Imagine twenty percent of those prawns are giant emperor prawns, while the rest are just your normal King prawns... yeah?'

'Yeah.'

'Well, the emperor prawns... they're your dark web. The dark web is a part of the deep web - the stuff we can't normally access - except this part of the web - '

'The naughty part,' Maya said.

'The naughty part,' he agreed, 'is especially difficult to access. And it's difficult because you need specific software to be able to do it. You've gotta consider what's on there to understand why. I mean, this is where your serious criminals operate.'

'Drug dealing, trafficking...'

'And the rest, man,' he said. 'Child porn. There's a lot of that. Really horrible abuse stuff, you know. Live murder and torture. I mean, this is really sick shit. But it goes on, believe me. Proper Satanic, you know. Then there's the drugs, the finance criminals, the fucking hitmen.'

'Hitmen?'

'Oh yeah,' he said. 'You can buy a hit man on the dark web if you know where to look. I'm not joking, man. Wish I was.'

'Are you serious?'

'Deadly,' he said. 'It's a very dangerous game to go playing around on there. Because if you don't know what you're doing, you can find yourself in deep, deep trouble.

Let your guard slip and potentially, your IP address is identified and boom - if you've rubbed someone up the wrong way, they're likely to come knocking at your door.'

'What's an IP address?' I said.

'Internet Protocol address. It's unique to the machine you're browsing from. In a nutshell, it identifies your location.'

'Jesus.'

'Exactly. So essentially, if you're lax with your security, you can be identified quite easily.'

'So, in the wrong hands,' Bob said, 'it's not worth the risk. Am I right?'

He nodded. 'That's a definite understatement. It's like being locked in a dark room with your worst nightmare. You can get trapped in these places. So can you imagine Laura noseying around? Without knowing what she was up against, it would be suicide.'

I knew more than anyone how Laura could be clumsy with these things, but she wasn't all dizzy blonde. Sometimes I don't know where I'd be without her, and it was her, after all, that had brought us to this point. But Dave was right. In the wrong hands, it would be dangerous and I wouldn't forgive myself if she got hurt doing what was essentially my own dirty work.

'So tell me about this site,' I said.

'It's a forum,' Laura said. 'I found the link to it deep in the Facebook pages of our friend, Colin Black. It wasn't the only link, but it stood out in a really creepy conversation I was reading between him and some other people.'

'Anyone you recognise?'

'No,' she said. 'But in the conversation, they were talking about something they called 'the plan' and one of them put a link up to this website...'

'Except the website,' Maya said, 'wouldn't let her in. Which she found odd until I mentioned it to Dave.'

'Who said it was probably on the dark web,' Laura finished. 'And I couldn't access it because -'

'You didn't have a Tor browser,' Dave said. 'But I did.'

'Go on.'

'Well basically, a Tor browser allows you to access encrypted websites that also use the same browser software.'

'So unless you have that on your computer,' Bob said, 'you can't access it?'

'Exactly,' Dave said. 'And the reason these sites use Tor is because it adds that extra privacy, that extra protection. But we're getting technical here so I'll be blunt.'

'Get to the point, Dave,' Maya said.

'I am.' He took a long drink and finished the can. I tossed him another. 'If you've got the right software, you can easily access these sites. But it's risky, like I said. Now you haven't got this software, Jim, and for a private detective or whatever, well, that's just plain silly. You need a serious upgrade of your gear, man.'

'Get to the point, Dave.'

'I will if you stop interrupting, Maya. Okay. Now because I have Tor and I know what I'm talking about, I brought my laptop up and had a look on this site Laura couldn't access. And here it is.'

'Doesn't look like much,' I said.

'Maybe not,' Laura said. 'But this is their forum.'

'Their chat room,' Maya said. 'Where they talk shit all day.'

'Are you saying this is where the E.N.D. hang around online?'

'That's it, Jim,' Dave said. 'To the layman, this kind of site is encrypted. And because we're talking extremism here, they want to stay hidden. But they don't bank on people like me poking around.'

'What about this IP address stuff?' Bob asked. 'Won't that give you away?'

'That's the fun bit,' he said. He stubbed out his smoke. 'Essentially, we've hacked into their party. So I've taken the precaution of calling their bluff. Someone on the other end - someone responsible for the site, let's say - will know there is someone new out there browsing their domain.'

'And they'll want to know who,' I said.

'Yes, but they won't know, you see. Because there's another little bit of software that allows me to override my IP address and create multiple fake ones instead.'

'Meaning,' Laura said, 'that he can hide within the system.'

'Changing the IP every thirty seconds,' Maya said.

'So that they don't know - will never know,' Dave said, 'who I am.'

It was pretty fucking clever, and I told him so.

'Thanks. But that's just the beginning. Now we come to the bit that will really fucking depress you.'

'I knew it was too good to be true.'

'No, nothing like that,' Laura said. 'It's the shit they're discussing that will piss you off.'

D ave and Maya left shortly after he'd given us the basics on how to behave on the site, with strict instructions to not engage in any discussion. We were just there to browse, and that was it. They had tickets for a gig up the road and he said he'd leave the laptop with us and pick it up afterwards as he'd be staying with Maya tonight anyway and would be in her flat nearby. I had to wonder if they were more than just friends.

'Are you sure I won't start World War Three?' I said before they left.

'You'll be safe on there,' he said. 'Don't worry about breaking it. If something goes wrong, like some weird shit, don't worry about it. I'll deal with it.'

'I'm not sure I can trust myself.'

'Jim, it's not rocket science, man. Just chill. But whatever you do, no matter how tempted you might be, don't register to join in the chat. It could blow everything, so it's just not worth the risk. And I'd think about upgrading your gear, man. Seriously.'

I knew it wasn't a bad idea at all, but like anything with these things, I didn't know where to start. I told him so.

'I'll help you out,' he said. 'But it'll cost you.'

'Name your price.'

'I meant for the gear - hardware and software.'

'Can you get this special software in for us?'

'It won't come cheap, if you want the best. And it needs upgrading constantly.'

I thought about what was locked in the cabinet. The cost was no object. 'No problem,' I said. 'It'll be worth it, I'm sure.'

Laura gave me a look. 'Does this mean I can get that swanky laptop I've had my eye on?'

'I suppose so.'

'I'll help you out, man,' he said, before downing the rest of his beer. 'We'll make sure you're well protected.'

Bob had found my brandy stash and was helping himself. I could see there was something on his mind, something else besides the obvious. I watched Dave and Maya cross the street as he necked a shot from one of Laura's coffee cups and sparked up. I felt like following his lead but thought it best not to, considering the information in front of me. The temptation to open my mouth on the forum would be too much if I were three sheets, and I couldn't jeopardise anything. Instead, I sparked up myself and cracked open another beer before facing it head on with my notepad at the ready.

'So,' I said. Laura was scrolling through the page, the layout of which was pretty much the same as any other Internet forum, only more basic. Right away I got the impression that whoever ran this site hadn't spent much on maintaining it or making it look nice. Then again, what did I know? 'What've we got?'

'All kinds of subjects,' she said. 'And separate forums for other, less extreme discussion. But the general gist of it is that these people like nothing more than to talk about the country's woes and how great it used to be when there were no 'Pakis' and 'Niggers' and 'Jews' here. Like they remember.'

'Twats.'

'Yeah,' she said. 'Or just thick. Either way, they're dangerous. But this lot are bordering on lunacy. Actually, scrap 'bordering', they are fucking lunatics. I'll go to this main page and show you the discussions they're having. The level of racism is disgusting, Jim, it really is.'

She moved onto the main page and slowly scrolled through. I counted twenty separate threads, each with a title as disturbing as the previous one. Would you ever fuck a Paki? Inbreeding Rife In Rochdale. The Final Solution - Part 2. No Irish, No Gypsies, No Coons. Kill All Immigrants. This Land Is Our Land. It's Whites They Hate...

'Makes you sick, doesn't it?'

Bob was standing over my shoulder, his head shaking,

cigar smoke permeating the room. The air was heavy with static. I could feel a storm coming.

'Makes you wonder where they get so much hate from,' I said. 'Their parents? The generation before them? I mean, how can so many people have such bitterness and hatred in them? I don't get it.'

'We're all human,' Laura said. 'That's where we're all equal.'

'Oh aye,' Bob said. 'But some of these people think other races are subhuman.'

'A whole new level.'

'Not new at all,' he said. 'But it does seem like it's on the rise at the minute and I'm wondering why.'

'Been on the increase the past four or five years,' I said. 'There's been a lot of groups parading their shit.'

'With the mistaken belief,' Laura said, 'that so many others share their hatred.'

'Fascism,' Bob said, 'has a long and disturbing history, not least the holocaust, of course. But it's never really gone away. Forget the politics. It's an ideology that attracts those who are geared towards violence against their fellow man. It's tribal. Backward. Warped.'

'Fucked up is what it is,' Laura said.

She wasn't wrong. I knew that all over Europe, all over the world, in fact, far right ideology was on the rise. White supremacy, neo-nazism, fascist nationalism. There were a hundred names for the same kind of people under the same political umbrella. But I also knew that most of these groups masquerading as political were also nothing of the sort and were so extreme that they were much further to the right than your average right wing political party. These groups, the kind the E.N.D came under, would not be satisfied until the people they hated were annihilated from the face of the

Earth. Poisoned minds, poisoned souls. I wondered just how many of these groups lurked on underground forums like the one before me. How many of them operated on the dark web. How many were ready to shed blood in the fight for their cause.

How many had killed already.

'You can see there's a fair amount of discussion,' Laura said. She clicked on the thread entitled 'Burn The Bastards', which I found particularly intriguing, for obvious reasons. Already, there was a lot of chat, even as we browsed, the content of which was nothing short of moronic. Yet they seemed as excited as primary school kids at the senseless violent talk. It was all about burning Pakis, burning Gypsies. There was even talk here and there of gassing them as well. Taking a leaf out of the Führer's book, as one put it.

I made a note of some of the user names to see if anything stood out or caught my eye. Something that gave me that itch. But no one was giving anything away. Most of the names were just a combination of numbers and letters. Others were more of a nod to their heroes. Himmler40, Adolf, JewKiller, KKK24, Blackshirt Bill. I suppose I shouldn't have been surprised. Though perhaps one or two of them were the reckless kind when it came to the Internet - when it came to life, for that matter - so I kept scrawling those usernames down, anyway. And, of course, some of the things they were saying. The nicknames they had for each other, especially when a name was mentioned in the discussion thread that wasn't being used. I knew that browsing this thing could take me forever, and time was something I didn't have.

Colin Black, where are you?

'So this thing you mentioned,' I said. 'The Plan. What is that?'

'That was on Facebook,' she said. 'A conversation between several people, one of whom was our man, Colin Black. Not a clue what the 'plan' is or was, but they were definitely discussing something. I'll show you.'

She went back to the Mac and found the page pretty quickly. Because it was Facebook, there wasn't a great deal of anonymity, but I could see that several had profile pictures that were clearly designed to be inconspicuous. Some even wore masks in a blatant effort of mock disguise. It was like they were taking the piss. I was more than convinced that they were. And the 'in' jokes spilled over to this dark web forum. It seemed an open secret that everyone knew about. SEE YOU AFTER DARK. CATCH YOU DOWN IN THE BUNKER. THERE'S AN AFTER PARTY TONIGHT. Etc etc, etc.

'From what I can make out,' she said, 'the 'Plan' simply refers to a gathering of like-minded people on a certain day, but I've an inkling it's more than that. But their conversation definitely seems to point to a meeting or a rally that they're all getting excited about.'

Bob and I read over the conversation she pointed out for us. Sure enough, a 'meeting' was planned for next Saturday, though it wasn't clear where. It also wasn't clear what the meeting was about or exactly who was attending. Not that it would be obvious on Facebook. But on the forum, I could only guess that one or two individuals were more relaxed about sharing the details.

'Twenty ninth of June,' Bob said. 'That's next week.'

'What do you think it could be?'

'A rally?' I said. It was as good a guess as any. 'A lynching?'

'Could be something less dramatic,' Bob said. 'Like a meeting in a pub or something.'

'A piss up,' Laura said. 'But why feel the need to discuss it on social media? Why not just ring each other?'

'Not the way things are done these days,' I said. 'Every man and his dog has a Facebook account.'

'Or Twitter.'

'Or both,' she said. 'And more.'

I nodded. Downed my beer. Thought for a moment and jumped when a clap of thunder roared right above our heads. The storm had well and truly arrived. I made a mental note of the meeting - Saturday twenty ninth of June - and collapsed onto the couch. Sparked up. Took that shit in deep. A flash of lightning illuminated the sky and soon after, the downpour finally came.

I sat and tried to put the pieces together, though my brain felt wired. It had been a long day. And my thoughts had turned to the conversation with Fiona and the hard drive locked in the filing cabinet. Also, the phone call with Karen was playing on my mind. I was beginning to get pretty fucking angry about my daughter living with her grandad, not to mention Karen's attitude to the whole thing. I could put it off no longer.

'Laura,' I said. 'And Bob, you too. If you don't mind helping me out on this..?'

'Got nothing better to do,' he said. 'For now.'

'Good. Because I haven't got time for this. I want you both to scour this forum for anything you can get. It might take a few days.'

'And what's in it for me?'

'I don't need to remind you, Bob, that you're staying on my couch. But if you need a bit extra, help yourself to the brandy.'

'I think you'll find it's my couch,' Laura said.

'Point taken, lad. But while we're doing that...'

'I've got a few things to do. Phone calls to make. Visits to carry out. I want to speak to Shannon again as well.'

'And what about the hard drive?'

I wasn't ready to tell Laura about that yet, but seeing as Bob had spilled it, I had no choice but to explain everything right there and then. They were both as eager as I was to view the data, but now wasn't the time. I wasn't even sure that viewing the hard drive here was such a good idea at all, given the gravity of the situation. You never can tell who's watching.

'You've forgotten,' Laura said, 'that Dave will be back for his laptop. He didn't recommend us delving any deeper into this without the right software.'

'Or knowing what we're up against,' Bob said. 'Though I've a good idea.'

'Do what you can for at least tonight,' I said. 'Maybe ask to loan it for a few days.'

'Would be better coming from you, lad.'

'I think it'd be better coming from Laura,' I said. 'She can sweet talk anyone into submission. And besides, Maya's her mate so it makes more sense.'

'Leave it to me,' she said. 'But where are you going?'

I didn't answer because I didn't know myself. I only knew I needed to get out of here. I unlocked the filing cabinet and took the hard drive. A sudden wave of paranoia overwhelmed me. It wouldn't be safe here. I took the window in the other room and went down via the fire escape, lifting my phone to my ear as I descended the stairs, a bright flash of lightning electrifying the air.

'Fiona?'

'Yeah?' she said. She sounded as drunk as I felt. 'That you, Jim Locke?'

'I need something.'

'You don't waste any time, do you? And look, I'm not sure this is such a great idea ringing me like this. You know the walls have ears.'

I reached the bottom and almost slipped on the last step as another loud thunderclap boomed overhead. The heavens opened. Steam rose from the streets as the rain burned off the heat. The smell was fantastic. I stood and let it cleanse me. This was my kind of weather.

'I need you to run a check on the PNC for me, as soon as you can. White Range Rover, registration CV15TYK.'

'Have you looked at it yet?'

'What?'

'I said, have you looked at it yet?!'

'No, but give me tonight. I need to be somewhere safe. Now there's something else,' I said. 'Colin Black. Make a note of it. I need everything you've got on him.'

'That name rings a bell.'

'It does?'

'But I can't think where.'

'Check it out. Tomorrow.'

'I will.'

'And listen,' I said, though I didn't have anything to say. I paused. 'Step out in the rain. It feels good. God, it feels so fucking good.'

I hung up and raised my face to the sky.

CHAPTER TWELVE

I walked back to the flat in the downpour, which served two purposes. It helped to both sober me up and cool me down, and the flat was cool too when I finally lay down on the couch in the dark. I fell asleep quickly and by the time I awoke, it was dark outside. I'd had several texts and a missed call from Laura. Sparked up and dialled.

'Have you been avoiding us?'

'Fell asleep,' I said, opening the living room window. Cool air rushed in. Glanced at the clock on the wall. It was gone eleven. 'Didn't realise how tired I was.'

'There's a lot of chatter on here,' she said. 'So I was just ringing to give you an update.'

'I'm listening.'

'Are you in bed?'

'No,' I said. 'On the couch. Bob still there?'

'I think he had too much brandy. He's asleep too. There was some kind of fight in the street earlier. Police everywhere.'

'When the sun comes out...'

'Nutters after a few beers. Anyway. This meeting. It

seems they've a rally planned for Saturday in town. And the anti fascists are marching too. It's not been publicised yet, but it's definitely happening.'

'Any idea where?'

'Albert square.'

'Great...'

'That's not all. It seems there will be others there as well. Other far right groups, I mean.'

'Wonderful.'

'Like a coalition of ignoramuses, if you like. And also, this Colin Black. Well, there's a guy with a username of 'Blackshirt Bill'.'

'I noted that, yeah.'

'And he's pretty active on here tonight. The interesting thing is that other users are referring to him as 'Col'. You think we might've found him?'

'There's a good chance.' I found her laptop in the bedroom and switched it on. Rummaged around for the hard drive I dumped in here just before I crashed on the couch. Plugged the USB cable in and let the machine fire up. 'Can you note down everything they say? I know it's a big ask...'

'Would be much easier just to print it but...'

'Not plugged in?'

'It's not that, it's just... well, it's Dave's computer. I don't feel right just using it like it's my own.'

'Know what you mean. Did you get a hold of Maya?'

'She got my text. Said she was in the bar at the gig. Would be back early hours as they'd probably go clubbing afterwards. Dave said he was cool with us loaning it for a few days, but wants to get you some new gear so we can do it ourselves. Said you can pay him later.'

'I suppose it makes sense.'

'So, the hard drive. I take it you've looked at it by now.'

'You know me too well, but I'm only just about to delve into it. I'm using your laptop. Hope you don't mind.'

'Well, you did say you would get me a new one, so go for your life.'

'Okay, I better go. I can't wait to see what we've got. So when are you coming home?'

'I'm gonna wait until Maya and Dave get back, then call it a day. I'm knackered. Plus, Bob's still knocked out here. Do you think I should wake him?'

'Christ, no. He's a moody bastard after a kip. Just lock up and leave him there.'

She laughed and said she had work to do, before hanging up. I realised I needed her more than I thought.

I brought the laptop into the living room and placed it on the coffee table. Poured a long drink and settled in. I looked at the desktop screen, pausing for a moment as I thought briefly of what Fiona had said. About the stuff on here being so incriminating and so naughty that I'd want to kill the bastard as soon as I discovered what it was. As if I didn't want to kill him already. Clocked the icon for the hard drive in the corner of the screen - BUF918T-Drive - and hovered the little arrow over it. Sparked up and clicked. Something told me I was in for a long night.

———————

I put the password in - DIRTYPSYCHOBASTARDGMP - which Fiona had sent me via text just after we parted earlier tonight. It was hardly something I could forget. Straight away, a long list of information came up. I scrolled down to the bottom, then back again. There was over a hundred individual files here.

Over half of them were JPEG images. The rest, word documents, audio files, even video. It would take me a while to
plough through it, but nothing would stop me. Immediately,
I knew I had to make my own copies, to nail the bastard
once and for all. This shit really was gold dust, and I
laughed out loud at the audacity of the young WPC. She
really had been busy these past six months.

I started with the images. Felt too wired to be reading
any documents and anyway, a picture paints a thousand
words. They certainly did with the first few images I
viewed, though I didn't expect those words to be dirty, fucking, and nonce. Jesus. Robertson was in some deep, deep
shit if this ever got out.

There were several images belonging to a set. One of
Robertson's BMW parked up near a school. I'd recognise
that plate anywhere. Pretty insignificant, until I moved
along a few more. A girl in a school uniform getting into his
car. Again, could be completely innocent. Just a father
picking his daughter up, although I knew he didn't have a
daughter. The third one was the clincher, though. I had to
take a closer look, but it was definitely the same girl, this
time without her uniform. Tidy cleavage, short skirt. Both of
them sharing a kiss outside a coffee shop on a summer's day.
Made me want to throw up. I looked back at the picture of
her with the uniform. Zoomed in. She had to be no older
than fifteen. Back again at the one without. And several
others of the same scene - coffee shop, sunny day - and in
these she'd pass as a young woman. He'd probably get away
with it in a pub, just. But it was the same girl, without a
doubt. Like a lot of teenage kids, she put years on herself
with a bit of makeup and a low cut top.

'You stupid, horrible cunt, Robertson,' I said, and dialed
up Fiona.

'Not a good time, Jim,' she said. 'I'm with someone, if you know what I mean.'

'Just one question.'

'I hope I'm not gonna start getting midnight phone calls every night.'

'How old is she?'

A sigh. 'Fifteen. I did some digging around and got some details. She's called Isabella Burns. Very pretty, wouldn't you say?'

'He's a dirty bastard. Fuck me, what does she see in him?!'

'And what do you think of the other stuff?'

'What, there's more?'

'Tip of the iceberg, Jim. Look, I'd better go. I'll be in touch soon.'

I was about to question her one more but she hung up. When I phoned her back, there was no answer. I tried a third time and got a dead line. I suppose she meant what she said. If this was the tip of the iceberg, I could only imagine what was coming next. But that was where this series of photographs ended, which was just one small file. This tiny bit alone would be enough to make the man weep, and I longed to see such a sight, so if the rest of it was half as bad, I could see why she was willing to give up her career to see justice prevail.

Already, I was planning on speaking to Dave to ask him to sort all this computer gear as soon as possible. I had to ensure this was protected. No wonder Fiona wanted it away from her flat. And there was surely no reason to take her off the murder inquiry she'd mentioned other than the fact that Robertson had somehow gotten wind of her activities. But could he have friends who'd look out for him? In top brass, yes. I wouldn't put anything past them. And Fiona had said she was certain that she was being watched. I knew that feeling.

More photographs. High resolution. The girl hadn't been messing around when she said she'd been watching him. Looked like these had been taken with a zoom lens from a good distance away. The first one showed the location pretty clearly - a supermarket car park, though not clear which one. And there, in the middle distance, walking towards the camera with shopping bags, was Robertson and a woman, different to the young schoolgirl and probably much older. But it was what was written underneath the photograph that really caught my eye.

Wife number one. Marie Dawson. And DI Rob Robertson, AKA John Dawson.

Which not only implied there was another wife, but another version of the man himself. Fuck me, was the silly bastard really living a double life? Oh, Robertson, what have you been up to?

I sat and stared at the screen, struggled to get my head around it. Just what on Earth did he think he was doing? I considered, for a brief moment, that perhaps I had been the victim of some elaborate hoax and here I was, the butt of everyone's joke. Maybe this was Robertson's way of taking the piss. Maybe he'd roped Fiona into reeling me in with her promises of sending the bastard down. A way to get me to tow the line.

But no. Couldn't be. Could it?

No.

I dug out a bottle of Glenfiddich I had stashed away and poured a stiff one. The rain was coming down hard again, and I listened to the distant rumble of thunder ripple through the night sky. Sparked up, thinking back to my time on the force. Had Robertson said anything about his marriage back then? Anything that struck me as odd? No, not at all. He was the epitome of a jobsworth prick in a pinstripe suit, no more a proper copper than I was a washed up rock star. Which meant that if all of this was true - and let's face it, the camera never lies - then he really had us all fooled.

I moved along and browsed through a lot more of the same couple. The Dawsons in the supermarket car park, better photographs and close up. The Dawsons in a pub beer garden. The Dawsons arriving home. 'John Dawson' putting the bins out. The Dawsons at a funeral, to name but a few. There seemed to be no end to the deceit. There also seemed to be no end to the photos. I counted thirty-three of this particular group. Had to wonder if Marie Dawson knew of the schoolgirl, Isabella Burns. I doubted it. And if she did, had she forgiven him? But when I moved into the next file of photographs, it had to be pretty clear now that Marie Dawson knew nothing about anything. Her husband had betrayed her in the worst way imaginable. It was pretty clear he wasn't just a liar, but a pathological one. Seemed the guy was a man out to gain everything for himself and fuck the rest. I wondered, and not for the first time, if Robertson could be a genuine psychopath. It was getting more disturbing with every image.

Wife number two, as Fiona had written beneath the next images, was called Amanda Michelle Robertson. I recognised her, no problem. Had seen her at police func-tions with the man himself. Had probably shared elbow room at the bar. And yet here she was, oblivious to her husband's lies. They'd been married at least ten years, I was certain, though I'd have to check with one or two of the coppers who did still speak to me. We had the Robertsons at the garden centre; the Robertsons walking the dog in the park with the kids in tow. Amanda Robertson cradling a baby at a Christening while Rob looked on, as innocent as they come. They probably had hundreds of photographs at home of them enjoying a good marriage. Two kids - the significance of which wasn't lost on me - and a semi-detached in suburbia. On the surface, a normal family, a normal family man. What, if anything, did Amanda Robertson know? Just how well was Robertson hiding this? How long had the other marriage been going on? And how the hell did he imagine he'd get away with it?

The questions kept on coming, and yet the answers were elusive. I called Fiona again but got a dead line. So I just stared at the photographs repeatedly, shaking my head in disbelief and smiling when I thought that, as well as sending the bastard down for a very long time, his marriage - both marriages - would be ruined. The innocent victims in all of this would never forgive him, and who in the world could blame them? Maybe that would be a just punishment.

I went back and forth, studying the images until I came back to where I started and Isabella Burns. She was just a kid, but there was no doubting she would become a beautiful young woman. Just how was he exploiting her? The kiss was enough to nail him, but what if there was more? The tip of the iceberg, Fiona had said. And after what she'd told me about him touching her up in the toilets, could we put anything past him? Did he really think he was untouchable? Fiona had said as much, but why? If he was that brazen at a police function - the annual awards ceremony - what was to stop him trying it on and, by the looks of things, succeeding with an underage girl?

I sparked up another, poured another stiff one. I knew I was getting an unhealthy taste for whisky and I'd have to rein it in. And I'd suddenly gotten an overwhelming urge to shut the laptop down. I'd reminded myself many times over the past couple of days that you never knew who could be watching. But I couldn't bring myself to do that just yet.

After some pacing around and several smokes, a cloud of bad shit circulating the room, I pondered on what the consequences would be for me if we nailed him anytime soon. Perhaps just sitting on this stuff would be enough to keep him compliant for now, and if I could let him know what he was up against - the danger he was in if he didn't cooperate with me on the things I needed - then the power was all mine. I could let the cat out of the bag at any time of my own choosing. Could pick the moment, to devastating effect. Could even let it drag on for years so that he would be the one looking over his shoulder. If you don't bend my way, Robertson, I'll spill everything. I could really make him sweat. The thought was tantalising...

I checked the clock. It was now gone midnight and, despite having had a few hours' sleep, I still felt drained. I knew I'd need as much energy as I could if I was to get to the bottom of Stevie's and Lloyd's murders. I felt angry at the senselessness. Angry that the police seemed to be doing fuck all and cared even less. Especially about Lloyd's murder, which they mustn't have seen coming. Lloyd, shot in the head and then burnt to death, if he wasn't dead already. I wondered what he knew to deserve such treatment. Had he been hiding something from me? Had he been somewhat creative with the truth? He claimed they'd been following him only after Stevie's remains turned up. But could they have been following him prior to Stevie's murder?

Fire burns away evidence. But the testimony of others doesn't go away unless you get rid of them, too. And maybe that was why they took Lloyd out. I also wondered if there were any witnesses to Lloyd's brutal attack. And if so, would they be willing to talk? Or, more likely, would they go out of their way to keep their mouths shut?

It was pubs where things got said. After a few drinks, when tongues get loose, rumour becomes counter rumour and the truth - or the lies - gets lost in the fog of drink and drugs. But someone must've known something. Someone must've seen. Someone must have a story to tell about last night. I thought about making a few enquiries around the Broughton area, perhaps meet Shannon to go over what she'd found out about those suicides, if anything. Kill two birds with one stone. Told myself that someone would talk. Or maybe I could make them talk, if that's what it took.

I thought of Lloyd's wife and kids as I shut the laptop down. About the agony they must be going through. One day he was here, a dad, a husband, the next... gone. Murdered in cold blood. Gunned down in the streets. Considered going to see his wife but wrote it off immediately. It was far too soon for any of that.

Pretty soon, after the laptop was safely stashed under the bed, I got in it and fell into a deep sleep as the rain battered down hard outside. Washing away the heat. Washing away a bad day.

I briefly woke when Laura found her way into bed, the sheets kicked off both of us. Seemed to remember her saying something about Bob being locked in the office. And then the night fell away, taking my dreams with it. Fire and blood. Blood and fire. And the screams of two men being burnt alive.

I left Laura sleeping when I was woken by the sun beaming through the window. Made a pot of strong coffee and sparked up. Found my mobile on the coffee table beside the opened bottle of Bowmore, and several missed calls and texts from Bob. Flicked on the TV and caught the tail end of the first morning news bulletin. It was 06:05am, twenty-four degrees and rising.

I could have phoned him back, but opted not to just yet. He'd probably spent most of his time scrabbling around in the dark, wondering why he was locked in my office alone. I guessed he'd be asleep again now, which was probably for the best. It would be a while before Laura would stir again, which gave me plenty of opportunity to resume my study of the hard drive. Removed the laptop from under the bed and left her snoring, comatose. Started the beast up and poured a strong one, black. The first rush of morning nicotine brought me back to the land of the living, but I still felt half dead. Besides living a double life and getting off with schoolkids, I wondered if Robertson had more skeletons in his closet. And if he did, how the hell did he find the time?

Once the machine came to life, I settled in, expecting more of the same. Began by scrolling down to the word documents, of which there were several. It was looking like this prick was up to his eyeballs judging by the statements I read, the first of which was signed by forensic scientist Dr. Samantha Webb, Bsc. As I read, I found myself shaking my head. Things were looking that bad for Robertson, I almost laughed. In the statement, Dr. Webb described the time in detail when DI Rob Robertson abused his power and touched her intimately when she was hard at work on a cadaver in the mortuary department. He tried to kiss her neck as he groped her backside when her back was turned. The statement echoed what Fiona had said. He'd said to Dr. Webb that he thought she'd wanted him to. Which, of course, she flatly denied in the statement here. When she confronted him about it, right there in the mortuary, he simply told her it was her word against his and that no one would believe her. She then told him to fuck off. He left the room then, blowing her a kiss on the way out to go with the wink as he calmly opened the door.

Dr. Webb said she wanted to state on record exactly what had happened to a trusted confidante, WPC Fiona Watson. The statement was signed and dated and written on GMP headed paper. I could only assume Fiona had printed out a hard copy. I made a note of asking her next time we spoke.

Then I read Fiona's statement, which was another detailed piece. It contained pretty much everything she'd told me, right down to the bare bones. A two-page summary of events, beginning with how she came to be a copper, to how she came to being sexually assaulted in the ladies' toilets on the annual awards night. If this was a film, I would be inclined to say it was unrealistic. Senior police officers don't behave like that. Yet with Robertson, I could believe it. Given his connections to top brass - and especially given that they had previous when it came to matters of vice - it really was no surprise. Fiona had said he thought he was untouchable. And I'd witnessed the corruption within the force first hand. Was it no surprise, then, that such behaviour went on? Perhaps the only thing that did surprise me was that he thought he could get away with it. But then, that's power. Delusions of grandeur must have gotten to his head. I could see no other possibility. Either that or he just didn't give a shit.

But it was the next document that sent my head spinning. This wasn't a word document, but a scanned item from a hard copy piece of NHS paper. An official medical letter, confirming a procedure. It was addressed to Isabella Burns and gave instructions for her attendance at an abortion clinic attached to the Manchester Royal Infirmary. Dated 18th July 2016, just shy of one year ago. A Friday. She would've been off school as it was during the summer holidays. Was Robertson the father? Did he go with her, to make sure she went through with it?

This callous bastard was really beginning to make me very angry.

I jumped when my mobile rang out. Answered quickly, so I didn't wake Laura.

'Where the bloody hell are you, lad? I can't get out!'

'Try the fire escape.'

'I'm not bloody burning to death.'

'Just open the window in the other room and get onto the fire escape stairs. I'll be there in ten minutes. I'll shout you breakfast.'

I found him sitting on the step out the front, smoking a Montecristo. He looked a bloated mess. With his shirt half undone, revealing curly white chest hair to go with his thick beard and an odour of stale brandy hanging around him, he looked like an off duty bad Santa.

'My neck hurts,' he said. 'You could've woke me up, lad.'

'Laura said you were out of it, so I thought it best to let you sleep.'

We took a short walk through the Northern Quarter to the Koffee Pot on Oldham Street. We were the first customers through the door as they'd just opened, and we must've looked like a couple of tramps to the girl on the counter. Ordered us two large full English breakfasts and a good pot of coffee for two. We got ourselves a booth in the far corner and settled in.

'I'm bloody starving,' he said, pouring a cup. 'Did you get done what you had to get done?'

'No. But I looked at the hard drive. Bob, this would make one hell of a story.'

'I'm retired and assumed dead.'

'Just as well. Because I'm not sure even you could take it in without wanting to throttle the bastard.'

'But I do have friends who are still very much in the game.'

'Who, George Thornley?'

'Among others. So come on. How bad is it?'

'Very bad. Seriously, this would be front page for days.'

I told him what I'd seen on the hard drive. The wives, the schoolgirl, the abortion, everything. If he was shocked, he didn't show it, just nodded intently between mouthfuls of sausage and bacon. When I'd finished, he sat back, poured hot coffee down his neck and stroked his beard.

'Would never have put it past that twat,' he said. 'His father was the same. But about the two wives. Has it crossed your mind that they might be aware of each other? Or that all parties are complicit in the arrangement?'

'Can't see it,' I said. 'As mad as it seems, and as deluded and incompetent as he is, I just can't see it. I mean, how sad would his wives have to be to agree to it? It's crazy. So not complicit, no. They might be aware of each other, but even then... would they just be happy to let it continue? Would they fuck.'

'Maybe you're right...'

'No two ways about it. And anyway, this double life he seems to have pales in comparison to what he's been up to with a school kid.'

'But we don't know for certain that he's been up to anything.'

'You've not seen the photographs, Bob.'

'Okay, the kiss, granted, but ...'

'The abortion appointment.'

'Still doesn't prove that he's been... well, that he's been fucking her.'

'Let's not skirt the issue, eh?'

'Well, that's what it comes down to, lad, isn't it? I don't want to put it plainly, but plain is what it is. No point messing about with flowery words. If he's been having sex with a schoolgirl, might as well say how it is.'

'Keep your voice down.'

'Okay,' he said. 'But you know the story. And I re-iterate, we don't know if he has.'

'The camera never lies.'

'Show me the one of him giving her one, then.'

Gotta admit, he was right.

'I'll speak to Fiona,' I said. 'And anyway, I've still not viewed everything on the hard drive. There's a lot of stuff I still haven't seen.'

'So what have you been up to all night?'

'Sleeping,' I said. 'I am only human, you know.'

'Are you sure?'

'And anyway, I've got things to do. Which brings me to the task I gave you and Laura. Any joy on that?'

'A completely joyless endeavour, lad. Kind of re-enforces what I always thought.'

'Which is?'

'Society is full of imbeciles,' he said. 'At least a good

section of it, anyway. Honestly, these people. I'm not even sure that they're sure what they want, you know? It's just blatant racism, blatant xenophobia. Us against them. And that's their mentality, you know. Tribal, like I said.'

'Laura mentioned this Blackshirt Bill character...'

'Ah, that would be 'Col'. At least, that's what everyone was calling him. Had a lot to say about Pakistanis and not much else, other than this meeting they have planned.'

'The rally.'

'Yeah, but more of a piss up from what we can gather, a come and have a go if you think you're hard enough type thing.'

'Like a bunch of football hooligans.'

'If you like,' he said. 'But much more extreme. Just a bunch of fascists making a lot of noise. These are people that aren't just looking for a ruck. They want to annihilate certain groups from the face of the earth. Certainly from the U.K.'

It was depressing, to say the least. It was almost eight and I was considering trying Fiona again. Outside, the bustle of the city went up a notch, as did the heat, and I knew it was going to be another long day. I knew I didn't want Bob coming with me for my next excursion, and he was probably of better use back at the office, continuing the job I'd given them last night. He wasn't best pleased.

'It's too hot to be stuck in there all day,' he said. 'Especially keeping an eye on the shit those wankers are talking about.'

'Just a few hours, then. I've got some family business to attend to.'

A sigh. 'Two hours. That's it. I do have better things to do.'

'What, like run from the Spanish police?'

It was a low blow, and I immediately apologised.

'No, but you're right,' he said. 'I need to get this sorted out.'

'What do you mean?'

A long pause as he looked beyond me to the window and the morning sunshine. 'I don't know, lad,' he said. 'I just don't know.'

I didn't know either. But what I did know was that I couldn't put him up much longer than what we agreed. A fortnight and that was that. I was aware he'd been making some phone calls, calling in favours. He'd said so himself. I had no clue as to what those phone calls were about, but I only hoped he knew what he was doing. He was up to his neck in it. I had to wonder why he'd bothered to come back at all. If he'd have disappeared to the Spanish mountains, perhaps he'd have been able to get away with murder.

'So what've you got planned? Gonna finally speak to that wife of yours?'

'No,' I said. I finished my coffee, by now cold, and left my seat, throwing a twenty down to settle the bill. 'Her father.'

CHAPTER THIRTEEN

The last time I'd been to Frank and Maureen's house was when we buried Maureen. She'd lost a short battle with cancer just before Christmas, which left Frank devastated and their daughter, Karen, in a state of shock. Our daughter, Nicole, had taken it all in her stride. She'd been upset like all of us, of course, but soon went back to her books, her drawing and painting and her favourite TV shows. She understood that Maureen was now in heaven and she wouldn't be coming home. We knew she was upset by it all, but she took it better than any of us. As everyone else around her grieved, she was more philosophical. On the day of the funeral, she told her grandfather, Frank, that Maureen wouldn't have wanted him to cry. And she was right.

But he did cry. And the crying continued, as far as I was aware, right up to today. Frank and Maureen had been married for fifty-odd years. They'd virtually never spent a day apart. So he felt the loss immensely, and I knew he was hurting. I also knew that Karen wasn't the best at spending time with her own father. That career thing again. Even with her mother gone, knowing her dad was alone, she couldn't bring herself to spend much time with him. I wondered if that was part of the reason for Nicole staying here. Our daughter could keep her grandad company as well as conveniently be out of the way, so Karen and Chris could do whatever it was they wanted to do without having a kid hanging around.

As I pulled in outside the house on Hillroyd Road, I noticed the front garden was overgrown. I guessed Frank hadn't felt up to it since Maureen left us. I couldn't blame him. Yet with the summer we were having, and the lack of rainfall, it was apt to go wild if it wasn't attended to.

I left the Volvo behind his Ford Focus. At least I knew he was home. I'd only spoken to him on the phone a few times since the funeral. Considered the odd man-to-man talk over a pint now and again, but bottled out at the last minute. Our relationship hadn't quite been the same since Karen and I split. I hadn't seen him for two years after she threw me out and we lost the house. Those years on the streets had taken their toll. It had been made clear I wasn't welcome at the in laws. But after I finally turned up here during the Angel case, the air had been cleared - but I was left with a bitter taste. I never got to say goodbye to Maureen, and our relationship was now strained, to say the least. For Frank, I just happened to be Nicole's biological father. He'd made it clear I'd let her down, and I had. I liked him - always had - but the good vibes had turned bad around him. I reckoned a part of him couldn't forgive the fact that I was a drinker.

I let the knocker drop twice, but I didn't need to. Nicole was at the window, parting the blinds as I stood at the door, an excited look on her face. Although I tried to see my daughter as often as I could - making up for lost time - it wasn't always easy and I never picked her up from here. Karen and I had agreed that a neutral place she could drop her off would be better all round. It suited me fine.

Seconds later, the door opened. Frank was standing there in his dressing gown and pyjamas, a week old stubble on his face.

'Morning.'

'You'd better come in then,' he said, turning his back and wandering off down the hall to the kitchen. 'I'll get the kettle on.'

He was doing his best, judging by the living room. He was an old-fashioned bloke, had no skills in the housework department, but he was trying. I remembered the last time I was standing here, holding Frank in my arms after he broke the news that Maureen was in the Christie Hospital, gravely ill. I knew he'd take it harder than most right then.

'Tea okay?'

'Fine,' I called out, sitting down on the couch and swallowing Nicole in my arms. My daughter. My flesh and blood. It felt good to see her, but every time I did, I was awash with guilt. I'd spent too long away from her. Missed important years down the bottom of a bottle, my mind lost, my heart broken. 'How's my baby?'

'Okaaaay,' she said. She wrapped her arms around my neck and squeezed tight. 'Bored. Are you taking me out?'

'I'm afraid not, sweet,' I said. 'Just thought I'd call round to see how you're doing.'

'And grandad.'

'And grandad too, of course.'

'Well can we go out at the weekend, then? I really, really want to see the new Ghostbusters film.'

'It's a date.'

'Mum's going to the Lakes...'

'Oh, is she now?'

'Yeah, with Claire and Paul.'

'And Chris.'

'Who else, dad?'

She was sharp. Always was. 'Listen, your mum said you've been having trouble at school. Want to tell me what's going on?'

'Not really...'

'Nicole, don't make me drag it out of you.'

'Drag what?'

'Your mum said you'd been fighting.'

'They deserved it.'

'Who deserved it?'

But with the energy of a typical seven-year-old, she tore herself away and bounded upstairs just as Frank came in with two mugs of tea. I don't know whether I was imagining it, but Frank was moving a little slower than normal. Maybe age had finally caught up with him.

'Karen said you were gonna phone,' he said. He crashed down on the couch. Dragged a hand through his stubble. 'Said you'd fallen out. Making a habit of that these days, aren't you?'

'She's no saint, Frank.'

'I know, I meant the both of you.'

'I was gonna call first, but... well, you know. Shouldn't have to phone just to see my daughter.'

'Not at all, Jimmy.'

'How long has she been here, Frank?'

A sigh. He took a gulp of tea and frowned. 'A few weeks. Since she got expelled from school. It's a good job it's the summer holidays, really. Gives Kaz a chance to find her a new one.'

I was almost taken aback by how casual this was for

him. Almost. No one would get in the way of Frank and his daughter. She could do no wrong. Perhaps if it wasn't for her, Nicole wouldn't be in this mess to begin with.

'Like she'll do a decent job of that,' I said.

'What do you mean?'

'She seems more concerned with her precious job than she is with our daughter.'

'I don't think it's like that, Jimmy.'

'Oh, I do,' I said. 'Always was. It's almost as if our daughter was an unfortunate distraction.'

'Come off it.'

'Can you see why I'm pissed off? Whose idea was it?'

'What do you mean?

'To stay here?'

'It was Karen's idea, but Nicole jumped at it. They're not getting on.'

'Yeah, and I wonder why that is...'

'You'll have to ask Nicole.'

'Frank, come on. What are you hiding? Why are you protecting her?'

'You what?'

'Karen,' I said. 'Seems to me like she should've known about the absences well before this fighting started.'

'Absences? What absences?'

'She said she'd been absent from school. Missing whole days, apparently.'

'Kaz said that?'

'Yeah.'

'You're kidding?' he said. 'Well, she never told me. She never mentioned anything like that. If I'd have known that I'd have worded her.'

'You really didn't know?'

He shook his head, shrugged. 'I just thought the kid wanted to stay to keep me company, you know...'

'Well, she probably does, but I can't help but think it suits Karen just fine, you know what I mean?'

He was quiet for a moment, nodding. I had a quick drink of tea and almost spat it out. I should've remembered that Frank had never made a good brew.

'That girl,' he said, shaking his head. 'I've a mind to give her a good bollocking, you know. So how many times has she been absent?'

'I don't know the details,' I said. Forced the tea down my throat, wishing it was something stronger. 'Just that she's not been in. Which begs the question...'

'Where has she been?'

'Exactly. Now can you see where I'm coming from? She's seven, Frank. Seven. And her mum - a teacher, for fuck's sake - should know better, you know what I mean? She should take her mind off her bloody job and start putting it on our child.'

'Point taken,' he said. 'And you're right. I'd be fucking livid as well.'

'I can't believe she's not mentioned it.'

'Not a dickie bird.'

Which was no surprise. If I had a fiver for every time that woman pissed me off, I'd be a millionaire by now. Sometimes I had to wonder why I ever married the silly cow.

'Has she said when she intends to take her back home?'

'She's been a bit vague, to be honest.'

'Figures.'

'But I'll be speaking to her, no doubt about that.'

'If you can get hold of her.'

'Aye.'

Nicole came bounding down the stairs then. It was time to have a good one to one, see if I could get out of her any more than what my ex wife was willing to tell me.

She came into the living room sheepishly, her head bowed. Handed me a piece of crumpled up paper from behind her back. It was like touching hot coals when I first laid my hands on it. It was a kid's picture, a scrawl really, nothing more, of a stick man walking towards a building. There was a sign jutting out from the edge of the child's crude rendition - four windows, a big door. The sign said 'The Pub'. I instinctively put my hand to my mouth to stop myself from swearing when I saw an arrow pointing to the stick man and the words 'your dad' written above it. It didn't quite work.

'Oh fucking hell, no...'

'What is it?'

I handed it to him and put my head in my hands, but Nicole had more. She still had her head bowed, and she was crying. She handed me more kid scrawls, which had more of the same stuff, plus little yellow post-it notes with horrible little bullying statements scribbled on them. 'Your dad a drunkard'. 'Your daddy pissed'. 'Your nana dead'.

'What the...'

'Don't,' I said. 'Just let's not go there right now.'

Nicole fell into my arms, blubbering.

'Is it true, dad?'

'Is what true, Nic?'

'Is that where you've been all this time? Is that where you were?'

'What?'

'The pub? Drinking beer?' She sniffed, wiped her nose on her sleeve. 'With that woman?'

'Woman?' I said. 'With what woman? Nicole? Who's done this? Who's been telling you stories?'

I lifted her chin, but she wouldn't look at me. I saw that Frank had his fists clenched.

'That's what they said. They kept saying it and saying it until I hit them.'

'And this is why you've not been in school?'

She nodded. Let her tears come harder.

'So you didn't have to listen to them say this stuff?'

This time, she ran back upstairs. Frank and I exchanged a look. I fell back into the couch, my head in my hands. How could I not have known my kid was going through this kind of shit? How the fuck did Karen not know? Or did she know and was keeping it from me? If that was really the case, then she was lower than I thought.

Kids or not, I'd like to wring their little bastard necks.

I phoned the school, then quickly hung up when I realised no one was there until September. It was the summer holidays, and the building would be desolate. I made a mental note of going there on the first day of the new term to speak to the head teacher directly. And if I could get the names of the kids doing this kind of mental harm to my daughter, I'd be round to speak to their parents too, sooner rather than later.

'I can't believe this,' I said. 'Frank, did you have any idea this was going on?'

'Not a bloody clue, Jimmy! Listen, son, if I'd have known you'd have been the first to know, you know that, don't you?'

'It's just so wrong...'

'It's kids,' he said. 'They have no idea of the harm they're doing.'

Karen was the next to receive a phone call, though it

just went straight to her voice mail. No doubt she was busy in yet another meeting. I left her a message to call me back, anyway. I'd be surprised if she bothered, and if she did, it wouldn't be in a hurry.

After the tears had stopped, and Nicole had come back downstairs, between us we got some sense from her. The bullying, it seemed, had been going on for some time, but had ramped up after Maureen died just before Christmas. So for the past six months or so, my daughter had been going to school expecting to be bullied by several kids in particular. It made my blood boil.

The absences were sporadic, spread apart over several months. Not too many to be of concern to her teacher, but they were enough for me. When I asked her where she was going on these days - the worst days - she said she went where she felt the most safe - her grandma's grave. It seemed the school hadn't done much to enquire as to why she was absent. No letter, no phone calls - certainly not to me - but I'd have to ask Karen for her side of things, if she bothered to take an interest in anything other than her job.

On these days, Nicole had taken her packed lunch and sat by Maureen's grave until it was time to go home. She'd walked around the cemetery, wondering why her dad was always in the pub and why he was with 'that woman' and not still with her mum.

It made my heart bleed to think she'd been carrying this on her shoulders for so long. And it made me sick with anger to think her teacher hadn't noticed any of this was going on. But I think what bothered me the most was the fact these kids knew anything at all about me and had chosen to bully my kid with such evil by choosing to tarnish me in the worst way possible in my daughter's little innocent head. It begged the question: where were they getting their information from?

After some persuading, Nicole gave up their names. Three little girls who knew no better but knew enough to know my kid was hurting thanks to their cruelty. The parents of Emily Martyn, Ashley Cross, and Mia Squires had better prepare themselves for a visit from me.

'I never liked that school anyway,' she said. 'None of my friends go there.'

It was true. I never wanted her to go to a Catholic school, but Karen had insisted. Just one of the many things we disagreed on. Her two best friends both went to the local state school up the road. Nicole had made it clear many times that she wanted to change schools. It was easier said than done. But now might be a good time to look into it. I'd make sure I had an input into things given the situation. Karen simply couldn't be trusted with the responsibility.

'I'm sorry, dad,' she said. She was sitting beside me on the couch, her head on my shoulder. Frank had gone for an overdue shower. 'I didn't mean to make you upset too.'

'I'm not upset, Nic,' I said. 'Just angry.'

'They deserved it.'

'Not with you, with them.'

'Oh,' she said. We were quiet for a moment. I was thinking about what I was going to say to the three kids who'd made her life a misery. She took a deep breath. 'Where did you go, dad? You know, when you disappeared for so long? Mum said you were up to no good.'

'Did she now?'

'Yeah, she said you were seeing someone else.'

'Well, it's not true, Nic,' I said. 'Far from the truth, in fact.'

But just how do you explain it to a seven-year-old? How

could I tell her that I lost my job, ended up on the streets, nearly took my own life? Drowned my pain at the bottom of a bottle...

'Look, I wasn't very well,' I said. 'We lost the house, remember? And your mum didn't love me anymore. I tried to call, lots of times, but your grandad...'

'Mum didn't love you?'

'No.'

She only ever really loved herself.

'And what about this woman you were with?'

I shook my head in despair, as much as disappointment that my kid had been lied to by her own mother. Karen knew there was no one else and never was. For me, that is. For the first time, it occurred to me that Chris might have been on the scene well before I left it.

'There was no woman, Nic,' I said. 'I promise. Just your silly daddy.'

'You're not silly, daddy,' she said. 'And I love you, even if mum doesn't.'

I consoled myself with those words as I drove away from the house. She was a good kid. A great kid. And I was proud of her for sticking up for herself, even if it took several months. I was proud of her even more for trying to ignore them, for walking away. I promised her that at the weekend, we'd go out for a burger and a movie and she could have as much popcorn and sweets as she wanted. We'd spend the whole day together, maybe even the weekend, and I'd put right what Karen had put wrong in her head.

I looked down at the kid scrawls on the passenger seat. The one of me walking to the pub. Toyed with the idea, for the briefest of moments, that I would put it up on the fridge as a stark reminder to steer clear of the booze. But then I knew it would just remind me of the pain and cruelty my girl had been through. I almost shredded it up with my one free hand as I steered the wheel, but quickly tossed it all into the glove box instead. Out of sight, out of mind. But I knew it wouldn't stay buried for long. Emily Martyn, Ashley Cross, Mia Squires. There was something vaguely familiar about one of those names, but I couldn't place it...

I sparked up. Took that shit in deep. Checked the clock on the dash and dialed up Fiona Watson. Got her on speakerphone as I headed back to the office. She took a while to answer, and when she did, there was an echo.

'I'll call you back shortly,' she said. 'Not a good time just now.'

'Make it quick.'

She did, less than two minutes later. I was approaching the city centre, my thoughts on Stevie and Lloyd and the shit that bastard Robertson had been up to.

'Good morning,' I said. It was another hot one, but I was pleased to see the thunderclouds were gathering on the horizon. 'Did you get what I asked for?'

'Depends which way you look at it,' she said. I could hear her blow smoke out. 'Anyway, we'll come to that in a minute. You first. I don't suppose you've got through all of it, but you must be up to speed on the major points...'

'He's a sly bastard.'

'You're not wrong.'

'Did she really have an abortion?'

'Oh yeah,' she said. 'I even interviewed her. I take it you've not got to that bit yet?'

'Fucking hell, you are good.'

'You wouldn't be the first to say that. So, come on. Am I worth it?'

'Every penny.'

I pulled over just before the Marble Arch and put my hazards on. Had one eye on the front door as we talked.

'And what do you think?'

'What do I think? It just gets better and better. Or worse, depending on which way you look at it. I mean, two marriages? Seriously? Is that guy right in the fucking head or what?'

'Mental, I know. But this is what he's like. It's all true. Every bit of it. Don't ask me just how he juggles this double life, because I don't know. But the camera doesn't lie, Jim. And don't get me started on Isabella. That poor kid.'

'At least give me something.'

'You'll read all about it if you spend some time with the hard drive.'

'The thought of it makes me want to throw up.'

'I know. But the general gist is this: Robertson is a friend of her father. Isabella, I mean. Not best mates or anything, but he knows him. Only he knows him as John Dawson. Jack Burns is a butcher - or was. He had his own business until it went to the wall like everything else during the recession. Dawson - A.K.A. DI Rob Robertson - used to be a regular customer. His wife - wife number one, Marie Dawson - used to drink in The Admiral pub with Katrina Burns. They used to work together a few years back. With me so far?'

'Just about.'

'Look, I've not got long. Just on a quick fag break, you know. Anyway. Isabella Burns told me that Robertson - and she had no idea of his double life as a senior copper, by the way - went to kiss her at a barbecue one summer night at the

Burns house. She said he collared her in the upstairs bathroom as she was on her way out. Took her totally by surprise.'

'Fucking hell.'

'And she was gob smacked, of course. But flattered, too. So she kissed him back.'

'Jesus.'

'I know, I know. She'd had a few drinks, you know, got all excited. It was a party. She was young and naïve.'

'Just how young are we talking.'

'Fourteen.'

'For fuck's sake...'

'And that's how it started. They began an affair. And from everything she told me when I interviewed her, he was the one controlling everything.'

'No doubt.'

'Although she admitted to being a willing partner. At least in the beginning. Of course, she didn't want her parents or anyone to know a thing. She told no one, not even her closest friends.'

'Hardly surprising,' I said. 'Though you'd think she'd confide in someone.'

'You're forgetting who was in charge here. Anyway, in a nutshell: Robertson goes and gets her pregnant. The kid's not been on the pill and that horrible bastard hasn't been using anything. She said they hadn't had a lot of sex, just two or three times.'

'Did he force her?'

'Apparently not, but that's not the point, anyway. She was underage, he knew it. She got pregnant when she was still fifteen. She admitted it all on tape.'

'What, at police HQ?'

'Fucking hell, no. She came to my house. She said she

wanted to keep the baby but felt pressured into getting rid. And, of course, she was scared. Bloody terrified, actually, of what the consequences would be if she did have it and the father's true identity came out.'

'Jesus...'

'The guy's a lunatic, Jim.'

'I know.'

'And I'm really beginning to think he is actually, you know... fucking nuts.'

'You and me both.'

'It's just not the behaviour of a respectable copper.'

'Not just a copper! Anyone!'

'Which brings me to the crux of it all,' she said. 'Can you see, now, that what he did with me and with Doctor Webb is just the tip of the iceberg?'

'This is proper psychopathic behaviour,' I said. 'I mean, this can't be normal, surely...'

'Isabella said that too,' she said. 'Now she's a bit older and a bit wiser, and she knows she's been manipulated all along - leaving a very bitter taste, I might add - she's beginning to wonder if she's to blame for everything. It was all her fault, you know...'

'Bastard.'

'And she's started self harming now too,' she said. 'Cutting her arms, that kind of thing. Basically, Jim, he's ruined that poor girl's life and now he's washing his hands of her.'

'The absolute cunt...'

'And swanning around HQ like the big boss he thinks he is.'

I was almost ready to put my foot down and speed straight to the horrible bastard, drag him out of his little fucking office, and beat the living shit out of him.

Instead, I sat there, one eye on the entrance to the

Marble Arch, wondering when it would open. It had to be soon.

'Jim?'

'Yeah?'

'Did you hear what I just said? I said she's willing to testify in court, when the time comes. Which I think is very brave of her.'

'Who, Isabella?'

'Of course.'

'Can I meet her?'

'I don't think that's a good idea yet. But maybe one day...'

'Do her parents know?'

'No. And they might never know. I'm taking Isabella's confidentiality very seriously. And you should too. But when you get a chance, catch up with what else is on the hard drive. I need you up to speed.'

I told her I would, naturally. But right now, I was just about taking it all in. I asked her about the information I wanted, taking my notepad out and tossing the fag out of the window.

'So I checked the number plate,' she said. 'CV15 TYK is registered to a guy called Liam MacNamara.'

'Address?'

'The vehicle's registered to an address in North Wales. Porthmadog, to be precise. Though it's a business address, not residential. A garage, actually. But when I checked the business out online, it appears it had gone under. And not only that, the garage, it turns out, had been the victim of an 'arson' attack late last year.'

'Insurance job?'

'Possibly. Anyway, that's the Range Rover. Liam MacNamara, whoever that is.'

I had an idea of who that might be.

'And Colin Black?'

'Ah, Colin Black. So this is where it gets interesting. Pin back your ears.'

'Just get on with it.'

'I'll be quick. I'm getting some funny looks right now. Was due back in five minutes ago.'

'Give me all you've got.'

'All right,' she said. 'I knew when you said his name that I'd heard it before. Colin Black isn't all he's cracked up to be. First off, that's not his real name. His real name is Trevor Hardy, fifty-nine years old. He's also been known as Peter Moore, Robert West and Terence Hammond, among others. This guy's got more aliases than I've had hot dinners. Well, maybe an exaggeration, but...'

'So why the aliases?'

'Oh, he's done time for all sorts, going right back to the seventies. GBH, robbery, assault, fraud. Trouble is, every time he came out of prison, he changed his name and started over again. He's been known as Colin Black since twenty twelve. Before that, he was known as Shaun Cox. He was locked up in Strangeways again for a serious assault as Shaun Cox, but when he got out, Colin Black made an appearance. He's been Colin Black ever since. He'd bitten a guy's ear off in a pub fight. GBH again. He's a violent man, Jim.'

'Sounds it,' I said. 'I'm surprised they let him out. He capable of murder, you think?'

'No doubt. Though he's not on record for any of that.'

'Look, I need everything you can get on this guy,' I said. 'I mean everything. And this Liam MacNamara too. Are there any links to the far right?'

'Not that I'm aware of, but I suppose I can check. Look, I've got to go.'

'Call me back when you can.'

'After work, okay?'

'My phone's always on...'

But she'd hung up before I could finish.

So. Real name Trevor Hardy. Last known as Shaun Cox. Now Colin Black. It sounded like this guy knew how to recreate himself, even if he kept getting caught, usually for violence by the sound of things. And if he was easily prone to knocking teeth out, perhaps he was prone to the most severe acts of violence too.

I sat and breathed deep, still with one eye on the door of the Marble Arch. Let the traffic rush past me and the sun blaze down. If I could escape to a desert island, I would, and I wouldn't turn back.

As the door to the pub opened, I turned the key in the ignition and moved off back to the office. Compartmentalised the drink I needed into a deep corner of my brain and locked it away. I knew I'd be scrambling to unlock it soon.

'Thank God you're back,' Bob said. 'I need to get right out of this bloody stifling oven you call an office and sit back on a sun lounger with a nice cold beer.'

'Don't we all,' I said. 'But we've got work to do. Did you manage to dig anything out?'

'It's been very quiet on here,' Laura said. 'Virtually no traffic whatsoever. Aside from what we know about the rally, there's nothing. Though Dave called in about half an hour ago. Said he's happy to do some shopping for you today if that suits? He can rig everything up. Did you see Karen?'

'No, her father. Is Dave with Maya?'

'As far as I know.'

'Okay, you go with him. Use the business account. Tell him no expense spared. I take it you're in the car today?'

But she was already phoning down to Maya. I turned to Bob, who was looking lost in his own world. I suppose he had a lot on his mind.

'Have you been in touch with Margaret?'

He broke from his trance and turned in his chair. 'Not yet, lad. But I will. I trust you've spoken to your ex?'

'Tried to. She's got a lot to answer for.'

I didn't see much point in discussing it. There were some things in life you just had to keep to yourself. And there was no use sharing any of it with Bob. It was pretty clear to me he had more important things on his mind than Karen and my kid. The anguish was written all over his face.

When Laura had finished on the phone and was getting her things together, I told them about Colin Black's aliases. Like me, they were just as confused.

'That's just made my head hurt,' she said. 'So you're saying he's now calling himself Colin Black, but that's not his real name?'

'That's right. He was born one Trevor Hardy in nineteen fifty-seven. And since his first sentence for GBH, he's changed his name, or at least he's been calling himself by something else. I've asked Fiona for all I can get on him.'

'Start afresh after every sentence,' Laura said.

'Or assume a new identity at every opportunity,' Bob said. 'So he can fool everyone. Character traits of a true psychopath.'

I couldn't help but think of Robertson. I reeled off the list of names Fiona had given me and Laura noted them down for later exploration.

'Whatever his motives, this is our man. And we've got our work cut out with him. The good thing is, we now have several more names to research. And also, I think I know who Liam is.'

'Who's Liam?'

Bob told her while I made a quick phone call. I was relieved to be leaving the car parked up. I had a bad case of the sweats. Nothing a cold, refreshing drink wouldn't sort out.

'You can't be sure, though,' Bob said, after I'd hung up. 'About this Liam MacNamara. Whether it's the same guy, I mean.'

'Can't be sure of anything,' I said, nodding. 'I know that. But according to Fiona, the PNC says the Range Rover's registered to him. If it's the same guy, that's more evidence the Range Rover - or rather the occupants of it - were directly connected to Stevie and, ultimately, Steve's murder. Then there's Lloyd, of course.'

'Yeah,' Bob said. He picked up a copy of the Evening Chronicle, the paper where he built a career as a crime correspondent. Handed it to me. 'Have you seen the paper?'

It was all over the front page. MAN GUNNED DOWN IN PARK. Beside it was a picture of the SOC tent. And below that, the proclamation of 'witnesses at the scene'. If the paper had found witnesses, then what were Robertson and the police hiding? Either the paper was lying through its back teeth - something Bob had readily admitted it had done in the past - or they knew more on the ground than the police did. I skimmed through the first paragraphs, shaking my head. Apparently, there were several witnesses who'd seen the gunman, but the facts were somewhat blurry, to say the least. It was clear, though, that a lot of people had seen the car go up in flames. That much we knew anyway.

'You reckon you can speak to someone at the paper?' I said. 'Maybe find out who these witnesses are? Get their contacts? Or am I clutching at straws here...?'

'I'm already on it,' he said. He stood up. 'I've made some calls.'

'Called in some favours?'

'Something like that, lad,' he said. 'But I need to go out, anyway. Got to see a man about a dog.'

'Anything I should know about?'

But he didn't answer, just fished a Montecristo from his top shirt pocket and put his leather fedora on. Laura called out as she was halfway out the door, said she'd be in touch later.

Bob sparked up. 'Could be these witnesses actually saw nothing, and the reporter had just added that in.'

'As if it didn't matter...'

'But it's more than likely to be the truth. And anyway, you saw Lloyd yourself, didn't you? So you know yourself he was shot before the car went up.'

'But if there are witnesses to corroborate what I already know...'

'It helps your case, I know,' he said. He blew a cloud of cigar smoke to the ceiling. 'I'd think about getting some decent air con, lad. Seriously.'

'Bob, where are you going? Is there something you're not telling me?'

He held his hands up. 'Just a few things to sort out. That's all. Don't you worry about me.'

'But I am worried.'

'It's all in hand.'

'You've been making a lot of phone calls lately. Is this Bob Turner making them or Alvaro Garcia?'

He looked me in the eye. 'Just leave it now, lad. All right? It's personal.'

He took a drag on his cigar, tipped his hat, and said he'd be in touch. I watched him leave the building and walk across the street. Whatever he was up to, I knew I couldn't stand in his way. Wouldn't want to, either.

I rummaged around for the brandy he'd been nailing and found the last measure sitting lonely at the bottom of the bottle. Unscrewed the cap and tipped it back. Felt the burn. Tossed the empty bottle into the bin and sparked up. Took that shit in deep.

Ten minutes later, I was on a bus to Salford.

CHAPTER FOURTEEN

The Wilton Arms was a typical nineteen seventies Holts pub in the heart of a run down council estate in Pendleton, Salford. It was the pub where Shannon and her friend had last night murdered several karaoke classics and had drank the night away with the other locals who no doubt fancied themselves as club singers belting out tracks by Meatloaf and Queen and the Bee Gees. I stepped up to the bar and got myself an ice cold pint of Diamond. I launched it back, let the stresses seep out, and immediately got myself another and a bottle for Shannon, who was sitting alone at a corner table near the back window. She assured me that my idea of the weekly karaoke night was spot on, but that it was the only night of the week she and her friend enjoyed.

It had been difficult going out for a drink, ever since the police knocked on her door to tell her of Stevie's remains. Like lots of people, she scraped by on a very tight budget, but her one night out a week meant so much more when she had good friends to help her through and the people who drank in here had done more than most to help her through the worst of times. This place was one of the few things that would truly make her smile.

'You can't smoke in pubs anymore,' she said, removing a cigarette from the packet on the table. 'The powers that be don't like it. But Norman,' she said, nodding to the big guy who was bringing a large plastic ashtray to us, 'doesn't give a fuck. Do you Norm? And if it's okay with the landlord...'

'Don't mind if I do,' I said. I sparked up myself and watched Norman disappear down into the cellar. The Smiths were singing on the jukebox about shoplifters of the world uniting and taking over. Looking around at the faces dotted about the pub, I doubted anyone could muster any enthusiasm for Morrisey's call to arms. 'Like a blast from the past.'

'What, the smoking?'

'And The Smiths.' I said. 'Anyway, on the phone you said you'd been busy asking questions last night.'

'When I could get a word in,' she said. 'Couldn't hear myself think over all the noise. It was hammered in here last night. Not like now.'

'Everyone's at work, I expect.'

'Or in bed,' she said. 'Or the bookies.'

I took a long drink. Asked her if she minded me recording the conversation. She told me to do whatever I wanted. I put the phone between us and saw no point in wasting time. Got down to the bare bones.

'The suicides,' I said. 'You said there'd been a few. One guy you knew...'

She nodded. 'Carl McDermott. He's the guy I knew, the one I was talking about. Turns out he hung himself. They found him on a Sunday morning. But I found out there were more. A lot more, actually.'

'Suicides?'

'Yeah,' she said, blowing smoke out. She drank the neck of her beer. Rummaged around in her pocket and brought out a slip of paper. 'Quite a few. I wrote the names down. Had to pretend I was writing down the songs I was lining up to sing, you know. People would think I was morbid otherwise. I mean, it's a pretty grim subject.'

I was impressed. I counted nine names. 'Who told you about all of these men?'

'A few people, actually.'

'Anyone in here now?'

She shook her head. 'But the interesting thing is that they all went to Ivy Brook. Like Stevie and me.'

I thought about what Bob had said about kids in care being linked to suicides in Lancashire and Wales. Shook my head, downed half my pint, and took the nicotine in deep. 'Did they all die by hanging?'

'Oh, they're not all dead,' she said. 'Five of them managed it while the other four had attempted suicide but survived.'

'Really?'

She was nodding. 'I mean, the care system was a cruel place. Really, really shit. I knew there were a lot of people sent... well, ended up coming out of the system worse than when they went in, you know. So to me it's no surprise. But nine is a lot, I know.'

'Did they all live around here?'

'Oh yeah, they were well known around here. Regulars in this very pub. I told you I'd find stuff out in here. Everyone knows everyone's business.'

I wondered if anyone had witnessed Lloyd's assassination, too.

'So, roughly how old were these men? I mean, are they

recent or what? I mean, of the suicides, how long ago did they...you know?'

She grabbed the list and spread the paper on the table, moving the ashtray aside to make room. Turned the paper around so we could both see. With her index finger, she went down the list one by one.

'So Carl McDermott, we know about. Hung himself not that long ago. Six months, so I'm told. He was found...'

'On a Sunday morning in his flat. You know his age?'

She shook her head. 'Similar age to our Stevie. Thirty-eight, thirty-nine. Or thereabouts.'

'Is it the same for all of them?'

'No,' she said. Took a hard drag. 'These deaths are going back a good few years. So I don't know how old they all were, but I suppose we can take a rough estimate. Between thirty-five and forty-five?'

'That'll do for me. Go on.'

'Okay. Jimmy Carroll. Hanging. They found him one Monday morning at a Metrolink station. They had to close the line all morning, apparently.'

'Jesus.'

'I know. Paul Lennon. Now he's one that tried but failed. Overdose. Norman told me it sent him nuts. Lack of oxygen to his brain or something. Anyway, he took a load of tablets with a bottle of vodka, but the paramedics got to him in time. He's now looked after in the community, you know. Has a carer, all that. Sees a psychiatrist once a month.'

'Mental health stuff?'

She nodded. 'Poor bastard. Now the next one, Alan Pickering. He's an interesting one. You might be able to speak to him yourself. He was even in here last night.'

'What, drinking?'

'When you could get him off the karaoke, yeah. They

usually let him have three goes. Always the same song. Anyway, he cut his wrists. I always wondered what the scars were and stupidly thought it must be from an operation or something. I mean, duh. He'd sliced himself up - in here, would you believe - on a Wednesday lunchtime. Strange one, really. In the men's toilets, you know. Someone found him on the floor, covered in blood.'

'How long ago?'

'About three years ago,' she said. 'Norman will tell you, I'm sure.'

I turned around to see Norman reading a paper he'd spread out on the bar. On the TV on the wall beyond, Sky News was reporting a military coup in Turkey.

'Mark Reynolds,' she said. 'He was forty. Threw himself in front of the 09:37 from Blackpool to Victoria on his fortieth birthday. Left two kids. Twin girls. His wife drinks in here, but only on Sunday afternoons. Got a new man now. They had a massive domestic, apparently. Then he went and did that. Absolutely fucking tragic.'

'What's his wife called?'

'Katrina. You know, like Katrina and the Waves.'

'Carry on.'

'Okay. Robbie White. Now he's another one that tried but failed. There's no telling he might have another go because apparently he's...you know.'

'No.'

'A bit... well, a bit mental. One of these ones that does really daft stuff, you know. He went into Sainsbury's and got his dick out. Drove a BMW into a petrol station and tried to blow it up. Stabbed a man in the neck. Not just any man, either. One of the Roberts brothers.'

'Gangsters?'

She nodded, dragged her smoke down to the filter, and

immediately sparked up again. 'John Roberts, the older one. Apparently he was pissing himself, swinging a pool cue around the pub with a knife sticking out of his neck.'

'What, in here?'

'No, the Flying Horse. Eccles. Anyway, just a few examples of just how nuts Robbie White is. He walked in front of a truck. Out on Eccles Old Road. Not that far from here. Smashed up both of his legs. Spinal damage. He's now confined to a wheelchair, poor bastard.'

'He drink in here too?'

'Wouldn't surprise me,' she said. 'Ask Norman. He knows everyone.'

'Next one.'

'John Forbes. Bizarre one, this. He threw himself into a quarry up in Bury. Ramsbottom. Though the verdict was suicide, a lot of people around here reckon he was bumped off, you know.'

'Murdered?'

She was nodding. 'Just because it was completely out of character. Now I knew him too. He was a nice lad. But a few reckon he might've got himself into trouble. Out of his depth with some drug dealers or something. They found his body at the bottom of this quarry. It was a long fall. But if he really wanted to kill himself, why not just jump from a building or something? You know, why there?'

'Seems odd, I agree.'

'Anyway. He's gone. The last two now. Dominic Pearson. Just a straightforward overdose. But he failed. He's another that might try again. Now he definitely drinks in here. Sits on his own in the corner.'

'Was he in here last night?'

'No,' she said, before taking a long drink. I did the same. 'He only ever comes in on a Tuesday night. His mum drinks in here as well. I suppose you might be able to speak to him yourself. And last one...'

'David Mitchell.'

'David Mitchell,' she said. 'Threw himself off a car park roof at rush hour. In town, this was. He wasn't messing about. But he ruined a lot of people's commute home that night, the selfish twat. They had to close Shudehill all night to clean up the mess.'

But I wasn't listening. Instead, I was standing on that ledge myself with Angel behind me, her peroxide blonde hair blowing in the wind.

'Jim?'

I snapped out of it as quickly as I'd fallen in.

'And that's it. As many as I could find out about, at least.'

'And the ones who failed - are they still living around here?'

'All of them, as far as I know. You might be better off speaking to a few other people yourself, like I said. Norman will probably be able to give you all you need.'

I looked around again and clocked Norman, still reading the paper. I'd probably collar him on the way out. In the meantime, I pulled the copy of the Evening Chronicle I had in my pocket and handed it over.

'It's Lloyd,' I said. 'A friend of mine. A friend of Stevie's. I think the people who did it might also be the ones responsible for Stevie's murder.'

'Oh my god, he was at the funeral, wasn't he? He's the one who got you to look into Stevie, right?'

'That's right.'

'Jesus.'

I watched as she read, shaking her head. A text message pinged on my phone. Resisted the urge, for now, to check it.

Instead, I scanned the room for anyone else who might look like they'd talk. There were probably less than a dozen faces scattered around, including the landlord. None looked too happy, their heads buried in newspapers or hypnotised by the TV. But maybe one or two would develop a loose tongue given the right amount of ale.

'Terrible,' she said. 'Gunned down? What, like, shot?'

I nodded. 'Then they set the car alight, with him in it.'

'You know, I'm sure I heard people talking about this last night.'

'Really?'

She nodded. This was interesting. The murder had occurred only two nights ago. I knew word could get around fast, but as far as I knew, it wasn't in the press until today. So who had been talking about it? Anyone who could've witnessed it? I knew that by the time I could feel the heat from the flames myself, a crowd had gathered. As far as I was aware, no one knew or could've known there was a dead man inside unless they'd seen something earlier. Had someone watched Lloyd drive his Vectra in a panic onto the grass at Albert Park, only to watch him get shot in the head before the car went up? Had someone seen the Range Rover, or better still, who was inside it? And would they be willing to talk? Or maybe someone or several people had witnessed the assassination but wanted to keep their mouths shut for safety reasons. Perhaps the killers were well known. The type of bastards who could easily hurt people.

'Says he's left a wife and two kids,' she said. 'God, that's awful. I can't imagine what they must be going through.'

Maybe they wouldn't have to be going through anything if I'd have done my job better. 'This Liam you mentioned,' I said. 'The guy who turned up with Stevie that day.'

'What about him?'

'I think I might have a name. Does the surname MacNamara ring any bells?'

She thought for a moment, then shook her head. 'Sorry.
Not really.'

'It's just... well, I think this Liam might be connected to
Stevie's death. I think he may be a key person in my investigation. Have the police mentioned anything about him to
you? Have they been to see you since we last discussed it?'

'The police? No. That prick detective? Robertson? No,
they've not been round. Makes me wonder if they're even
bothered about finding Stevie's killer. I'm not even sure they
think he was murdered.'

'I know what you mean,' I said. And given what I now
knew about Robertson, I wouldn't have been surprised if he
ever cared. Stevie - and now Lloyd - were just statistics in a
world full of noise. 'And that's the reason I'm involved.'

'I can't believe Lloyd's dead,' she said. 'Are you sure it's
him? He seemed like a nice man. He was Stevie's friend
from the Sanctuary place. Murdered? Why?'

'Exactly,' I said. 'Why him? Why Steve? Why anyone?'

'Well, this definitely can't be suicide, can it?'

'I very much doubt it, Shannon.'

'I don't get it,' she said, slumping back in her seat. 'I just
don't get it.'

I didn't either. 'Listen, have you seen anyone hanging
around your flat? Anyone you recognise - particularly this
Liam character - or anyone behaving strangely?'

'No,' she said. 'No one.'

'Any white Range Rovers knocking around?'

'No.'

'This kid you were with when we called to see you -'

'What, Jamie?'

'Whatever he's called. The kid who was in your bedroom. How well do you know him?'

She laughed, embarrassed. 'Just... well, he's not my boyfriend or anything. Just slept with him a few times, you know. It can get lonely sometimes at my age.'

'You know him well?'

'Well enough,' she said. 'Known him a few months...'

'Does he drink in here?'

'Sometimes,' she said. 'Look, what are you getting at, Jim?'

I didn't know if I was getting at anything. But I had a sudden itch to keep her safe. 'Nothing,' I said. 'Just putting feelers out, that's all. Just trying to make sense of things. But I reckon you should keep your eye out, just in case.'

'In case of what? Shit, you're scaring me now.'

'Don't be silly,' I said. I watched her drink up, then stood to get us another, but she stopped me.

'I need to go,' she said. 'Get some shopping done, you know. And I can get a bit too cosy in the pub if I'm not careful. Thanks for the beer.'

'Thanks for the information,' I said, pocketing the list she'd written down. 'And I'm still on the case. For Stevie, I mean.'

'Are you looking into Lloyd too?'

'Comes with the territory.'

'So you think it's connected?'

I nodded.

'Then I need to know why as well,' she said. 'Stay in touch, Jim. Keep me updated.'

'I will.'

Then she left, leaving me standing at a dead bar. Norman caught my eye and I sparked up, asked for the same again. I watched Shannon walk away through the window, thinking that young Jamie was a pretty lucky kid.

———

'Not seen you in here before,' he said, handing me a fresh pint. 'New to the area? A word of advice - leave.'

'No,' I said. I took out a business card and pushed it across the bar. 'Here on business.'

While he scanned the card, I scanned him and took the head off my pint. Felt good. Norman was a big guy, the kind of man who could handle himself in a fight if he ever needed to. I suppose he'd have to be if he was the landlord here.

'Private investigator, eh?' he said. 'That's a new one on me.'

'Not many of us around these parts.'

'Well, you can't do any worse than the police around here. Even the coppers are dodgy.'

'Don't I know it.'

'So what're you investigating? Anything important? Shannon been swindling the DWP again?'

'Nothing like that,' I said. 'You may have heard about her brother?'

He nodded, grabbed his brew from the shelf behind him. 'I heard it,' he said, pocketing the card in his top pocket. 'Never knew him, but Shannon was in a bad way for a few weeks. Must've been tough for the girl.'

'It still is,' I said. 'I'm looking into the circumstances surrounding his death. I don't think it was an accident.'

'Murder?'

'Oh yeah.'

'Thought as much.'

'Why's that?'

'Not many people go up in flames unless it's a deliberate act from someone else. And I've seen men burn. Done my share of active service, you know. Northern Ireland, Iraq. Can't say I'll ever forget the smell of burnt flesh under the blistering sun. Not nice.'

He wasn't lying, judging by the tattoos on his arms. I could make out a crest for the Lancashire Fusiliers on his bicep, among others.

'I'm sure it isn't.' I took another drink while I weighed up what I was going to ask him, but he went first.

'Much prefer pulling pints these days. Anyway, anything I can help you with?'

Took a long drag on the smoke. Took that shit in deep and blew a cloud above us. 'As a matter of fact, you might be able to help me.' Shook out the list Shannon had written and spread it on the bar. Norman put his specs on and leaned in. 'You might recognise some of these names.'

He took a quick look and nodded. 'I recognise them all. She was asking me about them last night. I did wonder why.'

'Yeah, well what I wanted to know,' I said, pointing to the ones who were still alive, 'is if any of these men come in here. Or if you know where I can find them. Would be a big help.'

'Can I ask why?'

I saw little point in pussyfooting around. 'Seems these men all have something in common,' I said. 'They all went to the same institution as Shannon's brother, Stevie.'

'What do you mean?'

'They all went to the same care home. During the eighties, maybe some of them before then. And I want to speak to a survivor - or several of them - to see if there's a pattern connected to the suicide attempts.'

'Yeah, well, you could just be seeing patterns where none exist,' he said. 'It's easily done. The only thing these men have in common is they're all fucked up. No one's fault. It's called life.'

'I reckon it's a bit more complicated than that. Just find it a bit strange that there's been so many suicides and suicide attempts from an age group ranging over ten years or thereabouts. From men who were all under the care of the same place.'

'And what's this got to do with the lad's death?'

'Maybe nothing. Or maybe something. I don't know. But I'd be a fool to not at least speak to the lads that didn't manage to pull it off, if you know what I mean. Ask them about Stevie, if they knew him. Ask them about Ivy Brook.'

'Ivy Brook?'

'The place they all went.'

'But wouldn't that be bringing back bad memories? You want to be the one responsible for them trying to top themselves again? You know, bringing it all back?'

There was a pause between us. Eyeballed him. 'I'm willing to take that risk.'

He shook his head and almost laughed. Grabbed a bottle of Auchentoshan from the top shelf and poured us both a dram. 'I like your style, Mr. Locke,' he said. 'A man who knows what he wants. Cheers.'

I downed it in one. Felt the burn. 'You don't ask,' I said, 'you don't get.'

He nodded, sparked one up himself and pointed over to the opposite corner of the room, over near the vault. 'You'll catch him in there in about ten minutes. Tall and thin, glasses. You'll notice the scars on both wrists. Name's Alan

Pickering. Obsessed with Buddy Holly. Tell him you're a friend of mine. That's the best I can do for now.'

I took the pint through and sat myself down at an empty table in a quiet room. It was a good opportunity to check the text. The lunchtime news came on, the volume on low. Sat back in a golden ray of thirty degree sunshine and checked the phone.

ALMOST DONE!! GOT SOME PROPER GEAR! Xxx

Dialed her up. She answered straight away.

'How much?'

'We're on the way back now. Three and a half grand.'

I could hear what I assumed was Dave's fancy car purring like a kitten. 'Jesus, Laura...'

'You said no expenses spared. We got some fantastic stuff.'

'I should think so. It better be worth it.'

'It is,' she said. 'Dave got us a discount as well. Two laptops, a brand new Mac, a new printer and a shit load of high end software. I think you'll be pleased.'

'Is he still gonna rig it all up?'

'As soon as we get back. The important thing is we're well protected whereas we weren't before. Dave's gonna teach us some tricks so that we can 'hide' when we're going about our business online. The software will go on both laptops too. Believe me, it's much better than what we've been used to. Like something out of Star Trek.'

'So you're able to beam me up whenever you require now?'

'Chance would be a fine thing.'

'Well listen, if you play your cards right, tonight might be the night.'

'I've heard those promises before.'

'Yeah, well, this time I mean it.'

'Must be the heat.'

'Making the blood go to parts I never knew existed.'

'I'll have to give you a thorough examination tonight, Jim Locke.'

'Is that a promise?'

'It's an order,' she said, which was enough to make me want to get started immediately. 'But on a serious note, I wanted to talk to you about Bob.'

'What about him?'

'Look, I know he's your friend and everything, and you're letting him stay on our couch because you care, but I really think you should have a word.'

'Any reason?'

'Jim, he's not all there at the minute. He's been staring into space all morning. And last night, he drank nearly all of that brandy.'

'I think he's got a lot of stuff on his mind.'

'Obviously, but you need to have a word. Or at least keep him away from the office. He's bringing me down.'

'I can't just ask him to leave like that.'

'We agreed a fortnight, so a fortnight it is. But after that, I want him out of my flat.'

'You're the boss. But listen, love - do you think he's coping?'

'In a word, no. But would you? To be honest, I don't care. He's not my concern.'

'Come on, love, have a heart.'

'I have got a heart. And the best thing for him, if you really want my opinion, is to go home to his wife. He's no use here. And you can forget about getting laid until he's gone.'

'Okay, I'll speak to him. Ask him to stay out of your way.'

'That's not what I mean. If I'm honest, I'm worried about him. Just... I don't know. Just have a word. Sort it out. Do what you're good at. Where are you, by the way?'

I told her. Looked at the pint before me, convinced myself - and her - that I was on the case.

'Just be careful,' she said. 'I want you back in one piece. And Jim?'

'Yeah?'

'Can we go back to housewives and dodgy builders when all this blows over? It's stressing me out.'

I knew how she felt. 'It's a promise.'

But I only half believed it. I hung up after her assertion that Dave was eager to get started now that they were around the corner from the office. Sat there at that quiet table with the TV on low, a taste for whisky going through me like an arrow to my brain. Turned to see if Norman still had that bottle on the bar through the other room, but he was gone. When I turned back, a guy I could only describe as Buddy Holly returned from the dead burst through the doors and stepped up to the vault bar. A middle-aged woman pulled him a pint of bitter with no words exchanged. I watched him carefully place his coins down and spark up a long smoke. Took my cue and sparked up myself, tipping my pint to him and motioning to the seat in front.

'You must be Alan,' I said.

He broke into song then. 'Peggy Sue' had never sounded so raw. He didn't need a second invitation and looked like he needed the company. He approached the table and plonked his bitter down, spilling a mouthful on the beer mat. The woman behind the bar laughed and shook her head. We get them all in here...

'February 3rd, nineteen fifty-nine,' he said, sitting down. 'The day the music died. It's been shite ever since.'

I nodded. 'I'm a mate of Norman's,' I said, offering my hand. We shook. I noticed the scars on his wrists, both vertical and horizontal. Worse on his right arm. 'Jim Locke. I'm a Private investigator.'

'What, a detective? Like Hercule Poirot? Sherlock Holmes? That kind of thing?'

'Something like that,' I said. 'I used to work for the police but I don't anymore.'

He nodded. 'So go on. What's he done now?'

I had him down as mid fifties, thick-rimmed glasses like his hero, a lanky frame and pale skin. The scars were paler than the rest of him. Hair overlong and slicked back. Got the impression he wished he belonged to a different time. Had a voice like someone had forced a Brillo pad down his throat.

'Who?'

'Norman. Is that why you're here?'

'No, nothing like that,' I said. 'As a matter of fact, it's you I wanted to speak to. I hope you don't mind.'

'Me? Well, why would I mind?'

'Just... well, it's not every day a private investigator wants to speak to you.'

'Exactly,' he said. 'So that's even better, eh?'

'I suppose so.'

'So, go on. Ask me anything. Anything at all. I'm a font of all knowledge.'

I doubted that, but got down to it. This could be tricky. Sensitivity was hardly a strong point. 'Okay, Alan, I'm gonna be blunt. You might not like some of what I say.'

'Try me.'

'I mean, it might be tough going over some of this stuff.

But I think it might be necessary if I'm to get to the bottom of things.'

'Bottom of what?' He took a sip of bitter and a drag on his smoke. Crossed his legs and waited. I was half expecting him to break into a chorus of That'll Be The Day.

I suppose he deserved an explanation as to why I wanted to talk. But I feared he'd take what I wanted to ask him badly. And like Norman said, I didn't want to be the one to break him. But I knew I had to give him a reason why I wanted to dredge up the past. And a difficult past at that.

'There's a woman who drinks in here,' I said. 'Shannon. She was in here last night.'

'I know her,' he said. 'Lovely girl.'

'Yeah, well, you might have heard about her brother.'

He nodded. Took a drink. 'Steve, I believe he was called. Found dead in town. Burnt to death, am I right?'

Perhaps this could be easier than I thought. 'So you knew him?'

'Not really,' he said. 'But I heard about him. Everyone heard about him because he was her brother, you know. Couldn't have been a nice way to die. You only hope that he was knocked out or something, you know, before he was set on fire.'

Or dead already, I thought. 'Did you know he went to Ivy Brook? It doesn't exist anymore. It was a home for young men in care. Boys, really.'

He shifted in his seat, took another drink and looked away. Massive sigh, followed by a long drag on his smoke. He took that shit in deep. 'I know the place,' he said. 'Like the back of my hand.'

'You went there too, didn't you?'

He nodded. Bit his lip. 'Yeah,' he said. 'And the others. Lots of people, you know.'

'Was it long ago, or...?'

'Early eighties,' he said. 'I was twelve in nineteen eighty-one. Ended up in there 'cause my dad was knocking my mum about. He was a drinker, you know. Fucked up. And my mum was like a little bird. She couldn't handle herself, never mind me or my little sister.'

'So you ended up there?'

He nodded. Swallowed. 'Sometimes I think I'd have been better off at home.'

It was a trend I'd heard before. Get taken away from your circumstances and end up worse off under the care of some charitable organisation or a place run by the state. I had to wonder why so many had spoken of their past in those terms. Shannon had said it. Stevie had told me some things, too. So they must've had good reason to feel so strongly.

'It was a broken system, you see,' he said. 'Still is.'

'What do you mean?'

'Like a prison. The only thing missing was the bars. They treated us like shit. I know a lot of lads were beaten up. After dark, you know. You could hear it. Could hear them screaming.'

'Were you beaten up, Alan?'

He nodded 'We all were, as far as I know. The rule was that you only got beaten up if you didn't cave in to them. But we all caved in, eventually.'

'Cave in?' I said. 'What do you mean, Alan? Cave in to what?'

'Well, what they wanted, you know.'

'What who wanted?'

'The screws,' he said. 'Well, they weren't screws, but that's what we called them. If it looks like a screw, if it behaves like a screw, then it probably is a screw.'

'And what was it they wanted, Alan? Why did some lads get beaten up?'

He looked away a moment. Out the window, down at the floor. Took a drink of his pint and put it down hard on the table. Looked me in the eye. 'They wanted us to suck them off. You know. That kind of stuff. And worse. Much worse. They had their favourites. If you didn't want to, they'd either force you or kick your head in. So the beatings were common. Almost every single night. Fridays were the worst. They'd let us have booze, get us drunk, then it would start, you know. And when the girls were sent away, it was open season. They were a lot more relaxed about it. Instead of taking you to their room, this back room they had down in the basement, they came to yours instead. You could smell the fear, and I mean that literally.'

I needed a stiff drink. Walked back through to the main bar and got us two pints and a shot each of Auchentoshan. I downed my whisky and carried Alan's through. He was still sitting there, composed, but staring at the ashtray that was filling up. He'd sparked up again, and I joined him.

'There was a kid that died there,' he said. 'Tommy Clarke, he was called. A Saturday night, they found him. He'd cut his wrists. Everyone said there was blood everywhere, all over his bed sheets, all over the floor. He was only fourteen, a bit older than me. They think he'd nicked a bottle of rum from an office or something and drank it all before...you know, before he did it.'

Once again, I looked at the scars on Alan's own wrists. Wondered if I should ask him about it or see if he'd come up with it himself. But then he'd clocked me looking at them and held up his arms.

'I don't mind,' he said. 'You looking, I mean. I don't try to hide it. People look at them all the time, and they try to hide it, pretend they're not looking, you know. But this is real life. I carry the scars. It reminds me every day of what I carried with me - still carry - for thirty-odd years. It took me that long to try and do it. You know, do myself in. I wish I'd had the balls to do it then, like Tommy did. But I didn't, and it went on and on until I finally fucked off from the bastard place.'

'Must've been difficult...'

'Not even the half of it. And you know something? I think it still happens now. Not there because it's gone, but other places.'

'You think it's a common thing?'

'More common than you think.'

We were quiet a moment. Gave me a chance to get stuck into my pint. I thought about where this conversation was going, and I didn't want Alan, who I was beginning to quite like, to have to go through all that nasty stuff. I didn't want him going home thinking about it. But then maybe he thought about it every night, anyway.

'How long did it go on for?'

'As long as I was there,' he said. 'I left when I was eighteen because they couldn't keep me there.'

'Did the police ever find out?'

He laughed. 'Did they fuck. No, people were too scared to say anything. They really had us by the balls, you know. No pun intended.'

I wasn't laughing. 'So the authorities had no idea?'

'Wouldn't surprise me if the authorities were involved, you know.'

'You know that for certain?'

He took a slow drag. 'No. But I've wondered for so long - and I'm not the only one - about how it was allowed to continue unchallenged all this time. And we never really found out why the place was closed down, you know.'

I had to ask him. 'Look, Alan. Tell me to fuck off if you want, but... the scars. How did it come about?'

He laughed. 'How did it come about? How do you fucking think? I got a razor blade and I fucking slashed them, didn't I? Right here in the toilets. I wanted to die that day, Jim. And do you know what else? I wanted it to hurt. Don't ask fucking stupid questions.'

'I'm sorry.'

But he said nothing, just got stuck into his pint, and then his whisky. There was a heavy silence between us. The empty room felt that little bit emptier. Maybe this was really a bad idea after all. I should've listened to Norman. I'd put my foot in it and couldn't get out of it now.

'I wasn't the only one,' he said. 'You know, the only one who tried to top myself. I think I'm through it now. But there were a fair few of us. And we all went to Ivy Brook. There was a time when it seemed like one after the other was dropping. We called it the suicide club, some of us in here. The ones who got away - the lucky ones - well, they're long gone. It's the ones who're still here that are still fucked up. Suffering, you know. Do you want another? I could do with a drink, but I've only got a few quid on me, you know...'

I sent him to the bar with a twenty. Told him to keep the change. He came back with two more of the same and two more whiskies. I knew this was my line. Once I crossed, there was no going back. But I was willing to dive in for the cause. I sparked up, thinking about delving deeper. I wanted to jog Alan's memory just a bit more.

'I know this is hard, Alan, but can you think back? To that time, I mean?'

'Well, what do you want to know?'

What did I want I know? A few things. 'The screws you talked about. Look, I know this is hard, but - ,'

'It's not hard,' he said. 'I've talked about it before, loads of times. It's no secret I was abused. Like I say, a lot of us were. I'm not ashamed of it.'

I nodded. Downed the whisky, felt the burn. 'Do you remember any names? From that time? Any at all...'

'How could I forget? Might as well be tattooed on my brain.'

'Go on.'

'There were three of them,' he said. 'Three ring leaders. All bastards. The older one was a fat bloke called Bill. Bill Williams, if I remember. Huge man. Overpowering, you know. Six foot, massive, must have been twenty stone. He used to get us to...you know...'

I'm not sure I wanted to know, but I could guess. 'And the others?'

'Bill was probably in his fifties at the time. He's well dead now, died about ten years ago, I believe.'

And good riddance, too. 'Go on.'

'The other two. They were much younger, but they were still men, you know. A tall guy. Thin, rubbery skin. He liked Fridays a lot. Kenneth Regan. Kenneth fucking Regan.'

'And the third?'

There was a pause. He took a long, slow drag on his smoke before stubbing it out.

'I think he was the youngest. But he was the worst. Definitely the worst. Stocky, muscly. And racist. He used to love beating the black kids. It was like he really didn't give a fuck, you know. He was really violent. Pretty much ruled the place. Everyone was scared of him. You'd better do whatever he said otherwise - otherwise, you were well and truly fucked. The other two loved him because they got to get what they wanted because he was such a psychopath, you know. Trevor, he was called. Trevor Hardy. A total cunt.'

And there it was. An opening I'd been looking for. I guess I knew it in my guts, but to hear his name gave me a strange kind of thrill. The hairs on the back of my neck tingled.

'Trevor Hardy?' I said. 'Did you just say his name was Trevor Hardy?'

'You heard right,' he said. 'He's someone I'll never forget. He's the bastard that had me first.'

A lan had gotten more drunk with every round, insisting we had a whisky chaser with each pint. I could hardly blame him and I felt I owed him one for opening up like that. Seemed my constitution was holding up well. But the line had been crossed and there would be no going back tonight.

I put him in a taxi around four o'clock, just as the evening rush hour was building up. He didn't notice, but I put sixty quid in twenties in his shirt pocket and paid the taxi driver in advance. He'd struck me as a man who couldn't forget, didn't want to forget. Those things we talked about were imprinted on his memory. Like old photographs, a few things had faded over time, but he still remembered everything. Like his scars, the memories marked him. He was even able to corroborate some of the names on Shannon's list and suggested I speak to Robbie White, if I could find him.

'He'll tell you the gory details,' he'd said as he finished the last drink.

But I was pretty sure I didn't want to hear them. I'd gotten what I needed. I returned to the bar, eager to speak with Norman again, but he was nowhere to be seen. Got myself one for the road and took it to the front step. I sparked up and watched another storm cloud come in from the east, thinking about the hell those kids had gone through. All the pain and hurt and fear. I could see Trevor Hardy's face in my mind, certain he was the scumbag I wanted.

As I left the empty glass on the step, from somewhere inside, the jukebox kicked in. That'll Be The Day. I wondered if Stevie's ghost had been sitting with us, that maybe the empty room hadn't been so empty at all.

BLOOD

CHAPTER FIFTEEN

By the time my own taxi turned into Piccadilly, I was bursting for a piss and eager for another pint. I called Bob just as the heavens opened and a clap of thunder tore up the evening sky. There was no answer, which I half expected. He'd said he had things to do. But after what Laura had said about his mood and the fact that she wanted him out of the flat as soon as possible, it got me thinking that little bit more about his state of mind. I had a feeling myself that something wasn't right. Told myself I'd try him again in half an hour.

I sparked up and walked through the rain to a hidden bar I knew around the corner from the office in the Northern Quarter. With the end of work commute picking up a pace, it wouldn't be long before the bars saw business, but this one had a quiet booth in a dark corner. It was my kind of place for throwing caution to the wind. It had been one of those days. My daughter bullied, three grand out of pocket, Bob keeping secrets and Alan's story was enough to make me crawl to the bottle and hide in it.

I turned into Hell's Kitchen around Back Turner Street

and the cool, dark interior was a welcome retreat. Took a quick piss in a toilet full of graffiti before stepping up to the bar. Got myself a bottle of good American IPA served up expertly by a young rock chick who barely looked me in the face. Passed on the whisky, knowing it would be a mistake. I took the drink out into the backyard and sparked up. It was stifling. So hot you could fry an egg on the stone floor. But the light had darkened too. I looked up at the rain clouds, so heavy and black. Saw a flash of lightning and felt the electricity in the air. The atmosphere reflected my thoughts on recent events. Trevor Hardy. What else had this bastard done? I had a feeling that something was about to blow. And then the thunder came again. It was as if the world moved in response to my mood. When the rain came, battering down on the handful of smokers brave enough to face it, I stepped out from a shelter and let it wash over me. I felt drunk. But that was okay. The water felt good and cool, even if it put my smoke out.

I stepped back inside just as my phone rang. Was pleased to hear Bob's voice when I answered.

'Did you see a man about a dog?'

'I did, but the dog was out,' he said. 'Where are you, lad?'

I told him. He said he'd join me in ten minutes and to get him a drink. I got him the same and retreated to my booth, thinking about Nicole and the bullying she'd been through. At least now that she was expelled from the school, we could find somewhere more suitable, and better. I fired off a quick text to Karen, just to say that I'd want a key part in deciding where our daughter would be educated. There was no way I was leaving this kind of decision to her alone.

I called Laura to see where we were up to with the computer gear. It had to be ready now.

'Dave's just installing the software,' she said. 'Not long

now. It's all great, by the way. And I love my laptop. How did it go?'

'Got a lot of information from Shannon.'

'Stevie's sister, right?'

'Yeah,' I said. 'I'd asked her to find out what she could about these suicides. Turns out there were quite a few. And of the ones who attempted suicide but survived, I spoke to one. Alan Pickering. And guess what?'

'You sound drunk, Jim. How many have you had?'

'Just a few. Anyway, he gave me names of three men who worked at Ivy Brook. Get a pen.'

'Just tell me.'

I took a drink first. 'Bill Williams, Kenneth Regan and Trevor Hardy.'

'Trevor Hardy? You mean our Colin Black?'

'Let's not complicate things,' I said. 'But yeah, our main man.'

'Well, that makes things interesting.'

'Doesn't it just?'

'And he worked there?'

'So he says. But it's what he was doing with the kids they were supposed to be looking after you won't like.'

'Go on.'

'No, now's not the time for details,' I said. I clocked Bob walking through the door. 'But basically he abused them.'

'What, physically? Sexually?'

'Both. And the other two. Look, Bob's here. I'll maybe have a chat with him about what we discussed earlier.'

'Jesus,' she said. 'I wonder if he abused Stevie.'

The thought had entered my head, too. 'Maybe. I suppose we won't know for sure. But it sounds like he was just as racist back then as well. I suppose he always was.'

'How do you know?'

'Just something Alan said. Look, I've gotta go...'

'Rein the drinking in now, love. You'll never get it up in that condition.'

'You can count on it,' I said, before hanging up and taking another long drink. The beer was going down a treat. I was hungry, though. I knew I should make the effort to eat, but I just couldn't be bothered. It might have to be another night for junk.

'You look half cut, lad,' Bob said, sitting down opposite. I could have said the same about him. Had he been at the brandy again? And those worry lines on his forehead were getting deeper. 'Been busy?'

'I was gonna ask you the same thing.'

'You first.'

So I told him about my meeting with Shannon and the suicides from the Ivy Brook attendees. Showed him the list and went through each one. I stopped at Alan Pickering and gave him the details of my conversation with him. The fact that Trevor Hardy had been named as one of the key perpetrators told us we were well on the right track. And it raised more than an eyebrow with Bob.

'Haven't heard of the other two,' he said. 'But it goes back to what I said about all those suicides in the seventies. Kids in care homes around North Wales and Lancashire. I wonder if Ivy Brook is just another in a long line of places connected to those kinds of deaths.'

'It's a long list,' I said. 'And that's just nine we know of. Only five of whom actually managed it. As for the rest...'

'Perhaps you could try and speak with at least one more,' he said. 'Just to see if Hardy pops up again. Do you know a timeline? I mean, the year he started, the year he finished, that kind of thing?'

'No, but maybe Alan will know. I could always get in

touch with him again. Though I do feel a bit guilty for bringing it all back to him.'

'It'll be on record somewhere,' he said. 'Guaranteed.'

Which reminded me. Fiona said she would call after work. I checked the clock on my phone. It had just gone five. I expected an update around about now. Perhaps she could give me more on Trevor Hardy and the others. I reckon I needed more on Liam MacNamara, too. Whoever he was, it seemed he knew Hardy well. I wondered just how long he'd been an acquaintance. It occurred to me that perhaps his image was already on a print I had from the CCTV footage Graham had given me. If I could dig it out and show Shannon, maybe she could make an identification. Maybe.

'Go on, then,' I said. 'Your turn.'

'There's nothing to tell.'

'Come on, Bob...'

'Seriously, lad,' he said. 'Look, I said I had a few things to sort out while I was here - the reason I came back. And I'm sorting it. So that's it. Nothing to worry about.'

'Laura's worried about you.'

'What? About me? What for?'

'She said you were nailing the brandy last night, you know. Like it was your last.'

'It wasn't like that,' he said. 'And anyway, lad, as you know, I do have rather a few things on my mind. When you kill a man like I have, something changes inside. It's not a good feeling.'

'No doubt. But I know where she's coming from, Bob. You're not yourself.'

'Well, would you be? And anyway, you can talk.'

He was right. I'd had my moments with the bottle. 'I know that, but -'

'I'm sorry,' he said. 'Sometimes I don't think. Listen, I appreciate the concern. Honestly, I do. But this is just something I've got to deal with alone, you know? Give a man a break, eh?'

'I get that, but... well, are you planning on going back?'

'Well I can't stay here.'

'Well, is there anything I can do to help?'

He shook his head. 'No. But you can stop worrying about me. I'm fine. I'm dealing with it in my own way.'

'Are you sure?'

'Absolutely.'

He told me to shut up then. I got myself an overpriced 'Dirty Burger' and ate while he told me of his enquiries about the witnesses to Lloyd's murder. The ones that were on the front page of the Evening Chronicle. He'd made some calls - the ones he was willing to tell me about, at least - and came up with two names.

'Yvonne Carlisle,' he said. 'And Jordan Bowman. Yvonne turns out to be Jordan's auntie. Seems both were in the vicinity at the time, walking up Great Cheetham Street, wherever that is.'

'That's the main road beyond the park.'

'Right. So, they're walking to Yvonne's house when they see the Range Rover do a U-turn at the main junction there. They watch the Vectra drive through the main gates and onto the grass. The Range Rover comes back down the road and follows the Vectra. A man dressed all in black with a balaclava over his face then gets out and fires three shots into the windscreen.'

'And they see all this?

'So George says.'

'George Thornley? He still the editor?'

'The very same and yes, he is.'

'So he knows you're not dead?'

'Keep your voice down,' he said. 'We'll come to that in a minute.'

'Go on.'

'So, three shots. Then the guy pulls out a bottle of something, like a water gun, you know, and sprays liquid over the bonnet. He must be really close. Slings a match and - '

'Whoosh.'

'Up in flames. And it doesn't take long for fire to spread, lad. Give it a fuel source, in this case foam seats, plastic, engine parts, not to mention the flammable stuff he's thrown over it.'

'A body.'

He nodded. Drank from his beer. 'Until it reaches the petrol tank. And then it's goodnight Vienna.'

I could almost feel the heat again as I sat there, half drunk. I saw those bullet holes, the spider web cracks, the blood splatter. Lloyd's open mouth. Saw it all again before the whole thing blew, could smell the smoke, see it billowing like a black death across the Salford night sky and the city beyond. The crack of the metal. The headlights bearing down on me...

'So do we know what happened to Yvonne and Jordan?'

'They didn't stick around,' he said. 'I mean, would you? They must've shit themselves, lad. Only natural, I suppose. They later told the reporter they fucked off, sharpish. Someone else must've seen something as well, because they said they could hear the police sirens as they ran to Yvonne's house. I can only assume they stayed inside after that.'

'So someone had called them?'

'Maybe. Probably.'

'Could've been Lloyd himself.'

'Jesus, I never even thought of that. Yeah, it could've been, lad.'

'He'd sent me text messages, probably from the front seat as he drove. So it makes sense he might've phoned the police as well.'

'Is there any way of finding out?'

'If he did call, there'll be a record of it somewhere.'

'There's always a record, lad. Are you eating those chips?'

'Help yourself.'

He did, taking several handfuls. In the end, I just pushed the plate over and drained the bottle.

'Did you get addresses, phone numbers, anything like that?'

'No,' he said. 'Was lucky to get the names, to be honest. See, the chances are there were more witnesses. Yeah, supposedly it was a quiet night...'

'It was.'

'But there's a large population in the area.'

'A lot of students.'

'Exactly. It was late but not that late, am I right?'

I nodded.

'And after the event, or during, depending on which way you look at it, a crowd was gathering. That's what you told me, right?'

'Yeah.'

'So there could well be someone else out there - or several people - that saw stuff. Finding them, though. That's the tricky bit.'

'Even if I found them, would they talk?'

He shrugged with a mouthful of chips.

'Would it even be worth my time?'

'Up to you, lad, I suppose. Anyway, that's all they gave

me. Yvonne Carlisle and Jordan Bowman. They were the ones who spoke to the reporter, and from that came the front page. Couldn't get anything else.'

My phone pinged then. A text message from Karen:

SO DOES THIS MEAN YOU'LL BE SEEING HER MORE THAN ONCE A YEAR THEN??

She was a cheeky bitch and she knew it. It wouldn't have surprised me if she wasn't just trying to push my buttons. It was the kind of woman she was. Bitter and twisted. I considered firing back an immediate reply, but what good would that have done? Instead, I pocketed the phone and watched the bar fill up as Bob disappeared for a blast on his Montecristo. Considered dipping into the top shelf. There was a time when Karen could push me over the edge so that I got so bad I had to hit the hard stuff. I settled for another beer instead, figuring I'd save the whisky for later.

When Bob came back, his cigar half smoked, he suggested we move on somewhere else. By this time the jukebox had kicked in loud, AC/DC hammering out Gimme A Bullet. Got me thinking again about that bullet through Lloyd's head. Although the music was getting the blood pumping, I knew I wouldn't be able to hear myself think over all the noise. The bar was filling up quickly, and I could sense Bob needed a quieter space to talk. We returned to the street and a hard rain. It was welcome, but the humidity was still high.

'The Angel?' he said. 'Someone might be tickling the ivories...'

It was as good a place as any. A resident piano in the corner invited anyone who could play to jump on. I suspected Bob would find the piano a bit more soothing than Angus Young's balls out rock n roll guitar riffs, though I begged to differ. Though my mood called for grit and dirty drinking, I knew we also needed to discuss a few things. With Fiona's phone call on the horizon as well, at least in the Angel I could hear the phone ring. I didn't want to miss her call.

'So, these suicides in the seventies you were on about,' I said. 'I assume it was in the papers at the time?'

'Oh aye, lad,' he said. We walked out towards Shudehill for the short journey to the next pub. 'Though it was hardly front page news. Certainly not in any of the nationals. But locally, it was big. It didn't stay on the front pages for long, though.'

'No? Why's that?'

'Well,' he said. He sparked up the rest of his Montecristo. 'That's a good question and one I can't answer. But maybe the powers that be at the time decided it wasn't newsworthy, if you know what I mean...'

'You mean it was conveniently covered up?'

'That's not what I said.'

'But it's what you mean, isn't it?'

'It's very easy to make two plus two equal five, lad. I'd be careful if I were you. Jumping to conclusions should be the last resort of a private investigator.'

'Come on, Bob,' I said, sparking up my own. 'The world and his wife know there was a lot of dodgy shit going on in these parts. Bent politicians, needy D-List celebrities...'

'Not just around the North West,' he said. 'Everywhere, particularly London. Secret parties and stuff, you know. But you're right, there was a lot of dodgy shit going on.'

'Do you think Ivy Brook might've been one of those dodgy care homes, then?'

'I suppose it's entirely possible, yeah. But maybe now we'll never really know for sure. It's gone for good, hasn't it?'

'But some of the victims are still around. And at least one of the perpetrators, as far as we're aware.'

'You sure it's the same Trevor Hardy?'

'Can't be that many, can there?'

'It pays to make sure, though.'

I thought I could maybe show Alan an up-to-date picture of the bastard. Maybe that would make it certain. Tomorrow I would get a hold of him, bend his ear just one more time.

'But what does your gut tell you about this, Bob?' I said. 'You know I trust your judgement.'

'I know you do, lad. And my gut tells me you should be careful. Very careful.'

'You'd say that anyway,' I said. 'Even if I was knee deep in a theft of cakes from the Women's Institute or something.'

'Give over. This is serious, Jim. If Hardy is the guy that killed those poor men, if he's the same bloke that abused those vulnerable kids, then do you really think he's gonna give a toss about you?'

'That's if he even knows I'm on his case.'

'You said yourself they had you in their headlights,' he said. 'So either they know who you are or you were in the wrong place at the wrong time when they blew Lloyd's car up. Either way, for you, this is dangerous, lad. You're playing with fire...'

'I know, I know.'

'But do you?' We'd stopped at a pelican crossing, the heavy evening traffic of Rochdale Road buzzing past. The Angel was just a stone's throw away. 'Do you really?

Because you could be knee deep in shit here, lad, and you'll have no one to toss you a life jacket when it goes down.'

The thought had crossed my mind, too. But I couldn't retreat now. I had to finish what I'd started, for both Stevie's and Lloyd's sake, or all of this would count for nothing. Was I really putting myself at risk? Was I really playing with fire?

'I'll be fine,' I said, though I wasn't certain I believed it.

'You don't know that, lad. Look at the type of bloke this guy appears to be. A racist, fascist, far right sex abuser who's done time for all sorts, including grievous bodily harm. If he and his associates, whoever they may be, are responsible for the deaths of those two men, then what the bloody hell's to stop him from sorting you out? Eh? Answer me that, lad. Because I don't think you're fully aware of what you're involved in here. Things could go tits up very quickly when you're dealing with pricks like this.'

'You sound like you know from experience.'

'Bollocks,' he said. The pelican crossing finally beeped us across. 'It's my round, lad. Move your arse.'

———

'You say you're worried about me,' he said, 'but I'm beginning to worry about you. I think you might've finally lost your mind.'

'Come on, Bob. I know what I'm doing.'

'I don't think you do. And I think you should walk away.'

'You know I can't do that.'

'I know damn well that you can,' he said. 'Of course you can!'

'Bob, I'm involved anyway. Like you said, they had me in

their headlights. They were parked outside the office when they were following Lloyd...'

'So taking you out - which they could easily do - would solve a lot of problems for them. Wouldn't it? It makes complete sense, lad.'

We were halfway through another ale, and I was really feeling it. I think Bob was too, because he was slurring his words.

'Look, I know what you're saying,' I said. 'And I can see why you're worried. But I can look after myself, Bob.'

'You know you've said that before and look what happened.'

'I know, and when I took this on, I didn't expect them to kill Lloyd as well. If it wasn't for him asking me to take it on because he knew I knew Stevie, I'd still be knee deep in bored housewives and spying on skiving employees. I didn't expect it to go this far.'

'But it has, lad. So my advice is to step away now, while you've still got the chance.'

'I can't do that, Bob. You know it. You're wasting your time trying to convince me otherwise, so forget it. You'd be better off putting your energy into helping me nail the bastards.'

'Best left to the police.'

'And look what a balls up they're making of it,' I said. 'You know above anyone just how corrupt they are.'

'Not corrupt enough to turn a blind eye to this.'

'Maybe not a blind eye,' I said. 'But they're incompetent, as you well know. And Robertson, being the SIO - do you really think he's got their interests at heart? Do you think he gives a fuck about Shannon or Lloyd's wife and kids? After what we now know about him, does he fuck, Bob. But some-one's got to.'

'But it doesn't have to be you, does it? Let someone else carry that weight.'

'Yeah? Like who? There is no one else. I made a promise I intend to keep.'

'Loyalty like that could get you hurt, lad. That's all I'm saying.'

I took a half arsed drink, looked around the pub. Someone had taken root at the piano, which sounded out of tune.

'What if they've got someone else lined up?' I said.

'What do you mean?'

'I mean, these killings,' I said. 'There's got to be a reason for them. Why did they want them dead? To shut them up? For what?'

'You're not making any sense.'

'I'm just trying to make a connection, that's all. Piece this shit together. I mean, who else do they want dead?'

'So these four suicide attempts,' he said. 'The survivors.'

'Go on.'

'Not sure where I'm going with this, lad. But did Shannon ever mention anything about Stevie attempting suicide? Could he be number five?'

'I don't recall her saying anything.'

'But if he had - in the past, I mean   could he have been bumped off because of something he knew? Something he was going to blow open?'

'To shut him up, you mean?'

He nodded. 'Come on, I need a smoke.'

We stood out on the lawn. A few of the tables had been occupied since the rain had stopped. The setting sun cast a golden hue over the city, and the humidity was still high despite the cooling downpour. I thought of what Bob had said as he took a phone call sheepishly a few metres away.

Whoever it was or whatever the call was about, it was clear he wanted it to be a private conversation. I left him to it. It was his business. If he wanted to discuss it with me, he knew he could.

Could Stevie have tried to take his own life and failed, like the others? I was tempted to make a quick phone call to Shannon, but figured I needed to think it over a bit first. And there was no telling, of course, that Shannon would have known even if he had attempted suicide. I suppose it wouldn't have been out of the question for him to go down that road. Young lad, probably a victim of the abuse just like the others. He would've been scared, had probably been threatened in the past, going off what Alan Pickering had said about the beatings. Had he disappeared from Ivy Brook with secrets and kept them hidden all those years he spent on the streets? Could he have gotten into drink and drugs as a way of coping with the past that haunted him? Maybe he'd wanted to slowly kill himself by doing the things that helped him forget. Maybe. Maybe he was just another kid whose life was ruined by the people who were fucked up enough to do so. The people who were supposed to be looking after him.

It was a lot of maybes and nothing concrete. And I never recalled him discussing a suicide attempt with me. And why would he? We were hardly best mates, just acquaintances. He helped me out when I needed it and that was pretty much it. Besides bedding down together around the back of Ho's Chinese bakery, there was no real close friendship between us. Like Shannon had said, he wasn't the type to confide in anyone, even people he knew and trusted. I knew very little of his past. Perhaps that was just how he liked it.

What Bob had said had brought up some pertinent

questions. If the suicides were all connected to the abuse like they were connected to Ivy Brook, was it convenient for Hardy that they were now dead? And if that was the case, was it inconvenient that the ones who'd tried to take their own lives and failed were still around and still a potential threat to him? I thought of each survivor and how the remainder of their lives were panning out.

Alan Pickering, obsessed with Buddy Holly, could be considered vulnerable? Paul Lennon, by all accounts another vulnerable adult needing support in the community. Robbie White, very much a loose cannon, confined to a wheelchair. Dominic Pearson, a frightened loner. All of them had the same connection. All of them could be considered vulnerable, eccentric, a little bit nuts... Not worth listening to. Unreliable, gotta take whatever those freaks say with a large pinch of salt. And maybe that was why they were still here. Their very vulnerability had protected them. If Hardy had kept an eye on them from a distance, only willing to step in if they opened their mouths, it helped to cover his arse. Because they were just a handful of crackpots. No one would believe a word they said anyway, even if they were to open their mouths. It was as if it was all hidden in plain sight. Had he kept them in fear of something, just to make sure? And if they didn't comply...

There were some suicides to consider, perhaps the odd one out being John Forbes, the one who'd jumped into a quarry up in Ramsbottom. Shannon had said that everyone doubted that one, that people thought he'd maybe gotten into some trouble with drug dealers or something and they made him pay by taking him up there and pushing him in. Like they wanted to make sure he was dead.

Could it have been Hardy? Could he have had help

from his mate, Kenneth Regan? Was John Forbes one of their abuse victims and was he about to spill?

There could've been others we didn't know about. And were the suicides really suicides? Of the ones who managed it, there were two that could've been something more sinister. Mark Reynolds had apparently thrown himself in front of a train after a domestic, while David Mitchell had jumped from a building in the city centre. Both could easily have been pushed. Could their deaths have been murders made to look like suicides?

So many questions, so few answers. A world of secrets and lies, with the truth hidden in the dark.

I tossed my smoke and was about to go back inside when the phone rang again. It was the call I'd been waiting for. Bob was still occupied, so I took a seat nearby and sparked up another.

'Locke.'

'Jim,' she said. 'You'll be glad to know I'm now home and in the bath, with no bent coppers to hear me scream. There's a bottle of wine with my name on it and the Chinese better get itself ready for my banquet order.'

'Sounds like you mean business.'

'Banquet for one, sadly. You're welcome to join me...'

Fuck, was she flirting with me? 'Yeah, I'm... I'm busy.'

'A bit tied up?'

'Something like that.'

'Shame,' she said. 'Anyway, I think you'll like what I've got for you tonight.'

Bloody hell, she was definitely flirting. Bob signalled he'd get us another, and I nodded.

'Sounds... interesting.'

'You might say it could be vital evidence,' she said. I could hear her splashing in the bath. 'And something

Robertson was apparently keen to either ignore or get rid of.'

'Sounds more than interesting.'

'It's a SIM card,' she said. 'From a Samsung. It's probably from Lloyd's phone.'

'You're kidding me.'

'I wouldn't joke about something like this.'

'And you have it?'

'Yep,' she said. 'Managed to sign it out under everyone's nose. It wasn't considered important, just what was found at the scene. There are some other bits too. Plastic, a glass screen, a few metal parts from inside the device, that kind of thing. I reckon he must've thrown it from his window before he was shot, you know.'

'Has it been analysed?'

'Not that I'm aware of, no.'

'And it's in your possession?'

'Locked in my bedside drawer.'

'Jesus, Fiona...'

'There's nowhere else,' she said. That splashing again. 'And anyway, they aren't bothered about it, they see it as insignificant in the investigation.'

'Clueless...'

'I know. So, do you want it?'

Did I want it? You bet your arse I wanted it. 'When can I get it?'

'I don't know. Tomorrow?'

'Works for me. Can you drop it?'

'Might be able to before work. I'm on a late. They've got me on the hen night beat until two in the morning.'

'Good luck with that.'

'I know. So I can drop it in your office around four, if that's okay with you? I'll let you know.'

'Sounds like a plan.'

And it was. I was more than intrigued by what the SIM contained. Already the possibilities were going through my mind. I thought of Maya's computer whiz friend, Dave. Wondered if he could help dig out what was on it. With any luck, it could piece together a timeline of events and tell us who Lloyd had been in contact with prior to his death. Perhaps it could shed more light on the reasons he was gunned down and torched. Or even the reasons he'd been followed ever since Stevie's remains were found.

'I thought you might like it,' she said. 'Though I should caution that it might be water damaged or something. There might not be anything on it. Are you able to see what it contains?'

'I'm working on it already,' I said. I glanced inside to see Bob holding aloft another pint. I was feeling drunk. My second wind had turned bad. 'You got anything else?'

'Well, I'm coming to that. You wanted more on this Trevor Hardy, didn't you?'

'And Liam MacNamara, if you have it.'

'Yes, well MacNamara. The only thing we have of him on the PNC is that he was done for possession of cocaine and ecstasy with intent to supply four years ago. Served fourteen months of a two-year sentence. It was a paltry amount, though, nothing like you'd expect from the big boys in the drugs game. He was still living in North Wales at the time...'

'He Welsh then?'

'No,' she said. 'Northern Irish roots, but no reason to believe he's from those parts, either. We believe he's spent a fair few years living in the Salford area and has connections all over Manchester and some in Liverpool, Birmingham and North Wales.'

'You've done your work.'

'But that's all,' she said. 'A qualified car mechanic...'

'Which would explain the Range Rover being registered to that garage in Porthmadog.'

'Exactly.'

'Any far right shit with him?'

'Nothing I could find.'

'And Hardy?'

'He's a tougher nut to crack,' she said. 'With his many guises, your guess is as good as mine. I can only tell you what I found.'

'Go on.'

'Like I said, he's been done for all sorts. Other than what you know already - the GBH, the robbery etc - there isn't much to go on.'

'You got anything on his past? History, I mean, not convictions. Places he might've worked, previous addresses, any acquaintances, that kind of stuff. Has he been married, has he got kids, you know...'

'So you want his life story?'

'Something like that.'

'Well, he's never been married as far as the records show. No kids, not much of a worker using any of the names he went under. He's been a bin man as Terence Hammond and a bus driver as Shaun Cox. That was when he bit that guy's ear off in the pub. Done time for that before his release a few years later. That's when he became one Colin Black. As far as we know, he remains unemployed.'

'Okay, going back,' I said. 'Right back, I mean. I'm talking the late seventies, early eighties. Maybe even the mid-eighties. He would've been known as Trevor Hardy then, right?'

'According to the records, yes, he was,' she said. 'But

that's a long time ago, Jim. You're talking thirty-odd years, as long as I've been alive. His employment history is paper thin, to be honest, but I did find something. Why do you want to go that far back, anyway?'

'Because,' I said, 'I think he might've worked at the care home Stevie attended. Ivy Brook, Salford.'

'Well, he lived in Salford during the eighties, we know that much.'

'Really?'

'Yeah, Lower Broughton,' she said, the significance of which wasn't lost on me. He knew the area like the back of his hand. 'And Weaste, for a time. But this care home you mentioned - Ivy Brook, yeah?'

'Yeah, but it's gone now.'

'There's no record as far as I could find,' she said. 'Doesn't mean he didn't work there, though. What as, anyway? A porter or something?'

'Doesn't matter what.'

'Nothing on Ivy Brook. But he did work at a place called St. Joseph's. Rochdale, this was.'

A lightbulb went off in my head. Could it have been the same St Joseph's Stevie and Shannon attended when they were just little kids?

'St. Joseph's? You got a specific period he was there?'

'I'll have to check again. Why, is this important?'

'It's just... Well, I think it was the same place Stevie went as a child. Then he was moved to Ivy Brook later, early eighties...'

More splashing. 'Interesting.'

But it was more than that. I had that feeling again, that itch, that gut instinct. 'Anything else? Do you know what his job title was, anything like that?'

'No job title, just 'Senior Position', it says. That's it. But without it in front of me, I can't really go into detail, not that I recall there being much, anyway.'

'Any other work?'

'Nothing other than a few bits of voluntary work.'

It was getting juicier. I looked back to see Bob on his own call again. He didn't look too happy with it. I once again wondered if this was Bob Turner talking or Alvaro Garcia.

'What voluntary work? Come on, Fiona, I need specifics.'

'Not much I can give, I'm afraid. But according to what he'd said in a previous police interview as Shaun Cox, he'd been working voluntarily at a homeless shelter. And before that, a care home for mentally handicapped kids.'

'You're kidding me.'

'No, why? Jim, what's up?'

'Are you serious?'

'Why wouldn't I be? I've got better things to do than make this kind of shit up.'

'Did he say where? Fiona, this is important.'

'Off the top of my head, no, he didn't. Does it really matter?'

'Yes, it fucking matters, it matters a great deal...'

'Okay, keep your pants on,' she said. 'But no, I don't think it's documented exactly where.'

'Can I get a copy of this interview? A transcript?'

'Might be hard,' she said. 'Impossible, even. I don't get that kind of access, Jim. For copies, I mean.'

'Okay, look, do what you can. But this voluntary work, it couldn't have been that long ago, could it?'

'It's a good few years,' she said. 'I mean, this interview would've been upon his arrest for biting that guy's ear off in the pub. He was then charged with GBH and sent down. So four years ago or thereabouts.'

'And he specifically said he was volunteering at this place? For how long?'

'I don't know, Jim,' she said. 'I can't remember the details, Jesus! Look, I'm going now anyway, I need to get out of this bath.'

'Just a few more questions then we're done.'

'You better be.'

'I am paying you for this, Fiona.'

'Just as well, isn't it?' she said. 'I got an extra lovely bottle of Rioja...'

'And I'm looking after your files...'

'But that benefits you too, am I right?'

She wasn't wrong, put it that way. 'Just a few more things,' I said. 'Then we're done - for now.'

'I do still have to order this Chinese, you know.'

'Okay,' I said. 'Any far right leanings, as far as you're aware, of Trevor Hardy?'

'Apparently, he was a fully paid-up member of the BNP,' she said. 'So he said in an interview, think it was the same one he had as Shaun Cox, when he -'

'Got done for GBH.'

'Right,' she said. 'But other than that, nothing.'

'Okay, Kenneth Regan and Bill Williams. Remember the names. I need all you can get on both of them. I reckon they might be known to Hardy too, so especially in connection with him. According to my witness, he apparently worked with both at Ivy Brook.'

'Aye aye, Captain.'

'And one more thing,' I said.

A sigh. 'Go on.'

'Do the surnames Squires, Martyn and Cross mean anything to you?'

'There's a detective sergeant Cross at work,' she said. 'On the Serious Crime Team.'

'He close to Robertson?'

'Let's just say he's one of his very few friends,' she said. 'Why do you ask?'

'Has he got kids?'

'I can find out. Why?'

'I'll explain another time. But for now, can you keep an eye on him for me? And maybe let me know his shift pattern if you can find out.'

'Right, anything else or are you done?'

'Just one more thing,' I said. 'The next time you invite me for a Chinese, I'd appreciate an advanced warning.'

She was quiet a brief few seconds, except for some splashing. 'It's a deal, love.'

I made a quick call to Laura before I headed back inside. She said everything was now set up beautifully, but that she was going home to Sara's house to look after Charlie.

'She's getting funny again,' she said. 'Not to the point that I'm really worried, but I think she's been skipping her meds.'

'She's done that before, hasn't she?'

'Yeah, and look where she ended up.'

I remembered it well. The disturbing visit I made to Wythenshawe Hospital will live long in the memory. 'Give her my love.'

'You need to come and see her,' she said. 'And Charlie. You know she likes you.'

'I know, and I will. But you know how things are at the minute. We'll sort something after all this is over. But listen, I need to bend your ear - or rather, Dave's. Is he there?'

'No, he left ages ago. Why?'

I told her about the SIM. 'Could do with his expertise.'

'I'm sure he'll be able to do something. You think it might be important?'

'There's probably stuff on there that would explain Lloyd's death, or at least point us in the right direction. If we can view it, great.'

'I'll text Maya.'

'Good girl,' I said, inching my way back to Bob. 'And listen: I think Hardy might've worked at St Joseph's, as well as Ivy Brook. Back in the day, I mean.'

'Wowsers.'

'And not only that. Seems he's quite the volunteer. I need to go to Sanctuary first thing in the morning and bend their ear about their records. So how long are you gonna be with Sara?'

'As long as it takes. Certainly overnight. Did you speak to Bob?'

'I'm on it,' I said. 'Leave it to me.'

'Jim, I know your heart to hearts involve the top shelf. You've had enough now. Time to call it a day.'

'I'm going back to the flat any minute. There's still a lot I need to check on Robertson.'

'Just be careful,' she said. 'You never know who's watching.'

It was the kind of statement that would be enough to give me the jitters, but the alcohol had left me with little care. 'I will,' I said. 'And Laura?'

'Yeah?'

'I know I don't often say it, but I love you.'

'I love you too, Jim Locke.'

'I mean I really, really love you.'

'Now I definitely know you've had too much. Just get home to bed. There's a pizza in the fridge.'

———

B ut I had one last pint to drink before I went anywhere. I found Bob sitting quietly and tearing up a beer mat. I knew he was troubled. It was written all over his face.

'Everything okay?'

He nodded slowly. 'Aye, lad.'

'Only you look like you've just seen the ghost of Jack The Ripper.'

'My business...'

'Bob, if there's something - '

'Just leave it now, eh?' he said. 'I'm all right. But I'm gonna head back and get my head down. I hope you don't mind. I just don't feel too good. Got a lot on my plate, you know.'

'I know,' I said. 'I'll come with you.'

'Just finish your pint,' he said, standing and draining his own. 'I'll probably be asleep by the time you get back.'

'But you were gonna tell me about George Thornley,' I said. 'You know, the fact that he knows you're still alive...'

'Another time,' he said. 'But needless to say - it's sorted. So nowt to worry about. I'll see you when I wake up.'

I watched him leave, his chin almost on the floor. I was beginning to think he was depressed. It was more than just the guilt he was carrying with him. The man just wasn't himself.

I sat a few minutes and drank, contemplating the day's events. My conversations with Shannon and Alan Pickering had shed some serious light on the investigation. And the revelations Fiona had uncovered about Robertson - the cunt was lower than a snake's belly - had really taken their toll. I was feeling tired. Perhaps it was time to get my head down, too. But it was Bob that dominated my thoughts as I sat and drank. I had a bad feeling about him. And when I had those feelings, I'd learned to not ignore them.

I downed the beer quickly and followed him.

CHAPTER SIXTEEN

The sun was setting over the city, the bright red and gold leaking across Rochdale Road and Shudehill, blending into the horizon like a wall of light. It was blinding when I looked down towards the centre of town, but I could just make him out in the distance when I covered my eyes. Wherever he was going, it wasn't exactly in the right direction for the flat. His pace was quick, as if he was in a rush. I couldn't help but worry. I crossed the road to get onto the same pavement and jogged until I was a decent distance back, but close enough to keep pace and stay on his tail. Bob was many things, but he certainly wasn't an athlete, especially now, so I had no qualms about keeping up. Maybe he wanted another drink alone, without my stuff to get in the way. Maybe he had to see another man about another dog. Whatever it was, I wanted to keep track of him and see where he landed. It wasn't like him to just cut off like that. I needed to know what he was hiding, for my own sanity as well as his.

If I could step in somehow, and address whatever was bothering him head on, man to man, perhaps everything would be okay. I didn't believe this was just down to him killing a man. He'd been living with that for a while now, although I'm sure it haunted his every moment. It had to be something else. Laura was right to be worried. She was better than me at picking these things up. I suppose having lived with a sister battling mental illness had made her sensitive to it, as well as hardened.

He passed the hotel and pubs down Shudehill and reached the tram tracks, where he took a left. I picked up my pace to catch up and when I did, turning left onto High Street, I just about saw him heading up the back alley behind my office. Was that where he was going? It was hard to make him out through the crowd of punters out drinking in the Northern Quarter, but I think he took one of the narrow back streets beyond instead. I jogged up until I reached the end of the alley, standing behind my office. I looked up the fire escape steps. No one, nothing. Turned to my left and thought I saw him pass by in a blur, but couldn't be sure.

It was the only option I had. I took it, even though I was only fifty percent sure it was him. I crossed the street and took another dark alley, where it narrowed the deeper I got into it. The shadows were deep down here, and it was deathly quiet, away from the crowds. A rat burst out from behind a leaking drainpipe and scurried beneath some damp cardboard boxes. I almost slipped in the slime it had been having a party in, and when I neared the end of the alley and the bustling city beyond, the traffic brimming with taxis and buses, I looked in every direction, knowing I'd lost him.

'Bastard.'

I caught my breath before I took out my phone and dialled him up. It rang for several minutes until it answered.

I could hear him breathing on the other end until it went dead. He'd hung up.

'Bob?'

Nothing. Just the noise of the night and a pounding in my head.

'Fuck.'

Had he caught me following him? And why the hell had he hung up? This wasn't like him at all.

I headed back to the flat, figuring he'd made it clear he wanted to be alone. As I walked back through the city streets, the night owls in full swing, I had a hundred things on my mind, not least the man I'd been sharing a beer with just half an hour ago. Then, of course, there was Robertson the psychopath, Hardy the abuser, Hardy the murderer. Stevie, Lloyd, Lloyd's family, St. Joseph's, Sanctuary, Fiona, Laura, Nicole, Alan Pickering and all the suicides. All I wanted to do was lie down on the couch and fall into a deep and dreamless sleep, forget about everything.

The flat was dark and eerily quiet when I opened the door. And as was usually the case after a session, time had seemed to melt away fast, the dying hours leaving emptiness and silence behind. I bumped into the kitchen sideboard, then hit my head on the door before bumping into the couch as I scrambled for the light switch. Out through the window, the sun was close to setting. Red sky at night, shepherd's delight. But the sky was the colour of fire, and as I crashed, feeling drunk, I was reminded of why I was even involved in all of this. Stevie dead, Lloyd dead; both consumed by the flames.

I sparked up and tried Bob again. This time it went straight to a dead line. Maybe he'd turn up back here once he needed to get his head down. At least, that's what I was telling myself. I also told myself I would keep trying.

I went to my drinks cabinet and opened it. There was a bottle of sixteen-year-old Bowmore and a bottle of reserve Jean Cave Armagnac staring back at me. I considered pouring myself a warm measure, especially now Laura wasn't here to keep me under control... I closed the cabinet. I knew I'd had enough, and I had more of the hard drive to wade through. I wasn't looking forward to it because I knew that now that I knew this stuff about Robertson - the double life, the second marriage, the sexual affair with a minor - things could never be the same again. It gave me power, and a power I knew could be dangerous, especially after a few drinks. Could I trust myself with this kind of information? When it came down to it, I really didn't know. I could take him down with one phone call if I wanted, yet I knew he'd be more useful bending over backwards for me instead of making others bend over for him.

Fuck it. I opened the cabinet and pulled out the Armagnac, pouring a large measure before I could change my mind. Threw it back, felt the burn. The burn felt good. Too good, if I'm honest, and I knew I'd need to be strong to not let this beast take over my mind. Poured another, this time to savour.

I sparked up and dug around in the bedroom for Laura's laptop. Found it where I left it, under the bed, and dumped it on the coffee table. Plugged in the hard drive. It took a few slow moments to load up - Laura was always leaving the machine running - so I sat and smoked while I waited, and let my eyes drift, staring blankly into space and thinking about Bob. I had to accept he was an adult, and he could make his own decisions. I glanced at the clock. It was just gone ten. Plenty of time for him to roll back in, even more drunk than I was myself. But this wasn't like him.

When the machine came to life and I opened the hard drive back up, those photographs of Robertson with his teenage lover and his two wives, I went through them all again one by one, shaking my head in disbelief as I did so. It wasn't just wrong; it was insane. No doubt about it. And yet he was getting away with it - had gotten away with it - for so long. But not for much longer. I couldn't wait to make the bastard sweat.

My thoughts went back to the phone call with Fiona and the revelation about where Hardy had worked in the past. It had to be more than mere coincidence. What did it mean? And not only paid employment, either. Seems the man had earmarked himself as a stalwart volunteer, a bastion of community contribution, a pillar of society. He was having a laugh, hiding it in plain sight.

He was taking the piss.

Just what was he up to? If he'd volunteered at one place, chances are he'd volunteered at others. There was no record, as far as I was aware, that he'd worked at Ivy Brook, yet Alan had identified him. And Fiona had said the voluntary work was at a homeless shelter, which meant that if this homeless shelter was the one Stevie went to - Sanctuary - then it linked Hardy to Stevie at all three places. St. Joseph's, Ivy Brook, Sanctuary.

Lloyd had volunteered at Sanctuary too. Had he known his killer? Was there any kind of motive to get rid of Lloyd? Did Lloyd know something other than what he'd let on to me? They'd been following him since Stevie's remains had been found. Was there a reason for this that wasn't connected to Stevie's death at all?

Then there was Liam MacNamara, the mechanic who owned the Range Rover. Lived in Salford, had contacts in major cities. But other than that, we knew next to nothing about him. Had he worked in any of the places Hardy had been known to work at? Had Lloyd known him, known either of them? Had their paths crossed in a life or a time prior to Lloyd knowing Stevie? What was the connection? Perhaps there was none. Perhaps I was searching for answers where none existed.

I was reminded, as I paced up and down the living room, that Fiona had offered me a SIM card, believed to be Lloyd's, which was found at the scene of his murder. It couldn't come soon enough and I was looking forward to her turning up with it. I was aware that any damage to the microchip could prove a problem and there was a possibility I could be totally wasting my time, but... what if there was stuff on there that proved significant? Could it be the key that would unlock everything?

I sat back down again and clicked through the files. It seemed Fiona was keen for me to read more, so I scanned for what looked like an interview document and found it near the bottom - IBInt070216/doc1

A t first glance, a lot of indecipherable digits which on closer inspection became pretty obvious. Isabella Burns Interview, 7th February 2016, Document Number One. I opened it up and sat back, resting the machine on my lap. Sparked up and read.

Date: 07/02/16

Location: Interviewer's home

Time: 12:30pm

Present: WPC Fiona Watson, Dr. Samantha Webb, Miss Isabella Burns.

(Interview conducted upon witness's request. Witness (1), Miss Isabella Burns, D.O.B 11/07/1997, interviewed by WPC Fiona Watson and also in the presence of Dr. Samantha Webb Bsc, acting as interview witness and appropriate adult for the benefit of Miss Burns).

Watson: *The time is 12:30pm on Sunday the 7th of February, 2016. Present here are the witness, Miss Isabella Burns, and Doctor Samantha Webb, who will act as interview witness and appropriate adult for the duration. For the benefit of the tape, I am now taking photographs of Miss Burns's bare arms, which are scarred with severe lacerations. These photographs will be kept on file for future reference.*

I went back to the documents listed on the drive and scrolled through the JPEGs until I came across twenty or so images of the cuts Fiona was talking about. It looked bad. I'd seen this kind of self harm before, and worse than this, but what I was looking at was enough to convince me the girl was traumatised and tormented. In the worst possible way, by the worst possible means. I could only imagine what had gone through the poor kid's head when she found out the truth about him. I read on.

PAUSE ON TAPE WHILST WITNESS 1 POSES FOR PHOTOGRAPHS

Watson: *Interview begins. Can you confirm your name and address, please?*

Burns: *It's Isabella Burns. I live at number 15 Sandbrook Road, Altrincham.*

Watson: *And your age, Miss Burns?*

Burns: *I'm sixteen.*

Watson: *Your date of birth?*

Burns: *Eleventh of July, nineteen ninety seven.*

Watson: *And can you confirm the names of your parents?*

Burns: *My father is Jack Burns and my mother is Katrina Burns.*

Watson: *Okay. You requested this interview yourself, is that correct?*

Burns: *Yes*

Watson: *Okay. In your own words, can you tell me why you asked for this interview.*

Burns: *Well, it's a long story.*

Watson: *Take all the time you need.*

Burns: *Well, I remember that you came to me once, outside school. This was when I'd lost the baby. And you'd told me about him being a copper.*

Watson: *Okay, Isabella. We need specifics, for the benefit of the recording. We'll go back to the time when you met DI Rob Robertson but for now, we'll just focus on how you came to request this interview. Can you remember the day I came to you?*

Burns: *It was a Friday, after school. About four o'clock, I think. You met me at the gates and asked me to join you for a coffee because you wanted to talk about John.*

Watson: *Who is John?*

Burns: *That's John Dawson. Robertson.*

Watson: *So John Dawson is also DI Rob Robertson?*

Burns: *Yes*

Watson: *Okay, carry on.*

Burns: *It was a Friday afternoon. We went to the local coffee place. It was a really grim day, I remember. Pissing down with rain. You got me a chocolate mocha and you just had a basic black coffee.*

Watson: *And I told you about Robertson?*

Burns: *Yeah.*

Watson: *So, for the recording, can you tell us what you now know about DI Rob Robertson? Again, we'll go over this in more detail later, but I just want to outline why we're conducting this interview.*

Burns: *Right. Well, I didn't know him as DI Rob Robertson; I knew him as John Dawson. He was a neighbour across the street.*

Watson: *From your parents' house?*

Burns: *Yeah, that's right. And I didn't know he was a copper or that he was living a double life. I didn't know anything until you told me and showed me the photographs of him. And of us. I didn't know what to think, really. To me, he was just John Dawson. A sort of friend of the family, you know. Anyway, I got pregnant and he made me get rid of it. That's why I wanted this interview.*

Watson: *So, we'll go into more detail soon but I just want to clarify that you specifically requested this interview with me, and in the presence of Doctor Samantha Webb, because the man in question - Dawson/Robertson - had gotten you pregnant and then had subsequently made you terminate the pregnancy. Is that correct, Isabella?*

Burns: *Yeah. Yeah, that's right.*

Watson: *And so can you confirm the reason why you wanted this interview?*

Burns: *Because I want to tell you everything. I want to be honest about it all.*

Watson: *About what, specifically?*

Burns: *About our affair. We had an affair and I slept with him a few times.*

PAUSE ON TAPE.

She was good. God, she was good. I lay there on the

couch and took it all in. How Robertson had manipulated this poor girl and gotten away with it was beyond evil. And for a man in such high power and authority, it was absolutely criminal. I went back and forth between the interview transcript and the photographs of her self harm. It was tragic. The scars were deep, and I could see there were fresh cuts too. I was no expert, but for someone to take a sharp blade to their arm like that meant they were very traumatised and something major had triggered the self-harming behaviour. There was no doubt as to what that was. The girl was young, naive, probably easily manipulated. I wondered if the bastard had told her he loved her, just to get her into bed. A troubling thought occurred to me. If he'd abused this poor girl - in so many ways, never mind the sex - had he done it with others? With other kids? I took a drink and read on.

Watson: *Okay, Isabella. Can you start at the very beginning? Tell us how you came to start an affair with John Dawson.*

Burns: *Well... It was a barbecue. My dad likes to have them every summer - mainly to show off what he has in stock, really - and there were a lot of people there. The whole street, it seemed. It turned into a proper party, you know. We loved it because we could nick a bit of booze here and there.*

Watson: *Who's we?*

Burns: *Me and the Thompsons. Chloe, Annabel, Ollie. Chloe was the same age as me, while Ollie and Annabel were a bit older.*

Watson: *So when you say you could 'nick a bit of booze', what kind of alcohol do you mean?*

Burns: *Just anything, really. Beer, wine. Vodka, Jack Daniels. That kind of stuff.*

Watson: *And so how much would you say you'd drunk that day? Bearing in mind also that you were all under age.*

Burns: *I just had a few bottles of lager. And some wine Annabel had in a bottle.*

Watson: *Is that everything?*

Burns: *Some vodka as well. We were messing about, playing games. Trying to get pissed for a laugh. No one noticed because they were all pissed, too. Everyone was.*

Watson: *Had John Dawson been drinking?*

Burns: *Yeah. He was one of the worst. He was really drunk.*

Watson: *Okay. Isabella, can you tell me what happened at this barbecue, with John Dawson?*

Burns: *He'd been looking at me all day, all night. I thought he was a perv. But I quite liked it as well. He made me feel...like a woman.*

Watson: *What exactly do you mean by that? How was he looking at you?*

Burns: *Like the boys did at school, only worse. Looking at my tits. Looking at my arse. You know, perving. It was a bit creepy. A bit odd.*

Watson: *And did the others notice it, too? Chloe and Annabel and Ollie?*

Burns: *Well, Ollie was off upstairs for most of the day, playing on my PlayStation. So I don't think he noticed. I don't think he would've cared. But Chloe and Annabel did. They just thought it was funny.*

Watson: *And were Chloe and Annabel drunk, too?*

Burns: *I don't think any of us were really drunk, just... merry, you know. Having a laugh, mainly.*

Watson: *I see. So Dawson had been looking at you. What happened then?*

Burns: *Well, nothing for ages. I had something to eat,*

about six o'clock, a few burgers, some chicken and salad, then I went upstairs for a bit to beat Ollie at FIFA. We had some vodka that Chloe had grabbed from the kitchen. And I had some smoke too. Wish I hadn't.

Watson: *Smoke?*

Burns: *Ollie had some weed. We didn't smoke a lot, honest.*

Watson: *Go on.*

Burns: *It made me feel sick, so I went to the bathroom to throw up but couldn't. So I just sat there. I used the toilet and freshened up a bit. And when I opened the door, he was there.*

Watson: *Dawson was there?*

Burns: *Yeah. He looked at me funny, then went to kiss me.*

Watson: *And did he kiss you?*

Burns: *Yeah. I let him. I kissed him back and we shut the bathroom door. He locked it and we...you know, I got off with him.*

Watson: *You got off with him? Was it just kissing?*

Burns: *Yeah, you know. I didn't want to go any further, so I stopped and he left the bathroom. He said he was sorry and that I should just forget it. He was drunk.*

Watson: *But you couldn't forget it, right?*

Burns: *No. Of course not. He was a neighbour; he was married, his wife was in the garden with my parents and he'd just been snogging me. I couldn't believe it.*

Watson: *And then what did you do?*

Burns: *I think I was in shock. He just... came out of nowhere. I knew he was looking at me all the time he'd been at the barbecue, but I just thought.... well, I didn't think he'd do anything. I didn't think he'd try to kiss me. I went back downstairs and he was just carrying on as normal, in the garden with everyone else. The music was louder by this time and there were some people dancing and messing about, so I just grabbed a few cans of beer from the fridge and went back to my room. Ollie had fallen asleep and the girls were watching Friends. And I just sat and drank and smoked some of Ollie's cigs.*

Watson: *Did he approach you again that night?*

Burns: *I saw him in the garden later on. This was about ten o'clock. He was a bit more sober by then. He just said he was sorry, and he didn't know what came over him. He should've known better and that he hoped I wasn't upset by it.*

Watson: *And were you upset?*

Burns: *Not really. Just freaked out. I mean, he was a man. I was fourteen. He could've been my dad.*

Watson: *He shouldn't have done it.*

Burns: *I know. But I quite liked it. He wasn't like the other boys at school that I'd got off with. He said if I wanted it to happen again, I could text him. Then he gave me his number on a slip of paper.*

Watson: *And what did you do with that number, Isabella?*

Burns: *I added it to my contacts on my iPhone.*

Watson: *And do you still have it?*

Burns: *Yes.*

Jesus. I downed the brandy and thought briefly about getting another when my mobile rang. Hoping it was Bob, I slung the laptop off me and sat up, scrambling for the phone. I was disappointed when it wasn't him.

'Laura.'

'Jim,' she said. 'You don't sound too happy to hear from me. Are you drunk? Oh no, you are, aren't you?'

'A bit,' I said. 'But it's not that. Bob's disappeared. He's not answering his phone, which is not like him. He even hung up on me.'

'Really? God...'

'I know. So I'm just waiting for him to turn up but I've got a bad feeling, you know. I don't know why.'

'Maybe you're worrying over nothing.'

'It's not like him.'

'Maybe so, but there's no point in panicking. It might be nothing. And anyway, he is an adult. He can do what he wants. Look, I just phoned to let you know I'm off to the hospital.'

'What?'

'With Sara. She's been off her meds, just like I thought. She thinks the FBI have planted tiny microphones around the house. And the neighbour said she was talking about leaving the gas on.'

'Jesus.'

'I know. So the upshot is that the crisis team at the mental health unit have managed to get her a bed tonight. She won't go without me.'

'And how's it looking?'

'I'm hoping they keep her in. But that means I'll be over here for a while longer. Charlie's gone next door for the night for an impromptu sleepover again with his little mate. So if you need me, I might not be able to answer my phone. Better to text.'

'Okay, but keep me updated.'

'I will.'

'Do you think she'll be alright?'

'We've been here lots of times before. Better go. Hey, did you eat that pizza?'

I told her I had, but it was the last thing on my mind. She went on her way and once more left me to a lonely flat.

I sparked up, thinking about pouring another brandy, telling myself I needed it to settle the nerves, but knowing I needed it like a hole in my head. I put the bottle back in the cabinet and wished I had a key to lock it. Considered reading more of the interview transcript but figured I could go back to it in the morning. For now, I needed rest. I could feel myself drifting and collapsed on the couch again, finishing my smoke quickly before I dropped it on my shirt. Slung my top off and lay back. Closed my eyes and soon found myself dreaming of Frank and Maureen.

———

I'd never been one to sleep lightly, so when the phone rang like some distant yet familiar alarm from somewhere out in the void, it took me several moments to realise it was meant for me. I shot up, still half drunk, and sent it flying off the coffee table. When I reached it, I answered breathless.

'Bob?'

'Fucking hell, finally.'

'What? Bob, is that you? You okay?'

'It's Norman,' he said.

'Norman?'

'Norman the landlord. At the Wilton? You spoke to me today about Shannon's brother. You know, Stevie? You gave me your business card. Listen, I thought I'd better give you a ring because - '

'Wait a minute.'

I sparked up and took that shit in deep. Knew it was killing me slowly, but it just felt too good. Norman? Did he have some new information? I walked to the window and let the cool air blow me awake. Heard the distant hum of passing traffic, even at this ungodly hour. Checked the clock on the wall. It had just gone three a.m.

'Listen, I know it's late.'

'It's just gone three in the morning,' I said. 'Don't think this is a good time, to be honest.'

'I know but I felt I had to call you to let you know.'

I let a heavy cloud of cigarette smoke leave my nose. 'Let me know what?'

'There's been a fire,' he said. 'There's still a fire, actually. And it's burning pretty bad.'

'What do you mean? What fire?'

'You're not awake yet, are you?'

'What fire, Norman?'

'You need some time to come round, I get it,' he said. 'But listen, Mr. Locke.'

'Jim.'

'Jim. Look, I'm phoning because I thought you might need to know that it's her flat. At least I think it is.'

'Whose flat?'

'Well Shannon's flat, obviously. At least, it's definitely the same building. I can see it from here.'

'Shannon?'

'That's what I said.'

'Is Shannon in there?'

'I don't know, I don't know.'

'Well phone the fire brigade, Jesus...'

'They're already there,' he said. 'They've been there a while, that's what woke me up. I could hear the engines from my bed.'

'Fucking hell.'

'I've not seen her since this afternoon, you know.'

'Is it still burning?'

'As far as I can tell.'

'I'm coming over.'

'I don't think there's much point.'

'I'm coming.'

I hung up and dragged my shirt on. Ran to the bathroom to splash cold water on my face. I needed to sober up fast. Sunk two pints of tap water and got my shit together. Phone, keys, smokes, wallet. Left everything where it was and stepped out of the flat into the quiet of the night. The streets were dark and desolate, and even when I reached the main Rochdale Road, heading towards the office where I'd left the Volvo, there was no life around except for a lone fox that hurried from behind an upturned bin the moment I ran past. I watched it run off down a back street while I ran as best I could back to the office.

I didn't bother going inside, knowing there would be no point. Instead, I got behind the wheel of the Volvo, knowing I was probably still well over the legal limit. There wasn't much I could do about that other than not drive at all, and that wasn't going to be an option. I opened the glove box in my search for a stray water bottle and some paracetamol, but found nothing other than what I'd left in there. The kid scrawl of myself walking to the pub. Nicole instantly came to my mind, and I immediately wanted to be with her. Then I was reminded of Karen's last text and the fact that I hadn't yet replied. It could wait until the sun came up, at least.

Started her up and put her into gear. The night shift talk show from the local station came on the radio, and I half listened as I pulled away from the office and the Northern Quarter. Through the city and across the River Irwell lay Salford and the block where Shannon had a flat - the very place where Bob and I had quizzed her about Stevie - and the flat was now up in flames. It occurred to me then that I was right to suggest she be careful this afternoon when we discussed the suicides in the pub. That instinct I had told me she needed to be on her toes. I hadn't anticipated any immediate danger. Of course, there was no proof yet that she had come to any harm, but if the fire was still burning, as Norman had said, there was every chance she'd just become another victim. I dug out my phone and found the previous received call. Dialed him up. I didn't need to wait long.

'Jim,' he said. 'Tell me you're not coming out here.'

'I'm on my way.' I put my foot down through the traffic lights at Blackfriars Road. 'You still at home?'

'No, I got in my car and drove over here. There's a lot of people around. Jim, this is as big a fire as I've ever seen. There's four engines here. At least six ambulances.'

'Fucking hell.'

'There must be four or five flats on fire.'

'Have you seen Shannon? Have you heard anything?'

'I've not seen her, I've not seen her.'

'She could be among the crowd or something.'

'She's not here, Jim. Just get here.'

I hung up and dialled Shannon but it just went straight to a dead line. I slung the phone aside and focussed on the road. In less than five minutes, I was driving up Salford crescent towards Pendleton and the fire. When I neared the group of high-rise flats and drove into the estate, keeping one eye out for Shannon in the vain hope that she'd somehow gotten away from it all, the air became thick with smoke. It must've been a bad fire indeed to take the early morning freshness from the air. I let my window drop and almost choked. Then the flashing blue lights of the emergency services illuminated the whole area, leaking over the Volvo as I got closer. Kept my eye out for anyone I might've recognised, but it was hardly the best environment for it, or the best light.

I got as close as I could without the heat becoming a problem. The place had been cordoned off and the building was still wildly ablaze. There was a wind too, which couldn't have helped matters at all, and the noise from the engines drowned out any of the chatter from the small crowd that had gathered.

I left the Volvo parked half on the road and partly on the kerb a short distance away, and ran towards the crowd, expecting to see Norman among them. I struggled through, the voices panicked and tearful, and I guessed that some of these people were friends or relatives of the occupants of the burning flats. But then I looked down towards the bottom end of the road and saw another group, their silhouettes black against the pale light of the night, their hands against their heads, their heads bowed, some of them falling to their knees. I realised these people lived in the very building that was now in flames. If Shannon was still alive, she had to be among them. I instinctively called out her name, but no one around me batted an eyelid.

'Shannon! Shannon Kennedy!'

No one, nothing, though even if she'd responded, I wouldn't have heard her. There was too much going on. Not too far away, several fire crews were busy with hoses. Two ladders had been extended to reach the level where the fire, I assumed, was seated, and I could see the water gushing in from two directions. Beyond in the other direction, away from the fire and the heat and the chaos, a line of ambulances were blocking the road, and the police were behind that, blocking the entrances to the side roads that were usually gated off but were now open to allow the fire crews access. Norman had said this was the biggest fire he'd seen in a long time, and now I knew what he meant. Yet there was no sign of him.

I headed towards the ambulances, pushing my way through the crowd. The people here, I knew, were freaking out. Perhaps some of them lived here, perhaps some didn't. Either way, a lot were hysterical. I nudged a few out of the way as I fought my way through, ducking under a police cordon tape out of sight of several coppers, and had almost made it between two ambulances when a hand grabbed my shoulder. I almost turned and decked him there and then, but I recognised the voice before I could push him off.

'Jim!'

'Jesus, for fuck's sake!'

'There's still no sign of her,' Norman said. 'I've been up and down this road twice and there's still no sign. It doesn't look good.'

'Too early for that.'

'It doesn't bode well, Jim.'

But I was already off, grabbing a copper who'd just sent a couple in their pyjamas away from the cordon.

'Stand back, sir,' he said. 'Keep away from the line and wait in the yellow area away from this cordon.'

'I'm looking for Shannon,' I said. 'Shannon Kennedy, brother of Stephen Kennedy who was found murdered and burnt to death under the arches behind the Park Inn hotel -'

'Move into the yellow zone, sir.'

'She's his brother, and I believe she was a target. I believe this building was set on fire because he knows I'm on to him. Hardy knows I'm on to him.'

'Move into the yellow zone.'

'My name's Jim Locke, I'm a private investigator. I used to be a DS on the serious crime unit. I know

Robertson is in charge of this investigation. Is he here? Is Robertson here? If he isn't I suggest you get him out of bed.'

'I won't tell you again, sir.'

I grabbed him by the collar, but he was a big lad and no doubt an enthusiastic rookie. He pushed me away as I clocked another copper heading towards us, and I saw Norman duck under the tape again and disappear behind the ambulances I'd intended to sneak behind. I was pushed back and fell on my arse, which pissed me off no end. But when I got back to my feet, keen to lamp him one but knowing it would be incredibly stupid, another bunch of people who were just as keen for answers were poking him in the face and demanding to be allowed through. It was my chance to slip away to plan B, but plan B wasn't necessary because Norman called me from beyond the flashing blue of the ambulances he'd got to. I ducked away and ran towards him.

'I think she's in there,' he said. He pointed back to the vehicle behind him. Its doors were shut and its engine was running. The siren blistered through the night and I knew it was about to move off. 'I'm sure it was her, before they shut the door.'

'What?'

'They wheeled her in on a gurney. Jim, I'm positive. She didn't look good.'

'What?! Are you sure?'

'Not one hundred percent, but sure enough! Jim, she's in my pub every week, I know that face, even if it is burnt!'

'She's burnt?'

'I think so!'

I went to haul open the back doors of the ambulance, knowing it would be more than enough to get me arrested, but Norman pulled me back. The ambulance was pulling away.

'It's either going to the MRI or Salford Royal,' he said. 'I know which is my guess.'

'Salford's closest.'

'And they have a specialist burns unit. I'll drive.'

'No, no, we'll take my car.'

And we ran. I started her up and spun it around with just enough time to spare to see the ambulance turn away onto the main road out. I put my foot down and crept up behind it, wishing I had blues and twos on myself.

'Why?' he said. 'Why her, Jim?'

'I don't know,' I said, and I didn't. I trailed behind, away from the scene, and by now it was easier to breathe. The air was fresher and with both windows down, we drank it in. Norman was coughing hard. I glanced at my phone and saw it had just gone four. The morning was young and pretty soon, the sun would be up. The authorities would then begin to piece together events, but I already knew how it had started and no one could tell me otherwise. Had Hardy been watching when I met Shannon in the pub just yesterday? Had he even been present, sitting on one of the tables in the lounge, keeping a close eye on our conversation? If not him, then one of his associates? MacNamara? Kenneth Regan? Had Shannon found out too much and had she now paid the price of opening her mouth? I couldn't help but feel this was all my fault. I gritted my teeth and drove.

'Do you think she'll be all right?'

'I don't know, I don't know!' I said. 'You tell me, you've been in bloody war zones...'

'She looked in a bad way.'

'I don't know anything about burns! I know next to fuck all about smoke inhalation! It doesn't sound good, does it?

Listen, do you know anyone close to her? Any friends, anyone?'

'Well, there's no family I know of.'

'She hasn't got any,' I said. 'I know that much. I just wonder who was the last person to see her alive.'

'You think she might be dead?'

'Well don't you? She's as good as, surely?'

'She might've gotten away with it,' he said. 'You know, they might've got her out in time.'

'Are you even sure it was her?'

'Look, I can't say for certain,' he said. 'But it was a woman. She looked like Shannon, she had black hair or what was left of it, and her face was white and black with blisters. Fuck's sake, Jim, the woman was burnt. She was screaming as well. She was really, really screaming hard.'

I kept my eyes on the road, knowing all this had just gotten a hundred times worse. If they could get to her, they could get to anyone. Me, Laura, Bob, Fiona. Nicole...

I knew then that none of us were safe.

My eyes drifted in and out of focus as I drove. Beside me, Norman was silent, his head in his hands. Then he turned and threw up out of the window. My head was pounding and I felt sick, too. It took a few moments for me to notice I was shaking, and even longer to notice the swastika sprayed in black across one of the glass panels on the back doors of the ambulance in front.

CHAPTER SEVENTEEN

W e drove right in behind the ambulance as it came to a stop at the Accident and Emergency entrance at Salford Royal, a hospital also known as Hope. Shannon would need a great deal of that now. It was still dark and the stark neon lighting hurt my eyes as they brought her out the back. I grabbed my phone and took several quick shots of the swastika that had been daubed on the back of the vehicle, then almost dropped it when I saw Shannon's face. It was very clear she was in a bad way. You could say she was almost unrecognisable - almost.

It was as if her skin had somehow liquified. Where it had blistered in bright white patches, and charred black in others, a sickly yellow pus that I thought might be body fat seemed to leak from her skin. Her face was also covered in a clear plastic film, which I assumed was to protect her features. An oxygen mask covered what was left of her nose and mouth. Her eyes were wide open, like yellow ping pong balls, their lids a blood red circle of flesh, the lashes gone, the eyebrows singed. Her lips had gone from soft pink to ruby red dotted with bright yellow and had fattened to twice the size. And from her neck down, the flesh hung off her in strips, as if the fire had simply torn her skin from her bones. Her black hair was pulled from her scalp and hung off the back of her head in clumps.

I saw her left arm and hand hanging loosely from the gurney, while the rest of her burnt body lay hidden beneath a black plastic blanket. God only knew what horrors were there, but from what I could see on her arm - the same blistered flesh hanging off in strips, the bright red meat beneath, the yellow fat leaking out, the exposed bones of her forearm and fingers - it would be no surprise if the rest of her looked the same, or much worse. The woman was half dead, and only the loud shrieking noise that was coming from somewhere deep down in what was left of her throat told me she was still alive at all.

The paramedics wheeled her in fast, and I sensed a few onlookers who turned away horrified as we followed them. We went through an area bathed in light, a few nurses here and there and several banks of chairs occupied by the walking wounded, the shrieking coming from what was left of Shannon piercing the quiet early morning with the sound of death. It was as if she was being cooked alive and the very air she moved through was a hot oil only she could feel.

They disappeared through a set of double doors, a flashing green light on the wall turning red as they closed behind them, and the gurney was wheeled away with Shannon's screams fading as they vanished somewhere into the depths of the hospital to a place, no doubt, where the real work would be done.

I turned to see Norman at a desk with a glass partition in it, trying to explain to the member of staff behind that we were with Shannon, the burning woman they'd just brought in. I guessed he was met with a brick wall, at least for now, and I knew I'd have to either turn on the charm or try to call in a favour in order to get to see her. I wondered if it was too early to call Fiona, and glanced at the clock on the wall. It was barely gone four thirty. Of course it was. I remembered she said she was on hen night duty tonight, so she'd need all the rest she could get. She was probably fast asleep. Yet I knew she could be of service if she could turn up here in uniform, though I guessed that wouldn't be required when I heard the familiar crackle of an air wave radio from somewhere behind me. It was coming from outside, and I stepped out, with Norman trailing behind, to get a better look at who was there.

The air was fresh. If ever I needed a smoke, it was now. I sparked up and took that shit in deep, thinking of the oxygen mask over Shannon's face as I blew a cloud above us. The Volvo was illegally parked and I clocked one of the coppers giving it a once over as they approached. I knew now would probably be a good time to move it, so I told Norman to stay inside and I'd find my way back to him soon.

'This yours, sir?'

There were two ways I could play it. I could either come clean, tell them who I was and why I was here, only to let them block me from seeing the poor girl, or I could wing it and blag that I knew her somehow, that I'd heard about the fire and raced over here as fast as I could. Either way wasn't going to be easy and, given what I knew about Robertson and what he knew about me and the Stevie and Lloyd case, it was only a matter of time before the bastard connected the dots and found me here anyway. With any luck, he'd still be in bed - and could stay there until sunrise at least - which would give me a short window to get to see her if there was any way. For all I knew, she'd be in surgery right now, and there was no certainty she'd survive at all. Weighing up my best chances, I had to blag it. I knew I had more than one enemy at the GMP and any mention of my name could get me sent packing quickly. Time was of the essence. The way things were looking, she'd be dead within hours. It was a good job Norman was here with me. He would just have to take the blame.

'Yeah, sorry,' I said. 'I had to come down here with a friend of mine. One of his neighbours - a good friend of his - has been involved in a bad fire in Pendleton. He heard she was in a bad way so we rushed to get here and I just parked where I could so he could get in to see her as quick as possible, you know. I'm moving it now.'

They didn't look convinced, but nodded for me to continue. I watched them head inside, and I knew by the way they were handling themselves that they were here for the same reasons I was. I got in the Volvo and spun it around, then spent ten minutes trying to find a parking space, which I managed around the back of the main hospital building. After spending a fiver on a three-hour stay, I made my way back through the hospital grounds, down brightly lit corridors, through automatic doors, past trolleys and gurneys and isolated wards and industrial floor polishing machinery. Thought about heading for the burns unit, struggling to see where the hell I was and where I needed to be, but then just followed the red signs to the A&E department. I called Norman's mobile as I walked.

'Any joy?'

'Not really,' he said. 'But then I suppose we should've expected it. They said a doctor might come to see us given that no family can be contacted. I suppose we'll find out soon enough.'

'I'm on my way back,' I said. 'I'll see if I can get things moving. Do we know where they've taken her?'

'I assume to theatre,' he said. 'You saw her, Jim. I think they've got a battle on just to keep her with us.'

I picked us up two mud coloured machine coffees and made my way back. Found Norman slumped in a plastic chair between a guy with a bloody bandage on his head and a drunk who'd seemed to have lost his shoes and had parts of his face chiselled away. I slumped beside him, feeling battered and bruised myself. A million and one thoughts went through my head. A thousand possibilities...

An image doesn't lie. I opened my photos on the iPhone and looked down at the swastika daubed across the rear of the ambulance, thinking that this had to be the work of the same people. I didn't believe in coincidences. This had the E.N.D written all over it. And when I compared it to the shot I'd taken under those arches where Stevie's remains had been found, there was no mistaking. Now they'd gotten his sister, presumably to shut her up - and there must've been reasons for that - the motives had become a little less clear and a little more unbelievable. But who had set the fires burning? Hardy himself? Or one of his associates? Thing was, I didn't have them down as simple pyromaniacs. They were much more than that.

I thought about the sexual abuse Alan Pickering had talked about, and he even named Hardy as being the main perpetrator. What did Stevie know? Had he been a victim too, and was he about to reveal his hand before they killed him?

'Got a light, mate?'

The drunk was beside me, and I rummaged around for a

spare lighter I knew I had. Judging by the look of him, there had to be more to his appearance than just an alcohol addiction. Our eyes met and he nodded, seeming to read my thoughts. He took the lighter and hobbled outside. A warm breeze swept through the waiting area when the automatic doors whispered open.

I took a sip of coffee. It was over hot and weak, but it was better than nothing. By now I felt sober, though I suspected I didn't look it. I was tired, which amplified the heavy bags under my eyes. If they got any heavier, I'd have to carry them home myself. It was still way too early, and time was drifting by slowly, but it wasn't too early to try Bob again. I was more than worried. It wasn't like him to keep me waiting. The way he'd hung up had unnerved me. I wondered if he'd caught up with a friend or two from the paper. I had George Thornley's number somewhere. If I could dig it out, perhaps he'd have a better clue where to find him.

I dialed Bob and was met once again with a dead line. I kept telling myself I should relax, give him some time alone. It had only been a matter of hours since he left me in the Angel, but every second counted. Like Laura had said, he'd clearly wanted to get away for a while. But I trusted my instincts. They'd never fooled me.

'That's the head nurse on duty,' Norman said, pointing over to the glass partition. 'You think she might know what's going on?'

But I was already heading towards her. 'Excuse me.'

She looked up from a computer screen. 'Can I help you?'

'Shannon Kennedy,' I said, aware of Norman on my shoulder. 'We're friends of hers. We know she's been brought in just recently, badly burnt. There was a fire and...'

She rummaged around for notes and picked up a phone, dialing internally while she held a finger up to us. 'Just one moment.'

'... I hope she can make it.'

We waited a few moments while she nodded and spoke with the invisible voice on the other end of the line.

'I see,' she said. 'Yes, of course. I'll tell them.' She hung up, then turned to us. 'She's in I.C.U.'

'I.C.U?' Norman said.

'Intensive Care Unit,' she said. 'She's not out of the woods yet, far from it. I will try to get a doctor to come and speak to you, but that may take a while. We're trying to contact her family but -'

'You won't find anyone,' I said. 'They're all dead. I mean, she hasn't got anyone. Not anymore.'

'We're the closest thing,' Norman said. 'Her friends are her family, you know?'

She nodded. I clocked her name badge. Staff Nurse Hannah McKenzie. 'I understand. But in cases like this, the police usually deal with any next of kin stuff. You'll have to speak to them.' She nodded behind us and I heard those air wave radios crackling again, a tinny voice from the central control room filling the air. 'But in the meantime, please take a seat and I will see if a doctor can speak to you soon.'

'Will she live?' Norman said. 'I mean, in your experience, with burns that bad? Will she make it?'

'She's probably suffering from hypothermia,' she said.

'What, with burns?'

'The body shuts down in shock,' she said. 'So its core temperature can drop dramatically. She's probably also lost a lot of blood and may be suffering from hypovolemia. I'm sure you're aware that she's in a very poorly condition and she's going to be in hospital for a long time, if she survives this. I'm sorry.'

'We need a doctor as soon as possible,' I said, as I led Norman away from the desk. She smiled sympathetically and nodded before picking up the phone again.

I turned my attention to the two coppers. They were both young and newly qualified, probably still keen. I knew I had to play the worried friend card again.

'Can we have a private word?' I said.

'What about, sir?'

He was young, fit, a square jaw and flushed cheeks. Probably barely a year into the job and exuding an overconfidence that bordered on arrogance. I'd seen his type many times before, and had a few under my charge before now. Before my career went down the pan.

'We just want to see our friend Shannon,' Norman said. 'She's the one from the fire. You know, at Birch Court? Pendleton?'

The other one, taller, handsome but filled out and built like a brick shit house, nodded. 'I'm sure you're aware that she's in safe hands in ICU,' he said. 'We don't know any more than you do, but it doesn't look good, does it?'

'As soon as we know anything,' the other one said, 'we'll let you know.'

Norman, as tall as copper number two and just as wide, insisted they take his number to update him as soon as possible while I was distracted by the drunk outside. He looked me in the eye and nodded knowingly before I was brought back to reality.

'Have I seen you before?' The smaller one said. 'You look familiar.'

I shrugged. 'I'm a good boy,' I said, forcing a smile. 'Never been nicked in my life.'

That seemed to satisfy him before he went to speak with the nurse on the desk himself. I got the impression the taller one was a little more experienced and sought to allay our fears.

'Look,' he said. He had a thick Welsh accent. I felt more relaxed knowing he wasn't from around here. 'I know this must be worrying for you both and we're doing all we can to find out what's gone on with this fire, but in terms of actually finding out how she is, well that's where we're as much in the dark as you are. But rest assured, I will give you a call just as soon as we know more. So you say there's no family?'

'We're her family,' Norman said. 'The only one she's got. There are other friends, of course. A lot of us. As you can expect, we're all very worried.'

The copper nodded. 'Understandable. And we know she's not the only victim in this. There are three more ambulances on the way and there are a lot of people and relatives keen to get a clear picture of what's happened, so...'

'What do you think might've caused this?' I said, knowing full well what had caused it. 'For it to be such a bad fire, you know?'

'We'll have to wait until the fire is out and we get the all clear from the fire service,' he said. 'Together we'll investigate and learn more as we go on, but I'm sure you'll understand that these things can take some time, given the nature of the situation. As soon as it's under control, we'll inevitably know a lot more.'

'Could it be arson?' I said.

'It's really too early to say.'

'But you're not ruling it out?'

'Of course not, sir. We can't rule that out.'

'So if some of the victims die - or all of them, even - then it could be a murder inquiry, couldn't it?'

He nodded. 'I guess you could very well be correct, sir, but I must stress that at this stage - very important - all we know for certain is that there has been a fire and several people are badly hurt. Now if you excuse me, gentleman, I need to speak with my colleague.'

Norman wanted to press him some more, but I stopped him. 'Let's have a smoke,' I said. 'There's nothing we can do but wait.'

———

So that's what we did. For another two hours. During that time, I'd called Bob three times and sent several texts, getting nothing in return. It was nearly seven o'clock and we were two more coffees down. The sun had come up about an hour ago, and already it was blazing. Not much change there. I felt like shit, needed a shower, and knew I had my work cut out. Norman had fallen asleep, which gave me a chance to wander the local corridors for any sign of a doctor that might tell us something. Though all I found were hospital staff rushing in for early duties and more walking wounded turning up as the day began. I was just outside finishing another smoke and thinking about my next move when a doctor called me from the doors. It was about time. Norman was hovering, bleary-eyed, behind him.

'Mr. Thompson?'

'That's me,' I lied. 'How is she?'

He took us to a quiet room nearby, one I suspected was reserved for relatives of the newly deceased, a place where the news of sudden death could sink in. There were tissues on a coffee table next to leaflets about grief. I feared the worst. We sat down on a soft and comfortable sofa.

'The good news is that she is stable,' he said. I clocked

his name badge. Dr. Sethi was calm and measured, a well-spoken man in his mid-forties. 'But she's very poorly indeed. She's suffering from hypothermia and hypovolemia, meaning she has lost a lot of blood. She will need skin grafts, blood transfusions, and a lot of care on our burns unit before we can even think about discharging her. I think she could be in hospital for a long time.'

'Is she gonna die?' Norman said.

Dr. Sethi was quiet for a moment, carefully considering his next answer. 'I'll be honest with you. She might die. She's certainly not through the worst of this. Her body has suffered a massive shock and has a lot of damage. She has third-degree burns to about seventy percent of it, mainly on her torso, but her legs and arms are badly damaged too. Her... face is also severely affected and in some cases the flesh is so badly damaged that her bones are exposed. Obviously, she's now bandaged up and it will take her a long time to recover even the most basic of functions. But it's not unheard of for someone to survive this kind of thing and we're of course doing absolutely everything we can to ensure she has the best possible chance of survival. It's going to take a lot of time and a lot of care before she's even on the road to recovery, but we've made a start and at this stage it's really all we can do. She's stable, but now we wait.'

'How long could we be talking, Doctor?' I said.

Again, he was composed and measured before answering. 'This kind of hospitalisation requires a lot of factors to fall into place before the patient is truly on the road to recovery. She will need plastic surgery, counselling, specialist nutrition, advanced nursing care. A lot of therapy. As well as the damage to the physical body - the blood loss, the skin grafting - I'm afraid Shannon will go through a very difficult time in terms of her mental health. She may suffer from anxiety and depression as a consequence of this, perhaps Post Traumatic Stress Disorder, you name it. Coming to terms with the stress she's been under in that fire will perhaps be her biggest challenge. So we say a person can never truly recover from this kind of thing, but in terms of her physical recovery, we could be looking at maybe a year, minimum, before she is anything like her more usual self. The more long-term damage could be psychological though, so she will need a lot of support. This is a big life change and it will require a lot of coping strategies. There will have to be a lot of multi-agency care put in place, including social care, before Shannon is considered for discharge.'

Anxiety, depression, PTSD. As if the girl hadn't been through enough in her life. I wondered if she'd be better off dead.

'So she's gonna be here a long time.' I said. 'We'll have to make sure she's well looked after.'

The doctor nodded. 'If she comes through this next period, this intensive care she will be under, then we can begin to formulate a plan for her more long-term care. For now, we work hard at keeping her stable.'

'Jesus,' Norman said. 'How can she survive this?'

'It will take a lot, from everyone around her, not least herself.'

'She's better off dead,' Norman said. I'm glad he was voicing what I myself was thinking. 'I've seen what that kind of damage can do to a person. Psychologically, you know. I'd be surprised if she doesn't wish she'd died in that fire.'

Like the good doctor said, there was nothing we could do but watch and wait. Norman said he had a pub to run, and I had a hundred things to do - at least, it felt that way. No doubt word would get out soon enough, and perhaps was already out, that Shannon had narrowly escaped death - for now. As soon as she was well enough for visitors, I'd be the first in the queue. But now there were another two people I felt I needed to speak to: her best friend, Claire, and her young lover, Jamie. I'd be interested to know who her last contact was with. I suppose it could even have been with me. But if she'd spent the night with Jamie, perhaps he'd been a victim of the fire too. I needed Fiona to do my digging for me. I dialed her up and left a message for her to call me back.

We'd already seen three more ambulances bring the injured to Salford Royal, and the coppers had hinted at more casualties that might've gone to another hospital, the MRI or North Manchester General being the main two that would cope with this kind of event. A fire of that magnitude would surely claim fatalities. And there were at least four flats burning that I saw myself. I expected more to come, for certain. It was a local tragedy, and when there is a local tragedy, local people get angry. Someone, somewhere, would know what went down last night. Someone would be pissed off enough to do something about it. I knew things didn't end here.

When I got back to the car, the morning now in full swing, I called Laura.

'How is she?'

'She's seen better days,' she said. 'But they're keeping her in, at least. Just until they stabilise her again. You?'

'It's been a long night.' I filled her in on events and

brought her up to speed, which took a few minutes over the chatter from the TV and Charlie complaining about having to go to school. If she was shocked, she didn't show it.

'It's on the news now,' she said. 'Hang on.'

'Are you at home?'

'Yeah, got to get Charlie ready for school. You know that. She's okay. Nothing we haven't seen before. She's in good hands now - I hope.'

'What's the news saying?'

There was a pause for a moment, and I could hear her gasp. 'Oh my God, there's been a gas explosion. A big one.'

'Oh fucking hell...'

'It looks pretty bloody awful. Hang on, let me just watch it a minute.'

I heard the TV in the background go up a notch, but couldn't make out what was being said. It was all just jumbled noise to go with the noise running around my head. I started up the Volvo and considered which way I was going to go now the traffic was building up.

'Yeah, a gas explosion,' she said. 'They reckon the fire had led to it somehow.'

'So there wasn't an explosion to begin with?'

'They didn't say. Jim, where are you now?'

'I'm just about to leave the Salford Royal.'

'So is she still alive? Will she live?'

'She is and she will - probably. It's complicated but there's a long way to go for her now.'

'Christ. And still no sign of Bob?'

'Not a dickie bird. Do you think he's all right?'

A sigh. 'Not really, no. But then I've thought that from the beginning. Jim, are you forgetting that he's on the run?'

'Not on the phone, Laura.'

'Well, you know what I mean.'

'I know what you mean,' I said. 'But he's been keeping secrets. Says he's got things to sort out, which I can understand, but...'

'Does he have to keep things from you?'

'Exactly.'

'Oh no.'

'What? What's wrong?'

'They're saying a firefighter's lost his life. And there are several fatalities.'

'Fucking hell, no.' Except I knew it. I could see it coming. 'I need to get down there again.'

'No,' she said. 'Don't be silly. You stay away from there, Jim, do you hear me?'

'We need to know more.'

'But do we?'

'Who painted the swastika on the ambulance, Laura? Whoever it was must've been there as it went up in flames. They could've been there watching it all in that crowd, they could've been watching me. And my bet is that someone will know that whoever set fire to that building will know he - or they - was there. They can't all look out for each other. Someone will know exactly what happened last night, and why.'

'Seems a bit extreme to take Shannon out and kill innocents in the process.'

'We're dealing with extreme people, love,' I said. 'This is how they operate.'

'And the irony is that they failed. She's not even dead.'

'But innocents are,' I said. 'Listen, can you get back to the office today? I think I need you there.'

'I'll be there, but what are you doing?'

'I've gotta see a man about a dog.'

'You don't keep secrets from me, Jim Locke.'

'I'm going to Sanctuary,' I said. 'Find out more about some voluntary work I've got my eye on. But listen, I'm expecting Fiona. She's got something I think will come in handy. She might just turn up at the office. And one more thing - can you get in touch with Dave? I need to speak to him about something.'

'Of course, but what is it?'

'I'll tell you later,' I said, 'but it might turn out to be nothing. I just want to run some things past him. Is everything set up properly now?'

'All ready to go,' she said. 'I've got to transfer some files onto the new computer today, so I'll be heading to town as soon as I drop Charlie off.'

'Speaking of Charlie - is he okay?'

'He's fine. I think he's used to all this now. But he misses you.'

'I miss him. And when all this is over, we'll all go out for junk food and stuff. Whatever you want.'

'I just want things to be normal for a change,' she said. 'Is that too much to ask?'

But I didn't have an answer and instead reminded her to phone me if anything or anyone turned up before it was time for me to head back.

In the meantime, I put the Volvo into gear and left the hospital car park, that image of Shannon's gruesomely burnt features distracting me from the road as I drove.

I was on the road for longer than I would've liked. The roadworks in and around the city centre were becoming a total joke, leaving traffic in absolute gridlock for miles around. When I eventually got to where I needed to be, I parked up down a back alley I knew before heading in. When I reached the door, it wasn't even open, so I crossed the road and slipped into a ramshackle looking greasy spoon cafe. Got myself a bacon roll and a large coffee, black, while I waited and pieced recent events together in my head as the rush hour traffic moved slowly past the window.

There was a TV fixed to the wall in the corner and I caught the tail end of the morning news bulletin. It was all about the fire and the gas explosion. I looked around and the few people that were in the place all audibly gasped when the journalist confirmed that there were at least four fatalities that they knew of, including the firefighter. I counted the dead. Stevie, Lloyd, four others. Six needless deaths. When the news finished and the morning's talk show came on, I turned away and wondered how many more they'd killed that we didn't know about. If Shannon lost her battle, that would make seven that I knew of. It'd be interesting to hear who else had perished in that inferno. From what I could make out on the news, most people had evacuated the building before the explosion. There was certainly a large crowd when I arrived, and a lot of them were keen to get past the police cordon while Norman and I were there. There surely couldn't have been many people left in there unless they were physically unable to get out in time. Nevertheless, Hardy and his associates, I was sure, had some major blood on their hands. The problem came in finding the evidence that they were responsible. I had to wonder if Robertson was yet on the case.

I got myself a top up and watched the front entrance to Sanctuary finally open from the inside. A handful of rough sleepers stepped out into the heat of the morning, their ragged belongings trailing behind them. I was reminded of my former life, a temporary tragedy that had almost cost me.

The bespectacled care worker waved them off before moving a door weight against the tiled wall and fixing it open to all. It was my cue to step out and see just how well Hardy had fooled everyone around him.

I sparked up outside and crossed the road, weaving between traffic that was still only moving at a snail's pace. Took that shit in deep. The coffee had been strong and had woken me up enough so that I was ready to observe with a critical eye. Trouble was, it had made me jumpy and I kept having a nervous urge to look over my shoulder. It was a good job I had nicotine coursing through my veins to help temper the mild paranoia.

I stepped inside. All was quiet. Looked through into the sitting area and there was an old guy I might've recognised in my previous life, but I couldn't be sure. He was staring into space, nursing a cup of tea.

'Can I help you?'

I looked up to see a young and good looking woman standing in the partition doorway. Beyond it, I knew, was a large kitchen area where most people, staff included, congregated over a coffee urn.

I saw no point in bending the truth. 'My name's Jim Locke,' I said. I handed her my card. 'I'm a private investigator. Lloyd was one of my clients, and I was looking into a case for him. Stephen Kennedy? He used to doss here now and again.'

She put a hand to her mouth, wide eyed, and turned around for any sign of her colleague. He was marching down the corridor, looking keen.

'Katie?'

'It's that private detective,' she said. 'Mr. Locke. Wants to speak to us about Lloyd and Stephen Kennedy.'

Had they been expecting me? It didn't show, but then I

guessed events could be too recent and the murders too raw. They didn't seem surprised that I was here. I didn't know whether that was a good or bad thing.

'You'd better come through,' the bespectacled one said. It was the same guy I spoke to the night Lloyd was killed, the one who'd just come on duty. 'I'm surprised it's taken you this long. We've been hoping you'd call in.'

'Oh really?' I said. 'Any reason for that?'

There was no reply as I followed them through to the kitchen area. He introduced himself as Damien and asked if I wanted a coffee. After the one I'd just had, the jitters still rising in me, I told him no.

There were a handful of service users, both homeless and in need of a detox - I'd recognise that look anywhere, having seen it in my own reflection before now - sitting around a large round table. There were several pots of tea and a mixed plate of biscuits, a few empty plates with the remnants of breakfast toast on them. There were nods in my direction as Damien offered me a seat. I felt obliged, but declined.

'Do you have an office we could go to?'

One of the homeless guys - a man dressed head to toe in combat gear - stood up. 'We're just going now anyway,' he said. 'Thanks for the bed and breakfast, Damo.'

Damien smiled and nodded as they left the table, then the building. It was probably best there was no interruption of any kind. I needed a clear enough head to nail down what it was I came here for.

'So how can I help, Mr. Locke?'

'Call me Jim,' I said. 'Lloyd did. Stevie did. Too formal otherwise.'

'Jim it is,' he said. 'But at least let me get you a drink.'

'Actually, a cold water would be good.'

'I'll get it,' Katie said, and went over to the fridge.

I had a quick look around. The place was familiar, since I'd been here a few times before, once when I came to rope Stevie into doing my dirty work on the Angel case, and before that as a service user myself when I tried to get housing advice and a hot dinner. It wasn't too long ago, but it felt like a lifetime. It was all best left in the past.

'As you may know, I'm investigating the death of a man who frequently took a bed here,' I said.

'Stephen Kennedy,' said Katie, joining us at the table. 'He was a lovely man, you know.'

'I know,' I said. But he had his demons, like all of us. Some of us have more demons than others. 'And I believe he was murdered. This was no accident.'

'Like Lloyd,' Damien said. 'That was certainly no accident.'

'No.'

'Do you think the police will find those responsible? I mean, they say he was shot in the head. Like a what do you call it...'

'A hit,' Katie said. 'Like they took him out for a reason.'

'Exactly,' I said. 'And the question is, for what reason?'

They nodded solemnly, shared a look between them. I downed the water and unashamedly asked for more. While Katie delivered, my phone pinged. Glanced at the text message. It was from Fiona, asking me to give her a call. It would have to wait.

'And now,' I said, 'Stevie's sister is in hospital with severe third-degree burns. Shannon Kennedy.'

'She was at his funeral.'

'That's right.'

'I didn't know he had any family,' Katie said.

'Well, she's the only one,' I said. 'And I believe she's

been targeted too. Except she's still alive while four innocents, including a firefighter, are dead.'

'You think it's the same people responsible?' Damien
said.

'I don't think it,' I said. 'I know it. Getting the police to
see it is another matter, though.'

'Jesus,' Katie said. 'Oh God, that's awful. What the hell
is happening?'

'It's a good question,' I said. There were a lot of good
questions and so few answers. But I hoped I would get some
here. I'd written the names of Hardy's aliases in my notebook and took it out. 'Now I've done some digging around.'

'Find anything?'

I was beginning to dislike Damien. He had a mild edge
of smarminess I found nauseating, like a cocky know it all
student who needed a good punch. 'It's my job to find
things,' I said. 'And yes, I believe I have. That's the reason
I'm here and I could do with your help just to confirm what
it is I'm thinking.'

'Fire away.'

I went straight for the jugular, wishing I was doing it for
real. 'I need a list of all volunteers, going right back to the
eighties.'

'Not possible,' he said. 'We didn't even exist in the
eighties.'

And I bet he was still swimming around his daddy's
balls back then, so he wouldn't have a clue what I'm looking
for. The connection. The proof that Hardy was here.

'But we were in the early nineties,' Katie said. 'Weren't
we?'

Damien rolled his eyes and stood up, scraping his chair
back on the cold, tiled floor. 'You'd better come this way.'

I followed him through a set of doors and down a long,

dark corridor that gave me goosebumps. Perhaps it was the sudden drop in temperature, perhaps not. But the place freaked me out. It felt like a prison, with rooms on either side that might have one day been cells.

'It used to be a prison,' Katie whispered beside me, as if she'd read my mind. 'Back in the day. The Victorians certainly knew how to give you the creeps.'

When we reached the end, we went through another set of doors and into a room carpeted in grey with a ceiling so low I instinctively ducked. Damien took a large bunch of keys from his jeans and rattled around in the lock of a narrow, steel topped door until it opened up into deep gloom. He found an ancient light switch on the bare brick wall and flicked it on. A sickly yellow strip light illuminated a row of grey filing cabinets and an old office desk with a single broken chair flushed into it. There was a shit brown couch against the back wall that reminded me of one my mum used to have. The room was bloody freezing.

'Have a seat,' he said. I told him I'd rather stand.

He rummaged around in all three cabinets until at the bottom of the third one, buried under a mountain of files, was an orange folder. He lifted it out and dumped it on the desk.

'It's all in there,' he said. 'Help yourself. I'll be in my office if you need me.'

I was glad he'd disappeared, and the echo of his footsteps down the corridor from hell was music to my ears. The fact that Katie saw fit to hang around was a bonus, too.

'Need some help?'

'Don't see why not,' I said. I opened the folder and took out half the paperwork stuffed in there. Handed it to her. 'Can you go through this? Just skim read it. I'm looking for some names. Trevor Hardy, Shaun Cox,

Kenneth Regan, Liam MacNamara, Bill Williams. Shaun Cox in particular, since that name fits the time period I want.'

She nodded. 'Anything else?'

'Not really,' I said. I took my share of the papers and began sifting through them. 'But maybe you can tell me about this place. You know, any of its history you might know of, how you came to work here, that kind of stuff.'

'There's not much to tell,' she said. 'I've been here a few years.'

'What, as a paid employee?'

She nodded. 'I ended up here after University. Thought it would be good to get some experience while I was doing my training, so I volunteered here during my degree.'

'In...?'

'Social work. And then when I finished, they offered me a job. It pays the bills, just.'

'So it's the kind of place that probably has a lot of volunteers going in and out of its doors...'

'You could say that.'

'So you'll have known Lloyd, then?'

'Oh yeah,' she said. 'He was a lovely man. He'd volunteered here forever.'

'Anyone you know of that came here but didn't last, for whatever reason? You know, someone who didn't hang around too long?'

She thought for a minute. 'No, not really. No one I know of, though Damien might know better. He's been here for ten years, at least.'

But I suspected I'd get very little from him. 'He seems a guarded kind of bloke.'

'Damien?'

'Yeah.'

She nodded. 'He can be a bit funny sometimes. I believe 'Up his own arse' is the correct terminology.'

'Glad it's not just me, then.'

'He can be a funny bugger sometimes,' she said. 'Don't take him seriously. I know I don't.'

'Any plans to stay here?'

'Actually, no.' Her voice became a whisper. 'I will be moving on soon but don't mention it to him.'

I nodded and smiled. I could see she was destined for greater things. 'So tell me about the place. How long have people been coming here?'

'I don't know for certain, but it's been here a good twenty years, at least. Maybe twenty-five, thirty years, even.'

'That would take us right back to the late eighties then.'

'I suppose.'

'But Damien said it didn't exist in the eighties.'

'Take no notice of him.'

'If it's thirty years, then nineteen eighty-six or thereabouts.'

'Yeah, but the building itself,' she said, 'has been here a long time. Like I said, the Victorians had it as a prison. A small place, I know, but at one time it was attached to a police station. Back in the day, I mean.'

'So these would've been holding cells then...'

'Yeah, I guess they would. Spooky.'

She wasn't wrong. There was a certain shiver going down my spine, come to think of it, and I didn't think it was just the temperature.

We were quiet a moment as we each shuffled through the papers. My phone pinged again and I checked the message. Fiona. Perhaps it was more urgent than I thought. I sent a quick reply and told her I'd be in touch within half an hour.

The papers themselves weren't much to look at and were hardly a wealth of information. They were just simple employee records. Names, addresses, phone numbers, next of kin. But it was gold dust for someone like me and for what I wanted. I only needed a scrap, just to confirm what I was thinking. And then it came.

'Here we are,' she said. She handed me a sheet of paper. 'Bill Williams.'

I took it and had a quick look. Bill Williams volunteered a long time ago, right back at the beginning of nineteen ninety. He was sixty-two at the time and living in Rochdale. This place would've been a long way for him to come, just to volunteer.

'Can I get a copy of this?'

'Photocopier's not working,' she said. 'But I won't say anything if you won't...?'

I pocketed the sheet and went back to my own pile. Spent a few moments leafing through the papers, some of it illegible, until I finally found what I came for. There it was, in black and white.

Shaun Cox. September 14th 2001 - January 8th 2002. So he didn't last long and probably never had the intention to. He was certainly no Mother Teresa. I wondered, as I looked down at the basic information before me, what had gone through his mind the day he first volunteered here. And had Lloyd been here then, too? I knew he'd been here a long time, but this was 2016. We're talking fifteen, almost twenty years ago now. Had he been here that long? Had he once worked with his killer?

'Any idea when Lloyd started here?'

She puffed out her cheeks. 'Not entirely sure. But if we find his paperwork too, then we'll know, won't we?'

Perhaps it was the lack of sleep or too much coffee and

nicotine, and my brain had begun to melt. I dug through and found Lloyd's information at the bottom of my pile. Seemed like none of this stuff was in any kind of order, as if someone had just thrown it all together randomly. The sheet of paper was turning brown with age, but everything I needed was there. Lloyd had begun his voluntary work back in nineteen ninety-eight. And we all knew how it ended. So he'd definitely been around when Hardy was here, Hardy who had fooled everyone into thinking he was Shaun Cox, a bus driver who somehow had the time to volunteer at a homeless shelter. A bus driver who would end up serving time for GBH. Who would end up killing innocents in order to cover up the abuse he'd carried out on a different kind of victim in the past.

Why did he want Lloyd dead? What did Lloyd know?

'Can I take this as well?'

'Don't see why not. It's been buried here for years without anyone batting an eyelid. I don't think it'll be missed.'

I was in need of a smoke, so it was time to make my excuses. But I needed to know one more thing before I cut off and called Fiona.

'Damien said you'd been hoping I'd call in,' I said. 'Is there any reason for that?'

She shook her head. 'Not that I'm aware of. But it's probably to do with Lloyd. A lot of the service users knew him and they want to know what's going on, you know? Some of them are scared, I think.'

I thought of Kyle Faulkner, of Bubble Coat and Stumps. Considered that when I'd last spoken to them, they'd kept some things quiet, for whatever reason. Were they keen to know what had gone down? Others too? Was it time for another talk?

I stuffed the paperwork I came for in my jeans pocket and motioned to leave. I needed to get the fuck out of here. The place was seriously giving me the creeps.

Katie followed me just a little closer than I would've expected. And I don't know whether it was just me and my imagination, but the corridor back to the kitchen seemed that little bit darker on the way out.

CHAPTER EIGHTEEN

'Now do you see why it was so important?'
        'I get it now. Absolutely. Just wish you'd made more sense at the time. Anyway, are you listening or do I have to repeat myself again?'

'I'm all ears.'

I was en route back to the car with the papers from Sanctuary safely in my pocket. Damien didn't have much else to say, and when I'd questioned him about whether he'd remembered any suspicious volunteers from his time here, he rolled his eyes and said he could barely remember what happened yesterday. The guy simply oozed cool. I thanked Katie for her help and left with my phone stuck to my ear. Fiona was keen to get down to business.

'So they woke me up at two a.m., asked if I could come in to help cover traffic because of the fire,' she said. 'It meant they could change my duty tonight, which suits me fine. I mean, Friday night around the Northern Quarter with all those fucking hen parties and stag nights? No thanks. So I'm about to head off home to bed. It's a win win. All I've been doing is standing around Salford Crescent, redirecting traffic. Not to say there hasn't been the odd twat to deal with though.'

'I bet.'

'And I've had it up to here with the traffic commissioner. Don't get me started.'

'I wasn't going to. Anyway, what've you got?'

'The six million dollar question,' she said. 'Bottom line is, they're all over it. Forensics are on top of it as we speak and shit's going down. They're putting everything into it. Even Robertson's keen. I've never seen him so fired up.'

'He on the case, then?'

'Oh yeah,' she said. 'They know all about Shannon Kennedy, poor woman. Four dead. Firefighter Tom Rawlings leaves a wife and a two-year-old.'

'Fucking hell...'

'I know, I know. It's awful. The other three are as yet unidentified, but I'm hearing they've pulled a body from Shannon's flat. They don't know if it's male or female yet.'

'Jesus. That could be Jamie.'

'Jamie?'

'Lad she was seeing,' I said. 'Half her age.'

'The innocents are always the victims,' she said, and she was right. I'd seen my fair share of it down the years. 'Just a young man, then?'

'Early twenties, I think. If it's him.'

'Well, I suppose it could be,' she said. 'But listen, it's chaos down there, and a lot of people are getting seriously pissed off. They aren't allowed back into their homes until a thorough investigation has been carried out. Four flats have been taken out, two of them almost entirely thanks to the gas explosion. It's a mess, Jim. I've never seen anything like it.'

'Do we have any kind of timeframe?'

'Your guess is as good as mine.'

'It could be days, couldn't it?'

'More than likely.'

'And those people are gonna get more and more pissed off.'

'Oh yeah,' she said. 'But they'll let them back in slowly, floor by floor. Make sure the whole building's safe before giving the all clear.'

It was to be expected, but no doubt a royal pain in the arse for the people that lived there. Chalked it up on the list of things Hardy and his associates had been responsible for as an aftereffect of their crimes. There were lots of people, not to mention families with children, who wouldn't be sleeping in their own beds tonight.

'Where are they gonna go?'

'Well, the council can't put them up,' she said. 'They haven't got a pot to piss in.'

'Yeah, that's what they'll tell you.'

'Times are hard,' she said. 'There's a few charities pulling together. Other than that...'

It was a problem everyone could do without.

'Listen,' I said. 'Did you look into those names I asked you about? Kenneth Regan and Bill Williams? Especially in connection with Hardy...'

'Well I was getting to that,' she said. 'Hang on.' I heard a car door shut and an engine start up. 'But did you get a chance to look at the hard drive again?'

'You first.'

'You got a pen?'

'Just text me the details.'

'Well, there isn't much,' she said. I could hear her car moving off. She must've had me on speakerphone. 'Kenneth Regan first. A long-time friend of Hardy and Williams. Like

Hardy, he's done time for grievous bodily harm. Battered an old lady with an iron when she finally clocked he was trying to rob her and threatened to phone the police. This was way back in the eighties. He'd blagged his way into her house and tried to nick her purse and some jewellery. Told her he was there to read her gas meter and got panicky when she came to her senses. So he hit her six times with her bloody iron until he knocked her out. Broke her nose and knocked a few teeth out too. He got eighteen months and served six.'

'Typical.'

'Yeah, some things never change. But get this: he's also on the sex offenders register. Been on it since nineteen ninety-two. He's a known paedophile. Has been active around Manchester and Salford but it's not known if he's been up to no good recently.'

'We got an address?'

'Last known address was a place in Crumpsall. A little maisonette on one of those damp council estates. This guy's been all over. He could be anywhere.'

'Is he even alive?'

'It's a good question,' she said. 'It wouldn't surprise me if someone hadn't bludgeoned the bastard to death by now.'

It crossed my mind that that someone might just be me should he prove to be connected to the killings. 'Can you text me that last known address?'

'Already plan to.'

'Good. Now Bill Williams. Anything on him?'

'Well, we know he worked at St Joseph's. A care home in Rochdale for orphaned kids and stuff.'

'Tell me something I don't know.'

'So is it the place Hardy worked as well?'

'Apparently so,' I said. 'And what's more, Williams volunteered at Sanctuary too.'

'Sanctuary?'

'Place where Lloyd volunteered. Speaking of whom....'

'We'll come to him,' she said. 'But some more on Bill Williams. He was a well-known character around the Rochdale area. Mixed with some very prominent local politicians back in the seventies and eighties.'

'These the ones that have been linked with sex crimes?'

'There was a paedophile ring, yeah,' she said. 'You'll know all about that, Jim.'

'You think he was a part of it?'

'Maybe,' she said. 'Probably. Most of those thought to be involved are dead now, including Williams. If he was involved, we'll never know.'

'Wouldn't surprise me.'

'Nor me. He was a member of the Masonic Order in Rochdale. Secret handshakes and all that shite.'

'Yeah, and the rest...'

'You can check their records yourself,' she said. 'The Masonic Hall is still there.'

'Maybe some other time,' I said. 'I've got enough for what I need for the time being.'

'He was a wealthy man,' she said. 'One of these philan-thropist types.'

'Like Jimmy Savile,' I said. 'And look at what he got up to.'

'I know. The charity stuff probably helped to cover his tracks. A respectful member of the community, pillar of society, all that. He probably didn't need a proper job, since he inherited most of his wealth.'

'Hiding it in plain sight again.'

'Come again?'

'Nothing,' I said. 'Just a pattern I'm noticing.'

'I'm not following.'

'It just seems they have no care of doing what they're doing,' I said. 'Or what they've done. Putting up a big fuck you to everyone and probably pissing themselves while they're at it. Getting away with it all right under our noses, you know.'

'I see.'

'And Hardy,' I said. 'He's still at it. Possibly Regan too.'

'You think they're both responsible? They're the two men in the Range Rover?'

'Either Hardy and Regan or Hardy and MacNamara. The car belongs to him, does it not?'

'Could he be the one putting a spark to a flame?'

'Exactly,' I said. I paused. 'Isn't that a song?'

'What?'

'Doesn't matter.' I reached the car and got in. 'But that brings us nicely to Lloyd.'

'Poor man.'

'This SIM card,' I said, digging around for my keys. 'You got it?'

'I'll be over this afternoon. Try and stop me.'

'Get some rest first.'

'I'm about to keel over. But listen, you sound shattered too, Jim. Why don't you get your head down as well?'

'I'll sleep when I'm dead,' I said. I suddenly thought of Bob and got a shiver. He still hadn't been in touch, and I was so caught up in this business that I'd forgotten about him. I felt a pang of guilt. 'Listen, I need to go. Got some things to do.'

'Four o'clock,' she said. 'Don't make me wait.'

I hung up, started the Volvo, and sped off towards the flat.

There was an eerie silence when I opened the door. It was just as I'd left it when I got the call from Norman. The glass I'd drunk the brandy from was left on the coffee table, sticky with the residue of alcohol. I sparked up and put a coffee on. Checked the time. It was almost 09:30. Took a quick piss and noticed Bob's bag on the floor by the bedroom. There were still some of his things in it - deodorant, toothbrush, some clothes - which indicated he'd be coming back. Wherever he'd gotten to, I assumed it was because he needed that time alone. One of the last things he'd said to me was that he was going back to the flat to get his head down. But he never did, and probably never had any intention to. I tried him again. Got a dead line. Had someone caught up with him? For what he'd done in Spain? I suddenly had a gut wrenching feeling.

I thought of his old friend, George Thornley, the editor at the Evening Chronicle. I knew I had his number somewhere. Made a quick call to Laura.

'So did you see that man?' she said. 'Dog suitable?'

'I got what I knew I'd find,' I said. 'Hardy had volunteered at Sanctuary, as did Bill Williams. And the thing is, Lloyd would've worked with Hardy too. He would've been around when Hardy turned up and then left the organisation in January two thousand and two. Except he'd have known him as Shaun Cox.'

'You think he had something on them?'

'Yeah, I do. But what, I don't know.'

'Maybe he knew they'd torched Stevie and they knew he was on to them. And that's why they were following him.'

'Probably, but I suspect it's more than that. You at the office yet?'

'Just got here.'

'Any sign of Bob?'

'Afraid not,' she said. 'He'll turn up, love.'

'I'm not so sure. Listen, I've been thinking of getting hold of George Thornley at the paper. They go back a long way.'

'You think he'll know where he is?'

'He could be kipping on his couch instead of mine as we speak. Though as far as I know, Thornley thinks he's dead.'

'Give me a minute.'

I heard her rummaging around in the office, so I put the shower on and got out of my jeans. The coffee was percolating nicely. Felt like I could sleep a thousand years and longed for the day when I could. But I knew I had work to do. I couldn't stop now. I glanced at the laptop on the coffee table. It was still running. Thought briefly of what I'd read over late last night. How Isabella Burns had first met Robertson. A family friend, the neighbour up the street. Felt sick to the pit of my stomach.

'You there?'

'Go on.'

'Got a pen?'

I put her on speaker and punched the number down on my phone's notepad. She said she'd get to work on transferring some files and asked when I'd be back in.

'Not sure,' I said. 'But Fiona's gonna turn up at four with the SIM card.'

'Dave said he'd be happy to help.'

'Good.' I glanced at the laptop again. 'Listen, I'm gonna go. If Bob turns up...'

'You'll be the first to know.'

'And listen, I still need you to keep an eye on that forum they use.'

'The dark web here I come. Such fun.'

'It's for a worthy cause.'

'Yeah, well now we have some decent gear I feel so much better about hanging around in there. Now get back as soon as you can. I want to see your face.'

I hung up and poured the coffee, black, before jumping in the shower. It did nothing to keep the weariness at bay. I felt more than tired. Got dressed, at last feeling the benefit of a good scrub down, and downed two painkillers with the coffee. Sparked up and crashed on the couch, dragging the laptop back to life. Took a deep breath and delved in once again.

Watson: *Do you have the phone now?*

WITNESS REMOVES iPHONE FROM HER JEANS AND HANDS IT TO WPC FIONA WATSON. THE DEVICE IS PHOTOGRAPHED AND PLACED IN A CLEAR SEALED BAG.

Watson: *You do realise that this device will hold vital evidence? Both the data within it and whatever is stored on the internet through the iCloud?*

Burns: *You can take it. But I need a replacement.*

Watson: *Of course. It's already been dealt with.*

WPC FIONA WATSON HANDS THE LATEST IPHONE TO THE WITNESS IN AN UNOPENED BOX.

Burns: *Thank you.*

Watson: *Okay. So after the barbecue, and what happened there, how did things continue?*

Burns: *I just went on as normal. But I couldn't stop thinking about it. I wanted it to happen again, you know?*

Watson: *I see. Tell us in your own words how the affair developed, Isabella.*

Burns: *Well, nothing happened for a while. A month at least. But I'd see him about three times a week leaving his house in the morning. You know, to go to work. I thought he worked away some nights, but now I know he wasn't.*

Watson: *Yes. Carry on.*

Burns: *So I'd see him and he'd look at me and I'd look away, then look back. I have to admit, I fancied him. He was much older, obviously. He was a man. There was something more that I wanted from that night at the barbecue. Eventually, I sent him a text.*

Watson: *Do you remember what the text said?*

Burns: *It's in the phone somewhere. I keep all my texts. Feel weird if I don't. But it was something like 'Can I meet you?' or something like that.*

Watson: *I see. And did he reply?*

Burns: *Almost straight away, actually. I remember it well because I was sitting in my history class when I checked my phone and got moaned at for it. He said he'd contact me.*

Watson: *How did you feel about this?*

Burns: *I felt... excited. And nervous. I couldn't think about anything else.*

Watson: *Understandable. Go on.*

Burns: *Well, I waited a few days. And when he didn't get in touch, I felt stupid. I thought he was messing around with me. That he didn't want to see me at all. I was just a silly little schoolgirl, you know.*

Watson: *Yes.*

Burns: *But then on the Friday, when school finished, he was waiting at the gate for me. I'd text him on the Monday, you see, and I had to wait all week for him to get in touch to arrange something. I thought he'd moved on, that he couldn't possibly like me, and I was just kidding myself. So when I saw him standing there in a suit at the gates... I think I might've done a wee.*

Watson: *So he just turned up? Did any of your friends notice him?*

Burns: *I don't know. Probably. Maybe. Anyway, we said 'Hi', you know, then we got in his car.*

Watson: *This was the BMW, right?*

Burns: *Yeah. The BMW. So we got in and he drove us to Heaton Park. We parked up near the lake.*

Watson: *The Sheepfoot Lane entrance.*

Burns: *I don't know, it was just near a lake. That's one of the places we always went.*

Watson: *That first time you went. What happened? Can you tell me that?*

Burns: *Same as what happened at the barbecue. But for longer this time.*

Watson: *I understand. And how did you feel? Did you feel under pressure or anything?*

Burns: *No, I liked it. I wanted it to happen and when it did, I felt happy about it.*

I stopped reading then, thinking what a horrible bastard the man really was. I went back to look again at some of the photographs of her cuts. Her arms were in a pretty bad way, and all because of the damage he'd done. I couldn't wait to wring his fucking neck.

If he was doing his job properly, he'd be at the scene of last night's fire right now. I knew that it'd be all over the news, so I spun around and sat up, then went online after I'd closed the hard drive down.

Sure enough, there it was. Top story on the Evening Chronicle website. They were running a live blog, which was still active, so I clicked through and read.

There was a brief statement from the Chief Fire Officer, Pat Morgan. He was adamant it was arson and the fire had started after someone had left a trail of petrol right up to the letter box of one of the flats. It didn't take long to spread its deadly flames, which had eaten its way through the building 'like a monster'.

There was also a statement from the Chief Superintendent of GMP, Sir David Michael Stephenson. They'd already concluded this was a serious arson attack on unsuspecting and innocent victims, and the hunt was now on to find those responsible and bring them to account using the full force of the law.

So the hunt was on. They needn't hunt for very long or very far. It was there in plain sight, right under their noses. I suspected Robertson already had a damn good idea who was responsible. That's if he wasn't too busy chasing after young girls. And if he didn't have a clue, he was worse than I thought. I didn't think he was covering up for anyone, although his behaviour - certainly with regard to young Isabella - paralleled that of Hardy and Williams and Regan. Abusive. Dangerous.

Psychopathic.

I scrolled down some more. Found a string of tweets from the handful of journalists that had been on the scene, read a few short statements from those who were now about to spend the night away from their homes. It was a shocking thing, a tragic outcome, a criminal act of barbarity.

They weren't wrong. And I knew I had to help bring those responsible to justice. The evidence was mounting. I examined the swastika that had been daubed on the ambulance, immediately thinking of Shannon and the agony she must've been going through as she lay in the back of it. The torment at knowing she'd be better off dead...

I downed the coffee and made a point of putting the laptop away under the bed. Instinctively called Bob again as I finished my smoke. Got a dead line to go with the shiver down my spine. The flat suddenly felt cold and empty. It was time to put my thoughts into action.

I dialled George Thornley as I left the building and walked towards the office. It was mid morning in the Northern Quarter, bright and bustling and full of life. There were giant, hand-painted murals on every corner, cafes and vintage clothes emporiums open to the trendy public, probably none of whom knew that just across the river somewhere in Salford lurked a fascist group of nutters intent on killing. I didn't believe any of it was random. There was no justification for it unless Hardy wanted to shut his victims up, and now I knew why he wanted to shut them up. I was convinced his victims were ready to finally reveal their hand. He had to put a stop to them if he wanted to stay out of prison. Their lives meant nothing, their deaths even less.

'Hello?'

'George Thornley?'

'Speaking.'

'You might remember me,' I said. 'It's Jim Locke.'

There was a brief pause, and I pictured him getting up from his swivel chair in his private office at the paper. 'Locke,' he said. 'To what do I owe the pleasure?'

'I'm not sure pleasure's the right word. You remember me, though?'

'Of course,' he said. 'I still have that Spider-Man satchel, if you need it back. And you owe me a pint.'

'Another time. Look, this may sound weird, but... has Bob Turner been in touch with you?'

Another pause, this time for longer, like he had something to hide. 'Bob's dead. I thought you knew that.'

'No,' I said. 'No, George. He isn't. He's alive and he's here, in Manchester. At least he was last night, but now he's disappeared. Look, I know he's been in touch with you. I know he's been on the phone to you at least once. So if he's sleeping on your couch, fair enough, it's just -' There was a silence on the line and I had to stop walking just to make sure he was still there and hadn't hung up. 'George?'

'Not on the phone. My office.'

'But...'

This time, the line did go dead. I was left standing outside the Night and Day Bar and Cafe, the temptation to step in for a pick me up as strong as ever. Instead, I sparked up and strode on the short distance to the paper's offices at Piccadilly Gardens.

As I got nearer, I could see Thornley standing out on the grass. The gardens were crowded with people catching a few rays in the never ending heatwave. He looked pale, like he'd just seen a ghost.

'Locke,' he said. We shook. 'Been a while.'

'Not too long. But I wish the circumstances could be better.'

He nodded. 'You'd better come up.'

I followed him up to the third floor. It was a lively place, busy with journalists at their desks and a lot of noise coming from one partitioned desk in particular, a gathering of hacks laughing their bollocks off over something on a computer screen. We shut them out when Thornley slammed his office door behind us, making sure, I noticed, that it was locked. The air con was blasting cold air through the room.

'Have a seat.'

'I think I'll stand.'

'Jim,' he said. 'Please. Sit down. You can cut out that copper shite with me. You're a friend of Bob's, you're a friend of mine.'

I sat down. 'Fair enough.'

He fell into his chair and sighed heavily. 'Like you, I thought he was dead. And like you, I also think he's a silly bastard for doing what he's done.'

'So he told you, then?'

He nodded. 'He came to see me a few days ago. Told me everything. At least, I think he's told me everything.'

'He's up shit creek.'

'You're not wrong there. They'll get to him, eventually. The Spanish, I mean. The Plod. But that's the least of his worries.'

'Go on.'

He clasped his hands together, looked me in the eye. 'Can I get you a drink?'

'Just spit it out, George.'

Another sigh. 'Okay. I met him in the Lass O' Gowrie. I couldn't believe what I was looking at.'

'Tell me about it.'

'He'd really changed, you know.'

'I know. Carry on.'

'We had a session,' he said. 'Not too heavy. He told me what he's told you, admitted you'd been putting him up, but that he wasn't planning on staying for much longer, you know.'

'Yeah.'

'And I reckon he was scared. And paranoid, just a little bit. He was talking about the Chinese and how he thought they might be onto him again.'

I thought that too. He'd said himself that it would only

be a matter of time. I nodded. 'Do you think they might've caught up with him?'

'I don't think so. I just think he was playing silly buggers, not thinking straight. Though I suppose,' he whispered, leaning in and keeping his voice down, 'that if you'd killed a man, one of their own, you'd be entitled to think they'd be coming after you.'

'He's been on the phone a few times,' I said. 'To several people, I reckon. Though I don't know why.'

'Or who?'

I shook my head. 'And now I've not seen him since last night. He left the pub and said he was going back to the flat - my place - but when I followed him he'd disappeared. I lost him.'

'And he's not been answering your calls?'

'No.'

'That's not like him. That's not Bob. I've known him forty-odd years, we've been rookie reporters together since the seventies...'

'I know.'

'Spent Christmas Day together before now. So I know him, you know what I mean?'

'Yeah.'

'Better than anyone.'

'Which is why I thought he'd be in touch,' I said. 'I'm surprised he didn't get in touch with you sooner.'

He left his chair and poured us both a coffee from the jug on the side. He handed me an ashtray and opened the window behind him. I sparked up, took that shit in deep.

'I knew he was in Spain,' he said. 'I knew just as much as you. But then after that Christmas Eve, when we heard nothing for months and months, I really believed he was dead. If he was still alive, he would've gotten in touch. I really believed that, so when he didn't...'

'It came as a shock to me as well. When he finally turned up back here. Did he not get in touch with you at all?'

'First I heard from him was two days ago.'

'Must have been a surprise.'

'You're fucking right it was.'

'Do you think he's done the right thing? Coming back, I mean?'

'Not really. I mean, do you? And let me put this to you - do you believe him? Do you believe any of it?'

'What, that he'd killed a man?'

'Yeah. You think he's capable?'

I thought about it. 'Why would he lie about a thing like that? And there's no reason not to believe him. And don't forget, he was on the phone to me before the gunshots went off. The only thing we got wrong was who was pulling the trigger.'

He looked out across the gardens, shaking his head. 'Maybe you're right. Maybe he really did get embroiled in some really bad stuff and lost it.'

'Did he show you the passport? Alvaro Eusebio Garcia?'

'No,' he said. 'Did it look -'

'Genuine? Yeah, it did. But the point I'm making is why go to all that trouble if he wasn't telling us the truth? You know? So yeah, I believe him. I've seen him the past week or so and I've heard him talk about it, looked him in the eye. I know he was suffering, you know. With the guilt...'

'Bob couldn't hurt a fly.'

'But in self defence?'

He shrugged. 'That's a different matter, I suppose. But I

still don't get why he came home. Why not just stay there? Hide away somewhere, like he said they planned to do...'

'He's been saying lately that he's had some things to sort out. You know what that might be?'

He shook his head. 'Not a Scooby.'

'Family stuff, he said.'

'Well he must've had good reason.'

'But I still don't understand why he's just disappeared like that. You think there's anywhere he might've gone?'

He shrugged. 'Well he could've gone home, I suppose.'

'Home?'

He nodded. Frowned. 'Jesus, of course that could be where he is.'

'Home?'

'Didsbury,' he said. 'The family home. He's been living there as long as I've known him and if he's come back to sort family stuff out, that's where he'll be. Won't he?'

'But wouldn't the authorities know it had been lying empty?'

'He's got a daughter here, hasn't he? She could easily have been staying there or popping in to keep an eye on his mail and that, at least until things died down. He only went to Spain temporarily, didn't he? It's not as if he was abandoning the country for good. So they were always going to come back.'

'Speaking of Margaret,' I said. 'You must know her.'

'Oh yeah. Almost as well as Bob.'

'Have you heard nothing from her?'

'Not a dickie bird.'

'Do you think she'll be coming back as well, then? If the family home's still there? Still in their hands, I mean.'

'Don't see why not. The dust on the corruption has settled. He was always planning on looking forward to living out his days there, having the grandkids around for sleepovers, all that stuff. I'm pretty sure all that police business wouldn't have stopped him, especially now that half of them are locked up.'

'But things have changed,' I said. 'He's killed a man. Accident or not, he's got blood on his hands.'

'True.'

'But if that's where he's gone, then it ties in with what he's been saying. The family stuff he needed to sort out. Maybe he just needed to pick some stuff up, you know, paperwork, that kind of thing.'

'Take a look at the old place before heading back to Spain to carve out a new life. Tie up some loose ends.'

'That's the impression I got.' He took out his phone. 'What are you doing?'

'Calling the landline.'

I watched as he waited. I could hear the faint ringing of the phone at Bob's family home. 'Still connected, then?'

'Someone's been paying the phone bill,' he said, nodding. 'But there's no answer.' He hung up. 'If he's there, he could've just nipped out to the shop or something.'

'Try it again later?'

'It's a start. Although we could go over there.'

'What, now?'

He shook his head. 'No, got stuff to do. But maybe later? Tonight, if you're free?'

'It's a deal,' I said, standing. 'Even if he isn't there, maybe we can clock if he has been, you know? I don't suppose you've got a key?'

'No,' he said. 'But I know he keeps a spare one hidden in the back garden. Shall we say eight? Meet me here.'

'I'll be here.'

'And Jim,' he said. 'Let's keep this quiet, eh? For now, at

least. I've still not even got my head around it all, tell you the truth.'

I nodded. Drained my coffee. 'Appreciate this, George. I need to know where he is.'

'You care about him,' he said. 'We both do. And there's nowt wrong with that.'

I left the paper's offices and stepped out, once again, into blinding light and the late morning heat. Wouldn't be long before the sun was reaching its highest point. Now would be a good opportunity to get indoors or stay in the shade, so I carried on with my plan to return to the office and crack on with the stuff on my mind. Hardy, the fire, the deaths of the innocents.

Stevie and Lloyd, we knew, were targeted attacks. But the other victims of last night's fire needn't have died at all. They were simply in the wrong place at the wrong time. If the trail of petrol had led to Shannon's flat - going off what the chief fire officer had said - then that would add more weight to my theory that she was targeted in order to shut her up. It wasn't lost on me that just hours ago, she'd been giving me information about all the suicides linked to Ivy Brook. And then so soon after that... more deaths. Someone was playing with fire like they didn't have a care for the consequences. But this time they were lax. They hadn't done their job. The one they wanted out of the picture was now lying in intensive care, likely to survive but to live the rest of her days in torment. And a firefighter was dead, leaving a wife and two-year-old son to cope with the hardest grief of all.

They were getting messy, allowing mistakes to happen.

And of course, they wanted to show me who was responsible. It was as if they wanted to be caught, that they were playing games with the swastika graffiti. Come and get us, it said. Come and have a go... I feared they were building up to something even bigger.

My thoughts turned once again to Isabella and Robertson. Fiona had struck gold with what she'd dug up on the bastard, and I knew she wanted him to suffer and to be punished appropriately for what he'd done, and rightly so.

But I couldn't help but feel that he'd be of much more use to me if he knew what I could threaten him with any time I chose. The minute he stepped out of line, just one phone call to remind him of the consequences of his actions would be enough to keep him co-operative for as long as I needed. And maybe that would be a punishment in itself.

When I reached the office, hot and bothered and ready for a long lie down, I stopped in my tracks. There, sprayed across the front door in electric blue, was E.N.D. Beneath it, and also on the side wall across the bricks, was a lightning bolt. I looked around for any sign of the Range Rover. There was nothing but the busy crossroads at Thomas Street, the punters out in the sun already. Seemed like no one had any work to go to. I turned the other way, but there was nothing there either. Looked across the street and through the windows of the bar opposite. Could someone be in there watching right now? I didn't doubt the possibility. I didn't doubt the possibility that they could be watching from anywhere.

I took out my phone and photographed several shots of the mess across my door. Wondered how the hell I was going to get it cleaned off.

I pushed the door open. It wasn't unusual for it to be ajar, but this time it felt different. Whoever had sprayed this shit across my door knew where my office was and therefore knew I was onto them. It didn't take a genius to logically go to the next step. Had they been inside? Were they inside now?

The old wooden stairs creaked as I ascended, and I unconsciously held my breath as I moved up, listening out for anything unusual. The hum of the afternoon traffic had faded as the door rolled shut behind me. Laura would be here alone unless Maya was sitting in with her, and I did ask for Dave again to help me out with some things, but still...as far as I was aware, she was alone up there.

My eyes fell on the large swastika sprayed in black on the landing, that same crude rendition I'd seen on the wall above Stevie's remains, the same one sprayed across the ambulance that carried Shannon to her living hell. I stopped halfway, feeling like my guts had somehow fallen out of me, and held onto the bannister. Listened out for any sign of Laura in the room above before I caught my breath and called out.

'Laura?'

There was a long wait and I was preparing myself for the worst when she answered.

'That you, Jim? You get things done? You want a coffee?'

I don't know whether I was relieved or not, because something about the way she answered troubled me. I paused on the step, trying to decide if I should go further. I pictured her sitting there with a knife at her throat or a gun to her head. Was someone there with her? Telling her to act normal? That was bad enough, but I think what troubled me more was the normality in her voice, as if nothing had happened and she hadn't even seen the graffiti. And that would suggest that as she arrived this morning, it wasn't there. It couldn't have been, and someone had scrawled it there whilst she was sitting in the office, oblivious to what had gone on right under her nose.

She came to the landing just as I was ascending again, my head spinning at the audacity of whoever had daubed this stuff across my property. I had my suspicions nailed down to a tee. Now they were definitely taking the piss.

'Jim?' she said. 'You okay?'

I looked through her, then into her eyes. 'Behind you.'

She turned and saw it. Audibly gasped and instinctively reached out to touch the paint before putting her hand back to her mouth. When I met her at the top, we embraced.

'Jesus, Jim, I had no idea.'

'How long have you been here?'

'God, since about nine or something.'

'And you've been in the office all that time?'

'Yeah.'

'And you heard nothing, saw nothing?'

'No! Oh shit, Jim, do you think they've been here while I -'

'Well how else have they been here? You didn't see anyone coming in?'

'No.'

'Are you sure?'

'Definitely!'

'Did you hear anything?'

'I've got the window open in there, you know yourself all I can hear is the noise from outside.'

I took out my phone and recorded everything in photograph and video before returning to Laura in the main office room. The window to the fire escape in the room attached was wide open to let the air in, and I stepped out onto the stairs. Whoever was responsible could've easily gotten into the building this way or made their way out from here as

Laura typed away next door. The fact that they'd been just metres away scared the shit out of me.

I looked down into the street. It was now approaching midday, and the area was as busy as usual. Could they be out there waiting for me to show my face? I looked around. There were plenty of businesses that had CCTV poised on the back block here. I cursed myself for being stupid enough to not have any installed on my own premises.

Dropped back inside. Sparked up and took that shit in deep. Considered a drop of the hard stuff, just to keep the nerves at bay, but then thought better of it. Alcohol was the absolute last thing I needed right now, but I knew it would come in handy soon enough.

I was tired. Sleepy. Recent events had caught up with me big time. I knew that if I didn't crash on the couch, I'd drop just as soon as I ran out of steam. With Fiona and Dave on the horizon, I'd need a clear enough head to focus. That meant getting some sleep, however minimal. I told Laura as much, and she agreed.

'You do look like the living dead have been taking beauty tips from you.'

Which was my cue to lie down. My head was spinning with it all, and there were only so many hours in the day.

'Lie down with me,' I said, crashing on the battered leather couch. I got no reply but instead felt a blanket, heavy as the world, fall over me. I covered my face and slumped into a deep sleep not even Jesus would resurrect from.

I dreamt of blood and fire and swastikas, Shannon's screams and Buddy Holly drinking whisky at the Wilton.

W hen I woke up, Laura was standing over me with a large mug of coffee, black. It was majorly hot outside and the evening commute was just kicking in.

'We've got visitors,' she said. 'Wakey wakey.'

I sat up and drank, knowing I'd need a few minutes to come round and get back to reality. Sparked up, recognising familiar voices next door. The fog of a deep sleep hung around my head like bitter black smoke, and I felt like I had to wade through it to get to the surface. The coffee was strong and the nicotine fired up my senses as I came around. I stepped out onto the fire escape and stretched. The Northern Quarter was bursting already with people keen for a good night out. I watched the trail of a hen party conga down the street before stepping back inside.

Fiona was standing there with a small piece of card between her fingers while Dave was busy typing away at the new Mac.

'Any sign of Bob?' I said.

Laura shook her head. 'Afraid not.'

I explained then about my meeting with George Thornley and the conclusions we'd come to. Checked the time. It was now creeping towards five o'clock. Would only be a few hours before I met him again.

'I made an attempt at cleaning it up,' Laura said. 'But your bog standard stuff just won't cut it. We're gonna need some industrial strength cleaner to get that off the walls.'

Fiona was shaking her head. 'I've already had a word with the bar across the road,' she said. 'Shown them my warrant card. They're downloading their CCTV to see what comes up. Can't do any harm.'

'Good job.'

'We'll get the bastards,' she said. 'It's only a matter of time.'

'I hope you're right,' I said.

What worried me, though, was that the police didn't seem at all interested. The killings were just more in a long line and, with Robertson at the helm, it didn't bode well. They weren't going to pull all resources, especially for me. Robertson, if word had gotten out about the shit daubed across my property, would likely be pissing himself about now.

Dave turned in his chair. 'We're ready to go.'

'I took the liberty,' Fiona said, 'of explaining to Dave here what it is we're after.'

'Piece of piss,' he said. 'Provided there's no damage to the chip inside. You got it?'

Fiona handed the SIM over and I watched him pop it into a little holder, no bigger than a matchbox. Moments later, the screen came to life, first black, then scrambled with a flash of code that skipped across the screen before a window popped up with several options on it.

'Told you.' His fingers jabbed away until a bar scrolled down through a list of information and back up again. 'You'd better come closer and tell me what you want to see.'

We gathered around. Dave went down the list one by one.

'Phone numbers first,' he said. 'You can see how when I highlight it, all I need to do is press return and there you go.' He did just that and another very long list of numbers popped up. Some were in green, others in red. They were clearly all phone numbers, some repeating more than others.

'What's with the different colours?' Fiona said.

'Calls made and calls received. So if we scroll down to

highlight a green one - calls made - we'll see that a little bubble window pops up and tells us all the specifics we need about that particular call: date, time, duration, even the location of where the call was made from. All you need.'

'Fuck me, Dave, you're a genius!'

He laughed. 'Well I wouldn't quite go that far... but you can do this with any SIM card, if you know what you're doing.'

'And how have you done it?' Laura asked.

'The information's just stored on the chip,' he said. 'Not always easy to access but if you have the right equipment,' he tapped the device that was connected to the computer, 'and are able to hack into O2's servers, like I've just done, it's a walk in the park.'

'You're kidding me?' I said.

He shook his head. 'Joking's not one of my strengths, Jim.'

'Bloody hell.'

'Jesus...'

I looked at the list of phone numbers and wondered if any of them belonged to anyone we knew. Had Lloyd been making repeat calls to someone, or had they been making repeat calls to him? Harassing him? Goading him?

'The red numbers,' I said. 'Are there any that come up more than once?'

'See for yourself.'

I sat down for a closer look. There were a lot of phone numbers in both colours. The green ones repeated a lot, especially one in particular. I guessed that could've been his wife. Of the red ones, there were a fair few 0800 numbers, the same number that repeated a lot in green - his wife again, maybe - but then there were some more that repeated several times. They were just numbers to us, they didn't mean anything - unless the data inside them had information that raised eyebrows.

'Click on that one.'

'Here,' he said. 'You do it. Have a proper look.'

There were two numbers I had my eye on. Both, by the looks of things, from mobile phones. I clicked on the first one and that little bubble window popped up: 11/06/16, 06:05, 20secs, Manchester City Centre. That would've been the latest call received from that number, but there were several more. I checked them all. The calls were made at varying times of day, but they were all from within the city and all of very short duration. It wasn't clear, from this information, what the calls were about. There was no indication of what was said, which left nothing but guesswork.

'They could just be cold calls,' Laura said. 'You know, have you got PPI? All that shit.'

'Maybe,' I said. 'But at six in the morning? Earlier than that, even. And from personal mobile numbers? I don't think so.'

I pointed out a call from a different mobile, this one timed at two a.m. precisely, just a day before Lloyd was shot in the head. The call lasted a mere 11 seconds. I got that shiver again, despite the heat. Who was calling him at that hour, and for what reason?

'Looks like someone was out to torment him,' Dave said. 'You know, waking him up at all hours.'

'Getting under his skin,' Fiona said. 'Would be interesting to know what was being said.'

'If anything at all was being said,' Laura added. 'Could've been just someone saying nothing at the other end of the line.'

She was right, I knew. A typical harassment call. The

sound of someone breathing on the other end before they hung up. Or maybe a one word threat to get them nervous.

'Just get the green numbers up again, Dave,' I said. 'Do any of these numbers tally with the red received calls, specifically these short duration ones?'

'Are you looking if he's made any return calls?' he said. 'That what you mean?'

I supposed it was. Dave once again took over while the rest of us hovered behind him. He tapped away, but shook his head.

'Doesn't look like it,' he said. 'At least from this phone.'

I noticed I was holding my own phone, ready to make a call.

'What about voicemail?' Fiona said. 'Can you get that?'

He messed around until he found an audio file lasting a mere nine seconds. Clicked so we could listen.

'Hi babe, just give me a ring back when you've got chance. Got some of that tea you like. Love you.'

His wife. It must've been. We exchanged silent looks. Dave pointed out that the voicemail was indeed from the same number that repeated numerous times, so it most probably was his wife. A quick visit would confirm it, of course, but now was not a good time. She was probably planning a funeral she thought she wouldn't have to plan for many years.

'Can you get photos?' Fiona said. 'Or video, even?'

'I've been waiting for you to ask me that,' he said, hovering the cursor over a drop-down menu on the top right. 'So if we look over here, you'll see a list of JPEGs. There isn't much to go on and I get the impression he wasn't much of a photographer.'

'Let's have a look.'

He brought them up one by one. A photo of Lloyd and

his wife that looked to be taken at a Christmas party. One of himself and his young son in a football kit, holding a trophy aloft. Another of all three in a garden in the summer. One of a dog. One of an older woman, perhaps a relative. One of a hot pan of steaming rice.

'That's it?' Fiona said.

There were two video files. Dave clicked on the first one. 'And this.'

It was the same one I had received the night he was gunned down. It showed the Range Rover following him down Portland Street and through the city. Lloyd's voice directly telling me he was going to a friend in Lower Broughton who could help him. Pointing out very clearly that they were following him.

When it finished, I asked Dave to show us the other one. I stiffened when it began playing.

He was sitting in the driver's seat, filming through the windscreen. He kept repeating 'no, no, no' over and over again, then 'There they are, there they are.'

The Range Rover drove onto the grass at speed and came to a stop. We could hear Lloyd fumbling around in the dark. The Range Rover's headlights were directly pointed at Lloyd. He turned the camera back to himself so we could see his face.

'Tell Alicia I lover her,' he said. 'Tell my kids I love them too.'

He turned it back to the Range Rover and we watched, horrified, as a man dressed head to toe in black stepped out and marched towards the Vectra.

'This is it,' I said, aware that Laura was gripping my arm tight.

The image went black, and I assumed it was when Lloyd had tossed the phone out of his window.

'No!'

The last, final cry before the gunshots hit the windscreen.

'Jesus..'

'Fucking hell.'

The video stopped and I lifted the phone as the girls let the tears come. 'Get me that number again, Dave.'

He brought it up and I tapped it into my phone. Dialing... It picked up. A voice as dirty and black as hell on the other end. I almost dropped it.

'You play with fire, you get burned. You play with fire, you get burned. You play with fire, you get burned.'

CHAPTER NINETEEN

'Well?' I handed Fiona the phone and her face screwed up. 'You play with fire, you get burned,' she said, hanging up. 'Over and over again. It's on a loop.' She handed it back. 'That guy sounds fucked up.'

'You think it's Hardy?' Laura said.

I shrugged. 'Maybe. Either him or one of the others.'

'It's as if they've been expecting you to call,' Fiona said. 'You know, waiting. Like they've done this recorded message just for you.'

Which is exactly what I was thinking. It was the kind of disturbing behaviour I'd come to expect from these people. There was a hint of pleasure in his voice, too, like he was really enjoying it. Like he was loving it, even. Added to the fact that there were far right slogans daubed across my property, it was pretty obvious they were watching me as much as I was watching them. It meant I wanted to close the office down sharpish, and get Laura somewhere safe.

'Tomorrow,' Laura said, 'is Saturday.'

'The far right rally,' I nodded.

'I'll be marching with the antifascists,' Dave said. 'We can't let these twats take over the city. It's not what we're about in these parts.'

'You think they'll be there?' Fiona said.

'I know they will,' I said. 'Question is, what are we gonna do about it?'

'The anti riot lot will be down there,' Fiona said.

'But they won't have their eye on Hardy,' I said.

'Or the others,' Laura added. 'At least, not that we know of.'

And she had a point. Perhaps they knew more, much more, than they were letting on. I discussed it with Fiona as Dave took screenshots of everything we found on the SIM card.

'I've not heard of anything relating to Hardy,' she said. 'Or any of the other names. But in terms of keeping a close check on these far right groups - especially the fringe ones - I'm sure we've got them well covered. There's been violence in the past, hasn't there? There'll be several Tactical Aid Units. If it kicks off, it'll be like a civil war.'

'I don't expect there to be a lot of the far right,' I said. 'They tend to travel down to the big cities from all the satellite towns.'

'West Yorkshire...'

'Further afield as well,' I nodded. 'The likes of the English Defence League are shrinking, so I don't think we'll see anything like in recent years. A few pockets of trouble here and there, maybe.'

'You never know, though,' she said. 'But now it's the little offshoots we need to think about.'

'The nutter fringe,' I said. 'The realm of the E.N.D. Where I expect to find Hardy.'

Now Laura chimed in. 'Are you going to this thing, then?'

I nodded. 'I reckon I should. Just to get a closer look at at the bastards we're dealing with.'

'You be careful, Jim.'

Fiona agreed. 'No one else will have your back. You need to stay out of trouble. I need you to help me nail Robertson, don't forget.'

'How could I forget that?'

'She's right, love,' Laura said. 'No one will have your back. Not the police, no one. I mean, what are you gonna do, anyway?'

'Take photographs,' I said. 'Get closer. See if I can pick up on anything they say we might be able to use as evidence in a court of law. Fucking hell, my job.'

'But they know who you are, love,' she said. 'And in case you hadn't noticed, they seem to have their eye on you too.'

'Bring it on.'

'She's right, Jim,' Fiona said. 'You can't be too careful.'

'If you're going, I am too.'

'Laura, no. You should be at home.'

'I'm off duty, Jim,' Fiona said. 'I could go with you.'

'I don't need any help,' I said. 'I'm only gonna be hanging around until the rally's over. But I need to keep an eye on things. I want decent shots of Hardy and his fucking entourage. If I can get anything that might nail these scumbags, I'll be happy. Now that's that.'

'If you want to nail them,' Dave said, spinning around from the computer, 'you'll need more than just a camera. I thought you said you were a private investigator.'

I left Fiona to do me that favour and view the CCTV from the bar across the road, while Laura and Dave checked out the chatter on the dark web. Maya had jokingly suggested she do me a couple of fake tattoos so I could blend in with the fascists more naturally. I thought it was a ridiculous idea, of course, and no one would be fooled, but Fiona said it wouldn't do me any harm and Laura suggested she'd be much more reassured if it meant I could hide right in front of their noses. Playing the bastards at their own game. I said I'd give it some thought, and maybe I would. But it was Bob that was on my mind right now.

I left Laura with the promise that she'd lock up the office just as soon as she'd painted over the graffiti - with Maya's and Dave's help - and reminded her to stay well away, at least until the dust had settled. Fiona had shared the CCTV footage with a few of her less bothersome GMP colleagues - putting it down to a random act by the very same far right types expected at tomorrow's rally. She assured me that it had gone out across various divisions, in particular the city centre division, who would now be keeping a closer eye on tomorrow's attendees.

I walked through the same backstreets where I'd lost Bob, wondering what was going through his mind as he escaped my trail. Wondered what, if anything, he had planned.

It was as busy as ever. The hot summer had brought out every nutter imaginable. It was silly season. I fought my way through crowds of students on the ale, through hen and stags parties meeting in the middle, through married couples on their monthly date night and young lovers on their first. Considered dropping in to the nearest bar for a quick cold one but instead marched on, keen to meet with George and find Bob once and for all.

I sparked up. Took that shit in deep. The nicotine reached the parts other things couldn't reach and took the weight of the day off my shoulders for the briefest of moments. But it was only brief. I longed for the darkest of nights, to hide away from all of this, to sleep so deep it'd take a marching band of millions to wake me. But I knew that night couldn't come yet, and maybe it would never come.

It was pushing eight when I walked onto the dried out grass at Piccadilly Gardens. I thought I'd have to wait for George, but he was actually waiting for me, casually looking out over the crowds of people passing through or lounging around. The aroma of marijuana hung in the air, and there were several groups launching back bottles of cider and cases of cheap lager from the local mini-markets, their rubbish strewn around without a care. There was a small group of young men hanging around under the tunnel beside the coffee bar. They were trying so desperately hard to intimidate people and failing.

'Locke,' he said. 'I wasn't expecting you on time.'

'I need to find Bob,' I said. 'Finally get this off my mind.'

He nodded and led the way. 'My car's parked up down Chorlton Street. We have a few spaces there specifically for the Evening Chronicle. It's not far.'

We cut across Portland Street, the traffic heavy and in full flow. It struck me how unusual this felt. How it might have felt for him, too. But I could see he was worried for Bob as much as I was. We knew the trouble he'd gotten into and the inevitable danger he was in. I had a bad feeling all of this could be too late.

'If I know Bob,' he said, 'on a summer night like this, he'd most likely be sitting in the back garden with a nice bottle of

Bordeaux. So with any luck, that's where we'll find him, deep in thought.'

'I think we'd have heard from him by now,' I said. 'I've been ringing and ringing, George. No answer, every time.'

He put a brave face on it, but I could see he was worried too. We reached his car, a Volkswagen, and stepped in. He started her up and took us off down past UMIST via Whit worth Street, then Upper Brook Street and right up towards Fallowfield. I watched the world pass by outside as he drove. It was still very light out, and the setting sun was casting red and gold across the land as far as I could see. I had to squint to see the road ahead. Thought of Shannon in her hospital bed, wrapped in bandages from head to toe. Thought of tomorrow's rally and how I should approach it. Thought of Robertson and Isabella Burns, those drives to the lake at Heaton Park. Lloyd's Vectra going up in flames with him lying dead inside it. Alan Pickering singing Peggy Sue at the Wilton...

'What's your gut feeling, Jim?' he said. We'd just turned off Birchfields Road and were heading towards Whalley Range.

'My gut feeling,' I said. I'd always listened to it and it had never let me down. 'My gut feeling is that we're too late, George.'

'You think he might be there?'

'Every possibility,' I nodded. I pushed the button beside the window and took out a smoke. 'You mind?'

He shook his head. 'Go for it.'

I sparked up. 'We'll find out.'

'You don't sound too confident.'

I said nothing. I felt that he could be there. What I was worried about was what state we'd find him in.

It was a large five bedroomed house, in a long tree-lined street just off the main Palatine Road and near to Barlow Moor Road to the south. The heart of Didsbury and south Manchester, where he'd made himself a home and raised a family for the past forty-odd years. The street was quiet and peaceful, even this close to one of the major routes into the city, and despite the hour, there was still a fair amount of traffic around. The gentle hum reminded us that though the street was quiet and leafy and you could easily be somewhere far out in the sticks, we weren't that far from civilisation. It was a street I'd have liked to have lived in, and it was easy to see its charm and appeal. No wonder he'd stayed here for so long. The place was full of character and would've been a welcome retreat to return to every evening.

George pulled up in front of the house and killed the engine. 'You ready?'

I opened the door and stepped out. George followed and led the way down the front path. The first thing we noticed was that the curtains were drawn in every window out front. There was a side window down the east of the house. I peered into an empty kitchen, the plants dying on the sill. Saw dust motes gently floating through the sunbeam cascading in from another window inside.

'Round the back,' George said. 'I'm sure he keeps a key under a rock near the back door.'

The garden was overgrown. I had to wonder what the neighbours had been thinking. But like most streets, gossip had a life of its own. Perhaps they knew that Bob and Margaret had fled to Spain and thought little else of it. When they returned, the garden would return to normal, they must've thought. I looked around. Bob's fences were high. Was that because he wanted to keep the privacy he so valued?

There was music and laughter coming from one of the gardens next door. Perhaps neighbours he'd known for a long time, perhaps not. By the sound of things, there was little concern for the house lying empty beside them. Seemed a party was in full swing.

George lifted a large rock beside a much larger plant pot. 'Bingo,' he said, picking up a small Yale key. 'I think it's for this back door.'

'One way to find out.'

He mounted the few steps to the door and put the key in, which slid in perfectly. Turned until it clicked and the door budged open.

A black and white cat burst through the gap and disappeared into the bushes. Had to wonder how long it had been inside. But as the door creaked open, the cat was the last thing on my mind.

It was the smell that hit us first. Sharp and sweet and not very pleasant. We exchanged a look. I think we both knew what was coming. It was warm inside and the lights were on. We could see the orange glow of electric light mixed with the natural sunlight on the staircase wall down the corridor to the left. We stepped into the kitchen, warm and stifling but with a feeling that it had been lived in not too long ago. I noticed two empty bottles of wine on the dining table and the tell-tale sign that Bob had been here. There were several cigar butts in a glass ashtray beside the stained wine glass. George, having been to this house several times before, led the way. But by the look on his face, I doubted he'd seen the place quite the same as he was seeing it now. Despite the heat, a quick shiver buzzed my spine.

The walk to the living room took forever. We passed family photographs on the wall, saw Bob in another, happier time. Then we stopped. A terrible, monstrous cry came from somewhere deep in George's throat, and he dropped to his knees like the life had simply vanished from his legs. I almost did the same but clung on to the doorframe for support as my head swam and the sight before me in the living room began to make sense.

Bob was in the armchair at the back wall, his head thrown back so that he was almost looking up at the ceiling. I guessed that was how he must have ended up immediately after the bullet came out the back of his skull. There was a cone shaped blood splatter on the cream wall behind him. I could tell it was still sticky, and there were lumps of what I assumed was bone and brain on the wall, like a bowl of porridge had been nonchalantly slung against it. The rifle he'd used was lying on the floor in front of the fireplace. In the corner, an expensive stereo hummed on a wall unit, still switched on, a bunch of CDs scattered around. There were photographs here too, albums that were left open, black and white prints dotted about the carpet, which was also stained with his blood. In his lap, a framed picture of himself and his wife, a photograph taken on their wedding day, when the world was theirs. His eyes were still open, but they were colourless now. His skin was pale white, cold and dead. His leather Fedora was sitting on the couch at the opposite wall.

When I finally let out a breath and helped George to his feet - who quickly retreated to the kitchen - my first instinct was to take photographs. I took out my iPhone and snapped away. I must've taken a hundred shots in quick succession of everything I could see. The walls, the floor, the rifle. The body. I realised I was shaking as I did so, a million miles away, somehow spaced out from reality, as if I was living inside a film. But I knew, deep down, that I needed to do this before the authorities got here. Also, while George was out of the way, I felt I had to do this dirty work in case it came back to haunt us later. I knew GMP couldn't be trusted to do a thorough job, and I'd never get to see the evidence. At least now I had the chance to gather up what I could before they made a mess of it. Already I could hear George stifling sobs on the phone to the emergency operator. It wouldn't be long, for sure, before the police arrived. Best to get this done now.

When I finished with the photographs, I took some video, making sure I got some close up footage of the rifle and the body and the blood stains. I pocketed the phone and stepped over to the stereo. The CD in the player was a live recording of a David Bowie concert from the nineties. I wondered during which song he'd pulled the trigger or whether he'd waited until the very last note. Oh, Bob. It was then it began to really hit me. I turned to him lying there, mouth open, bullet hole in his forehead. Had he done this to punish himself for what he'd done in self defence back in Spain? I knew my own sobs were a delayed reaction. I suddenly felt very nauseous and knew right then I'd be needing a very stiff drink.

I spotted his cheap mobile on the mantelpiece and pocketed it without a second thought. Then I grabbed the Fedora and went out into the garden. The light was so bright I had to close my eyes to it. I sat down on the step and sparked up. Took that shit in deep.

Felt a hand on my shoulder and George sit beside me. 'He's dead, Jim.'

'I know,' I said. Took a long drag on the smoke and blew a cloud above us. 'How long?'

He nodded, trying to hear them over the noise from next door's party. 'I think I can hear them now.'

You could say I felt numb, but I don't think that would accurately describe it as I stood out on the front lawn when the police had turned up. It was more a feeling of disconnection, a denial that what I'd just witnessed had taken place at all. Bob, dead? No. No, it couldn't be true, it couldn't really be him. Yet as I looked down at the Fedora he could never do without, and I glanced over at George, who was giving a statement to a detective I'd never seen before, I knew it was true. I even had the evidence that he was truly dead on my iPhone. The camera never lies.

I told myself I wouldn't mention the photos to George, though. At least, not yet. It wouldn't do any good and he'd think it was a weird and ghoulish thing to do, and he'd be right. It was. But I knew it had to be done. I reckon Bob would've understood too.

I took out the phone and resisted the urge to look at the photos I'd just taken, instead going straight to my contacts to call Laura. I looked to the sky, longing for rain. She answered after six rings.

'He's dead,' I said. Saying it out loud hit me hard, and I choked. Took a hard drag on my smoke to stop the tears from coming. 'Suicide. Looks like he shot himself.'

'Oh Jesus, no...'

I nodded, as if she could see me. 'The police are here now.' I looked over to the house, where half a dozen SOCOs were swarming around the front and back door. A few onlookers had gathered at the front gate. 'They're gonna be here some time, I reckon.'

'Shot himself?

'That's what it looks like,' I said. 'Though I've learned to take nothing for granted, love. Bottom line is he's gone. He probably went on Wednesday night, the last time I saw him alive. I knew I should've done something sooner, I should've known why he wasn't answering his bloody phone!'

'There was nothing you could do, Jim. He'd made his mind up.'

'I could've stopped him.' There was silence on the line. I suddenly felt very hot as I saw George walking towards me. 'Look, I'm gonna go.'

'Come home, Jim.'

'I can't, I've got things to do.'

'You need to sit down at home and take this in. I've locked up, the office is closed. Where are you gonna go?'

'I need a drink.'

'Jim...'

'I need to send him off, love. And I need to think.'

'I want you home by midnight.'

But I couldn't guarantee that. I hung up, and George grabbed me in a bear hug. He couldn't stop himself from letting it flood out, and we stood there, on Bob's front lawn, the blue light cascading over us as they dealt with the body inside.

———

'I 'll have whatever you're having,' George said. 'Then I'm going home.'

'Two large brandies,' I said over the noise. 'And two pints.'

George had parked the car back where he'd left it on Chorlton Street. Said he'd get the bus back home and pick it up in the morning as he needed to call into the office, anyway.

He'd got us a seat over by the jukebox, neither of us in the mood for music, though the hairs on the back of my neck stood up when a Bowie track came on. Wondered if Bob was hanging around, having a laugh.

'Get that down you,' I said, handing him a drink. He downed it in one and I did the same, sitting opposite. Took the head off my pint and let out a massive sigh. My head was banging and all I could see was Bob's front living room.

'I just wish he'd have come to talk to me,' George said. 'You know, pick up the phone, call into the office. Anything! You know I'd have sorted things out...'

'I know you would have.'

'Poor Margaret,' he said. 'She'll have no idea.'

'Unless he told her what he had planned. She might've known something.'

He was shaking his head. 'It's not straightforward, Jim. There'll be a proper investigation, an inquest. You name it.'

'Post Mortem,' I said. 'Though why, I don't know.'

'Seems pretty obvious to me. I mean, let's face it - there's no grey area.'

'There'll be dusting the place for prints,' I said. 'If they have any sense. Especially given what we know about why he upped and left.'

'After we went to press, you mean?'

'Yeah.'

'So it's not exactly cut and dry.'

'You said yourself, George. We both know he thought the Chinese were onto him. Could they have caught up with him? Made it look like suicide?'

He took a long drink from his pint. 'Nah, I can't see it. It's a bit too elaborate. Not how they operate.'

'So you think he definitely did...you know?'

'What, do himself in?'

I nodded. 'Yeah.'

'Probably,' he said. 'Seems the most likely. Though I never had him down for any of this, Jim. Especially with a bloody rifle.'

I didn't either. I was struggling to get my head around it and I knew George was, too. I thought about the scene we'd left as the sun was descending rapidly over the city. Half a dozen SOCOs combing through the house, several squad cars, a private ambulance, a handful of detectives I didn't know. And they'd still be there now, trying to piece things together, however obvious things appeared.

What got my attention the most, though, was the rifle. Where had he got it from and who had supplied it? Who had he been on the phone to that night he went missing? I thought back and remembered how his mood seemed to have changed dramatically. How he'd disappeared from the office and kept saying he needed to be alone, to sort a few things out, to see a man about a dog. What had he been up to?

'Do you have any contact with Margaret?'

'No,' he said. 'I did have, but not anymore. I don't know where she is.'

'When they left,' I said, 'they went straight to Spain. After he'd killed that guy -'

'Keep your voice down.'

'Okay, after he'd killed that guy,' I whispered, 'he roped in this bloke Sergio to help him out.'

'They disposed of the body at sea.'

'Until it washed up on the shore.'

'And then,' he said, 'they fled to the mountains. At least, that's what he told me the other day.'

'What he told me, too,' I said. I took a drink and noticed myself shaking. 'So she's probably still there, oblivious.'

'He must've been in touch with her,' George said. 'They'd been married decades, he wouldn't have just come here again without staying in contact somehow.'

I took Bob's phone from my pocket and held it up. 'It was on the mantelpiece. Battery's dead but I can soon sort that out.'

'Jesus, Jim, leave it to the police.'

'I can't do that, George,' I said, knowing that if he knew what I had on my own phone, he'd have kittens. I could almost hear Bob in my ear, telling me to keep my mouth shut. 'I'll get it checked out, find out who he's been calling, it'll probably have Margaret's number in it.'

He nodded. 'I suppose it won't do any harm.'

'And, not forgetting, anyone else he might've been in touch with. Come on, George. I'm a private investigator. I'm just doing my job. Is it your round?'

He shook his head and downed his pint. Dropped a fiver on the table. 'Sorry, not for me. I should get back.'

'Just one more.'

'I'll be in touch, Jim. I'll try to find out what's happening with the... with the body, you know.'

'Don't leave it too long,' I said, as he stood to leave. 'Oh, and George. One more thing. Do you happen to know anything about this far right rally tomorrow?'

He shook his head and almost laughed. 'Bunch of flag waving twats keen on a ruck,' he said. 'What else do you need to know?'

But I was out of my seat by then and ordering another

shot as he left the pub and a crowd took his place and our table.

I downed the brandy and felt the burn. Caught my reflection in the bar mirror and placed Bob's Fedora on my head. I could almost smell him. Then I turned and left for Salford.

CHAPTER TWENTY

Visiting time on the burns unit had closed over an hour ago, but when I flashed the only nurse on the front desk my old warrant card, she agreed to let me through. I found Shannon at the end of the ward, a long and narrow room with occupied beds on either side. No special side rooms for her. The lights were low. The NHS was on its arse, as was evident here, and I knew that those responsible for its demise couldn't have given the slightest fuck about people like Shannon.

She was wrapped from head to toe in special bandages and had what looked like a thin, filmy sheet of plastic moulded to what was left of her face. She was wired up to all sorts and there was a monitor beside her, which I assumed was to measure her heart rate, among other things. I stood at the foot of the bed and saw she had her eyes open. She was looking right at me. Had she been expecting me, or had she lost her mind? I didn't know.

'Shannon,' I said. 'I'm sorry.'

A blink. A stare.

This is all your fault.

'Do you know what happened?' I said. 'Do you... remember?'

Her mouth was open, a black hole against the pure white, and a gel substance coated her fat lips.

'Can you hear me, Shannon?' I said. 'Do you know who I am?'

Her lips moved, a tiny twitch before an almost silent croak creaked from her throat, a moan that was low at first, then became an audible murmur, until finally the moan abruptly stopped. A strange gurgling sound replaced it.

I stepped closer to the bed and moved to the side so I was as close as I could get. Her eyes followed me. I glanced at the machinery that was keeping track of her condition. Didn't have a clue what any of it meant, but she was in a bad way, for certain. There was that gurgling sound again. I removed my hat - Bob's hat - and slowly reached out my hand to touch her arm. It was lying stiff as a board against the bedsheet, but I didn't get that far because this time the moan was loud, as if she was warning me to get away. I took an intake of breath and stepped back. Swallowed hard, wishing I could spark up.

She slowly turned her head toward me.

'Can you tell me what you saw?' I said. 'What happened, Shannon? Do you know why you're here?'

This time, the moan was loud, and it caught me suddenly and off guard. I instinctively flinched and stepped back some more. Then the moan became a gurgle again, and I watched as she took in rapid breaths and reached for an oxygen mask that was hanging beside her. She sucked it up loudly, and I could see that she was gritting her teeth as she did so, her eyes wide and bloodshot. She looked like she was clinging to life and would most likely prefer, as Norman had said, to be dead.

I'd be a liar if I said I didn't feel a little bit scared by what I was seeing. Somewhere inside this woman was Shannon, the real Shannon, but I knew that most of her had been lost in the fire. Now she was merely a prisoner in her own body.

'I'll make sure those responsible are brought to justice,' I said. I was aware of my own breathing, low and slow, and yet I wasn't sure if I even believed my proclamation. I thought of how I'd warned her when we met to discuss the suicides at the Wilton. Had she taken what I said on board? No, I didn't think she had. 'I'm pretty certain it's them. Hardy and his lot. The... the fire service reckons there was a trail of petrol running right up to your door. So it was definitely arson. A targeted attack.'

I guessed she hadn't been informed of anything else relating to the fire, and really, would she have cared?

She was looking right through me. Daring me to say another word. Were there tears in her eyes? Probably. She must've known what she'd been through, and she probably wanted to kill for it. What had she been doing when the flames were licking at her door?

I jumped when my phone trilled in my pocket. Fumbled around until I removed it and saw that it was Fiona calling. Aware that I was disturbing the silence, I ended the call. Whatever she needed could wait. But then, when I turned back to Shannon, I clocked a nurse from the corner of my eye.

'I'm sorry, sir, but you're disturbing the patients,' she said. 'I'll have to ask you to leave.'

I nodded. 'Just one more minute?'

'One minute,' she said. 'And then come back tomorrow.'

As she left, I waited a moment and turned back to Shannon. 'She wants me to go,' I said. 'Stupid phone, eh? But you hang in there, love. It'll get better, I promise.'

But I didn't believe it. Not one bit. As I left her bed and crept slowly down the room, I heard her moaning again. Something told me she'd given up already.

'Not like you to not answer your phone. Just checking you're okay, that's all. Laura gave me the news. I'm so sorry, Jim.'

I watched a porter wheel a trolley of blood and plasma past the coffee machine and into the ward I'd just left. 'We've all got to go sometime.'

'Yeah, but still. Not nice, eh?'

It wasn't. And right then, I was standing in Bob's living room all over again. Saw the blood splattered all over the walls.

'Where are you, anyway?'

'Just needed to see someone.'

'It's Shannon, isn't it?'

'How did you know?'

'I know the kind of detective you are.'

'Was.'

'Whatever,' she said. 'But listen, I'd be careful. I heard Robertson was gonna be down there tonight. He might've left already but - '

'What does he want?'

'Well, he's investigating the fire, in case you forgot?'

'But it's late,' I said. 'Too late for the likes of him.'

'Maybe so, but I wouldn't put anything past him.'

She was right about that. 'Any word on that CCTV?'

'Well I looked at it. Was gonna fill you in tomorrow, but

there's nothing much to say, really. A man dressed in black - tracksuit bottoms, a hoodie - turns up with a spray can or two and just does his stuff right there in the middle of the street. Daytime, of course. Time stamp said it was 09:09. Then he runs off. No one seems to give a toss.'

'I expected as much. Did you see anyone go through the door? Anyone go upstairs?'

'No, nothing.'

'Which would mean they probably got in via the fire escape.'

'Looks like it. One other thing on our man in black. He was wearing red trainers. Quite distinctive Adidas. Gazelle, so I'm told. Red trainers with a dark blue stripe, if that's any use.'

'I suppose it narrows it down a bit.'

'Do I detect a hint of sarcasm?'

'Well, you know. It's hardly like we've got a decent image of his face. Or have we?'

'Afraid not,' she said. 'This guy kept himself well hidden.'

'Figures.'

'I suppose so. And I'm afraid there's no one else on the CCTV. Just him. He's got some audacity to just stroll up like that.'

'Doesn't mean there isn't more than just him involved.'

'No. But there you have it.'

'Can we get a copy?'

'Already sorted.'

'I knew you'd come in handy.'

'Yeah, yeah. Now listen. Tomorrow. I'm coming with you.'

'I don't think that's a good idea.'

'No ifs, no buts. My decision is final.'

'But Fiona...'

'Someone's got to keep an eye on you, it might as well be me.'

'I don't want you getting involved.'

'I already am.'

'But I don't want you getting hurt.'

'Jim, you're forgetting I'm a copper.'

'Exactly.'

'And what's that supposed to mean?'

'Nothing,' I said. 'But listen, if you must come -'

'I insist.'

'Fine. But you do whatever I say, when I tell you.'

'You're not my boss.'

'But I beat you in rank.'

'Not anymore.'

She was right, of course. 'But this is my case and you'll do as I say.'

'I quite like it when you're angry.'

Was she flirting with me again? 'Not angry, just being firm, but fair. You can come with me but you do what you're told.'

'Aye aye, captain.'

'Now, any news on the fire? Anything going down on site?'

'Nothing more than what we know already. There's a large presence down there but they're letting people back in the building, albeit slowly.'

'Any identification on the body they pulled from Shannon's flat?'

'Not really, but I'm hearing it was female.'

'Female? Really?'

'So they say.'

'So it's not Jamie, then.'

'Apparently not, no. Though there's nothing concrete, so don't quote me on that.'

'I wonder if it was her friend, Claire.'

'Who knows? So anyway, come on. How is Shannon?'

'You want the truth? She's better off dead.'

'Shit, really?'

'It's not good, Fiona.'

'Did she tell you anything?'

'She can't talk,' I said. 'I think she's trying to though.'

'Poor girl.'

'Poor girl doesn't even nearly cut it. I feel like this is all my fault.'

'Don't be ridiculous.'

'I should've known this was gonna happen.'

'Don't talk shite, Jim. You know better than that.'

But the feelings of guilt were real. I couldn't deny that. I had a feeling the way she was looking through me was going to haunt me for a long time yet.

'Listen, I'd better go. I need some sleep.'

'I know. You've had a long and crappy day. And again, Jim - I'm so sorry for your loss.'

'Just wish he'd have spoken to me, you know.'

'Was it definitely suicide?'

'Looks that way,' I said. 'Though we found no note. Unless the police find anything, it's all up in the air, so it's too soon to tell. I suppose no one will know for sure.'

'I'm sorry, love.'

'I know. Listen, I'll phone in the morning. If you're coming with me, you'll need to be ready. I plan to leave at nine.'

'Okay, I'll be ready. And Jim, remember what I said. Word has it that Robertson's down there, or at least has been.'

'Fuck him,' I said. 'The way I'm feeling right now, he'd be the perfect person to take my anger out on.'

I hung up and headed back the way I came in. The corridors were empty and partially dark. It was lights out on some of the wards and I was hardly surprised. It was getting late and for those who were suffering - Shannon in particular - sleep was an escape from a hell that must never seem to end. God knows I'd seen enough death and misery to last me a lifetime. It was time to get out and go home.

I reached the exit, the same way I'd come in, and wondered if there was a late bus I could catch into town. I didn't fancy paying a small fortune for a taxi, but I knew it would get me home much quicker. I stepped outside and sparked up. Took that shit in deep. Looked out across the car park, which was less than half full and illuminated by sixty foot tall lamp posts. Watched the smoke curl in the night air. I was having my doubts about being able to cut it as a private investigator. I was in way too deep. People had gotten hurt, thanks to my stupidity. I should've known better about Shannon and should've warned her more strongly than I did. I could've told Bob he was making a big mistake and driven him straight back to the airport myself. I could've told Lloyd to inform the police about the Range Rover and to hell with the job. It wasn't as if I was being paid and no one could bring Stevie back from the dead, least of all me. Shit, I could've refused point blank to get involved there and then.

But Stevie was a mate, and I owed him. Plus, I was intrigued. Sometimes I couldn't help myself but get involved where I knew I'd be better off out of it. I made a vow right there and then to knock this shit on the head. I'd lost a dear friend, and I'd have to live with it forever. I mean, who was I kidding? My heart wasn't in playing coppers anymore. From now on I'd stick to the boring stuff. I'd keep strict nine-to-five hours and have a life outside of tailing two-timing husbands and the work shy on the sick. It was mind numbing stuff, like tracing long-lost relatives. But it would keep a roof over my head and the wolf from the door. And it would keep me a lot safer than I felt right now.

I stepped through the car park and weaved my way through the vehicles, headed towards the exit. I couldn't bring myself to get Laura to come and pick me up, though I knew she would. It wouldn't be fair, and I needed her at home, where I knew she was safe. After all the shit recently, I felt it was my responsibility to keep her well out of it. The graffiti on the office walls could just be the tip of the iceberg. My gut told me she needed to be kept at home.

As I walked on, my shoes click clacking on the floor, I had a sudden sinking feeling and felt I was being watched. I stopped, looked around. Took a long, hard drag on my smoke before tossing it. The moon was bright and the sky was clear. I turned a three sixty and picked up my pace, stepping that little bit quicker towards the gate out front.

Then I saw them. Two figures, silhouettes against the black of the trees behind them and the main road illuminated by the bright street lights beyond. They were standing together, looking right at me.

Waiting.

Watching.

I'd recognise that cunt anywhere. I relaxed and moved closer, considering quickly what the hell it was he wanted. To warn me off the case? No doubt. To screw what he could out of me? Probably. Had he known what Fiona was up to? Maybe, and that's what excited me most. I felt a rush of blood. Words wouldn't come cheap. I suddenly saw Isabella Burns in my mind, those cuts to her arms, the shame she felt.

Saw the bastard leading her into her own bathroom, snaking his arms around her waist, picking her up from school in his fucking BMW. I gritted my teeth as I approached and tried not to put him on his arse too soon. How to play it? I'd wing it the best I could with an emphasis on being smart and quick. I knew he was slow out of the blocks. Always was. If I could hit him where it hurt first, he'd squirm. I came to a stop and looked him squarely in the eyes.

'Locke,' he said. 'Well, well.'

'Robertson. Nice evening for a stroll, eh?'

'You're on my patch again, Locke. I thought I'd warned you to steer clear of this case? Police matters, I'm sure you understand.'

I nodded. Clocked the uniformed copper beside him and had him down as one of the gobshite rookies I used to get palmed off with when they wanted me out of the way of the important stuff. The kid was barely out of school and looked like he'd only just taken up shaving. Face like a baby, but one you wanted to punch. He'd probably make a good politician one day or, better still, police chief. He looked like he'd been dragged into the job by an over enthusiastic father. Keeping it in the family, like they do. Just like Robertson and his father. Get them young and you've got them for life. I eyeballed him and watched him look away like the jumped up little shithouse he knew he was.

'Heard about that bloody journalist,' he said. 'Not surprised, really. He's been up our arses for God knows how long, as you know. Was only a matter of time before the pressure got to him. He was a friend of yours, I believe?'

'What do you want?'

'Me? Shouldn't the question really be about what you want? You're still fannying around playing at coppers like some kid in the playground while the big boys do the dirty work. You have no relevance at all, Locke. I mean, look at you, for fuck's sake. Why don't you just get off the fucking booze and go out and get a proper job? I mean, you're one miserable bastard. You'd probably make a good bus driver or something...'

It was almost funny. But then I thought of his double life, his two wives, his poor innocent kids and Isabella, poor Isabella, so fucked up in the head she was into self harming. All thanks to him.

'Seen much of John Dawson lately?' I said.

There was the faintest glimmer in his eyes, the faintest twitch. One side of his mouth curled up and he half blinked, as if he wanted to test he wasn't dreaming.

'What?'

'Dawson,' I said. 'John Dawson, you know. Married to Marie. Sometimes works away from home...'

'You're not making any sense...'

'Oh, I think I am.'

'No, I'm sorry, I don't know what you're - '

'Detective Inspector Robertson would like to remind you that - '

'Stay out of this, Colin,' he said. 'In fact, go back to the car and see if you can get hold of DS Crane, there's a good lad.'

'But, sir.'

'That's an order, Colin.'

'Run along, Colin,' I said, as I watched him slope off. Shit, he really was a kid. Even in the moonlight, I could see his cheeks reddening as he fumbled with his air wave radio. The squad car was parked up under a giant oak about twenty metres away. A decent distance, but not far enough for what I was about to do. Ah, fuck it. The worm had turned. The power shift was about to crack.

I turned back to Robertson. Stepped a bit closer and watched him squirm as he backed off.

'John Dawson,' I said. 'You know him, don't you? Got all mixed up and got himself involved with a school kid. You know, one of the neighbours. The butcher's daughter, of all people. Dangerous game, that. Imagine the damage he could do with a meat cleaver, eh? Could be brutal.'

'I don't know what you're talking about, Locke.'

But he did. I could see the fear in his eyes already, could almost hear his guts churning over as his lips quivered, desperately searching for a way to gain back control. I had him on the ropes and knew it was time to move in for the kill. He'd been found out, and his whole world was about to crumble. His mouth dropped open, but before he could utter a pathetic little word, I had him by the throat and pushed him back onto the pavement behind him and up against the metal railings.

'Not only are you not content with two wives, but you take advantage of a fifteen-year-old kid,' I said, shaking my head at what was coming from my mouth.

'No...'

'You got off with her at her parents' barbecue, gave her your phone number knowing she'd call you eventually, and then when she did you systematically took little pieces of her innocence away bit by bit by bit until you'd taken it all.'

'Get your fucking hands off me - '

I pushed him back against the railings, squeezing the bastard's throat hard and holding him there. I turned and saw Colin get out of the car and hesitantly step towards us with a truncheon held out as if it was a grenade that might go off in his bare hands.

'I've not fucking finished yet,' I said, gritting my teeth. I squeezed harder, wanting to choke him. 'It was your little secret, wasn't it? Right from the very start. You took this girl, this kid, and you moulded her, told her you loved her, took her out in your fucking BMW just so you could get in her fucking pants and look what you did.'

He was reddening, struggling to breathe. Colin was building up the courage to lunge, but I'd be ready for him.

'You got her pregnant and you made her get rid of it. You even drove her to the hospital, you fucking spineless little cunt.'

I brought my knee up into his balls and he doubled over. I let go of his throat and let his head drop, but before he could retaliate, I grabbed what was left of his hair and dragged him to the floor. Colin ran at me, all guns blazing, and I put him on his arse with a quick jab to his nose.

Grabbed the truncheon and slung it over the fence.

Then I laid into him. I hit him hard a good five times, felt his teeth crack against my knuckles, watched his nose explode in crimson, saw the fear and the dread in his eyes.

Stamped on the bastard's neck with my size nines.

Behind me and rolling around on the floor, Colin was on the air wave, calling for backup. Robertson mouthed something incomprehensible, spitting blood and fillings down his shirt. His eyes were bloodshot and watering.

I got down and face to face. Got him by the lapels and pulled him up. He was gasping for breath, catching the air in loud gulps as he weakly flopped back.

'This time, cunt, it'll be you looking over your shoulder,' I said. 'Because I can take you down any time I like, any time I choose. All it takes is one phone call and I ruin your life for good. Are we understood?'

'You're - you're f-fucked, Locke,' he said. 'You're on f-fucking camera, you stupid c-cunt.'

I laughed, knowing he must've been referring to the dashcam.

I hit him again, hard in the face. 'No, you're fucked,' I said. 'We know what you've been up to.'

'You've g-got no f-fucking evidence. Prove it.'

'We've got it all,' I said. 'Photographs, video, statements, you name it. Make no mistake, we can send you down any fucking time we like.'

'Bollocks...'

I laughed again. Behind me, Colin was back on his feet and staggering back to the squad car. I could hear the radio noise even over the pounding in my head, but couldn't make anything out. If more coppers were on their way, I'd better move fast.

'You answer to me now,' I said. 'You don't call the shots anymore. I could ruin everything at the drop of a hat. Your career, over. Your marriage - or rather both of them - over. And you know what, I think it's better this way, because it means we can finally work together again. If you want to keep your cosy little secret lives then you give me what I want, when I want it, is that clear?'

'You're out of your m-mind, Locke.'

'You can fucking talk.'

'You don't understand, you d-don't know what you're doing.'

'If he doesn't get to you first,' I said. 'You know, Isabella's father, the butcher - then I will, the minute you step out of line. I should cut your fucking cock off right now.'

Nothing would give me greater pleasure. Although enough was enough if I wanted to sleep in my own bed tonight. I marched back to the squad car and hauled Colin from the passenger seat. He was tending to his bloodied nose like a kid in the schoolyard. He backed off and stayed on his arse as I yanked the dashcam out and stamped on it. It smashed to pieces and I crushed it into the ground.

Then I turned back to Robertson, who was clambering to his knees. I suddenly saw Bob in my mind and almost heard him in my ear.

Give him one from me, lad...

Thought again of what he'd done to that poor kid and how he'd ruined everything for her, how he'd used her for his own gratification, how she'd become tormented by her experience.

I ran back to him and kicked him hard until he rolled onto his back. Then I kicked him again, where it really hurt, once, twice and a third time for good measure. That last one was Bob's.

'I'll make it simple for you,' I said, as he rolled around on the floor. The moans of agony were music to my ears as I circled him. 'There'll be no arrests for assault. Do that and it all goes down. I tell them everything, and I mean everything. Like I say, we've got it all covered. I could go to the papers as well, no problem. I could do that tomorrow.' I took out my phone and waved it around. Opened the camera app and started filming. 'Just one phone call, just one. That's all it takes. That's all we need to see you sent down.' I zoomed in on his bloody face, a triangle of red dripping down his chin. 'We got a deal?'

He looked up and spat blood. If I could put a bullet between his eyes right now, the kind of bullet Lloyd had taken, I would.

'Actually, there are no deals,' I said. 'From now on, you have your work cut out. I'll investigate what I want, when I want, where I want and who I want. I don't answer to you or anyone. And as soon as Isabella wants me to take things further, I will. Your fate could come at any time, Robert.'

'Please...'

'No bargains, Robert.'

'I can - I can explain everything.'

'So now do you see it's you that's fucked, Robert? Now do you see?'

'Please don't do this.'

'Everything is in place for when the time is right. Everything we need.'

'You bastard, Locke. You bastard.'

I stopped recording and pocketed the phone. Heard the squad car start up behind me, the engine turning over and the headlights shining right on us. It was time to get the fuck out of here.

'I'm watching you,' I said. It was my turn to catch my breath. 'All the time. The clock's ticking.'

I sparked up, my hands shaking and stained with his blood. Took that shit in deep and walked away into the summer night. I didn't once look back.

When I got back to the flat, I found Laura in a deep sleep. I almost tripped over Bob's bag, which had been left in the middle of the kitchen floor, some of its contents spilled out. I could only assume Laura had been through it. I tossed the Fedora on the side and went straight to the drinks cabinet. Grabbed the bottle of Glenfiddich I knew would knock me out and didn't bother with a glass.

I sat down and sparked up. My hands were still shaking as I blew a thick cloud to the ceiling. Robertson's blood was still drying on my knuckles. My mind was racing with everything. Finding Bob, his lifeless body slumped in the armchair; Shannon on the burns unit, her flat demolished; the fascist graffiti daubed all over my office; Lloyd with a bullet hole in his head and his car up in flames; the fat blue-bottles under the arches where Stevie had burned to death; Alan Pickering singing Peggy Sue and the scars on his wrists; Isabella Burns and her self harm; Robertson and his two wives...

I felt dizzy with it all. Nauseous. I ran to the sink and threw up. My stomach was empty so I just brought up bile until I was dry heaving dead air. My head pounded and I scrambled for painkillers. Took four with a pint of water, then returned to the coffee table. Launched back the whisky like it was a coke. Winced as I felt the burn. I knew it was bad, but I also knew it would put me to sleep quick. And it was that darkness I needed.

The flat window was open, blowing in cool air. The night was loud and lively, Friday night in the city in full party mode. I let the breeze blow through the room and hoped it would freshen my mind.

I returned to the sink and washed Robertson's blood off my hands, knowing that what I'd done would either give me great power over him or get me in a lot of trouble. I kept telling myself he'd be one stupid bastard if he came right back at me. I didn't know what Fiona would say, and it occurred to me that she might see it as one big fuck up given he now knew I was onto him. She'd either be seriously pissed off or completely delighted. Either way, things had changed. Only time would tell if it would come back to haunt me.

When I crashed on the couch, I took out my phone and watched the few moments of footage I'd taken of Robertson and his grovelling. Gotta say, it gave me great pleasure -

though I felt a little bit disturbed by my behaviour. Was that really me? Had I really been capable of that? Perhaps my demons had started to possess me.

I looked through the photographs I'd taken of Bob's living room. The photos scattered around, the blood, the rifle, the mess.

The body.

My friend, dead.

I let the tears come, stifling my sobs so that Laura wouldn't wake. But I knew I wasn't just crying for Bob.

When I fell into that darkness, that comforting deep black out, I dreamt of bluebottles and blood, of bandages and tears, of Buddy Holly and Shannon Kennedy, and of Lloyd, who came to tell me I needed to stop and that the end was coming sooner than I thought. When I asked him what he meant, he turned his face away, the hole in the back of his head white with bone and the smell of burning so strong I began to choke.

CHAPTER TWENTY ONE

I was aware of Laura pacing up and down the living room, throwing the windows open and emptying what was left in Bob's bag onto the kitchen unit. Sunlight beamed onto my eyelids and I flickered them open as the morning breeze whispered through. My mouth was drier than a desert bone, my head heavy as lead. I needed water, fast. Clocked the time. It was just before seven and I felt I'd had barely an hour. I turned to Laura, who was half dressed.

'I take it you may want to keep some of this stuff,' she said. 'Especially the booze, let's face it.'

I took in several deep breaths and stretched. She'd put an ice cold pint of water on the coffee table, followed by a greasy bacon sandwich, which made me want to throw up all over again. No two ways about it, I felt like shit, like I'd left my mind somewhere else. It was more than just a hangover. I felt half dead. I sat up and launched the water back in several desperate gulps and saw the bruises on my knuckles. Then I felt how tender they were too, and it all came rushing back. I wondered how many of his teeth I'd removed and had I broken his nose or not?

'I see your hands are a mess,' she said. 'What on earth have you been up to, Jim?'

'It's nothing,' I said. But my hands were shaking when I held them out.

'You must think I was born yesterday.'

'Nothing he didn't deserve, anyway.'

'I worry about you, Jim Locke.'

'I know you do.' I sparked up. 'But you should see the state of him.'

'Who was it? Are you eating that or not?'

I pushed it away. Took a long, hard drag, felt the nicotine bleed into my veins. 'Robertson. He had it coming.'

'Jesus, are you off your fucking head? They'll arrest you.'

'They wouldn't dare.'

'You're out of your mind.'

'That's what he said.'

'I can't believe I'm hearing this. How bad is he?'

'Bad enough,' I said. 'Bad enough to avoid looking in the mirror for a while, at least.'

She was silent for a moment, except for an exasperated sigh. 'I'll be glad when this is all over.'

I left the couch and circled my arms around her waist. Her bottom half was warm and soft. I'd forgotten how good she felt. Kissed her neck and held her close.

'It needed to happen, love,' I said. 'For Isabella, for Fiona. For me. For him, too. He knows that any hold he had over me is over. There'll be no arrests. He'll be hiding away like a frightened rat. He knows his worst nightmare could come at any time.'

'And when do you plan to nail him?'

'Maybe never,' I said, aware that she was waking me up good. 'I think it'd really be better if I could prolong the bastard's suffering for as long as I can.'

She kissed my hands, then my face, changing the subject. 'I've missed you. You've prolonged my suffering for long enough.'

A s much as I'd have liked to have stayed in bed, I knew I couldn't. Laura, by now fully naked, was standing over the coffeepot as it percolated nicely. It was my cue to get a shower. It felt like days since I last had one and my body had been through the mill. Told myself I needed more mornings like this and vowed to do just that when this was all over. Laura was right. I'd be glad when we saw the back of it too.

But there was work to be done before we could see the end. Though at least now I could see a light at the end of the tunnel. I'd be on the phone to Robertson before he had a chance to make a dental appointment. The evidence we had to connect Hardy and his boys would be shared as soon as possible so that he could make arrests and proceed with charging the bastards, whether he liked it or not.

It would be a good opportunity to test my theory.

Besides, there was enough to convict them with. We had MacNamara as the owner of the Range Rover, the clear video evidence from Lloyd's phone footage, the CCTV from both the Park Inn and the bar across the road from my office. The graffiti matching at the arches where Stevie was found, and the ambulance that carried his sister to her new temporary home. Not to mention the shit that was scrawled across my property. Hardy and Regan and Williams all connected to the care home where Stevie spent his formative years, the testimony of Alan Pickering about the abuse, the documents showing Hardy had worked voluntarily at

Sanctuary with Lloyd. The video evidence Lloyd had sent me before he was assassinated. But I knew it was primary evidence we needed most. Real proof their hands had gotten dirty at the business end of murder, and that we didn't have - yet.

I knew I'd need more, which meant that today's events could be pivotal and could see a major turn in my fortune. But it meant I'd have to get inside their heads, closer than I'd like but a necessary evil if I was to get the job done. I was beginning to think Robertson and Laura were right. Maybe I had lost my mind after all.

I pulled on a pair of jeans and the thinnest shirt I could find. It was set to be yet another scorcher and I was feeling it already. With any luck, the heat of the day would kill any kind of enthusiasm for a rampage down at the rally, but I knew that I was relying on hope. I wasn't looking forward to mingling with these idiots one bit, and the sooner it was over, the better.

'I don't want to alarm you, babe,' she said, pulling her own jeans on, 'but I was hanging around in that chat room yesterday and there was a lot of talk about the rally and what they were expecting to go down. Seems like a lot of them are going prepared for a fight.'

'They'd love nothing more.'

'I'm worried,' she said. 'Are you sure this is a good idea? What if it all goes wrong?'

'I'm kind of hoping it won't.'

'You can't rely on that.'

She was right, of course. But I needed to do something to get closer to the action, however desperate it seemed. The more I had on them, the better. If what she was saying was true, all the more reason to have her and anyone else well out of harm's way. I was beginning to think Fiona coming along was a bad idea.

She looked me in the eye and grabbed my hands, holding them tight. We'd talked about it already as we lay in bed, but she brought it up again. 'It must've been awful, seeing him like that.'

'It was,' I said. Like George, I didn't think she was ready to hear about the photographs I had on my phone. 'But what's done is done. He won't be coming back.' Instead, I took Bob's cheap phone from my pocket and handed it over. 'Keep it in the safe at the office. It's Bob's. I want to try and analyse what's on it but now's not the time.'

'What, like we did with Lloyd's SIM card? Who he'd been in contact with, that kind of thing?'

'Pretty much.'

'You think he killed himself, Jim? I can see the doubt in your eyes.'

Was it that obvious? 'I just don't think he had it in him.'

Plus, there were people who wanted him out of the picture, no doubt. The Chinese, to name but one group. Though Bob had a long and distinguished career as chief crime correspondent at the Evening Chronicle behind him, so he'd probably pissed off a few people over the years. Enough to warrant him being taken out? Maybe. If anyone had any inkling of who else might've had it in for him, it was George. I told myself I'd put it all on the back burner until more emerged, until a bigger picture was painted. But then, a painting of a tree is just a painting of a tree. Bob may have had a damn good reason for doing himself in after all.

'We think we know people,' she said. 'Don't we? Until they do something wild and we realise we don't know them at all.'

But I wasn't in the mood for philosophy. It was fast approaching half-past eight. My knuckles tingled and my gut ached. Something didn't feel right. My instinct was kicking in.

'I should call Fiona,' I said. 'She insisted she come with me.'

'I'm glad about that. But she said she'd meet you at the office. And Dave wants to be there too.'

'Fucking hell, we might as well have a party, eh?'

'I think he's got good reason, though. Said he had an idea.'

———

It seemed everyone wanted in on the action. What concerned me was that my plans would be blown, that they'd get in the way and fuck things up. It was the last thing I needed.

We walked the short distance together to the office. The streets were getting busy already. As we approached the corner of Thomas Street, we saw a small group of men trailing a large Union Jack behind them. It had begun already, and I knew that soon they'd be coming out of the woodwork like cockroaches.

Fiona was standing on the pavement outside the office, smoking hard. Beyond her, I could see Dave approaching. He was carrying a small box. What was in it was anyone's guess.

'Morning, you two,' Fiona said, slinging her smoke into the gutter. 'Nice day for it.'

Laura opened up and went upstairs while I stood out in the street. Fiona clocked my knuckles straight away.

'Please tell me he came off worse.'

'He came off much worse.'

'The man himself?'

'Put it this way,' I said. 'I'd be surprised if he even turns up for work on Monday. The next time you see him, he might have a new set of teeth.'

She laughed, excited. 'You didn't?'

'He deserved it.'

'You're a naughty boy, Jim.'

'No, he's the naughty one,' I said. 'He just got an overdue telling off.'

It was Dave's turn to chip in then. He held the box aloft. 'Hope you don't mind,' he said. 'But I couldn't let you go in there without this bit of kit.'

'What is it?'

'Let's go and find out.'

'I'm not sure getting wired up like this is a great idea.'

'Seems pretty sensible to me,' Fiona said.

'I'd feel a lot better if you were,' Laura added. 'And if Dave says he'll be nearby...'

'Have to be for it to work properly.'

'It's just an added bit of insurance,' Fiona said. 'I'd feel better too.'

'Tell me again, Dave.'

He took the black disc and placed it under my shirt. It was no bigger than a penny and as light as a button. When I saw how inconspicuous it was, my unease subsided.

'So it's basically a microphone,' he said. 'It'll pick up sound even from twenty metres away, so it's really sensitive.'

'It's like something from a spy novel.'

'Yeah,' he said. 'But you're a private eye, aren't you? This is just common practice in the game.'

'So what's the coffee cup for?' asked Laura.

He smiled. He took it from the box, a simple white cardboard coffee cup, weighted at the bottom. 'It's so cool. One of those things that's obvious after the event. But it's so inconspicuous and effective, it really does hide in plain sight, you know?'

'Yeah,' Laura said, 'but what exactly is it?'

'It's a receiver,' he said. 'Picks up whatever comes through the mic - the black disc - and then records it as well as lets me listen in real time.' He took a set of well-made headphones out, the kind you'd see the kids wearing on the Met, bopping their heads to tunes they thought passed as cool. 'With these. Look good, don't you think?'

Maya was leaning on my desk, sipping a black coffee and swinging a set of hair clippers. 'So what do you plan to do with it?'

I was interested to know too.

He sparked up and we followed. 'Jim wears the disc and does whatever it is he plans on doing.'

'I'll be in with the nut jobs.'

'Right,' he said. 'So I'll be as close as I can get to pick up the signal and listen in to what's going on. You can give me a running commentary if you want. At least that way we'll know what's happening as it happens. No guesswork.'

'Sounds good,' Fiona said, and I suppose it did. 'How does it work?'

'It's just a Wi-Fi signal. Dead easy. The disc will be set up to send information to my coffee and I just listen in on the headphones. To the man in the street, I'll just look like your average Joe standing around listening to -'

'Ed Sheeran,' Laura said.

The room went silent.

'Give me some fucking credit,' Dave said. 'Jesus...'

'Okay,' I said. 'But I'm not sure about the running commentary bit.'

'Like I said, that's up to you.'

If I was to blend in with these people, I'd need to keep my mouth shut where it mattered. Whispering into a hidden mic would no doubt give the game away. I couldn't be too careful.

'So you have to be near to him to pick anything up?' said Fiona.

'Pretty much, yeah. It's like any Wi-Fi signal. Move too far away and it fades. So I plan to be within a stone's throw of the action, at least.'

'You said you'd be with the anti fascist crowd,' Laura said. 'Still planning on that?'

'I thought it might be a bit tricky,' he said. 'It could be too noisy and it might get rowdy. Don't want to damage the equipment.'

'I think being a casual observer would work better,' said Maya. 'Maybe stand on the corner and watch proceedings from there.'

'Exactly.'

'I suppose the good thing,' I said, 'is that if I get into any trouble, you'll be able to hear me.'

'Absolutely, I'll hear everything.'

'We,' Fiona said. 'Mind if I stand with you?'

'Be my guest.'

Which made me feel better. 'Will I be able to see you?'

He shrugged. 'Maybe. Depends what happens. But we'll be keeping a close eye on you so we'll try not to lose you in the chaos.'

'Is it really gonna be that bad?' Laura said.

'A few thousand there, apparently,' said Maya. 'It's all over the local news.'

'Mostly the anti fascist league,' said Dave. 'But it'll be busy, no doubt.'

'I'm hearing there's a fair few of the others on their way in too,' Fiona said. 'We've got crews out at all major routes into the city, tactical aid units at the train stations, you name it.'

'Sounds like they expect it to kick off,' I said.

'Well, don't you?'

You could feel the tension in the city, in the country even. The far right had been slowly on the rise for a few years, the kind in suits knocking on people's doors and asking for their votes, the other kind putting their boots into brown faces and burning down mosques. Though I could barely tell the difference these days. We had a right wing government hell bent on ripping the country apart and not apologising for it one bit, but then a divided country is easier to control and half an hour from the shifty bastards on Question Time told only a tiny part of the story. The inner cities were on their knees, especially the northern ones, and the working classes were the ones who had to suffer the hardest. The real tragedy was that some of their own were deluded into thinking that the right way to go was a return to a nostalgic England that was never going to come back. So the nutter fringe had donned a suit and campaigned for a free Great Britain, except the Great had left it long ago. The sad thing was they got what they wanted, or at least what they thought they wanted. And the rest of us had to stand by and watch it turn to shit. Did I think it was going to kick off? You're fucking damn right I did.

'Without a doubt,' I said. 'The question is, how bad can it get?'

'We need arrests, Robertson,' I said. 'You either do that or it all goes tits up for you.'

'Locke, this is ridiculous,' he said. 'We can't just arrest people for doing fuck all.'

'They've not done fuck all,' I said. 'Hardy's got previous, MacNamara owns the Range Rover, and I've got CCTV evidence of my office being vandalised in fascist slogans. We've also got the footage Lloyd sent me before being shot in the head and blown up. What more fucking evidence do you want? And either way, I couldn't give fuck one. Arrest the bastards or you'll be going down faster than the bloody Titanic.'

A sigh. 'It's not what you think.'

'I wonder what Isabella Burns would have to say about that?'

'Locke, please...'

'Like I said, you've got your work cut out. How's your teeth, by the way?'

'You're a prize cunt, Locke. I'll get you back for this, mark my words.'

Had to laugh at that. Standing out on the street watching the likes of the EDL and the BNP march past was making me feel uneasy. But Robertson had surpassed their hatred and bullshit in one fell swoop. I knew I had to keep him on his toes before I got sucked into this nonsense. I had the phone on speaker and behind me, Fiona was listening in with a wry smile on her face. We had him by the balls and he knew it.

'So you're gonna follow my orders, then?'

'Follow your orders? I don't take orders from failed coppers, Locke.'

'You do if you want to stay out of prison,' I said. 'You'll go down for a very long time, as you know. Let's see. Sexual and emotional abuse of an underage girl would put a good few years alone on your sentence. Then there's forcing her to have an abortion. You're a classy little fucker, aren't you?'

'Please...'

'Claiming a false identity...'

'Please...'

'Sexual harassment in the workplace...'

'Jesus, Locke...'

'Not even Jesus can help you, Robertson. You're fucked. Make the arrests. Do the right thing for once in your pitiful little excuse of a life.'

But he didn't reply. The phone went dead.

'Bloody hell,' Fiona said. 'I don't know whether to laugh or cry. This is a dangerous game, Jim.'

I nodded. 'But he knows he's guilty. He knows he's ruined that poor girl's life, and he knows I wouldn't hesitate to make him pay for it, should I see fit. I've got him right where I want him. It's perfect.'

'I hope you're right.'

'There's no going back now,' I said. I cocked my head over my shoulder at the crowd of flag waving knuckleheads marching past. 'And as for this bunch of wankers, we'll see what kind of scum they really are. Do I look the part?'

She reached out and ran a hand across my shaved head. 'I prefer your hair longer, but what do I know?'

'Not sure why she felt the need to do my hair either.' I turned my hand over and examined the E.N.D. across my knuckles and the lightning bolt beneath my sleeve. 'Thought the tattoos would be enough to blend in.'

'I think the shaved head really shows off your Union Jack tattoo really well. Gotta say it, you look the part.'

'It better come off.'

'She said it would.'

Dave and Laura stepped out then, with Maya trailing behind them. Laura locked the office up and turned to me, looking worried.

'I'll be fine,' I said. 'You can trust me.'

'You'd better be,' she said. 'There's been a lot of talk on that forum. I've got a bad feeling something big's gonna go down, Jim. Listen, I'm gonna find a place to sit it out and watch from a distance. Have you got your phone?'

'Check.'

'We're ready then,' Dave said. 'Just remember, Jim. I can hear you loud and clear. Any problems, let us know.'

I nodded. Took a deep breath and sparked up. 'It'll be fine.'

Though I wasn't sure I even believed it myself.

CHAPTER TWENTY TWO

I started making my way down to Albert Square, walking
in line with the small crowd of fascists on either side of
me. I could tell a lot of them knew each other, and there
were smaller pockets of groups who'd made the journey to
the city from the farthest reaches of the country. There
were Southerners, there were Northerners. Londoners and
Geordies, Brummies and Scousers, all mixed up in a kind of
horrific soup. All wearing the colours and symbols of their
relative neo-nazi affiliation. I felt sick already, and I wanted
nothing more than to get away as fast as possible. My
instinctive feeling was that I was rubbing shoulders with
some very bad people indeed, people who could do some
serious harm if they knew who I was or why I was really
among them. I knew I had to tread a fine line and walk the
walk. As much as it pained me, I had to become one of them
if I valued my safety. I didn't trust any of them one bit.

   I must've been convincing because I felt hands on my
shoulders now and then, all boys in it together, a few back
slaps and roars of laughter at the racist jokes, a lot of verbal
abuse thrown at the innocent public and general lairiness I

didn't feel at all at home with. It was a different kind of camaraderie I'd not experienced before, and I didn't want to experience it ever again. I was surrounded by misguided fuckwits in all their various guises, a parade of the truly deluded. The only bonus was that someone was passing crates of cider around and I pocketed two cans while I drank a third and some ginger twat draped a St. George flag over my shoulders with NATIONAL ACTION emblazoned across it. I tied it around my waist and marched on down Mosley Street towards the town hall, keeping my eyes peeled for Hardy or any of his associates. Of course, they could've been with any other group, yet all were said to be meeting in Albert Square for a standoff with the antifascists. There would be plenty of time to move around once the march came to a stop, but for now I felt the need to keep moving and get into character, which didn't come easy. I felt like a reluctant method actor studying a role I couldn't take seriously.

I stayed with the crowd, doing my best to look and act like one of them, joining in with their racist and xenophobic chants and feeling like an utter twat for doing so. As we walked, the crowd grew and I felt relieved to see the Tactical Aid Unit leading the way at the front of the procession I'd fallen into. There were coppers walking on either side of the road, and as I occasionally glanced over I was reassured to see Dave and Fiona walking casually along too, cordoned off from the march and safe among the police.

In less than five minutes, we were penned in inside a large cordon within Albert Square itself. All around me I saw people pulling balaclavas and scarves over their faces, hard men that were keen to hide themselves away. I was nervous already, but now I was more than uneasy. The tension was building and there was the strong possibility of violence. The police, of which there were probably less than a hundred, had rushed in to kettle us into a corner and put barriers in place. Police dogs kept the few nutters at the front at bay, but there was a lot of booze going around in the crowd and I knew that alcohol and hot sun didn't mix well. It was only a matter of time before someone lost it and it only took one fool to light the fuse.

I looked up and saw a helicopter circling the square. A loud speaker echoed through the crowd, a deep voice instructing us to remain calm and comply with police requests. There were a few laughs around me, shouts of 'Fuck the police!' among the clearest words I'd heard all morning. Yet I knew that police crowd control could get out of hand very quickly, their kettling techniques more likely to aggravate than keep the peace.

'Wankers!'

It was someone beside me, an overweight fifty some-thing in an England rugby shirt. He smelt of alcohol, the dirtiest of spirits, and was launching a can of Stella down his throat between making hand gestures at the police on horseback nearby and shouting 'Fuck off home' to the group of Asian men who were trailing past to join the opposing crowd just metres away.

'I'm telling you, mate,' he said, his London accent grating already, 'if I could get near those cunts right now, I'd fucking bang their heads into next week. Why can't they just fuck off home?'

This is their home, I thought, careful not to say it out loud. I quickly realised the hardest thing about this was having to listen to guys like him and their vile bullshit. I wondered, as I nodded my head in agreement and forced a smile, what exactly it was he wanted. A return to a whites only England? Did he want the government to just kick people out of the country? Did he want a return to a pre-war past that could never return? Paki bashing?

'It's the same with the fucking niggers, innit?' he laughed. 'I mean, all this Black Lives Matter bollocks, who the fuck do they think they are, coming here and dictating this, that and the other to people like us, to people who defend Queen and Country and all that?' He laughed again, took another swig of his can before tossing it. He offered me one from the paper box at his feet. Naturally, I obliged, nodding my agreement in all the right places. 'I'm not racist, but enough is enough, eh? You can't just fucking come here and start demanding shit. I mean, how many of these cunts have got proper jobs? They're just sponging bastards, the lot of them. They came here in the fifties and promised they'd contribute and all that shit, then they had kids and those kids had their own kids and all any of the fucking kids want to do is deal drugs and smoke fucking weed all day. Am I right or am I wrong? And don't get me started on all these immigrants coming in...'

'Yeah,' someone said from behind us. It was a younger kid, a scally from Liverpool in a red and white Adidas track-suit. He blew thick smoke over our heads, the strong smell of skunk permeating the air. 'But their weed's fucking great, la.'

'Gotta be good for something, then,' the fat guy said. He held out his hand and I shook it. His grip was firm, the blue tattoo on his knuckles reading E.N.D. 'Terry Glover. And you are?'

Shit. Who the hell was I? 'Norman,' I said. 'Norman White. White by name...'

'Yeah, funny,' he said. I saw him clocking my own E.N.D. tattoo and watched his eyes twitch. 'White by nature, eh? Unlike some of these cunts around here. Who you with, then? Manc like you must be with some of Colin's lot, I bet. So where's the rest of 'em?'

That's what I wanted to know. 'I've no idea. You mean Colin Black?'

'That's him, yeah. Big bloke. Organised all them meetings, you know. Talk of something going down today. Something big. You must've heard?'

'Yeah, course I have,' I said. 'But I've only heard as much as you have. Chance of something major happening, like you say.'

'Well, there's rumours and there's rumours,' he said. He leaned in so I could really smell the booze on him. 'But between you and me, some of these fucking Muslims are gonna get a taste of their own medicine, if you know what I mean?'

'What, you mean...?'

He grinned, cracked another can open, and launched it down his neck. I thought about what he could be referring to, but I didn't have time to think too much. The crowd had swelled, and I could see that from some of the side streets a few hundred more had been ushered in by another Tactical Aid Unit. Everyone was kettled into the same small area and the noise had gone up a notch. I could hear hip hop drum beats from somewhere, like it was being pumped through a P.A. Heard someone behind me say the anti fascist lot was playing nigger music to drown out the patriot songs.

I elbowed my way through the crowd, keeping my eyes peeled at every turn for Hardy or any of his associates. I was getting dizzy with all the Union Jack flags, most of which had far right motifs on them. I spotted several pitbul type dogs and didn't fancy getting anywhere near them. From the look of their owners, I could hardly trust the animals to have a bark worse than their bite. I didn't want to leave it to chance, so steered well clear. All three looked fired up, spittle frothing from their mouths, their sharp teeth bared, their jaws packed with muscle, their brown eyes not so innocent looking. It wasn't worth the risk.

Someone tapped me on the shoulder and I spun around, expecting to see Glover, but there was no one there for me. I looked up again at the circling helicopter. It came to a stop, hovering over the square as several flares were lit and held aloft by some nutter at the far end. I drank from my can, thinking all of this was a waste of my time, the noise drowning out my thoughts entirely, when I felt the touch upon my shoulder again and I spun around to find the same thing. No one, nothing, except for the crowd around me.

Then I saw him, slinking away behind a group of fat fucks in army fatigues.

Jamie. Shannon's lover.

He was grinning as he ducked through the crowd, occasionally looking back at me as I wrestled my way through.

It was like being at a busy gig, except there was no music and the energy was all wrong. I tried to weave my way through so I could get nearer, but he was more lithe, more athletic, and it occurred to me that he was probably much more used to this kind of event. Had I missed something with him? What had I got wrong? Shannon was in hospital, not dead, but feeling like she might as well be, and he, her lover, was out here in this?

He must've been less than twenty metres away, yet so out of reach. Without thinking of the consequences or who could hear what I was saying - I suppose I must've thought the noise was too loud and who would really give a fuck anyway - I spoke into the mic beneath my shirt and finally gave Dave that running commentary I said I wouldn't.

'It's Jamie,' I said. 'Shannon's boyfriend. He's here, for fuck's sake! And I don't know why!'

I ducked beneath some barriers and found myself on the steps of a pub, the doors of which had long since been shut against the baying hordes. I surveyed the crowd from my vantage point, standing on my tiptoes to see over the heads directly in front of me.

I spotted him heading towards the front of the barriers, beyond which was a police cordon and the opposing crowd. I dropped down again and fought my way through until he was back in sight. As I got within metres, I reached out between two skinheads and grabbed him by his hoody, but he yanked himself away, grinning as he pulled back.

I fell off balance, tripping to my knees. Someone's boot went into my jaw, but then he pulled me up.

'Sorry mate, you okay?'

'Yeah,' I said. I caught my breath and stepped away. Felt my phone buzz in my pocket as I spun a three sixty. I'd lost him. 'Laura?'

'Jim, can you hear me?'

She was faint, but I could. 'Just about. What's up?'

'Just checking on you, it looks crazy in there!'

It was getting worse. 'I'm okay, I think.'

'You think?'

'You know what these fucking nut jobs are like.'

'Be careful what you say, love.'

I checked around, clocked one or two heads looking my way. I backed off and returned to the pub steps in the hope I'd get a clearer view of where Jamie had disappeared to.

'I'll be all right,' I said.

'See anyone?'

'Funnily enough, yeah,' I said. I filled her in on Jamie and the fact that I'd just as quickly lost him.

'What do you think he's doing in there?'

'Not a clue.' I rummaged around in my pocket and found a smoke. Sparked up. Took that shit in deep. 'But he's goading me. I think I might've missed something, love.'

'You just be careful, Jim Locke.'

'You can count on it. Listen, where are you?'

'I'm standing on the street, just over from you. I can see a few people throwing bottles. The police are getting pissed off.'

'It's gonna go off,' I said. 'There's talk of something going down. I knew something was gonna happen, but it's hard to say what. Did you pick anything up on that chat room?'

'Nothing, really, it was all just bloody code words or something, you know how they are.'

Just then I spotted Jamie, back over near the front of the barriers. He wasn't looking in my direction, so I dropped down into the crowd again as he pulled his hoody over his head.

'Listen, if you see anyone I should know about, make sure you tell me.'

'Well, that's partly why I'm phoning now,' she said. 'The Range Rover's parked up down an alley off Princes Street. I saw the reg - CV15TYK, right?'

'What!? Anyone inside?'

'Not that I saw, no.'

'Do me a favour and phone Fiona. I've got my hands full at the minute.'

'Okay. But don't you think that's odd? I mean, why there?'

'Got to be a reason,' I said. 'Just get on to Fiona, she'll deal with it.'

'Jim?'

'Yeah.'

'I love you. Don't do anything stupid.'

I hung up and pocketed the phone, keeping my head down but my eyes peeled on Jamie. As I fought my way through, thinking of what I was going to say when I got to him, a loud bang shook the sky and a bright red flare billowed smoke across the square. Loud cheers rang out, followed by a chant about the IRA.

A police loud hailer demanded order but got nothing of the sort. These people didn't give two fucks, and the laughter that surrounded me was of a kind I didn't want to involve myself in. I felt uneasy. Suddenly, the helicopter's rotor blades were chug-chugging a lot louder than before. Despite the heat, I felt a chill. Seemed everyone around me was getting ready for a fight. I saw a few heavies pull out chains and coshes. Heard the dogs barking that little bit louder.

And then he appeared again, right at the front of the barrier. I found a space several metres behind him, not too close for him to notice but close enough to take him in. Like the others, he was shouting obscenities to the police and the opposing crowd, his arms in the air and his fists clenched tight. He was all in black, including the scarf I watched him pull across his face. I took out my phone and took several shots, though I wasn't sure why. Force of habit had dictated I do so whenever my gut didn't feel right, and it didn't feel right now.

But it was when I started filming that it all began to make sense. I thought about what Fiona had said to me on the phone as I left the hospital last night. The guy the CCTV had caught spray painting my office was all in black, a hoody and tracksuit bottoms. Pretty much what our friend Jamie was wearing. But the clincher came when I moved the camera down to his feet.

He was wearing red trainers.

Adidas.

Red trainers with a dark blue stripe.

'You little fuck...'

I saw his grin in my mind and wanted to rip his tongue out. Instead, I put the phone away and spoke into the mic beneath my shirt.

'Jamie, Shannon's lover. I'm pretty sure he's responsible for the graffiti on the office. Possibly more. Jesus, what the fuck did she see in him?'

But then right away I knew he was one of them. He was hiding it all in plain sight, like the others. I remembered the day I went to her flat with Bob and he was there in her room, half naked and his torso covered in tattoos. He'd kicked the door shut on us with a scowl on his face. Just a kid punching above his weight. I wondered what he might've been doing behind that door as we met with Shannon for the first time.

I took a deep breath as the crowd moved around me like an angry sea. With my eyes fixed on his back, I marched toward him, my jaw tense. I had my fists clenched too.

I got within spitting distance when my phone buzzed again. I pulled it out and checked the caller.

Nicole.

Shit.

'Nicole?'

'Morning, dad,' she said, all bright and cheery. I could just about hear her. 'So what time's the film? You still picking me up?'

'What?'

'You said you'd take me to the cinema.'

'Did I?'

There was a pause, and I knew she was hurting. I had

promised her. I'd promised her a lot of things and let her down a dozen times. How could I have forgotten?

'Yeah, see, Nicole, I'm sort of a bit busy at the minute and I -'

'Dad...'

'I tell you what, we'll definitely do it next weekend, what you reckon? We could -'

The world went black, and my head felt like it had been hit with a cricket bat. The phone spun from my fingers and I fell to the deck, scrambling for it. I saw stars and felt my temples pounding. The earth spun and I went dizzy as I grabbed the phone and gripped tight. Spat blood into my fingers and looked up to try and see who'd hit me. My vision had blurred, as if I was looking through murky, rippling water.

I thought I saw Hardy standing over me, but in a moment he was gone and the lights went out.

CHAPTER TWENTY THREE

I felt two hands grip my shoulders and pull me up. My head swam and I felt a wetness leaking from my skull, the blood dripping into my eyes. I wiped them with a shaking arm, making sure my phone was safely tucked away deep in my jeans pocket.

'You all right, mate?'

I blinked, shook my head, let the blur clear. Took a lungful of air and looked down at my shirt, which was now blooming in crimson. He poured water over my head and I began to wake up. The noise came back and I got my breath, slowly coming back to the world. I tried to focus on the guy but struggled to see who it was, as there were several men around me.

'How long have I been out?'

'Just a minute,' a voice said. 'Listen, the police are gonna send in the horses if we aren't careful.'

I looked around for Hardy, for Jamie, but it was all a mess. I was standing in the middle of an escalating riot, and I wasn't the only one dripping blood. I looked up at the static helicopter just hovering above. The chug-chug of the rotor blades and the cacophony of the far right scum bags around me was all I could hear, and in the confusion, my rescuer, whom I thought might've been Glover, had vanished.

I spun around, then back again. The coppery taste of blood in my mouth would take a while to go away, and I launched back a can of cider I had in my pocket. The other one must have spilled away when I fell, but this was enough. I swilled it around, swallowed half, and spat the rest out. Several bottles landed in the crowd and smashed, one of which was just metres away. It prompted a response from some twat who thought it was a good idea to light a petrol bomb in return. He launched it at the line of police horses that were separating the two crowds. I watched as several of the beasts kicked back, their riders fighting with the reigns.

I instinctively ducked as another missile landed behind me. Glass smashed at my feet. Now would be a good time to move. I covered my head as the missiles rained down. Rocks and street furniture struck the ground as the crowd dodged out of the way. I saw one guy get hit by a piece of rubble, his head bursting in blood just above his eye.

Both sides were as bad as each other and the police horses had visibly had enough. I watched several gallop into the crowd as the two opposing sides were mixed up and the barricades were launched into the street. Fists flew in all directions, and in the melee I saw Hardy swinging a cosh at someone. It was definitely him. He looked in his element, like this was all he ever wanted. There was something about him I found odd, though. He looked more bulky than anyone else, and I didn't think it was just his build. He looked like he was wearing a stab vest over his blue shirt.

And he was wearing a long coat too, which was bizarre, given the heat.

I turned the other way and saw Jamie standing off with several anti fascists. He had his arms outstretched, ever the hard man. So this was the bastard that had gotten into my office. Had he started the fire at Shannon's flat? I had to get to him to find out.

By now, the riot police had come out. The place was a war zone. I spotted a police truncheon on the floor and grabbed it, looking up at the town hall. Albert Square was where the city held markets and mini festivals throughout the year. Now it was a hellhole. People were getting hurt, and the police were losing control. At the far corner, I saw a water cannon rolling in, spraying several people off their feet. I had to get to him now.

'It's Jamie,' I said into the mic. 'He's the one responsible for the shit all over my office. And he's Shannon's boyfriend. He's involved somehow and I think he might've started the fire at the flat. Fiona, if you can hear me, I'm coming out just as soon as I get the little bastard by his fucking bollocks.'

And then I ran, weaving through flailing arms and legs and falling bricks, my eyes firmly fixed on the bastard. He still had his arms raised, goading a group of men in a stand off, but as I got nearer and time seemed to slow down, he turned as if he knew I was coming for him, and grinned.

I dived at his legs and brought him down in a rugby tackle, and now, instead of time seeming to slow down, it sped up until things happened so fast it was almost as if I was living inside a film and had somehow left my body to witness what I was doing from above. I pinned him down by his throat as the riot crashed around me, an epic war between three armies.

'It was you, wasn't it?' I said, gasping for breath. 'The

graffiti on my office, the fucking swastikas and the lightning bolt.'

He went to spit at me, so I let my head fall swiftly onto his nose. Blood sprayed across my face and I watched a black blood crack line the bone. The little fucker was laughing.

'And the arches,' he said, blood tainting his lips. 'Don't forget that. Or the ambulance.'

The arches where Stevie's remains were found. The ambulance that carried Shannon to Salford Royal.

'Did you kill them? Was it you, Jamie?'

But he just laughed again and I couldn't stop myself from hitting him hard with the truncheon. Did Shannon know anything about him? No, of course not. He'd fooled her, had probably found Stevie through her, had been the perfect one to get under their skin. And if he had killed Stevie, had he killed Lloyd too? Had he been the one pulling the trigger and throwing the flame? Had he been involved with Hardy all along?

'It wasn't me,' he said. 'But I was there the night he set him alight.'

'Who?'

'You know who.'

'Who?!'

'Stephen Kennedy.'

'And you fucked his sister afterwards, yeah?'

'She had no idea.'

'Who killed him, Jamie? Tell me!'

'Trevor Hardy killed him.'

'To stop him from going public with the sexual abuse, yeah?'

'Maybe to stay out of prison.'

'Did he kill the others too?'

'I don't know what you're talking about.'

'The suicides,' I said. 'All those men from Ivy Brook, all of his victims...'

'I don't know who you mean.'

'Did you kill Lloyd?'

'He was getting in the way.'

'Did you pull the trigger?'

'Fuck you.'

I hit him again and pressed the truncheon on his throat. I'd get those answers from him somehow.

'He was innocent,' I said. 'Had a wife and kid, his whole life ahead of him.'

'He was a nigger cunt.'

The rage was rising within me. I brought a knee up hard into his balls. I'd strangle the little bastard right here and now. I watched him turning blue, choking, his eyes popping out.

I let go. 'Did Hardy make you do it?'

More choking, more coughing, more blood. 'I wanted to do it,' he said. 'I like the killing time.'

'You sick fucker.'

'It's meant to be.'

'No.'

'I wish I'd have killed her as well.'

'You set fire to the flat, didn't you? Took a trail of petrol to the door and lit it.'

'Walked a trail of petrol from the door, idiot.'

'You left her there.'

'Her and her fucking rotbag mate.'

'Claire.'

He laughed again. I went to hit him one more time but was pummelled off him with a boot to my ribs. Another boot went into me as I rolled on the cobbled floor, followed by a hard punch to my nose. It was my turn to spit teeth. I'd been through enough, saw the world turn dark as if God had dimmed the lights. I wanted out. I wanted out right now.

'Gonna kill some fucking Pakis now,' he said, kneeling over me. 'No one's taking me alive, now that I've done you.'

I felt one final punch to my guts, this one damn hard. I screamed out, knowing it was a bad one. Rolled over, squinting through tears as he ran off to the white Range Rover that was waiting for him on the corner. I went to hold my abdomen in a pointless and desperate effort to stop the pain. He'd done me all right. I watched the car screech off as the chaos abounded around me. I felt like I was only half in the world as I looked down at the blade that had punctured my belly, the blood pouring over my hands like a fountain.

CHAPTER TWENTY FOUR

I must've passed out because when I awoke, the pain excruciating, I was in a completely different place, my head facing the sky and the strength gone out of me. I felt limp and claustrophobic and took in huge gulping breaths in a desperate attempt to cling onto whatever life I had left in me. Was I close to death? I didn't know, but I felt it, and I was ready to go too. I'd be happy with that.

An arm held me by the throat, almost choking me so I could barely speak. As far as I knew, the knife was still in me, sticking out at a right angle, my blood soaking the handle and slick on my shirt. So this was what it felt like to be stabbed. And now, whoever had me by my neck might want to finish me off. Perhaps I'd let them. I couldn't fight it any longer. I could feel the life flowing out of me with every tiny thought as he held me close to his huge body.

I tried to speak, but it was pointless. All I had now was hope and the nerve to accept whatever my fate would be.

'You're coming with me,' he said. He squeezed that little bit tighter, the voice the same as what we heard when I called the mobile from my office. Filthy and dirty, like the devil himself. 'You play with fire, you get burned. That simple. I've had enough, you've had enough. It ends here, right now.'

'Hardy.' It took every effort to choke it from my lips.

He laughed, and I could smell him as he dragged me across the square. We must've been invisible in the chaos because no one seemed to care I had a blade in me. He smelt of death and alcohol, of blood and sweat. I thought of a million buzzing bluebottles in the hot sun. Saw the oily fat from where Stevie's remains were, against the wall beneath those arches. Thought of Laura, of Nicole, of Shannon in her hospital bed. Thought of a happier time I knew could never come back. This was it.

'It's over, Locke.'

'It'll never be over for you,' I said. He loosened his grip to let me speak as I felt his warm and putrid breath in my ear, still dragging me from the crowd. 'You'll have to live with what you've done for the rest of your life. I know about it all, Trevor. The abuse, the killings. Your desire for control runs deep, doesn't it? You'll end up doing time again. Prison's where you belong.'

'I'm ready to die,' he said. 'And you're coming with me. It's about time someone gave these fucking Muslims a taste of their own medicine, anyway. It might as well be me and I might as well take you down while I'm at it.'

'What are you talking about, Trevor?'

'All those suicide bombers,' he said. 'The warped belief in a greater cause and the willingness to kill themselves in order to murder others just to get their fucking point across. For their bloody religion or their ideology. It used to make my blood boil, but then I realised they were onto something. What's good enough for them is good enough for me.'

'What?'

'I've got a bomb strapped to me.' He squeezed me once more. 'Nails, ball bearings. A kilo of Semtex on my back. Thought it would be the best way, to go out in a blaze of glory and all that, you know. Take you with me just so I can make sure you're dead. Good idea, eh?'

'You're fucking crazy.'

'It's not me that's the crazy one.'

'You'll achieve nothing by blowing yourself apart.'

'It's the best way to go.'

'No one will give a fuck about you,' I said. 'You think anyone will care?'

'Everyone around us will be dead too.'

'The innocents will chase you into hell.'

'Hell ain't a bad place to be.'

'Is that how you want to be remembered? A cold-blooded murderer? A suicide bomber? What's your cause, Trevor?'

He laughed again, a sickening laugh that cut right through to my bones. I had to ask myself if he really was mad enough to blow himself up in this crowd and I concluded pretty quickly that indeed he was. Could I do anything about it? No.

I tried to get a feel for where exactly I was. It had to be still in the square because I could make out the roof of the town hall, but the noise and chaos around me was like a whirlwind and we were at the heart of it, somehow invisible to others. The riot was still in full swing, the police horses riding back and forth, the riot police too busy to care that I was bleeding to death.

'My cause?' He laughed once more and spat blood to the floor. I was fading out again. 'There is no cause, Locke. But I'm not going down again, not for anyone. What's done is done, you hear me? I can live with being a killer, but I can't live in prison. So I'm out.'

'Why kill them at all, Trevor?'

'You know why.'

'Because you abused him, didn't you? You and your mates, Regan and Williams.'

'No.'

'You took advantage of innocent boys and you forced them to have sex with you.'

'They wanted it too.'

'So you had to shut them up, didn't you? How many more have you killed, Trevor? Make it look like suicide and no one cares, right? And now you're gonna kill me as well.'

'Putting you out of your misery.'

'I don't think you've got the balls.'

But I nearly shat myself when a massive explosion tore through the sky. The square audibly jumped too, and with the horses spooked, the crowds ran in every direction. There must've been a few thousand people here, all of whom were walking wounded on both sides. And then I realised exactly where he had me. He dragged me up several steps and we were standing at the foot of the giant Albert Memorial statue. I made my peace with the world and was ready to go.

'That's my cue,' he said. 'Just one more minute now. Say goodbye to it all, Locke. Ask yourself if it was really worth it.'

My phone rang in my pocket and my daughter came back to me, the last call I had with my own flesh and blood, and I'd let her down badly. I closed my eyes and took a deep breath. At least it would be over quickly.

'Was that one of yours?'

'The Range Rover,' he said. 'Rusholme. Jamie will have killed them all.'

'You murdering bastard.'

'Not any more.'

The bang was deathly loud, bursting my ear drums first, and then the blood came, thick and fast. He let go of me and dropped and I fell down too, rolling down the steps, aware that I had his blood on my face as they pulled me away. My feet dragged across the cobbles and all I could see was blue, all I could smell was burning and all I could hear was a loud ringing in my ears. They dropped me to the floor and there were boots beside my head, and I felt bodies over me before my eyes blinked out. Perhaps this was it. There was nothing to fear, and it wasn't so bad.

'He's gonna do it!'

'No!'

And then the world turned white.

CHAPTER TWENTY FIVE

'You heard what the doctor said, love. You need lots of rest. Time to put your feet up for a while. I promise I'll give you anything you want or need just as long as you promise me you'll stay out of trouble from now on.'

'Anything?'

'You've a one track mind.'

'Got some catching up to do.'

She smiled and kissed me before helping me into the back of the cab and joining me on the back seat. The driver pulled off towards home. 'As long as you take it easy, that's fine with me.'

Four weeks ago, I thought I was dead. After the sniper had shot Hardy in the neck, allowing me to be dragged to safety by Dave and Fiona, a crowd of coppers and civilians had worked hard to stop the bleeding before I was rushed to hospital in the back of a squad car. At least, that's what they tell me. I can't remember that part, but the stuff before it is all too real. The world was much better off without that bastard, but he took nine others with him and injured plenty more, including two police horses that had to be put to sleep. I was the lucky one. I could've been blown into four parts, my life over in an instant. Instead, I woke up two days later, after they'd stitched me up. I was lucky that the blade Jamie used hadn't punctured my bowel. Maybe someone was watching over me that day.

'I'm so glad to be out of there, love,' I said. 'I'm so glad it's over.'

'You and me both. But it's just the beginning of your recovery, Jim. You heard what he said in there. Plenty of rest and no stress.'

'I want to get back to work as soon as possible,' I said. 'Got to earn a living somehow.'

'Not yet,' she said. 'But when the time comes, can we please go back to the normal stuff? No murderers, no bombs, eh? Just stick to the usual crap and come home for tea every night. You're not cut out for this, love. You could've died, Jim. I was that close to losing you.'

'But I'm still here.'

'I want you to keep it that way.'

When we got back to the flat, and after dumping my bag in the kitchen, we spent the rest of the day in bed making up for lost time. I was still in pain from the wound, which was still bandaged up, replaced every two days by Lisa, the nurse whom I'd gotten to know quite well during my time on the ward. But I got through the pain barrier with no problem. Laura made sure of that. She was a woman of her word.

My scar was seven inches long, like a bear claw mark down the left of my abdomen, a line of tissue the surgeons had frantically stitched up once they found none of my organs had been damaged. The blade had missed my lower intestine by a fraction. It was a miracle I'd lived to tell the tale. Jamie had died thinking he'd killed me first. The kid was a stupid, misguided little prick, another one who wouldn't be missed by anyone. The Range Rover had exploded as it travelled through the curry mile. The car bomb killed eighteen people instantly, including six children. Witnesses had said he was smiling as he sat behind the wheel, his lightning bolt flag trailing out the window before it went up.

It had been wall to wall coverage for weeks and the city was sick of it, and rightly so. I switched off from it whenever it came on the news in the hospital. I didn't need reminding of any more than I already lived with. I thought about what happened every day, thought about how things could've so easily been different. I'd stared death in the face and came out the other side. But it wasn't so for plenty of others, my good friend Bob included.

If I'd have done what I promised my daughter, taken her to the cinema and got us both some junk food, I wouldn't have had to go through any of it and I'd have seen what was really important in my life. My kid deserved better, and for once I'd make sure she saw much more of me than she was used to. She was the last thing I thought about before the bullet hit Hardy's neck, and I'd thought about her every day since. I finally realised I had a big role to fill. It was time to step up and be her dad.

I sat up the night I returned home, going over everything in my head one last time. Counted the victims, of which there were many. All those lives destroyed. All those people left behind, the ones who had to pick up the pieces. Shannon was still on the burns unit at Salford Royal, but I stayed away, at least for now. From the Ivy Brook victims to the firefighter leaving his wife and son behind, from the bomb victims in Albert Square and Rusholme to the cold-blooded murders of Lloyd and Stevie, Hardy had ripped out hearts and left this world with the blood of many on his hands. I could so easily have been one of those victims too, and in a way, I was. The scar on my belly wasn't the only one I carried with me.

As I settled in back home, retreating into a lifestyle of morning TV and overdoing the coffee, and working slowly on the physio I'd been advised to do daily, I gradually worked my way back to somewhere nearer the level of health I had before all this. Though I'd taken a heavy blow to the head - which, I'm told, turned out to be a punch - the prognosis was good despite a few memory problems. The doctor said I'd been having one or two absence seizures, which he expected to tail off over time. I'd been through significant trauma and stress and my body needed proper recovery. Alcohol wouldn't help, he'd said, so he advised me to steer clear. But my soul was hurting too, and I found the solace I'd been craving as much in a fresh Guinness as in the summer air.

The summer had been the hottest on record, and the everlasting heatwave seemed to finally come to a stop the minute I left the Manchester Royal Infirmary. Fiona had joked that the sun putting his hat away was all my fault. I didn't mind. Was glad to see the back of it, if I'm honest. As part of my recovery, I went walking around the city in the rain and I enjoyed letting it wash over me. It seemed to cleanse away the bad stuff and helped me forget, at least for a while.

I hadn't heard a peep from Robertson. It was to be expected. If I'd have died that day in Albert Square, all his hopes would've come true. I'd have been out of the picture and he wouldn't have to be watching his back the way I'd been watching mine. It wouldn't have stopped Fiona though, and she'd told me that herself. She also told me that she and Dave had heard everything going down before the main event itself, thanks mainly to the hidden mic down my shirt. I had a lot to thank Dave for. I hadn't quite realised how handy modern technology could be in my job. A simple Wi-Fi transmitter had saved my life. Fiona had called the bomb in after Laura had phoned her to tell her about the Range Rover. After it sped off with Jamie at the wheel, both she and Dave went into action. One of the Tactical Aid Units had put several snipers on the roofs. It was the one on the town hall roof that had taken Hardy out. Unluckily for Robertson, Fiona had earned massive respect among her peers. An off duty copper as on the ball as her could go a long way in the force, if she wanted to.

The sniper had saved me, but many others were not so lucky. Hardy had pulled a cord beneath his coat that triggered the bomb as he lay dying, his neck blown open so wide the blood flowed from his jugular vein like wine from a smashed barrel. The bomb had put him out of his misery. He got what he wanted.

No one had come out of this a victor. In the end, everyone had lost something.

One Friday night, after Laura had gone over to Sara's house for the weekend, I settled in with a few beers and a good book. Tried to take my mind off things. All I'd been thinking about was getting back to the office and getting some work done. I'd contemplated packing it all in for good but then realised I'd always struggle to hold down a proper job in this world. I was meant to do what I was doing, whether I liked it or not.

When it turned ten o'clock and I was about to dig into

my fourth bottle, AC/DC blasting out of the stereo to help
me escape my woe, I got a text from Laura:

Forgot to tell you. When you were in hospital, I finally
got around to emptying that bag Bob had left and found a
bottle of Bowmore. It's in my wardrobe. Thought I'd keep it
out of your reach until I thought you deserved it. Love you x
x x

I didn't need a second invitation. The rain tapped the
windows as I brought the box into the living room and
placed it on the coffee table. I took my whisky glass from the
drinks cabinet and set it down, thinking what a pleasure it
would be to share a dram with the man himself. I glanced at
the shelf where his Fedora was sitting and thought briefly of
him before I opened the box up and delved inside.

It was a twenty-five-year-old in a finely cut presentation
bottle, the label black and gold. I unscrewed the cap and
immediately noticed it had been opened already. Bob
must've had a wee dram himself and let's face it, who could
blame him? But when I poured, a sealed plastic bag came
out along with the whisky.

I opened it up and took out the paper inside. It was a
letter, printed out in black ink, no handwriting. I grabbed a
smoke and sparked up. Took that shit in deep. Unfolded the
note and read.

J*im,*
    Like all the good films, this one ends on a poignant
    *note. By the time you read this (couldn't resist, sorry) I'll
be gone. It will have been quick and painless (I hope) but no
doubt messy. In whatever circumstances I am found, please
know that I did my best and I don't regret my actions. It had*

to end this way, for me at least, and I suppose a part of me always knew it would have to be like this. Don't be angry, don't be sad. It's just the way it is and, well, that's it. It's for the best.

I hope it all works out for you. You're a good lad, a little bit nuts, a little bit stupid. But God loves a doer and a risk taker and I know your heart's always been in the right place. But be careful, Jim. I know I might sound like a broken bloody record, but there are dark forces at work and they don't care about you or anyone else. Stay out of trouble and always do the right thing.

You might wonder why I did it. The truth is, I've had enough. My world turned to shit the minute I let Margaret down. She's forgiven me, but the shame haunts me. It would never have been the same if I'd have carried on. We could never do what we wanted to do, you see. Hiding away in the mountains might've been a peaceful life and a fitting retirement, but I quickly learned I'd never really escape what I did until the day I died. And I needed that escape, lad. I hope you understand.

It's a fine whisky. I know you're probably sitting there with a dram, cursing at me for being a soft, stupid old bastard. But I don't care. What's done is done and there's no going back now. So this is a gift for you. I've left you a Montecristo in there too. A fine cigar for a fine friend.

God bless you, Jim. Maybe one day we'll meet again. Maybe. But always know I'll be just a thought away. So now I'll say farewell and goodbye.

Your Friend,

Bob

I sat and stared at the letter for several minutes, but my mind was empty. He'd gone, and he had his reasons. He wasn't coming back. I took the cigar from the box and turned it over in my hands. I left it on the table, thinking I'd find a better time than now. I topped up the whisky and went over to the window. Pushed it open and smelt the rain. Watched it fall across the city and heard the night alive, drifting through the air. Wondered what the future held as I ran a hand across my scar and sparked up. Took that shit in deep and downed the whisky. Felt the burn.

Tomorrow was a brand new day.

COMING SOON

Read an excerpt from the next book in the Jim Locke series...

Coming in Winter 2021

BLOODLINES

Two families. One deadly game.

Aisling Connolly is seeing a Badowski and the Connollys can't have that. So when Seamus Connolly asks Locke to trail his youngest daughter, it's easy money, his bread and butter. But the families don't see it that way.

Blood is blood...Then a high profile copper is found butchered in the river.

A long standing feud is re-ignited.
And Locke wants out...

BLOODLINES

"**A**re you a gambling man, Locke?"

Was I? Not really. I don't think I'd ever set foot in a bookie's in my life. I wouldn't know where to start with placing a bet, couldn't give the slightest fuck about horse racing, not even the Grand National. My poker face was just my usual expression and I wouldn't know a card game if I tried. I never was one for chasing a win and a tip was something I gave to the barmaid if I thought she was doing a good job at keeping me in beer. I occasionally bought a lottery ticket if it was a big one and I sometimes took risks - dangerous risks as Laura kept reminding me - so that was probably as far as my gambling went. I'd gambled with my life, many times, and yet I'd always came out the other side relatively unscathed, except for the seven inch scar across my abdomen. You could say those gambles mostly paid off. But was I a gambling man? Did I place bets? No.

"Not really," I said. "Can't say I am."

Seamus Connolly looked me in the eye and smiled. His youngest son, Kian, had returned to the table with a bottle of Jameson and two glasses. Grinned as he joined us and sat down. His older brother, Shane, the middle of the three brothers, lifted a Guinness and drank.

"I'm surprised by that," Seamus said. "I really am. But then what's a little bet now and then, eh? This one's just for fun."

"I suppose I could give it a go," I said, eyeing the bottle. "Looks a decent drink."

"Smooth as a baby's arse," Kian said. His accent was pure Mancunian, as was his brother's, when he bothered to speak. Seamus, on the other hand, was a mix of heavy Dublin coated in Manc and somewhere in between. He popped the cork from the bottle and poured two good measures into each glass, pushing one to me.

"What do you say we drink a dram each until this bottle is finished and the last one standing gets to take this home?" He dipped into his trouser pocket and pulled out a large wad of cash in twenties. Dropped it on the table. "A grand. Yours if you can keep up."

"A grand?" I said. "You'd seriously give me a grand if I'm still standing after this?"

"That's what I said."

"I couldn't, Seamus. It's a lot of money."

"You'll have earned it."

"And if you win? I have to give you a grand, is that how it works?"

"Ah, we just call it quits. Just for fun, like I said."

"But you're still willing to give me a grand? That's a lot of money to lose, if you don't mind me saying so."

"I don't intend to lose," he said, leaning in. "But I'm a man of my word. The cash is yours if you manage to finish on top. What do you say? Come on, it's St. Patrick's day. Live a little."

I looked down at the whiskey. It was one I knew well.

Could I match him, dram for dram? On a night like this?
"Are you sure about this?"

"Deadly."

And then the band kicked in, a six piece fusion set, kind
of like a cross between The Pogues and Toss the Feathers. If
it wasn't lively enough it was about to get that bit livelier.
When the drums counted in a one-two-three-four, and the
tables began to bounce, Kian and Shane jumped up to join
the party and Seamus and I raised a glass and drank it in
one. I poured us another and told him I was planning on
savouring this one. I saw him laugh and he mouthed something that I think was meant to be funny but I couldn't hear
him over the noise. Instead I caught his daughter's eye, a
pretty young twenty-something standing over near the bar
with a handful of men around her. She looked over her
shoulder at me sitting with her old man when Kian whispered something in her ear. Then she turned away and
moved into the crowd. I suspected she had no idea she was
the reason he'd brought me here in the first place. And I
needed to know that reason too. Last night's phone call had
taken me by surprise. "Meet me at Mulligan's," he'd
said. "I've got a proposition for you. I'll make it worth your
while."

So here I was, beginning to feel drunk, weeks of sobriety
falling away like rocks down a cliff. All of a sudden I was
back in at the deep end.

Seamus left his seat and joined me on the bench,
squeezing in between a fat girl who was half asleep. He
nudged me and downed another dram. Urged me to do the
same. I did, thinking that this could end messy, and watched
him top us both up again. It wasn't a drink to be reckoned
with. Best not to treat it as a session whisky but I doubted
Seamus Connolly would agree.

"So," he said. "Like this cash sitting right here," which he pocketed in his shirt breast pocket, "this job I want you to do for me is easy money. I wouldn't even call it work, to be honest, but if anyone can do this kind of thing, I suppose it must be you, eh?"

"What kind of thing?" I said. I'd also have liked to ask him to get to the fucking point, but you don't challenge Seamus Connolly, not if you value your teeth. "How can I be of service?"

"Surveillance," he said. "Just the straight forward kind."

"Meaning?"

"Just keep your eyes open," he said. "And report back to me on a weekly basis or as and when, depending on what you find."

"And who am I watching, exactly?"

He nodded into the crowd and I followed his gaze. "My youngest daughter," he said. "Aisling. You see her?"

How could I miss her? She was beautiful and alluring, dancing away to the band in a short brown dress, her black hair tied up in a green velvet band, her blue eyes sparkling. Slim but curvaceous in all the right places and an arse that wouldn't look out of place in anyone's bed. She was a young twenty three, a party girl if the rumours were true, and every kid in town was in love with her. It was easy to see why.

She was also untouchable given that her father was the patriarchal boss in the family, a family whose tentacles stretched into every corner of the country. Protection, drugs, loan sharking, prostitution even, if the latest reports were to be believed. I knew that Seamus had various properties scattered around, and his eldest son, Connor, was about to invest in the latest skyscraper apartment boom in a big way. Gangsters that even the gangsters feared. It was well known they'd fuck you up if you crossed them. Well known that Seamus and perhaps some of his boys were responsible for far more than breaking fingers. Bodies had shown up just recently that had their stamp all over it, though in this town, Seamus was king. I had no doubt he'd kept the local politicians happy in exchange for their protection from the law. Rumour had it he'd kept the police quiet too, and it didn't surprise me at all. Despite all that had gone down in recent years, the smell of corruption had never really gone away. It was just the faces that had changed.

"So she's your daughter then?"

"Youngest," he said. "My elsest, Siobhan, is settled with her own family back in Donegal. She's thirty five now. Two kids, a boy and a girl, and her husband, Kevin, has taken over his dad's farm. Pigs, mainly. They never run out of bacon."

If it was meant as a joke, I didn't find it funny. I looked at him, this old man pushing seventy five but still sixteen stone of raw muscle and hands like shovels. Not a rare breed for an Irishman but I knew people often wondered why he kept himself in the game at his age. I felt it was because he loved what he did. It kept him young, gave him something to live for. Kept the blood pumping through his veins. He topped us up again, and I saw the bottle was slowly going down. I thought about what I could do with that grand he had in his breast pocket.

"So why do you want me to watch her?" I said. "Make sure she's okay, that kind of thing?"

He shook his head. "She can handle herself," he said. "She's like her mother. Soft on the outside, hard on the inside. Won't be taken for a fool, you know? No, she'll be okay, I'm sure. I just don't want her to be taken advantage of, if you know what I mean."

"Not quite."

"A little bird tells me she's been seeing a fella."

"No surprise there," I said. "She's a good looking woman."

He nodded. "Young lad, about her age. But I worry about her because of who he is."

"You know him then?"

"Know of him," he said. "And the rest of his family. Anyone else and I wouldn't normally give a fuck. But this lot..."

"Sounds like you're not too happy about it. But kids are kids, Seamus. It'll just be a fling, I'm sure."

"If I find out he's fucking her, I'll murder the bastard."

"Who?"

"One of the Poles," he said. "Lukasz. Lukasz Badowski. You may have heard of his father."

I had. Wiktor Badowski was a well known career criminal around Manchester. He'd done time back in the eighties for manslaughter but everyone knew he was a murderer. His younger brother, Oskar, had taken over the reigns for a few years while Wiktor counted the days inside, making connections and striking up deals in unlikely places. But then Oskar was found dead in a reclamation yard out in Cheshire and it kicked off a war among the Poles and the Irish and the Italians. A few people were killed, including one of Connolly's boys, a young Cork man called James Dunne. Since then, the Connollys have not been best of friends with the Polish, least of all Wiktor and his lot, having long suspected him of being involved in Dunne's demise. They'd found him hanging from the Stockport viaduct, a hundred feet from the ground, on Good Friday in nineteen eighty nine. Since then, it's said a truce was called and patches respectfully not crossed. The Connollys and the Badowskis had agreed to leave it at that and move on with their respectful businesses. But there had always been the suspicion among both sides that either one was up to no good. So for Aisling Connolly to be romantically involved with the young Badowski kid, Lukasz, things had appeared to have taken a turn in a very different direction. And judging by the look on Seamus's face, I guessed he wasn't too keen on his daughter getting involved with the enemy.

"I find it hard to trust anyone," he said, "let alone a Badowski. See, Aisling likes to thinks she's streetwise, and she is to a certain extent, but I just don't trust these bastards. Which is where you come in."

"You think he's got an ulterior motive?"

"Something like that, yeah. And if he has, I'd like you to find out what that might be."

"As well as follow Aisling around and keep you informed of what she's up to?"

"That's right," he said. "You'll be well sorted for anything you need. All you need to do is ask. Cars, assistance, whatever."

"I like to work alone in cases like this," I said. "Too many cooks and all that."

"Let's just make something clear from the outset, though. I don't want you to feel like I've got some kind of power over you, you know. You know my reputation, Mr. Locke. I don't want you to feel like you're working for me. I'm your client, I'll pay you an excellent rate. Only fair for what I'm asking you to do."

"Normally I'd charge a straight five hundred per week for this kind of surveillance job. That covers my time, petrol allowances, the spying kit, you name it."

He waved this away like he was swatting a fly. "I'll double it. A grand a week, cash in hand. Shall we say every

Sunday? Just come to my house and we can sort everything there."

It was silly money and he knew it, and I knew I could drag this shit out for as long as it took. A grand a week in cash in my pocket would do very nicely, thank you very much.

"When do I start?"

He finished his whiskey and took the wad of cash from his breast pocket. He put it between my twitching fingers. "You win," he said. "I'm done anyway. No time like the present. We can iron out any paperwork you'd like me to deal with on Sunday. That's when you'll get your first payment."

"Seamus, this is good enough. Forget the bet, I don't gamble anyway. It feels wrong to just take this money."

"I never shirk on a bet, Locke."

"But I couldn't, really."

"You can and you will." He stood up and I did the same, suddenly feeling high and light as a feather. I was drunk and the party was beginning to kick in. Someone - I think it was Shane - put a fresh Guinness in front of me then vanished into the crowd. Seamus and I shook to seal the agreement. It was easy enough.

"We'll look forward to learning what she's up to," he said. "And remember, Locke. She's my daughter and I love her. I want to know everything, for her own good."

"I'll need some details," I said. "About her. Where she likes to go, who her friends are, that kind of thing."

He nodded. "Come to mine on Sunday. I'll give you everything you need."

"Just one thing to start me off," I said. He nodded but looked impatient. He was ready to call it a night. "Who told you she might be seeing Lukasz?"

"You'll have to speak to Kian," he said. "He knows all about that."

I glanced around for Kian, who was watching from over at the bar. When I turned back to Seamus, he'd gone. I watched him walk away out the side door and into the night.

I sat for a while, just minding my own business and watching the party get into full swing before the last band was due to come on. It was only just gone ten o' clock and I was beginning to think about one for the road. Thought about the job Seamus wanted me to do and his reasons for it. I suppose he'd do whatever it took to feel better. I just wasn't entirely sure I was the man for the job. If he didn't like whatever I had found out, how would he react? I'd heard my share of bad things about the Connollys over the years. There was no telling what these people could do given half a chance. I decided right there and then to do the right thing and be cautious with the truth if I knew it would make relations go tits up. My initial thoughts on this romance was that it was destined for disaster, but then what did I know these days? Not much.

My phone buzzed and I drained my pint and pulled it out, stepping outside via the front door. Two bouncers moved aside as I stumbled into the street. The night was noisy and beyond, the traffic on Deansgate moved like an electric snake.

"Laura."

"You said you'd be home by now."

"When have I ever been governed by time?"

"That's a point. So, you on the way back then?"

I glanced back at the pub. It was bouncing. I felt a temptation - no, more than that - an urge, to get back inside and get acquainted with the subject of my new job. Well, that was my excuse. What I really wanted, I knew, was another pint.

"I'm on the way."

"I've been waiting for you," she said. "It's lovely and warm in bed."

I knew what she wanted and was more than willing to oblige. But already a new case had whetted my appetite. It had been a while since I felt the buzz of it again. My last major case had gotten me hurt and had been enough to put me off the job for life...until I got bored hanging around the flat all day. It was time to get back in the saddle. I could only take so much of insurance fraud. Surveillance was my bread and butter and a job that paid as well as this was enough motivation.

"Sounds like an invitation," I said. "How could I refuse?"

"Just hurry up. But anyway, what did Connolly want?"

I told her.

"Seems easy enough, eh? A grand a week would be just fine."

"That's what I thought. Cash in hand as well. Bonus."

"Just make sure you keep him sweet."

I instinctively felt my scar, which was something I found myself doing of late. Since the stabbing, there had been a strange itch, a kind of ethereal pulse. It made me want to move my hand there as if the scar itself was some kind of oracle to forces unknown.

Or maybe I was just drunk. I turned away from the pub, figuring the further away I got, the further from my mind it became.

"I'm gonna walk," I said. "I'll be half an hour, tops."

"I'll be waiting."

I hung up and walked down to the river, lingering on Victoria Bridge as the night revellers buzzed past.

The Connollys. The Badowskis. Bloodlines that that ran deep.

I stared into the murky water as the rain began to fall. It was dirty, the colour of hell itself.

I took Bob's Fedora from my jacket pocket, a bit crumpled up but perfect in every way, and placed it on my head.

Then I turned away and walked into the neon lights of the city.

ACKNOWLEDGMENTS

Special thanks to my better half, Kelly-Ann, for the Punch Publishing Logo design, and also for putting up with my expert procrastination again. Thanks and appreciation must also go to Stuart Bache at Books Covered for the awesome cover. And a nod to a few others who've helped along the way, most notably fellow author Andrew Lowe.

ABOUT THE AUTHOR

P.F. Hughes was born in Manchester in 1976. He's worked in many jobs over the years - which has contributed strongly to his writing - and continues to work on the Jim Locke series, among other forthcoming projects.

He currently lives in Ramsbottom, somewhere between the city and the countryside, with his partner Kelly-Ann, their two children and his guitar. He is currently trying to escape the real world.

Join the author's mailing list for regular updates on forthcoming releases and more.

Printed in Great Britain
by Amazon

23727071R00265